The Last Day Of Summer

JF SMITH

ISBN: 1481929380
ISBN-13: 978-1481929387

<010105>

Disclaimer

This work contains references to certain sports teams, broadcasters and news agencies by name. All references are used fictitiously and are not intended to imply any endorsement of this work by these entities or any connection to this work or to the author by these entities. All other characters and events in this work are strictly fictional and any resemblance to actual persons (living or dead) or events is purely coincidental.

Contents

The Last Day Of Summer

Prologue

"But Dad!"

"Uh-unh! No buts! No son of mine is going to be a ladybug in some play! It's not... NORMAL!" There was an emphasis on the word that signaled it was to be the end of the discussion, no back-talk. He knew that sound in his dad's voice very well. He heard it whenever he liked something that his dad didn't. He heard that voice a lot.

"But I wanna have a costume with black polka-dots! Why not?"

"Because I said so!!"

His father muttered under his breath, "Cripes, I can already hear the guys at the office riding me on this, but good!"

His father shot him a look that dared him to argue any further about it.

He stood bewildered. He had been so excited to be in the play, to get to dress up like a bug that was bright red and had awesome black polka-dots all over it. But all of his daydreams of being up on the stage, singing with the rest of his class the song they had learned, seemed to be crashing down around him. Why was his dad like this? Why was he being punished this way? Didn't his dad understand how much better a ladybug was than some stupid spider? Or a bee or a mushroom?

Satisfied that this problem had been squashed once and for all, his dad wheeled around and marched out of the kitchen.

With his father's parental guidance over and done, his mom knelt down next to him and wiped away the tears that had formed in the corners of his eyes.

"Shhh, sweetie. I'll talk to him. You'll get to be the ladybug, so don't cry, ok? I promise!"

He nodded and felt better. A little bit. It still felt like his dad hated him and he didn't understand why.

A week later, when his mom had finally finished working on his costume, he couldn't wait to see it finished for the first time. He felt like he would pass out from excitement. He could see the shiny red shell with black polka-dots in his mind. He could already see himself racing around the house, pretending to be flying, just like a real ladybug.

His mom seemed to be excited, too, and he couldn't wait to try the costume on. What she pulled out of the box she had kept it in, though, had no red or black anywhere on it. Instead, there were a lot of arms, and it was plain old green. A centipede, she called it. But to his 7-year-old mind, all he could manage was "tentpeed." And tentpeeds didn't have black dots! Not a single one! He looked up at his mom's face, heartbroken.

She had promised. Promised it would be the ladybug! And when a mom promises, it's a cross-your-heart-and-hope-to-die kind of thing.

His mom's smile faltered. She explained, "Darling, this is just as good, ok? Look at all the arms on it! Isn't that fun? It's better!"

"But you promised!"

"I know, but your father is right. You'll learn to love the centipede costume even more!"

But all he learned was that arguing was stupid. Getting people to see your point of view didn't work.

He shook his head to get rid of the memory that had replayed in his mind, and then he stared down at the red t-shirt with black stripes on the sleeves.

Suddenly, he wasn't interested in the red shirt anymore and threw it all the way into the back of his closet. For several more minutes, he sat on the side of his bed, staring blankly at the ratty, mottled carpet before he eventually managed to rouse himself. He dug around again and then tried to decide between the white knit shirt and the blue v-neck. He glanced at his phone to check the time and his teeth gritted together.

Shit, Mike's gonna be pissed, he thought.

Chapter 1

Rett rushed in and found where Mike, Doug and Jonathan-not-Jon-and-definitely-not-Jonny were already at a table. One glance told him that he was three-quarters of a pitcher of margaritas late to dinner. It was one of those chain Mexican restaurants, the kind that's usually on a major four-lane commercial road. Judging from the number of TV's hanging up in it, it had probably been a sports bar before it had turned Mexican.

He ignored Jonathan, gave Doug a squeeze on the shoulder to greet him before finally settling into the seat next to Mike. He leaned over and gave Mike a quick kiss on the cheek, and got a gentle look of reproach for being late in return.

Mike smiled and put his arm behind Rett on the back of his chair, picking distractedly at his blue v-neck shirt in the process. "You need to see the menu, Rett? Or do you already know what you want?" he asked.

Rett unfolded his napkin to put it in his lap. "Uh, no. I think I know what I want. We can go ahead and order."

Jonathan commented dryly, "Well, that's good. I'd hate to have to wait for you and then wait even more for you to review the menu just so you can finally decide on the veggie burrito, which we *all know* you're going to order. All while I'm fading away to nothing over here."

Not bloody likely, thought Rett. *Civilization would crumble to sand and dust before that muffintop on you faded away to nothing.*

For the life of him, he couldn't fathom what Doug, who was a pretty decent guy, saw in Jonathan, who was a self-satisfied jerk. And Rett noticed that Doug was still looking through the menu, anyway.

"Actually," said Rett, ignoring Jonathan and turning to his boyfriend instead, "Mike, I thought maybe you'd like to split an order of the chicken fajitas tonight. Is that ok?"

Mike thought about it a moment before agreeing, "Yeah, that's good. Let's get that."

Jonathan wasn't quite ready to let go of Rett yet, though. "Splitting an entree? Sounds like still no success on the job hunt, huh, Rett?"

Doug popped a tortilla chip in his mouth and added, "Yeah, still coming up oh-fer on the job hunt?"

Rett looked at Doug, completely lost by the comment.

In explanation, Doug jerked his head up and Rett glanced back over his shoulder to where Doug was indicating. Over the bar of the restaurant there was a TV playing a ballgame. Rett still didn't understand.

Mike gave Rett a pat on his shoulder and said, "He's still looking. I worry that he's gonna start charging me for sex if he doesn't find something pretty soon."

Doug finally put his menu down and laughed, "Really?"

"We'll see if he's worth it," added Mike, grinning.

Rett was glad the lighting in the Mexican restaurant was low enough that they couldn't see his face flush pink at the comments. He disliked when they talked like this about him, but he hated it especially when *Mike* talked about him like this. It all messed with his usual sense of humor for some reason.

To make matters worse, Mike added, "But maybe that'd be a good opportunity to do some comparison shopping," which got a good laugh out of Doug and Jonathan.

Rett looked around to find their server, or any server, that he could grab to take their order and end this line of the conversation. Looking for work after getting his physical therapist certification was bad enough, but being the butt of jokes about it was worse.

Fortunately, their waiter appeared and the four of them focused on ordering dinner instead. As expected, the waiter wanted to see Rett's ID before bringing him a margarita glass. Rett was used to this; his slight size, pure-gold blond hair and faint dusting of freckles on his nose tended to make him look younger than the twenty-five years of life he had in his pocket already, and the result was near-constant server distrust.

Conversation turned to other things for the rest of their dinner together, and Rett tried to keep the antagonism towards Jonathan to a minimum. But in the background, his mind continued to chew on Mike's comments a little more than he knew he should allow.

Finally, after their waiter cleared their plates at the end of dinner, Doug poured the last swallow or two of margaritas into his glass mug and asked Rett, "So when are you moving in with Mike?"

Rett said, "We've never even talked about it." That wasn't strictly true. Mike had brought it up once, but it was along the lines of an innocuous "one of these days when you're ready, and you can pry Val from your side." Rett was glad Mike hadn't pushed any more than that one comment that one time. Valerie had been his roommate, best friend, and classmate during the last five years of physical therapy school at Alabama State University in Montgomery, and he was very settled in his place with her.

Another smirk surfaced on Mike's face, and he said, "He's going to run out of options before too long, I think. I'll be the only man in Alabama with a licensed physical therapist as my house boy."

Rett glared at Mike out of the corner of his eye, studying Mike's thin face and pointed chin. He had a constant shadow on his face like he only shaved on yesterdays. Mike was the same age as Rett, but had been working as a paralegal for two years before they met three months ago and subsequently starting seeing each other. This condescension on Mike's part was grating on Rett more and more lately. He needed to call Mike out on it.

As luck would have it, Doug and Jonathan wanted to hurry and pay and get out of there because there was a TV show Jonathan wanted to catch and had forgotten to record it. Rett made a point of saying goodbye to Doug and ignoring Jonathan.

But as soon as their dinner companions had taken their leave, Mike said, "I know you're supposed to get to that thing with Val in a little bit, but there is something that I wanted to give you."

Rett was still a little caught up in Mike's comments from earlier, but looked at him curiously. "Give me?"

Mike put his hand in his shirt pocket and pulled out a key and put it on the table in front of Rett. Rett didn't know what to say. He was still slightly put out with Mike from earlier, and now Mike was trying to take their relationship to the next level by giving him a key to his condo.

"Mike, I need to think about this."

Mike's mouth dropped open slightly, clearly not expecting that particular reaction.

"Why? What's to think about, Rett? I'm not asking you to have a three-way," he said, defensively.

Rett needed to tell him what was on his mind, but what came out was, "I... this isn't... I just need to think about this some."

Mike looked at him blankly.

"Besides," added Rett, "I don't know what's going to happen with my job situation. I might not even be able to stay in Montgomery, you know?"

Almost as an afterthought, Rett said, "I've got an interview for a job out of town. Next week." Rett twitched a little since he was completely lying about having any job interview the following week, much less one out of town.

Mike asked, "You do? With who? Where? You didn't say anything about it!"

"You know I don't like to talk about those because I don't want to jinx them," deflected Rett.

Mike started to press, but Rett told him he needed to leave so he could meet up with Val and he'd talk to him later. He was getting very uncomfortable with the conversation and really wanted to end it as fast as possible. He gave Mike some money for his dinner and got out of there as fast as he could.

He dashed out to the parking lot, feeling like he was escaping prison, the early June heat still oppressive even in the late evening. Typical of his luck, his crappy 16-year-old Jetta didn't want to start and he began cursing at it loudly. He dreaded Mike finally leaving the restaurant and finding him there, still trying to start his piece-of-shit car. He beat on the dash a few times, which magically seemed to wake the car up, and he got out of the parking lot of Los Banditos in record time.

As he pulled out, he glanced in his rear-view mirror praying he didn't see Mike behind him.

He drove off, feeling it gnawing into him in the pit of his stomach; this whole thing with Mike wasn't going to work.

~~~~~

Rett got home with a single thing on his mind, having forgotten all about any other plans for the evening. He passed through the dingy living room of his and Val's apartment, where they'd lived together for five years now, past the bathroom they shared and into his bedroom, tripping over the tear in the tan carpet in the doorway to his room, the one that he constantly snagged his foot on. Tonight more so than other nights, Rett noticed how Val had started to spend a little bit of money on some newer things for the apartment and her room since she had gotten hired as a physical therapist two months earlier. Rett didn't have that luxury by a long shot.

He pulled his laptop out and let it start cranking up while he went into the bathroom. He splashed some water on his face from the tap, and looked at himself in the mirror. But he didn't let himself get too caught up in feeling lost and alone. He'd made it this far without anyone else and he could make it through this, too. He just needed to focus and keep at it.

What had started out as a desperate lie at dinner, and something he had actively avoided in his job search thus far, now became his preferred plan of attack. Tonight had lit a fire in Rett, and it surely beat the alternatives that seemed to be surfacing at dinner that evening with Mike.

Even giving it a few minutes, his laptop wasn't done with its usual bout of wheezing and coughing while it pulled itself together. He got impatient with it and went to make himself a rum and coke while it slowly got to a point where it could give him its undivided attention.

Back in his room, he grabbed his laptop and flopped down on his bed, which squeaked as he did so. But then, it squeaked even when someone merely stood in the doorway and looked at it directly. He sat up against the wall and opened up the browser on his laptop to begin looking. He checked again for openings for physical therapists there in Montgomery, just in case, but there wasn't anything he hadn't already seen. The few listed all seemed to want people with years of experience, and he had already contacted pretty much every medical practice and office in Montgomery that hired physical therapists, some multiple times. So there was nothing new there.

He had avoided looking outside of Montgomery because, despite it being a pretty desperate town, he had gotten used to it. And there was Val, who he was really close to. He had started from zero when he moved to Montgomery and entered the physical therapy program at the university there, and he had avoided the thought of moving and starting from zero yet again.

But tonight, he felt differently. He started looking at job listings in other cities. He found one opening up in Birmingham, and so he sent off his resume and other information there.

He noticed another opening in Dothan, but he wasn't nearly that desperate yet. He'd move to Georgia, or, God forbid, even Mississippi, before going back to his hometown.

There was an odd opening listed in Mobile; it seemed perfect for him, but it gave no clue about which hospital, practice or office it was in. He skipped it and found another ad for a position at the University of South Alabama Medical Center, so he applied at that one as well. He went back and looked at the oddball listing again and thought about it a minute or two. He decided he had nothing to lose by applying, so he followed the instructions to submit his resume there as well.

He closed his laptop and tossed back the rest of his drink, letting the rum finish the job that the margaritas had started earlier.

~~~~~

An hour later, Rett stopped digging around in the back of the closet, stood up and looked back over his shoulder.

Standing there watching him was a petite girl with glossy, jet-black hair hanging down just past her shoulders. Her nose was a little more prominent than most guys would have liked, at least until they saw it on her in person. It gave her a very distinctive and exotic look, further enhanced by her deeper, Mediterranean complexion.

She pursed her lips at Rett and said, "If I find out you've been using my vibrator, I will kill you slowly, you know."

"Gimme a break," joked Rett. "I stopped using that thing of yours three years ago."

A lightning bolt of realization struck her face. "Oh my God! *That's* why the batteries suddenly started lasting so much longer!"

Rett continued to stand in the mess of stuff he had pulled out of Val's closet, twisted around so he could see her. "Wait... what the hell happened to your lips? They look like squashed chili peppers."

Val vamped for Rett and said, "You like? It's Oxblood! Alluring, no?"

"No," he deadpanned. He added, "And, it doesn't surprise me one bit that you would kill an ox just to make your lips look like *that*. Probably with your bare hands."

"I didn't kill the ox! They make some little Thai children on the lipstick farm somewhere kill the ox! You know, down in Argentina. Or Paraguay."

Rett sighed and resumed digging around in her closet again. "You mean in Thailand?"

"Don't be stupid. They don't have lipstick farms in Thailand."

Rett began to laugh at this point, unable to continue without letting it out. Val came the rest of the way into her bedroom and threw herself onto her bed.

She asked, her voice sultry and using a finger to twirl her hair seductively, "For what are you looking for, for real?"

Rett shifted over a little further to continue looking. "My Preten-" He stopped when he picked up some items out of her dirty clothes hamper and found what he was looking for right underneath. He wheeled around and held it up in triumph.

"My Pretenders t-shirt!"

Val shook her head and said, "Oh, that's not yours. That's mine. That's from my favorite band... The, uh, The Pret Enders."

Rett smirked snidely. "The post-industrial Ska gospel group?"

Val played along and nodded.

"Miss Papadakis, you wouldn't know a good band if it came up and fucked you between the tits." Rett then asked, "Why do you even want this to begin with? It's way big on me, which means it's gotta be *huge* on you."

"I sleep in it."

Rett looked horrified. "You've been wearing my favorite t-shirt without giving it the benefit of a bra? Ughhh... I'll *never* get the sweaty Greek-tits smell out of it!"

Val's forehead furrowed. "What the hell is *that* supposed to smell like?"

"How the hell should I know? I hope I *never* know! Milk and ouzo, maybe?" He sniffed at his beloved t-shirt tentatively.

"Ewww..." puled Val.

"Damn straight ewww! I feel like my innocence has been stolen!" howled Rett.

"Ha! Innocence?!" Val started writhing around on the bed and giggling helplessly.

"Kiss my lily white ass!" growled Rett. "I'm still in the summer of my youth and virtue, despite your five year campaign to tarnish me!"

Val wiped at the tears in her eyes before her laughing fit finally died down. She dropped the parlay they had going, frowned, and said, "You know, I expect you to be late. I don't expect you to ditch on me entirely, Everett."

Rett knew that whenever she wanted him to know she meant business, she used his full name. It usually never had any effect whatsoever on him.

He extricated his feet from the mess he had made going through her closet and, dragging a pair of Val's panties on his sneaker in the process, walked over to lay down on the bed next to her. "I had something come up that I wanted to take care of, Val. Sorry," he apologized.

Val's hand started inching its way over to where Rett's prize t-shirt was resting on his chest. "Did Mike talk to you tonight?" she asked.

Rett's head jerked over to face Val, instantly wary. "Yeah," he said.

"So you've got a key to his place now? When are you going to move in with him?"

"You *that* ready to ditch me?" he asked. Her hand crept inconspicuously closer towards Rett.

"I never said that," said Val. "You move and I'll still expect you to come over to vacuum, like always."

"I don't *vacuum* here! I've *never* vacuumed here!" scoffed Rett.

"Well, *I'm* not about to... Oh Jesus, no fucking wonder the ceiling feels like it gets a little lower every passing month!"

"I told him I wanted to think about it."

"About vacuuming?" said Val, intentionally not making the connection.

"Not vacuuming, stupid! About moving in with him!" snapped Rett.

"Think what? What's there to think about?" Val's hand discreetly shifted a little bit closer to the t-shirt again before Rett pulled it off his chest and dropped it on the floor where she couldn't get to it.

"I dunno," said Rett, turning on his side to face Val fully. "He made some comments at dinner. They made me feel a little weird."

"And you took him to the carpet on it, right?"

"Yeah. Well, no. Maybe. Stop obsessing about the carpet! I'll think about it," vacillated Rett. Why did she always want him to be so aggressive?

"These weren't the first comments, right, Rett?" she said more than she asked.

Rett frowned, "No."

"So, put a stop to it."

"Because I'm not Kendra the hairy-armed-Greek-she-beast like you!"

"That hurts, Rett. I'd *never* call myself... Kendra. It's too... too... *twee*," pouted Val. "Anyway," she continued, "if you don't like the comments, tell him to knock it the hell off."

Rett sighed. She always oversimplified everything. "Just let me deal with it."

Val didn't look at Rett and the sum total of her reply was a grunt brimming with annoyance.

They lay on the bed next to each other in silence for a few more moments.

Finally Val aggressively pushed him onto his back and straddled over his pelvis. She started running her hands through her hair and bouncing up and down on his groin. "Well, you know I'd love to have my stud roommate stay here to service my feminine needs, of which there are many."

Rett huffed and resumed his teasing, "Ugh! You can borrow *my* vibrator for that! At least it's not worn down to a pencil nub like yours is."

Val rolled off of him and put her hand on his chest. She watched him closely for a moment before he glanced over to see what she was thinking.

"It'll work out, Rett. I promise."

Rett nodded before taking her hand and kissing it affectionately.

"In the meantime..." started Val.

"I'm not *fucking vacuuming!*" shouted Rett.

Chapter 2

Rett thumped on the steering wheel of his Jetta impatiently. He should have known that today, when he really needed it to behave, it would choose to act like it had the automotive equivalent of a hangover. He had spent fifteen minutes, dressed in a coat and tie, trying to start it while the car managed only a slight, vaporous grunt before going back to sleep. Then he spent another few minutes looking under the hood of the car before he realized the sheer idiocy of his attempts to diagnose engine problems, especially in a dress shirt and tie, when all he could recognize under the hood was metal and wires and what looked like an old, dead rat. He kicked the front bumper a few times before he got back into the driver's seat and tried to start it again. After another ten minutes of trying, pleading, begging, and praying to every god he could think of, it roused itself enough to actually crank. Apparently, the deity that was working customer service that day was Odin.

Once he managed to get on I65 headed towards Mobile, he pushed the car hard to try and make up the thirty minutes he lost trying to get it cranked.

As soon as he got on the highway, his mind panicked by the car trouble, he remembered back to something from years before. Back when he had barely turned fifteen and had just gotten his learner's permit for driving.

Rett looked up at his dad. His father was a few inches short of six feet, but still had three or four inches on Rett nonetheless, so he seemed huge.

"Rett, darn it, I don't care if you don't want to learn! A man knows how to take care of a car. All we're talking about is learning to change the oil and change a tire here, not rebuilding an automatic transmission. Even Bo's already learned these basics and he's four years younger than you!"

"Then I can let him do it if he loves it so much," countered Rett, sullenly.

"Well, Bo won't always be around to do it for you!"

"Yeah? I can't seem to ever get rid of him, so maybe you don't know what you're talking about!" Rett was treading on very thin ice talking to his father this way. Plus, he was being nasty to his little brother. Bo was the one person in the family that he truly felt close to. But he didn't want to let that get in the way of making his point.

"Damn it, Rett!" his father sputtered. "You're gonna learn to be a man if it's the last thing I do! No son of mine is going to turn out like this!"

Rett knew he'd crossed a line with his dad since he was now using actual cuss words. But rather than back off, it made him dig in even harder. He glared at the man before him.

His father finally had enough of Rett standing there and yelled, the veins in his forehead throbbing, "Be a man, Rett! BE A MAN! I'm gonna make you a fucking man whether you like it OR NOT!"

Rett looked at his father, shocked. For the first time ever, it hit him that this wasn't really about oil changes, or playing little league, or going fishing, or the hundred other things they butted heads about. It was all about... something else. Something that Rett himself had only started to become dimly aware of in the last year. But in the blink of an eye, it came into crisp focus.

Rett dropped the quart bottle of engine oil he had been holding and it started running out all over the driveway. He ran off and hid and cried and didn't come home for the next six hours.

Rett didn't like thinking of his family. But in the last week or so, memories had popped up. For the last three years of his physical therapy studies, he'd managed to barely think of them at all. But lately they were in his mind. Mostly bad memories of his father, unfortunately. He didn't think much of his mother; when she wasn't just sitting doing nothing, she had been the shadow of his father, always going along with him and never really challenging anything his father did or wanted. It was *always* his father and what *he* wanted, how *he* saw the world, how *he* saw his family. How *he* saw Rett. His father never could stand *anything* that challenged that.

He had not seen or heard from them since he had walked out the door at eighteen, and he had kept it that way — almost seven years now, the time it took to get his license as a physical therapist. He'd racked up a huge amount of student loan debt to do it without them, but he had managed. He thought that now, done with school and hopefully on the verge of getting a job if today went well, he'd be totally focused on the future. But then these unwelcome memories would creep in.

He checked his rearview mirror to make sure he didn't see any cops, but the highway barely had any traffic at all. He pushed the Jetta to go a little bit faster to make up some more time.

~~~~~

Rett was sweating as he raced into the hotel, partly because the June heat in Mobile was even worse than in Montgomery, but even more because he was still ten minutes late to the interview. He was at least grateful it was right off the highway so he didn't have to go driving around Mobile trying to find the place.

He ran up to the reception desk and asked the red-headed clerk there if she knew where Rosemary Karan was. The clerk asked if he was there for an interview and he nodded. She pointed him in the direction of a handful of small conference rooms around a corner that were being used for the interviews.

As an afterthought, Rett asked the clerk if she knew which doctor's office or hospital was conducting the interviews. She shrugged an unhelpful response, and Rett ran off down the hallway in the direction she had pointed out. He glanced at his watch; it said ten minutes past two.

He had received the invitation to the interview the day after he had submitted his application, but even then there was still no indication of who he was interviewing with. It had started to make Rett a little bit suspicious, but not suspicious enough to not go. After all, desperate times called for desperate actions. Maybe it was all a front and he was going to be kidnapped and sold into white slavery. He thought about it, and white slavery for some Slavic crime boss perhaps deserved a little career consideration at this point. But since the invitation had requested he attend an interview only a few days later on the next Monday, he had not had a lot of time to think about it one way or the other.

He spotted a very dainty, immaculately put-together, silver-haired lady with small reading glasses around her neck on a thin silver chain sitting very erect at a table set up along a wall in the wide hallway. There were a few other people in chairs sprinkled around, but only a few.

He stopped running just as the lady he assumed was Rosemary Karan looked up at him. She glanced down at a piece of paper as he approached her table before looking back up.

Rett smiled broadly, trying to be very friendly and not look like the frantic wreck he was.

"Mr. Dougherty?" she asked.

Rett said, "Yes, ma'am. I'm here for the..."

Ms. Karan cut him off abruptly, "You're very late."

Rett stood, his smile faltered, and his heart started to pound. Surely ten minutes couldn't be that big of a deal.

An almost evil smile crept into the heavily applied powder and rouge on the elderly lady's face. She looked like a shark in a modest, floral-print skirt. "I suggest you arrive on time for your future interviews."

She added, caustically, "Elsewhere." She picked delicately at her hair a moment and finished, pleasantly enough, "Nice try, though."

Rett's heart felt like it was going to bust out of his chest and start running around the hallway in little, panicked circles.

He said, "I apologize for being a few minutes late. My car..."

"Excuse me," she said, interrupting again. "We're on a *very* tight schedule and there are others that chose to show up on time. I'm *very* sorry." She said she was very sorry but it was clear to Rett that she was anything but.

Rett backed a step or two away, deciding that no amount of arguing or begging was going to change her mind, and he was doubtful bribing would help. Rett stepped away a little further. He gritted his teeth and wondered how this could be happening.

Maybe he should have expected it. Maybe he deserved it. He hadn't even spoken to Mike since he had left him at the table at Los Banditos five days earlier. He knew he should have and needed to, but he hadn't been able to screw up the courage to actually do it. Plus, this interview happened so quickly, he thought that... he didn't know what to...

Shit, he thought as he exhaled heavily, *I don't know what the hell I was thinking. Fucking karma.*

A man in a sport coat had sauntered casually down the hall from the direction of the restrooms and came towards Rett and the lady at the desk.

The man gave Rett a slightly puzzled look and said, "Hi. I'm sorry. You're...?"

"Everett Dougherty. Rett," he said. He wasn't sure if the man had something to do with the interviews or not.

The man was wearing a tweed sport coat, khaki pants and sneakers, and looked a little like a college professor. He had to be in his fifties, mid- to late-fifties probably, with gray mixed in his dark hair, except on top where he was balding. The man's casual smile was a welcome change after the lady at the desk.

"Rett," the man repeated. "And you're here for...?"

The lady at the desk cut in at this point, "He's ridiculously late, George. *Not* a good candidate."

The man ignored her for a moment and looked back at Rett.

"Oh, uh," Rett said, finally realizing he should answer the man's question. "I'm here for the physical therapist position?"

That clicked for the man, George, and he smiled broadly and nodded at Rett. He glanced at his watch, then said over his shoulder, "C'mon! *Ten minutes*, Rose! And we're not even ready to talk to him yet. We're still negotiating in there."

He put a friendly hand on Rett's shoulder and said in a low voice, "Rosemary's a little bit of a pit-bull."

He stood back up and held out his hand for Rett to shake, "I'm George Hastings, Rett." George guided him over to a nearby chair and added, "Go on and have a seat, please. We're finishing up something, so if you can give us a few extra minutes, we'll be right with you. Ok?"

"Sure, Mr. Hastings."

"George, please."

Rett smiled and nodded at the man, who then turned around and held his arms out at Rosemary in mock surrender. "Rose, you're killing me here!"

Rosemary gave him a serious look indicating that maybe George didn't care if chaos reigned, but she did and wasn't about to allow it.

George walked back off down the hall and into one of the conference rooms. Rett stole a glance over at Rosemary, but she was now occupied with telling another person waiting in the hallway that he wasn't allowed to have a bottled water.

While he waited, Rett wondered what this was all about. Why were they interviewing at a hotel instead of in their offices? Was George Hastings a senior therapist? A doctor? Or was he the business manager for the medical practice?

Just when he was deciding he'd have to wait to get the answers he was looking for, a couple of guys came out of the conference room that Rett had seen George disappear into, and a more mismatched pair Rett had never seen.

One was probably in his late thirties or maybe very early forties. The guy was exceptionally well dressed in a dark suit with a very bright purple, blue and white tie. His hair was spiked up in a way that normally would have made Rett laugh at anyone that age attempting it. But this man was pulling it off pretty decently.

Walking next to him was, obviously, Bigfoot. The guy was huge and had to have at least five inches over the guy in the suit, but he was younger. Rett guessed he was about his own age. No, he decided Bigfoot was even younger when he got a better look at him as they got closer. But way taller than Rett. He was dressed more comfortably than the other guy, in khaki pants and a dark green knit shirt. His hair was shaggy and messy, but looked right on him. Rett did a double-take when he saw the size of the guy's arms coming out of the short sleeved shirt. The guy was freaking huge.

As the two approached where Rett was seated, Bigfoot was holding back a smile and he started to say to his companion, "Man, that went..."

"NOT a word until we're out of here!" said the guy in the suit sharply, cutting him off immediately.

Bigfoot closed his mouth, but looked like he was going to explode if he held that way for too long.

Rett watched them as they wandered around the corner. The guy in the suit didn't look old enough to be the other guy's dad. He wondered if the guy in the suit was a doctor. Maybe *this* was the Slavic crime lord and his hired muscle.

After about another ten minutes, another man that Rett had not seen before came down the hallway, dressed in dark pants and a white dress shirt. He was clearly Indian and had a very thick, luxuriant mustache. He came up to Rett, who stood to greet him.

"Hi... Rett?" the man asked. He had no real trace of an Indian accent at all.

Rett shook his hand and replied, "Yes, Rett Dougherty."

"Good, Rett. I'm Dr. Arun Balasubramanian."

Rett groaned inwardly, *oh, I am so fucked if I have to repeat that name.*

To his immense relief, Dr. Balasubramanian said, "But you can call me Dr. Bala. It's easier for everyone."

Rett sighed as he relaxed. "Thanks, Dr. Bala. It's nice to meet you." This started to feel more like something he was used to now that a doctor was involved.

As Dr. Bala walked Rett down the hallway, he asked casually, "Did you catch the game last night?"

Rett almost panicked. He didn't want to start off not being able to converse with the guy, but he didn't want to try and lie his way through it, either. He decided that getting caught lying about whatever game Dr. Bala was asking about would be worse.

Rett asked, "Uh, which game?"

"Oh, the Joes-Tigers game last night."

Rett wasn't even sure what kind of game that was. A residual effect of life with his father was that he adamantly avoided sports.

He regretted having to say it, but replied, "No, uh, I don't really follow any sports in particular." Rett wasn't even in the interview room and already had a knock against him.

"Oh, ok," said Dr. Bala as he led him into a conference room.

The room was a standard sized conference room, probably big enough to hold twenty people, but there was only a single table set up in it with a single chair on one side and three or four chairs on the other. Dr. Bala motioned for Rett to have a seat in the single chair while he took his place on the other side of the table.

To Rett's relief, there was nothing unusual about the next forty-five minutes. Dr. Bala asked all the standard questions about his education and any work he had done while in school that was relevant. He also asked to see Rett's physical therapist's license, which Rett had ready to present to him. Rett was very relieved to get the impression that he was doing well in the interview.

When Rett sensed that Dr. Bala was winding down with his questions, he took advantage of a quiet moment to ask, "Dr. Bala, do you mind telling me which hospital or doctor's office I'm interviewing with? I haven't seen anything yet that would tell me where this opening is, exactly."

"No, not just yet," replied Dr. Bala, which seemed really strange to Rett, and his suspicion meter started ticking up again. Dr. Bala shuffled through some papers on the table in front of him, which Rett could tell were resumes. The doctor seemed lost in thought for a few moments, but then suddenly said, "Wait here for a moment, please, Rett. I'll be right back."

Dr. Bala left the room and Rett wondered what the hell this was about. He'd never been in a single interview like this one.

A few seconds later, Dr. Bala walked back in with the man Rett had met earlier in the hallway, George Hastings. Rett now assumed he must be a doctor, after all. Rett stood up to greet him again, saying, "Hello, Dr. Hastings."

George Hastings laughed good-naturedly and said, "Oh, I'm not a doctor."

All three sat down at the table, and George asked Rett a few general questions about his grades at school, what drove his interest in physical therapy, did he mind travel, and even if Rett had anything that would limit how soon he could start. Rett took that as a good sign until Dr. Bala seemed to be a little irritated with George for asking it.

Before Rett could ask yet again who he was interviewing with, Dr. Bala and George stepped out of the conference room. When Dr. Bala stepped back in a couple of minutes later, he seemed in a much better mood.

He resumed his seat across from Rett and leaned over the table slightly in anticipation. "Rett, I'd like to offer you a job."

Before Rett could demand "With who?" Dr. Bala continued, "But... there are some aspects of this position that you need to be fully aware of in considering your response."

Dr. Bala spent the next few minutes explaining to Rett that the position was fairly intense. He would be expected to work six days a week, sometimes seven. Hours typically would be from 2pm to around 11pm at night. There would be extensive travel involved. There was also very limited time off in terms of vacation and holidays. Rett grew more and more concerned about the job as he listened. The whole slavery thing had started as a joke, but real-world indentured servitude wasn't as funny.

Dr. Bala finally said, "But, on the plus side, from November through January, you are totally free, but still paid at full salary. And most of the time, it's early October through January that you'll have off at full pay."

Rett had never heard of any physical therapy position with this kind of crazy schedule, but the three months off went a long way towards making up for the rest of the year. And then Dr. Bala told him what his starting salary would be, which was at least thirty percent higher than what he expected to get starting out in the field.

Dr. Bala ended by asking, "So, does this sound like a position you'd be willing to accept?"

The whole thing was so strange that Rett didn't know what to say. But the first of a long line of student loan repayments was staring him down very quickly. And to be honest, deep down inside, his uncertainty about Mike and his reluctance to face him made this offer immediately attractive.

Rett took a deep breath and said, "I still have no idea who this job is with, but yeah, I suppose I'd be willing to take it." If it turned out the mob or some eastern European crime syndicate was hiring him to be a physical therapist, he'd just change his mind and bolt. And he was damn close to believing that this was who was hiring him.

Dr. Bala nodded at Rett, very pleased.

"Great! Welcome to the Mobile Joes, Rett!"

~~~~~

"Ouch. It went that bad, huh?" Val made a face that looked like a bandage had just been ripped off her rear end.

"I told you they hired me," insisted Rett. He shifted over to get off that one lumpy spot in the couch that was always uncomfortable.

Val rolled her eyes. "Bullshit! A major league baseball team? Really? The only reason you'd make up *that* kind of a lie is if whatever interview you *did* go on went really bad. I know your freaky sense of humor, lily white." She eyed Rett, letting him know she was on to his little game.

"It's ok, Rett," she said, taking a more genuinely sympathetic tone. "You can stay here and I'll cover your rent a little longer until you get something."

Rett looked at her, offended. But everything that had happened that day had taken on a surreal quality for him as well, so he guessed he couldn't really fault her for her disbelief. It definitely wasn't a typical job, and he was still trying to process all of it. Rather than argue, he went to his bedroom (tripping on the torn carpet in the process) and grabbed the paperwork that Rosemary had grudgingly given to him after he had been hired.

He handed it to Val with a smug smile.

She started looking at the paperwork — details of his job on Mobile Joes letterhead, directions to the team's restricted parking lot at the LeBayonne Portyards in Mobile, and a sheet about what to bring and what to expect on his first day.

Val looked over the paperwork, her large, dark eyes getting even bigger with each passing second.

She finally said, her nose still buried in the papers, "You have GOT to be shitting me! You have GOT..."

Her head jerked up and her eyes narrowed at Rett. "You don't know *dick cheese* about baseball!"

Rett threw up his hands and shrugged, "I *know*! How fucked up is that?!"

She grinned widely at her beloved friend, but the grin faltered and drifted rather quickly until a shade of melancholy took over her face. "You're moving. Like *really* moving. Away."

It stung Rett, too, and his smile faded just as hers had. He had thought about it on the drive back from Mobile earlier, but it had been something like an abstract concept then, on the periphery of the relief of actually getting a job. But now, with Val in front of him, live and in person, it made the consequences painfully real. Both of their lives were going to change very drastically in the one week he had before his first day at his new job. That gave them almost no time since he had to find an apartment and move to Mobile in that interim. He went and hugged his friend, his very best friend, and tried to comfort the both of them, "I know, Val. But it's just Mobile... barely a few hours away. You'll be able to come visit. And I'll have time in the winter to come see you, too!"

Val tried to smile, but it took some effort to make it convincing.

She grabbed Rett's hand and started pulling at him, "C'mon, you."

Rett stumbled along behind her. "Where are we going?"

"We," she said emphatically, "are going out to get celebratorially shit-faced!"

Chapter 3

"Goddammit!" muttered Rett under his breath. He was
already late, and in his rush he had left in his car all of the
paperwork he needed with him for his first day. He turned
around, ran all the way back and grabbed the paperwork sitting
on his front seat. He was half out of breath when he made it back
up to the main gate at the LeBayonne Portyards, across the Mobile
River from the heart of downtown, and found the nearest security
guard. He let the guard know he was there for his first day,
showed him the hiring paperwork Rosemary had provided, and
the guard radioed in to have another guard come show Rett how
to get to the clubhouse. While he waited, he looked at the baseball
stadium in front of him and thought to himself how strange it
was that he would now be working there. He never would have
thought in a million years he'd be doing something like this,
mostly because he'd never given a spit-shined fig about baseball.

He had read some of the background information that had
been provided in his paperwork and knew that the stadium itself
was not quite two years old at this point. It had been paid for and
built by the LeBayonne family on part of the port land near the
USS Alabama Memorial Park. The LeBayonne family pretty much
had made an ungodly amount of money in shipping and
effectively owned all of the commercial port and associated
businesses in Mobile, hence the stadium name — LeBayonne
Portyards.

The same family had also worked with Major League Baseball to establish the Mobile Joes the season prior as an American League Central Division franchise expansion club. That same year the MLB had also created the Portland Goshawks as an American League Western Division team.

The team, the Mobile Joes, was named after Joe Cain, a particularly colorful character in Mobile history. Mobile was always proud of the fact that its celebration of Mardi Gras predated even New Orleans', and Joe Cain was a way for Mobile to get back at New Orleans for having the more widely renowned celebration. Joe Cain, the person, was credited with almost single-handedly causing a re-emergence of the Mardi Gras celebration in Mobile during the Civil War, where he paraded up and down one of the main streets as the character Chief Slacabamorinico in a mule-pulled coal cart. So the team became the Joes to honor this bright moment in a very dark time in the city's history, and the team mascot was aptly named Old Slac.

Rett wondered if he was the only person in all of Alabama to not know *any* of this. But he was already getting a crash course in it.

The other guard showed up and led Rett into the stadium and around the main stadium concourse before turning off into an employees-only area, down a floor in an elevator and along a service corridor before passing through a final locked door. The guard announced that this was the clubhouse and turned and left before Rett thought to ask him how to get to Rosemary's office. He wasn't fond of the idea of dealing with Rosemary again, but that was who he had been instructed to find when he first arrived. He hoped that maybe her attitude would improve now that he was an actual employee there.

The hallway he found himself in was a cream color with teal pin-stripes spaced evenly along its length. Facing the door to the clubhouse was the Mobile Joes logo, with Old Slac's feathered crown hanging off the "J". The hallway went in both directions, so he picked one and set out to find either Rosemary or someone he could ask. He didn't go far before he ran across a rather tall fellow wearing shorts, a pale blue knit shirt, and a baseball cap with the Joes logo on it.

"Hey," said Rett, glad to find someone, "sorry, but can you point me to Rosemary Karan's office?"

The guy got a rather comical pained look on his face and said, "Yeah, back that way," while pointing back the way Rett had come. "Here, I'll show you."

They walked back towards the end of the hallway as it curved around slightly and the man leading Rett said, "Up this way on the left. Hope your rabies shots are up to date!"

Rett's hopes that Rosemary would get easier to deal with sank significantly.

An acidic voice came out of the open doorway on the left that said, "I heard that, Topher."

Topher gave Rett a good-natured grin and led him into the office where Rosemary was seated primly behind her painfully organized desk.

She regarded Topher like he was a cockroach in the middle of her kitchen table and she had a rolled up newspaper in her hand. "Are those cleats you're wearing? You *know* what I've told you people about wearing cleats on this carpet!"

Topher turned to Rett and silently mouthed the words "good luck" before saying out loud, "Sorry, Rose! I'm leaving! I just needed to drop someone off first."

Rett was sorry to see Topher leave. He glanced around the office he was in, which had a nice seating area opposite Rosemary's desk. There was a new leather couch and upholstered club chairs arranged around a contemporary wood and glass coffee table.

Rett spun back around when he heard Rosemary exhale heavily, as if her day had just become unbearable, and say, "Well. This time you're twenty minutes late. I anticipate that, soon, you won't even bother to show up at all. But I'll imagine you'll still expect that paycheck to arrive like clockwork!"

Rett flushed a little red in the face and started to try and explain, only to be cut off again.

"Please. Just stop. I'll let George know you're here. *Don't* sit down! I mean it!"

Rosemary stepped through a door behind her desk and Rett managed to exhale for the first time since he had walked into her office.

She appeared again a moment later, eyeing Rett suspiciously, like she was certain she would catch him sitting on the forbidden couch.

She motioned Rett to the doorway behind her as she resumed her seat at her desk.

At the end of his job interview, Rett had found out that George Hastings was the General Manager of the Mobile Joes, and that was whose office he found himself in now. George was dressed more casually than he was when Rett met him during his interview — still with khaki pants, but a gold knit polo shirt with the Mobile Joes logo embroidered on the breast.

George stood and greeted Rett with a smile and had him sit down so they could talk. George's office was furnished every bit as nicely as Rosemary's reception area out in front, but his was an eruption of clutter and papers compared to the rigid organization of Rosemary's. The walls displayed a number of signed pictures of ballplayers and team pictures. George's desk had multiple stacks of papers scattered around and dangerously close to merging into one huge pile.

"It's great to have you here, Rett! I'm meeting with you first to go through some of the general crap we have to do to get you on board, and then later, I'll turn you over to Dr. Bala so you can really begin what you're here to do. It's great to have you join us, by the way!"

Rett said he was very happy to be there, and was finally able to relax a little bit. George seemed to be a very likable man, confirming Rett's first impression of him when had interviewed. Rett wondered how he and Rosemary managed to work together.

As George started pulling some things together for him, Rett noticed a small placard standing on his desk that read:

"This is the test of your manhood: How much is there left in you after you have lost everything outside of yourself?" — *Orison Swett Marden*

Rett snorted internally. His father had always talked of manhood and making him a man; it seemed to be a big deal to his dad. But what his father saw as manhood seemed to have nothing to do with what this quote talked about. At least that was the sense Rett got of Mr. Marden's intention.

George pulled the things he needed together and was able to begin with Rett. First up was a tour of the stadium to help Rett start to learn his way around, along with a stop off at the security office to have his ID made. George then took him to where he could use his clothing allowance (which he had no idea he was getting) to buy some team-only Mobile Joes shirts since he would be required to dress in teamwear on the job. Rett bought as many knit polos as he could with the allowance, along with a few t-shirts, plus a warm-up jacket and a cap. George then explained to him how the travel worked since Rett would be expected to travel with the team on away series. He made sure Rett was properly included in the travel coordinator's plans for the series in Boston against the Red Sox starting later in the week.

When they wound back up in his office, George glanced at his watch and said, "Rett, I need to cut this off now to get ready for Seattle, ok? Let's go find Bala and he can handle the rest with you."

"Oh, you're heading out to Seattle tonight?"

George laughed heartily, "No, no, Rett. Seattle's here!"

Rett looked lost.

George laughed again. "The Seattle Mariners? It's who we're playing tonight. You know... baseball?"

Rett felt himself turn every possible shade between stupid and mortified.

George was still grinning, though, when he added, "You really don't know *anything* about baseball, do you?"

Rett looked at his feet and wondered how this was going to work. How would he be able to fit in at this place? His desperation for a job had made him gloss over the fact that he'd be trying to fit in with a bunch of professional jocks. Every day. These guys would smell the ignorance on him within five seconds. How the hell was this ever going to work?

"George," Rett finally said, pushing the dejection out of his voice, "can I ask you a question?"

"Of course."

"Why did you hire me? I mean, you're totally right... I don't know much about baseball at all. There had to be a hundred physical therapists out there that are huge baseball fans and would kill for this kind of job."

If Rett had been there for any length of time more than the few hours he had been there already, was any more invested in this job, he probably would have found it impossible to ask that question, but right now he felt like he had nothing to lose by being really blatantly honest. If he needed to start looking for another job quickly, then he'd do that and bail on all of this.

George regarded Rett easily for a moment before he spoke. He said, "You're right, there are plenty out there. It was Bala's idea to stay away from those guys, and I agree with him on this. We didn't hire you to be the hitting coach for the team, Rett. We hired you to do physical therapy and to *focus* on that. The last guy we had acting as the team's physical therapist was a huge baseball fan, and frankly, it got in the way of him doing his job. We don't need another person with a strong opinion on how this team should play ball; we *need* a physical therapist. That's why we were careful not to talk about who the open position was with until we were sure we wanted to make an offer."

It made sense to Rett, and it made him feel a little better. But he was still wary of being at a serious disadvantage with the people he was supposed to be working with. He wasn't totally sure it would work out, but what was the harm in letting it play out a little to see what happened? He nodded to George.

George added, picking up on the doubt still in Rett, "Don't worry about the baseball stuff, Rett. You'll pick up on all that fast enough. You'll eventually understand it better than the know-it-all recliner coaches out there... because you'll be seeing it from the inside. Don't be afraid to ask even the most basic questions. Frankly, I think it would benefit a lot of the guys on the team to really think about the basic concepts some, but that's Ahab's job."

He clapped his hand on Rett's shoulder and said, "Just enjoy it, Rett! There's a lot of great individuals here, and sooner or later, we're going to turn into a team. And when we do, we're all gonna be in for a hell of a ride!"

George walked Rett over to Dr. Bala's office, having armed Rett with the paperwork he needed to finish up as a part of the hiring process.

Dr. Bala sat Rett down and spent some time with him making sure he understood the sensitive nature of patient/player confidentiality he would be expected to maintain. Rett, from school and his intern work in a few doctor's offices, was fully aware of the strict rules of patient confidentiality in any medical setting. Dr. Bala very seriously explained, though, that Rett would get pressed hard to talk about the players in a way that he'd *never* get with typical patients. Pro baseball players were celebrities; plus, a lot of money, legal and illegal, rode on MLB teams. As soon as people found out what Rett did for a living there would be tremendous pressure to talk about what Player X was like, or if it was true that Player Y was playing with a mild hamstring issue rather than go on the DL. (Rett had to interrupt and ask what Dr. Bala meant by the "DL" since he had no idea what that was, which led to Dr. Bala explaining the 15- and 60-day Disabled Lists in baseball). Dr. Bala was the one that made the call as to who went on the DL and who didn't. He warned Rett that he was never to talk about any player's condition to anyone outside the club without his explicit permission first.

He also made sure Rett understood he was there to do his job. He wasn't there to be the players' advisor, except in terms of physical therapy. He wasn't their coach. He wasn't their friend. He instructed Rett to keep it professional and let the players focus on what they were there to do. All of this made sense to Rett given what George had said earlier, and he surely wasn't going to be handing out baseball advice to anyone.

Dr. Bala then took Rett on a tour of the clubhouse itself since George had run out of time and hadn't gotten to that part. He started down at one end, the end nearest George's office and showed Rett the clubhouse kitchen and dining area, which had food, like real food, *good* food, provided for lunch and dinner on home game days due to the schedule the team kept. There was a sizable media room for interviews and presentations, along with an adjacent room with stations, Dr. Bala explained, where players could watch videos of themselves or opponents. There was a family lounge area for players that needed or wanted to have their immediate family nearby. Next to that, they got into the area that Rett would spend the most time in — there was an office for all the athletic trainers and a small desk for Rett to call home. The far end of the trainers' office led into a huge, full-sized gym for the team to use. To the right of their office was a treatment room, and Rett was impressed when Dr. Bala showed him they even had their own small X-ray room on the other side of the trainers' office. Past the treatment room and also opening up into the gym was a wet area with a couple of whirlpools and a high-end SwimEx.

Past a hallway that split off to Dr. Bala's office and the coaches' office was the main locker room for the team itself, but it wasn't like any locker room Rett had seen before. It was large and spacious, shaped like an elongated hexagon, with stations for each player around the entire periphery. Each station had the name and number of the player it belonged to along the top, with the player's uniform, which was cream with teal pinstripes, hanging in it. In the center was a grouping of expensive leather couches as well as a small conference table with high-backed ergonomic chairs. Hanging from the ceiling were a number of TV's, mostly showing ESPN at the moment, if Rett guessed right. Off the far end of the locker room was a living room/lounge room set up for the players. Also at the far end was the entrance to the team showers and restrooms.

When Rett stood in the middle of the room, he noticed a banner running around the periphery of the entire locker room above the players' stations. It read:

> *"Impossible is not a fact. It's an opinion. Impossible is not a declaration. It's a dare. Impossible is potential. Impossible is temporary. Impossible is nothing." ~ Muhammad Ali*

The entire clubhouse was finished much better than Rett was expecting, but that was mostly because his only real experience with any sports was the locker room at the gym he used at school. Prior to showing up that day, Rett's expectation for his working environment wasn't very high, but he was fine with the crow he was now eating on that count.

Between the locker room and the coaches' office, Dr. Bala took Rett down a staircase. Below the clubhouse was a private indoor area for batting and pitching practice. They went down a long hallway and Rett was once again surprised to see that when they came out, they were in the Joes' dugout and on the baseball field itself.

Dr. Bala told Rett, "Given your position on the team, you pretty much have access to anywhere in the stadium, so feel free to wander around. Just, you know, use common sense and don't be a jerk about it. You've got full use of any of the facilities in the clubhouse, including the gym and the wet area if you want, but players always get first crack, Rett. Always."

Rett acknowledged that he understood.

Back inside the clubhouse, Dr. Bala outfitted Rett with his laptop and showed him his desk again. Once Rett settled in a little, he gave him an orientation as to how they tracked the therapy for team members who were having problems that Rett or the trainers would focus on, whether they were on the DL or not.

Two of the trainers, Ryan and Wally, had already shown up and Dr. Bala introduced them to Rett. For the next several hours, and as more people and players showed up for the game that evening, Dr. Bala had Rett shadow him, Ryan, and Wally. Rett began to get a feel for what they did, what kind of problems they worked on with the players, and how they planned and tracked their efforts.

About thirty minutes before the game itself began, Ryan and Wally took Rett into the main locker room. Everyone had gathered and was standing around for a quick conference that Melville "Ahab" Delrossi, who Rett assumed was the coach although Wally had referred to him as the manager, wanted to have with everyone present.

The locker room started to get pretty crowded, so Rett tried to stand inconspicuously in the back. For one, he was brand new, and two, when Ahab stood up on a small stepstool so everyone could see and hear him, he looked rather angry. Ahab already seemed to be sweating and his brown hair with gray at the temples was soaking wet. He brushed his hand down his goatee impatiently and stubbed his foot at the stepstool a few times.

When he was satisfied that everyone was present, Ahab launched into an angry tirade, "Every person in this room is a goddamn cocksucker and, tonight, if you people want to take another long-dicking like we took in the series with the Marlins, I'll go drill a glory-hole in the visitors' clubhouse myself and you can bend your queer asses over! But I swear to God, when you get out on that damn field tonight, I'd better see everybody's, AND I MEAN EVERYBODY'S, head in the game! The ass-rape we just submitted to in Miami better not be repeated, shitheads!"

Ahab paused with his hands on his hips, his thick neck throbbing. Rett was completely shocked and shrunk down as much as he could.

"Focus, people! Concentrate!" bellowed Ahab.

Ahab paused to let it all sink in for a moment as he scanned the room, his face bright red from shouting.

He pointed at the Muhammad Ali quote circling the locker room and said, dialing back on the fury some, "When I say 'let's get out there and do the impossible,' I *do not* mean see how many cum loads the opposing team can bat down our willing and waiting throats, guys! Christ!"

For the first time in quite a while, Rett became extremely self-conscious about the fact that he was gay. He could feel himself blushing even though he knew Ahab's rant had nothing to do with him. But at the same time, he didn't think he'd be admitting his sexual orientation to anyone here anytime soon.

He cautiously looked around the room to see how everyone else was taking the dressing-down from Ahab, but it was difficult since he was shorter and smaller than most everyone present. The trainers, Ryan and Wally, didn't seem too put off by it. On his other side was a black guy with blond-tipped dreadlocks in a uniform with the number 9 on it who didn't seem to take it too personally, either.

Ahab sighed and scratched his head a little before continuing.

"Next item, and I can't believe I've got to stand up here and lecture you morons on this..."

He rubbed his eyes for a second and looked up at the ceiling like he was having to screw up the courage to cover the next topic. He seemed helpless to prevent the ironic grin that started to creep onto his face. "Guys, if you want to pick your goddamn nose, don't do it in the DUGOUT!"

The whole room exploded in laughter and catcalls, and even Ahab gave up trying to keep the smile off his face.

"Jesus, guys! If you go prospecting for gold nuggets while in the dugout, the cameras *will* pick it up, in *hi-def*, and you *will* be on ESPN that night!"

The whole room was cracking up and joking with each other while Ahab said, "If you wanna dredge the swamp for little green bodies, ladies, be my guest! *Just do it in the fucking tunnel, ok?*"

Ahab had to stop for a second and shake his head to keep from completely losing his composure and laughing with everyone else. He held up his hands again to try to get the conversation and laughter in the room to settle down.

"Now, I'm not going to be indiscreet and draw attention to the player who gave birth on live TV last night... because you know that's not my style." The laughter in the room started fresh and someone yelled, "C'mon, Ahab!!"

"But his initials are Luis Ojeda!"

The room erupted again and Rett saw a bunch of towels and t-shirts fly through the air, all aimed at a Hispanic guy with the number 3 on his uniform not far away. The guy was blushing, but waving at the room and he seemed to be taking it all in a good humor.

Ahab yelled over the laughter and taunts, "Focus, guys! Concentrate! Go do the impossible!" He stepped off the stepstool and the crowd started to disperse.

The black guy next to Rett, number 9, turned to him with a grin and said, "Feels like first grade recess sometimes!"

Rett laughed along with the guy.

Number 9 asked, "You the new trainer starting today?"

Rett shook his hand and said, "Well, physical therapist. But yeah, I just started today."

"That's cool. I'm JJ Troyer."

"I'm Rett. Rett Dougherty. What, uh, what do you do, JJ?"

JJ grinned crookedly at the question and said, "Well, when I'm not picking my nose just so I'll get some play on ESPN, Gunnar throws balls at me and I catch 'em. Sometimes, on a good night, I hit balls with a stick."

Rett felt like a complete idiot for asking such a stupid question. He was about to apologize, but JJ clapped him on the shoulder a couple of times and said, "Welcome to recess, Rett!" before heading out to the game with a happy grin.

As the crowd dispersed, Rett was about to go find Dr. Bala or one of the trainers to see what he should be doing next. He glanced over and saw Topher, the guy that had shown him to Rosemary's office when he first arrived, chatting with two other people, both in uniform. Number 39 was a trim guy with dark brown hair and a nice tan; he had keen eyes, but his face and demeanor looked like someone forty-ish. But it was the other guy who caught Rett's attention. He knew that guy. It was Bigfoot. He had seen that guy when he showed up for his interview, with the guy in the suit. Bigfoot, also dressed in a uniform with a 72 on the front, had a very serious look on his face and was listening intently to what Topher and 39 were saying to each other.

Dr. Bala found Rett a second later and told him to take a break for a while since the game was starting. Rett decided to get the last of his forms filled out so he could get them back to Rosemary. That completed, he went and got something to eat in the clubhouse dining room, and then wandered around the stadium. He grabbed a program and made his way up to some of the upper stands which had huge sections of empty seats, where he settled in to watch a little professional baseball for the first time in his life. It was a little odd to Rett to look down on the pitcher's mound and see number 39 that he had been in the locker room with earlier. Checking the program, he figured out that 39 was Gunnar Lang-Smith, the Joes' starting pitcher. And number 9, JJ Troyer with the dreadlocks, was the catcher. Luis Ojeda, the guy that everyone razzed for picking his nose, was the third baseman.

The day's heat was dissipating now that the sun had sunk down low in the sky, and the stadium was designed so that downtown Mobile was visible over one wall. Overhead, a few seabirds distracted from the bay flew around. Thinking about his day, Ahab's angry shouting had been a little disconcerting, but George seemed like a great guy. And he had gotten a good dinner in the dining room for free. Rett had enough of the starving student in him that "free" was still his favorite cuisine. He had gotten his license expecting to have a very run-of-the-mill physical therapy career — helping people recover from surgery, or minimizing the effects of debilitating diseases, or fighting the effects of aging. Here, it was still physical therapy, but completely different than what he had ever imagined a physical therapy career would be like. He decided that it could still turn out good or bad, but he was willing to try it and find out.

As the game got near the end, with the Joes losing to the Mariners 2—0, Rett headed back down to the clubhouse as Dr. Bala had asked him to do. Once there, one of the other trainers, Rikky Kato, introduced himself to Rett and asked him to help with icing down Gunnar's arm.

Walking over to the treatment room, Rett got a text from Val asking how his first day was going. He texted back briefly that he was busy and he'd call her later.

Rikky explained that in the 8th inning, Gunnar's arm had started hurting and Ahab sent in Ernie McGowan, one of the relief pitchers. Normally, they preferred not to ice an arm unless there was swelling or pain, but Gunnar definitely was feeling the pain that night.

Rikky introduced Rett to Gunnar, who was sitting up on one of the exam tables with his uniform pants on, but only his t-shirt up top. Rett had to internally admit to himself that Gunnar was in great shape. The tight compression shirt didn't leave anything to Rett's imagination, and it was clear that even for someone Gunnar's age, he had a really amazing upper body. Rett mostly listened as Rikky chatted with Gunnar about his pitching that evening and checked his arm and shoulder briefly.

Rikky asked Rett to grab one of the ice sleeves out of the freezer they kept in the treatment room. As he was fetching it, Gunnar asked him, "So what'd you think of the pitching tonight, Rett?"

Rett near-panicked for a second, but then shrugged as he came back with the ice pack and said, "I doubt anybody in this clubhouse could have done any better."

Gunnar laughed out loud and said, "That's a perfect bullshit answer if I ever heard one, Rett. You're gonna fit in fine here!"

Once Gunnar had the ice sleeve secured on his arm and shoulder, Rett helped Dr. Bala and the trainers with a few other players that weren't necessarily hurt, but "feeling it" now that the game had ended. Sometimes this consisted of gentle massages to keep the blood flowing, sometimes it was testing range of motion and pain levels to make sure there wasn't anything more serious going on, and sometimes helping players with the SwimEx.

Around 11pm that night, the clubhouse had rapidly started to clear out. Dr. Bala asked Rett to put his notes from the day's work into the computer and then study up on the therapy plans for the next few days, especially for Booker Joy and Brian Thorn, the only two players currently on the Joes' Disabled List.

By the time Rett had finished entering his notes and was about to start looking at the plans, the clubhouse seemed completely empty. He had almost decided he was the only person left and was going to review the therapy plans, but he became aware of some soft voices coming through the cracked doorway from the trainers' office into the weight training room.

Rett was going to glance to see who might still be there when heard a voice growl, "I pay you too much, you know, you worthless faggot!"

Rett stopped short from going into the training area when he heard that. But there was a trick of how the doors were arranged so that Rett could see through the treatment room to the far end of the training room, nearest the hallway between it and the main locker room. He caught a glimpse of the back of somebody in a dark suit walking out of the training room to the hallway between it and the main locker room. Whoever was in the suit reached his hand up at the last minute and flipped off whoever had made the comment to him.

Rett knew the person in the suit would be coming down the main hallway on the other side of his office if he was leaving the clubhouse, so out of curiosity he headed out that way to see who the person in the suit was. He went out the door at the other end of the trainers' office and walked down the main hallway towards the locker room. As he walked, the guy in the suit came around the corner from the cross hallway.

He didn't expect to recognize the person, but he *had* seen this guy before. It was the same guy he had seen in a suit with the big guy while he was waiting on his interview. He wondered if it was Bigfoot that was in the training room and had called him a faggot.

He went back to his office and waited a minute or two. He could still hear somebody on the weight machines out in the training room, so he knew the guy was there. Once he had waited long enough, he nonchalantly used the training room as a shortcut to get to Dr. Bala's office. He knew Dr. Bala had already left, but it was a convenient excuse. As soon as he got into the training room, he was able to confirm it. It was the big guy he had seen. What he had heard, plus the size of the guy made Rett make a mental note to avoid that one. Well, that guy, and probably Ahab, too, actually.

~~~~~

"I have no idea who that is, Val."

"Josh Kilfoyle!" shouted Val over the phone.

"Oh, you mean the guy that invented duct tape?" said Rett, giving up on trying to get Val to explain who Josh Kilfoyle was.

Val had sent a text telling him to call her when he got done with his day, no matter how late it was. It was well after midnight when he had called, and she immediately started asking about some person that Rett had never heard of.

"God, you're a dumbass!" heaved Val. "Josh Kilfoyle! The Australian guy! He plays right field for the Joes! He's like a... *co-worker* of yours! Wow, that's so fucked up to say that."

Rett said, proudly, "Hey, did you know the Portyards sells ten different flavors of Moon Pies? Some of them are available *only* at the Portyards!"

Val went berserk. "I swear to God, I'm going to murder you! I'm going to wiggle through this fucking phone and strangle you and watch the life drain out of those irritating blue eyes of yours, Rett! And then, I shall *dance*!"

Rett stayed silent, and there was an eerie silence on Val's end for several seconds.

"Anyway, he's hot," said Val, plainly.

Rett laughed and said, "No, I didn't get to meet him today. And there's a number of guys on the team that are good-looking, for your information. For jocks, I guess, anyway." For some reason, the image that popped into Rett's mind was that of Topher, Gunnar, and the human Monster Truck standing together in their uniforms in the locker room and talking.

Val managed only a disappointed grunt.

Rett tried a consolation prize. "Hey, do you know who Gunnar Lang-Smith is? The pitcher?"

Val perked up. "Of course! He's the star pitcher! The senior team member!"

"I *did* get to meet him. Actually, I got to help ice his arm down after he left the game. He's a cool guy."

Val was almost breathless. "You are so totally shitting me! Please tell me you're shitting me!"

"I do nothing *but* shit you, Val. It's kinda my thing," he said, stifling a yawn.

"Seriously, though. You got to, like, touch him?"

Rett rolled his eyes. "Yes, Val, I got to touch him."

"Awwwwwwwwwwwwwesome!" groaned Val.

"I'm hanging up if I hear a vibrator in the background."

"I'll turn it down to low," said Val. "You know, come to think of it, I don't think I've ever used the low setting on this thing. Why would a vibrator even have a low setting to begin with? That's sort of like having a shotgun that shoots marshmallows *or* buckshot. Shoot to kill, I always say."

"I got to meet JJ Troyer, too," said Rett. "The catcher dude? Have you heard of him?"

"Oh my God! He's amazing! He's like the coolest guy ever! He was interviewed on the news tonight right after the game ended!"

Rett said, "Yeah, he's a pretty funny guy. He probably thinks I'm an idiot, but he was totally laid-back about it."

"Ok, that's it, you lucky bastard! I'm coming down to Mobile this weekend, Rett!"

"Ok, I'll leave a key for you under the mat. I'll be in Boston with the team."

"Shit! You are so unworthy of that job, it's not even funny. You know that?" said Val.

"So? Why you say?"

Val said, "You think third base is anal sex."

"*I do not!*" said Rett, fully offended at the very idea. "Third base is felching!"

"Oh, Lord, I miss you so much already!" said Val, wistfully. "Seriously, do you think you'll become a baseball fan now?"

Rett sighed and said, "I don't know. It was sorta fun watching some of the game tonight. You know I've never cared much about sports, or jocks, or anything like that, though. Some of the guys seemed pretty cool. Others... maybe not."

Val paused before asking, sincerely, "So, what do you think your dad would think of what you're doing?"

"Who cares," said Rett, far more a statement than a question.

"Do you think he still would have turned you out if he could see you now?"

"Val, you know I don't like talking about this."

"I just wonder if maybe he'd find something in you he could..."

"Hey, I've got an idea! Let's not talk about this!" insisted Rett.

"I mean, you and I cut up, but it's not like you're some ditzy, limp-wristed flamethrower! You're masculine and could play sports if you wanted to! All those people that I told you were gay were completely and totally surprised! Don't you think your parents..."

"I'm *not* getting into... Wait... how many people did you tell I was gay?"

"Uh... Montgomery?"

"Val..."

"Oh, get over yourself. I kept it to just those inside the city limits. I didn't have time to cover the entire greater metropolitan area."

There was an uncomfortable lull at this point, broken only by an exaggerated sigh from Rett.

"Have you talked to Mike?" asked Val.

Rett didn't like the new subject any better than the previous one. "Yep, I'm hanging up now."

"Are you *serious* that you *still* haven't had a real talk with him?" Val was shocked.

"New job. Crazy sched..."

Val interrupted, "What a douchebag!"

Rett's early joking aside, now he really was tempted to just hang up. But instead he complained, "Jeez, you've turned into a big nag!"

"You haven't had a mom in your life for going on seven years, Rett, so here's Momma Papadakis speaking to you now — you can't fuck and run, sweetie. Call Mike up and *fix it* with him or *end it*. This dangling you're doing to him is ass-wipery. And I've seen you do it before!"

Rett sat quietly, but that gave Val a chance to push again. "You dated all eight available gay guys in Montgomery, not counting the truckers you'd blow when they'd pass through town, and I don't think you ended it gracefully with *any* of them!"

Rett felt like he had ants crawling all over him. He *had* left things completely unresolved with Mike. But he really didn't know how to approach it. Just ending it seemed unfair since he had issues with some of the character traits Mike had exhibited. But getting into all that now, after he had freaking moved, seemed stupid and incidental. So he had settled into a sort of denial stasis instead. The whole thing with Mike was like a big pile of unfolded laundry sitting on the kitchen table; he'd just look the other way every time he went into the kitchen and hoped somebody else would deal with it. Except... he lived alone now.

Mike had called probably three times since the night at Los Banditos, but had never left a message, and Rett had always found some excuse to not answer the phone.

Val seemed intent on waiting for some kind of reply, some kind of defense, valid or lame, from Rett. Rett said, "You hate me."

Val groaned and said, "Yes. From day one. That's why I scratched my ass with your toothbrush for five years. You know that one rashy spot that looked like Tom Hanks that never would go away? I scratched that."

"I'm sorry, Val," sniveled Rett.

"Oh, Jesus Christ! Not me! Talk to *Mike*!" bellowed Val into his ear. "Tell *him* you're sorry! Or tell him you're done! Or tell him you love him! Or tell him he's a dick for the list of reasons to be published in a full page ad tomorrow in the *Montgomery Advertiser*! But the silent treatment, Rett? Really?"

"Ok, fine! I hear you!" snapped Rett, desperate to stop Val from talking this way.

He added, "I will. It's just never been easy for me."

"Ok, I'll stop now. I don't like nagging any more than you like hearing it. And it's, shit, *really* late now and I need to get to bed, anyway. I've got a couple of arthritics tomorrow that we're starting on hydrotherapy exercises. How's that for glamour, asshole?"

"Oh, Valerie Papadakis. I do miss you, you know?"

"Hey, Rett?"

"Yeah?"

She cooed, "What flavors of Moon Pies?"

Chapter 4

The next day, Rett sat at the table in the middle of the locker room waiting for Brian Thorn, the relief pitcher that was on the Disabled List, to arrive. Brian had an acromioclavicular separation, or shoulder separation, that Dr. Bala had initially graded as mild. Rett was going to work with him since his time on the 15-day DL was nearing the end and they needed to decide if they were going to shift him to the 60-day DL and maybe recommend surgery for his shoulder if it seemed worse than originally anticipated.

A few other players had arrived and were hanging around before they got dressed for pitching and batting practice. Rett had torn out the team roster page from the program he had picked up the night before and was starting to use it as a cheat sheet to learn the players and coaches as he spotted them. One of the guys that had come in was an exceptionally handsome guy, with especially thick black hair and piercing dark eyes. He went to the station that had the number 5 and the name Arthur O'Creaghan over it. Rett looked him up and found out he was a catcher, like JJ Troyer was.

A second later, JJ himself showed up in a tight spandex sleeveless shirt and running shorts. He sat down at the table with Rett, who immediately tried to hide his cheat sheet. JJ was smiling but motioned for him to hand it over.

Rett knew he was busted so he slid it across the table to JJ. He looked away from him, down at the table, expecting that most anyone else would probably have already memorized all of these players and all about baseball before they ever started a job like this. He hoped JJ didn't think too poorly of him for not knowing these things. The AC separation he could handle, the rest still worried him.

JJ glanced down at it and was about to make a comment when Rosemary came striding purposefully through the locker room and using it as a shortcut to the coaches' office, completely indifferent to the player to the side that was in the process of changing.

All conversation in the room froze as she entered and Rett could feel everyone tense up. Everyone in the room seemed to be worried she was coming for them. When she had safely passed through, there was a collective sigh of relief. JJ looked at Rett and they both started laughing when they realized how they had all reacted.

JJ leaned across the table and said, "You know, there's a rumor going around that Rosemary is the one that trains all the Drill Instructors for the Marines."

Rett laughed out loud and Arthur, who was changing his shirt, said, "Aye! Your lady Rosemary there... Heard she eats live rats out of a brown bag for lunch, she does!"

JJ laughed and said, "Man, that's bullshit!"

Arthur said defensively, "'s not shite!"

They would have continued the discussion, but Rosemary appeared again. She seemed to sense something was going on and she stopped right inside the locker room, her eyes narrowing suspiciously and her thin, painted on lips pulling down. Arthur quickly tried to look busy and pretended to dig around in his locker station. Rosemary glanced from side to side to try to pick out who was up to no good, found no one she could immediately fault, and proceeded on through and out of the locker room.

JJ waved Rett's paper at him, "Crib notes?"

Rett nodded while JJ handed his paper back to him and said with another friendly smile, "Not a bad idea."

As he took the roster list back from JJ, Rett noticed a faint tattoo on his left forearm. It looked like nothing more than two short, crossed lines, like an "X". It didn't look like much of anything specific that Rett could pick out.

His curiosity got the better of him and he asked JJ, "What's the tattoo there?"

"Yeah, just a tattoo," the catcher replied, offering no more explanation.

A beat passed, and when JJ remained silent, Rett pushed a little further. "When you gonna get the rest of it?"

"Nah, that's it. It's nothing more than what you see," said JJ quietly.

Rett's interest was definitely piqued by that reaction, and he was weighing whether or not to pursue it a little more. Before he came to a decision, though, Rikky, one of the trainers Rett shared an office with, came into the locker room, leading another guy that Rett had barely caught a glimpse of on his first day, despite him being the most distinctive guy on the team. Aside from the guy being really lean and tightly muscled, he had a short, bright-green mohawk, and elaborate tattoos on both arms — lots of skulls, skeletons, daggers, crosses and guitars all in an elaborate Day of the Dead motif. Today, as he followed Rikky in, he only had a pair of baggy, shiny basketball shorts on and no shirt. Like his arms, his chest had a fair number of tattoos crossing it.

Rikky pointed the player in the direction of Rett, who immediately looked behind him to see who he was directing the player to, but there was no one behind him.

JJ watched all this in amusement and told him, "Good luck with Skunk, buddy!"

Before Rett had any chance to react, "Skunk" had run over and started pulling him up anxiously.

Rett stumbled out of his chair with Skunk still pulling on him roughly towards the treatment room.

Skunk was saying as he practically dragged Rett away, "You gotta come now! Man, you gotta fix this! Shit, this is all so fucked up! Rikky said you could do this. You're like the new doc, right, so you can tell me what the hell to do!"

Rett tried to explain that he wasn't a doctor, but Skunk wouldn't shut up long enough for him to get a word in. Skunk pulled him into the treatment room, still freaking out, "I don't know what the hell, man! I'm fucking freaked, though, doc!"

Rett tried to glance over in the trainers' office to see if he could grab one of the trainers, but Skunk planted him in front of one of the treatment tables and then jumped up on it in front of Rett. He stood up on the table, half-crazed, and in one swift motion he pulled his shorts and his jock strap down and grabbed his dick so it was only a few inches away from Rett's face.

"What the fuck is this, dude? What's that shit dripping out of it? Doc, you gotta fix this! It's burning like a son-of-a-bitch!"

Rett stammered "Holy shit!" and practically jumped back into the other treatment table behind him.

Skunk continued to waggle his dick at Rett. "Do you see it?! It's oozing something! What the fuck's going on? It's not gonna drop off, is it?"

Rett winced when he realized that Skunk's dick did, in fact, seem to be oozing a little. He backed up even further and looked up at the naked player standing on the table with his shorts down around his ankles.

Rett said forcefully, "Dude! I'm not doing anything until you stop... *splattering* everything around you!"

Skunk was still holding onto his dick, but he said, "Huh? Oh. Yeah. But you can fix it, right? You know what this is, right? It feels like goddamn fire ants in there!" To Rett's relief, he stopped shaking it around.

At this point, Rett could hear Rikky and Ryan and Wally behind him in their office laughing. Rett said to Skunk, "I'm not a doctor, uh, Skunk. I'm just a physical therapist, no matter what

Rikky told you!" He emphasized the last bit to make sure Rikky heard him in their office and knew he was on to them.

Rett added, "But... it looks like the clap."

Skunk panicked anew. "Oh, shit! How bad is that?"

Rett grabbed a paper cup from the wall dispenser and handed it to him.

He said, "I'll go get Dr. Bala."

Skunk nodded nervously. "What's the cup for?" he asked.

"The oozing is late stage. If Skunk Jr. falls off before I can find Dr. Bala and get him back here, just put it in the paper cup and we'll figure out what to do from there."

Skunk's eyes got as huge as baseballs and he choked out the words "Falls off?" There were now howls of laughter from Rikky, Ryan, and Wally in the adjoining office.

Rett opened the door from the treatment room to the weight room, only to see JJ, Arthur, Topher and a couple of other guys all laughing and scattering from where they had been listening at the door. Skunk finally realized he was being played and threw the paper cup at Rett. He pointed his cock at the guys in the weight room and shouted angrily, "You faggots better not leave any open drinks sitting around unless you want some runoff added!" He jumped down and sat on the table to wait, sulking.

Rett found Dr. Bala on the phone in his office. When he ended the call, Rett let him know what was going on with Skunk. Dr. Bala scratched at his mustache wearily, and muttered to himself, "I'm an orthopedist, for crying out loud."

He told Rett, "Skunk probably picked it up in Miami. Some of the guys, well... there's always groupies and..."

He gave up trying to explain and said, "I hope it's *just* gonorrhea."

Dr. Bala went to a locked cabinet and took out a syringe and a small bottle. He said, "In case it is."

As they walked back to the treatment room, Dr. Bala said, "It probably gives you an idea of how frequently this happens that I keep a little ceftriaxone on hand."

Back in the treatment room, Dr. Bala put on some gloves and confirmed that gonorrhea was, in fact, what Skunk had picked up. He gave Skunk the shot and told him to go get checked for other STDs just in case.

Rett stuck his head into his office where Rikky, Wally, Ryan were pretending to be busy. The other trainer, Freddie, had now walked in. Rett looked at Rikky and the others, who were now pretending to be very busy, and said, "Nice. Real nice."

Rikky said, "Hey, we've all had a trial-by-Skunk. No free rides here!"

Freddie looked around and said, "What'd I miss?"

Rikky started to fill him in and Rett left to go wait again in the locker room for Brian.

~~~~~

In the 4th inning, the Joes hadn't shown up on the scoreboard at all and the Mariners already had 4 runs. Instead of Gunnar pitching, today's program said the other starting pitcher, Ric Velasques, was on the mound. Rett had asked Gunnar about his arm earlier in the day, and he said it was feeling fine, so he thought maybe Ahab was giving him a little extra time for it to recuperate. Or maybe they alternated pitchers anyway since pitching was a fairly demanding role on the team. He checked the score again and started to wonder if the Joes had ever scored a run at all.

It was a lot hotter than the night before, and the humidity was worse, so it wasn't as comfortable watching this time around.

Scanning around the stadium, Rett saw that a few of the fans were already giving up on the Joes and the humidity and leaving the game, too.

Arthur was catching instead of JJ, and Rett paid attention to how Patrick "Skunk" Hanneman, in the jersey with 24 on it, was handling center field. Rett had to laugh to himself at their encounter earlier, even if he had gotten the feeling that it had pissed Skunk off a little bit. Skunk definitely seemed to be scratching his crotch a lot, even for a ballplayer.

Shortly into the 4th inning, his phone rang. Rett wasn't sure what to do when he saw that it was Mike, but his conversation with Val from the night before was fresh in his mind. He managed to waffle on what to do long enough that the call flipped over to voicemail, effectively making the decision for him, which was a little bit of a relief to him.

Rett was surprised when a voice mail actually did come through this time, though, unlike the other times Mike had called in the last week. He was tempted to ignore even the message, but finally couldn't stand the anticipation anymore and played it back a few minutes later.

Mike's message said, "Hey, Rett. Uh... I can only assume what's going on here. I wish you'd answer your phone because I know you always did before until now. I guess you've decided that it's over between us and that's the message you're trying to send. I'd like to know why, but I don't get the feeling I'm going to find out. But... message received, I guess... ok?"

There was a pause in the message before Mike finished, "Yeah, so good luck. In, uh, Mobile now, from what I hear. Bye." Rett could hear the disappointment in Mike's voice.

He stared at his phone in his hand for a while after he finished listening to the message. Val was right. He shouldn't have left things hanging like that. Mike wasn't perfect, but he wasn't a bad guy, and he deserved better treatment.

Rett tried to understand what made it so difficult to do what Val had suggested — to tell Mike about the things that had hurt his feelings, or to explicitly end it with no other discussion. He decided it was because he didn't know which of those was the right thing. And it bothered him that he couldn't figure out what he wanted from Mike, then or even now.

It was all moot after the phone call, though. What he couldn't seem to pull himself together enough to do, Mike had done in a message tonight, and he was off the hook as a result. It should have made him feel better that it was done, but it didn't.

But what bothered him worse was that he knew he wouldn't be able to bring himself to call Mike back and explain. To do Mike the simple favor of telling him he was a good guy, but that what they had wasn't working for him, and now that he had a hectic job in a different city, it was better this way. Or whatever excuse Rett wanted to come up with for ending it.

Rett spent the rest of the 4th inning trying to rouse enough courage to call Mike back and talk to him. He eventually gave up in frustration and went back to the clubhouse.

The clubhouse was pretty deserted, and there wasn't much for Rett to do at the moment. He decided to use the gym to try and clear his mind of his thoughts about Mike while he had some time. When he got in, he was glad to see JJ in there as well, Ahab having let him go for the rest of the game since Arthur was catching and the other catcher, Bert Cardona, was available to step in if necessary.

They chatted as they worked out, and Rett was very glad to have the distraction. Plus, he was really starting to like JJ, who was remarkably easy to talk to. Rett had assumed that all of these guys would want to talk about nothing but baseball, but JJ seemed happy to talk about anything.

In spite of feeling like he could bring anything up, Rett was the one that steered the conversation back to baseball. Or the team, at least. JJ had seemed pretty willing to help Rett learn, and so he decided to take advantage of it. He asked about Arthur and his accent. JJ explained that Arthur was Irish and his parents had moved to the US when he was ten or eleven. He had just been traded to the Joes from the Detroit Tigers prior to the start of the season.

JJ also volunteered that Rett had handled Skunk pretty well that afternoon. He said that Skunk was a conceited jerk for the most part, the kind that expected women's panties to spontaneously fall down merely because he had walked into a room. He said Skunk's only saving grace was that he was a solid fielder. Otherwise, he was a publicity whore, a slutcock as Rett had found out the hard way, and a "Mendoza line limbo star." Rett had to get him to explain what the hell *that* meant, and JJ's short explanation was that Skunk was worthless as a hitter.

At the start of the 9th inning, it was clear the Joes were going to lose again. A few other players started drifting back into the clubhouse, and so Rett headed to the showers and JJ followed less than a minute later.

Rett had never been nervous about showering with other guys in gyms. Since he rarely had a thing for jocks, and didn't care about sports, he worried very little about getting caught checking the guys out or suddenly getting a hard-on. So being in the showers with JJ didn't even enter Rett's mind as a concern. The shower stalls had chest high walls between them, but were open above that, and JJ and Rett continued their casual conversation as they cleaned up, this time talking more about Rett's schooling.

When Rett had gotten out and was toweling off and answering a question JJ had asked about his friend, Val, from school, Rett noticed someone else entering the shower area.

He glanced over and saw the Bigfoot guy coming in with nothing but a towel wrapped around him. Rett answered JJ's question, but his eyes involuntarily locked onto the guy, and despite hearing him call his agent or whoever a faggot the night before, Rett couldn't help but stare. The guy was fucking built. He had an incredibly muscular chest and huge arms. His pecs were well-defined, almost squared off, with a coating of golden brown hair that went with the shaggy hair on his head (which was a little damp with sweat around the edges from being outside in the heat). His stomach was flat, and he could tell the abdominals were powerful even if they were under a modest layer of natural body fat. The chest hair came down in a line, crossing his abdomen before fanning back out into a broad patch surrounding his navel and disappearing under the towel.

The guy stopped as soon as he saw Rett toweling off outside his shower stall. His eyes locked onto Rett for just a moment before he frowned almost imperceptibly and looked pissed. He twitched slightly and turned around and left the shower area without a word.

Rett involuntarily watched the guy's broad back, as equally sculpted as his front, while he turned back out into the locker room.

JJ had said, "So this friend of yours, you should bring her by one night."

Rett's eyes lingered a moment where the guy had left as he answered JJ, "I doubt I'll be able to keep her away. She wanted to come this weekend until I reminded her we were on the road. She almost passed out when I told her I met you last night."

JJ grinned widely and said, "Really? That's cool!"

"Don't get too excited," explained Rett. "She also wigged out when I told her the Portyards has ten different flavors of Moon Pies."

Rett started to get worried about Bigfoot's reaction. Maybe he had noticed Rett staring, and had now already figured Rett as queer. Maybe that's why he didn't want to be in the shower area with him. He thought about asking JJ who the guy was, but decided that would seem a little weird to ask right then. He warned himself he should be a lot more careful. The last thing he needed was to piss off some homophobic ball player in his first week.

~~~~~

By the time he was leaving the clubhouse a little after 11pm, Rett's mind was back on Mike, bouncing back and forth between returning his call and just leaving it where it was. He leaned towards leaving it where it was since talking to Mike wasn't going to change where things stood between them; with his schedule, there was no way they'd be able to realistically attempt to continue *any* kind of a relationship.

That reminded Rett he needed to focus on his job anyway, which was going to occupy huge amounts of his time. He wasn't sure how he'd even be in a position to meet a guy in Mobile, what with the frequent travel and working most evenings and weekends.

Hell, for all that, he needed a sofa far more than he needed a boyfriend. As he got in his car, he pictured his mostly empty apartment; all there was in it was his bedroom furniture and one Goodwill-quality easy chair in his den. His place was empty besides that. Back in Montgomery, everything in their apartment had been Val's. The apartment had been in her name, and all the utilities and phone and cable had been in her name. Even his cell phone had been on a family plan, under her name. Val seemed fine with leaving it all that way while they lived together, and Rett was fine with that arrangement, too, given his family situation. He had only transferred his cell phone number to his own account the day before he started working with the Joes.

All of these thoughts crapped out on him when he tried to crank his car and it sat passively, totally ignoring Rett.

Rett tried cajoling first and muttered at it, "C'mon baby, you've always come through for me before!! Don't let daddy down, baby!" A few more attempts at turning the key in the ignition yielded nothing, not even a hiccup.

When that didn't work, he got angry and yelled at the car for a bit. And when that didn't work, he started running through his list of gods, trying to see who was up and could be distracted from their late-night TV enough to help.

"Odin? You there, my man? A little help, maybe? You were a rock star the last time!!"

Nothing.

"Saint Christopher? You're a car nut! Give her a little nudge for me! Just a tiny one is all it takes!"

Nothing.

Rett got desperate. "Ahura Mazda? Flying Spaghetti Monster? Vishnu? Anybody?" He sat in silent frustration for a moment, feeling his own pulse in his neck. "Hey, Quetzalcoatl, why don't you take a turn at it? Surely a fucked up little Jetta doesn't intimidate you, does it, big guy? Come on, Quetzy, show this motherfucker who's boss!"

Nothing.

He beat his fist on the dash in frustration.

Rett popped the hood and got out of his car. He wondered if maybe JJ had already left for the night and if maybe he could bum a ride from him. He stood under the parking lot lights of the Portyards employee lot and looked at the mysterious and confusing car engine, again wondering why he had entertained any thoughts at all that this would be useful. Did he expect a flashing neon sign that would say "Jiggle this" or "twist that" with a helpful arrow? He poked at a random wire or two and then wondered where he could wipe his finger now that it was sooty and greasy.

He exhaled heavily and thought about giving up and sacking out for the night on one of the treatment room tables in the clubhouse, leaving the car to be dealt with in daylight.

He said aloud to his car engine, "Hey, Quetzalcoatl! Suck my dick, asshole!"

He slammed the hood of his car back down to go back inside when he saw, standing a few feet away and watching him, none other than the Bigfoot dude.

They stared at each other in silence for an awkward moment before Bigfoot said, "Er... Did you just tell... Quetzalcoatl... to blow you?"

"No," said Rett, trying to be evasive, but mostly just being embarrassed.

"Are you sure?" the guy asked again.

"No. Yes," said Rett firmly, sticking hard with the evasiveness tactic.

The guy looked at Rett, his forehead knitted in confusion.

Rett said, "Is there something I can help you with?"

The big guy looked a little surprised, and then he said with a smile, "Well, I was going to see if *you* needed any help. With your car... And all." He gestured at the black Jetta to make sure there was no misunderstanding which car he was referring to, despite the parking lot being almost totally empty.

Rett ground his teeth almost hard enough to crack a few and thought to himself, *God dammit, why does there have to be dimples? Perfect fucking dimples! I'm so totally fucked!*

The big guy stepped forward and held out his hand and said, "I've seen you in the clubhouse a few times, but we haven't met yet. I'm Cory. Cory Pritchart."

Rett couldn't look away from the guy's smile and his obscenely perfect dimples no matter how hard he tried. He wanted to turn and run the other way as fast as he could before he caused problems for himself he couldn't fix.

Instead, he held out his hand and shook Cory's. "Hey, yeah, I'm Rett Dougherty." His hand felt tiny compared to Cory's.

Cory said, "So... you need a mechanic or something?"

Rett forced himself to look over at his car. "A morphine drip and hospice, more likely."

Cory laughed out loud, and the dimples showed back up. "Hospice! And a morphine drip for the car! That's pretty good!"

"Well, the morphine drip is really for me. I need it and this piece of shit doesn't deserve it!" Rett glared at his car and kicked the nearest tire just so he wouldn't have to look at Cory's dimples.

He was getting nervous around the guy, which was something he rarely felt.

Cory nodded in sympathy, but then seemed at a loss for what to say next. So Rett locked his car door and said, "I'm just gonna get a cab and deal with this tomorrow." He pulled out his phone and started to search for a phone number for a taxi, just so he still wouldn't have to look at Cory.

Cory shifted his weight from one foot to the other while Rett fiddled with his phone. "I, uh... could... If you want... you know. Lemme give you a ride to your place. I mean, I was heading out myself for the night, so a taxi seems kinda stu... I mean, unnecessary."

Rett stopped fiddling with his phone, but continued to stare at it, just so he wouldn't have to look at Cory. He tried desperately to decide if he wanted to risk accepting a ride from one of the guys he had told himself to be careful of. Right now, he seemed like a pretty good guy, so it was difficult to refuse. In his mind, he played back Cory calling that other guy a "worthless faggot" to remind himself why this was a bad idea. For good measure, he reminded himself of Skunk calling a bunch of the guys "faggots" today as well. But then, the thought of paying for a cab before he had gotten his first paycheck and while money was still tight wasn't very appetizing.

He was about to refuse when Cory pointed at his truck and offered, "I'm parked right there, and a cab'll take twenty, thirty minutes to get here. We're on the same team, right? Let me help you out."

Shit, thought Rett, *he had to play the fucking teammate card, didn't he?*

He looked up at Cory, who, for whatever reason, suddenly looked panicked.

Great. Now he thinks I'm a jerk.

Rett folded. "Ok, sure. You're right. A ride would be great." He tried hard to make his voice sound sincere.

He grabbed his laptop and followed Cory over to his truck, a large blue-and-white crew cab thing that looked even older than Rett's own traitorous VW. Cory cleared a baseball bat and a glove out of the passenger side, and Rett had to push a few baseballs on the floorboard out of the way so he could get in. Cory cranked the truck up and Rett told him to use the Bankhead Tunnel to get back over to downtown Mobile.

An uncomfortable silence settled on them as they started out, and Rett started to regret giving in and accepting the ride. But since Cory was busy driving, he took advantage of the chance to sneak another look or two at the guy. Judging from the face, even with a faint unshaven look that had probably accumulated over a couple of days, Cory looked young. Rett estimated him to be one of the youngest guys he had seen on the team. Cory had on a Joes baseball cap, with his walnut-colored hair curling up from under it. He had on black cargo shorts and a tight fitting white polo shirt. The cargo shorts had thick, strong legs sticking out of them and ending in beat-up sneakers. But it was the polo shirt that worried Rett. It worried him because it was tight. "Tight" producing the same effect that so many reality shows produced — impossible to look away even though it was really, really, really in your best interest to do so. It perfectly fitted Cory, showing off his chest, shoulders, and arms exactly right. And Rett, who rarely found jocks attractive, found this guy *very* attractive.

He swallowed hard and told himself that getting hung up on one of the players was the worst thing he could do, especially this one. He would be better off selling steroids from a card table in the locker room.

"So, I heard a rumor that you gave Skunk the clap," said Cory out of nowhere, snapping Rett out of his thoughts.

"What? Hell, no! *He* gave *me* the clap!" blurted Rett. His sense of humor had somehow gone on autopilot with remarkably bad timing. He cussed himself out under his breath for letting that fly without stopping it.

Cory laughed, though, and Rett felt relieved that the player seated next to him didn't take either the rumor or his reaction to it as anything but a joke.

Rett tried to change the subject. "You know, the day I interviewed for my job, I saw you. It was in the hotel out by I65 about a week ago."

"Really? Yeah, I was there. I had just been a first round draft pick and we were there negotiating my contract. It all happened so freaking fast! MLB rules are that I'm only supposed to get a minors contract as a part of the draft, but with two expansion franchises opening, they waived it for the first two seasons, and I was able to go straight to the Bigs. Just a few days after that, it was done and I showed up at the clubhouse."

Rett shook his head to try and get those words to mean something. He frowned and decided he needed to be upfront with Bigfoot. "Ok. Cards on the table... I didn't really understand a word of that. I'm a physical therapist and I don't really know much about baseball. And by 'not much,' I mean 'nothing at all.' George said it was Dr. Bala's idea to hire somebody like me. Uh, ignorant, that is."

Rett waited for Cory to sink back into an uncomfortable silence now that he knew he wouldn't be able to talk baseball with him.

But Cory glanced over at him, grinned, and said, "Well, you know some stuff, right?"

"Not by y'all's standards."

"I mean, you know that the pitcher throws the ball and the batter tries to hit it, right?"

"Yeah," said Rett, grateful he knew at least *that* much.

"And you know the batter tries to run around the diamond before he gets touched with the ball after he's hit it, right?"

"Yeah."

"You know what first, second, third bases are, right?"

"That's an ongoing topic of discussion with a friend of mine."

"And you know what runs and outs are, right?"

"Yeah."

"Well, that's ninety percent of it right there," explained Cory. "The rest is just a bunch of arcane rules that have built up over the last 130 years or so, especially in the majors."

They emerged out of the tunnel and into downtown Mobile. Rett spent the remainder of the ride directing Cory to his place on Chatham, which was right outside of downtown and off of Government Street. Rett pointed his place out and Cory stopped along the curb between a couple of tall live oaks. There was a front walk leading to an older house that looked like it had been converted to a few apartments.

As he got out of the truck, Rett said, "Hey, Cory, thanks. I really do appreciate the ride."

Cory said, "Yeah, no problem."

Rather than pull off, Cory sat in his truck and picked at the steering wheel for a second. Rett could see him under the streetlight, considering something. Cory looked up and said, "Hey Rett, it's kinda good, you know, to know someone else that's brand new to this as well."

Rett realized he hadn't thought of it from Cory's perspective at all. The guy obviously knew baseball, but in a lot of ways he was as new to all of it as Rett was.

Rett waved and nodded at Cory from the bottom of the outside staircase to his upper unit, and Cory put the truck in gear and drove on off into the night.

Inside, Rett didn't even get a light turned on in his apartment before he sat down on the floor in the dark, the dappled light from the security floodlight outside playing patterns on the bare and scratched-up hardwood floors.

He didn't understand Bigfoot. The image of Cory catching Rett looking at him as he tried to enter the shower, then turning around and leaving, really didn't seem to line up with what had just now happened. The easy assumption was that, in the shower, Cory had decided he was queer and didn't want to be around him. And there was the other guy he had called a faggot, too. But tonight, Cory had seemed like a really nice guy. Maybe he was making more out of the shower thing than there was. Some guys stayed shy about showering with other guys their whole lives. That seemed a stretch for a guy that been a hard-core jock for probably a long time, however. Maybe it didn't have anything to do with Rett. Maybe it was JJ that Cory didn't like. Or maybe he had just forgotten something in his locker. Maybe he didn't want to interrupt Rett and JJ's conversation. Or maybe he had had a vision of the lottery numbers he should be playing that exact fucking minute.

Rett sighed to himself. He was being ridiculous now and not getting anywhere useful.

He pictured Cory driving his truck, his handsome face looking at Rett sideways, grinning and dimpled. That body magnificently concealed beneath the white shirt that still managed to show off every muscle exactly. That sloppy hair casually sticking out from under his Joes cap. That smile. God, that smile. That *perfect*... smile.

Rett shook his head and resolved to stop being so damn starry-eyed over a jock. A professional jock, no less. Besides, he had to work with the guy. Getting all goo-goo had an upside of exactly jack-shit, and plenty of downside.

God, he could hear Val tearing into him now about all of this, teasing him within an inch of his life.

Then he decided he needed a rug for his apartment floor before he even needed a sofa. Because when he finally killed Val for laughing at him, he'd need something to wrap the body up in.

Chapter 5

"Ouch!" muttered Rett as he pulled the toast out of his oven, and burning his fingers in the process. He threw the toast on an already-used paper plate, and then awkwardly tried to butter it using a popsicle stick, which currently constituted the sum total of all eating utensils in his apartment. He wondered why he hadn't just stolen a lot of Val's silverware rather than live like this.

He sat down in his one chair in the virtually-empty wasteland he charitably referred to as a den, punched the remote on his stereo to start playing some classic Fleetwood Mac, and started eating his toast. At least he wouldn't have to put up with Val's obsessing about his choice in music any more. He didn't make it 60 seconds before he realized he missed Val's obsessing.

Rett had planned on going and looking at sofas before heading in to work, but a dead car sitting at the Portyards now made that impossible.

That reminded him briefly of his ride home with Cory the night before, but he let the thought slip through his mind without latching onto it. After he had decided that trying to puzzle out or dwelling on Bigfoot was bad hoodoo, he had spent very little time on it, and wasn't about to start screwing around with that formula this morning.

Rett finished his toast and brushed the crumbs off his bare chest before he walked back into the kitchen barefoot. He decided the paper plate had reached the end of its useful life and tossed it in the trash, but carefully washed the popsicle stick and set it out to dry on the counter. Back in his den, he grabbed his work laptop and started to poke around online to pick a local mechanic he could have his car towed to if it still didn't start once he got back to the Portyards. He was really holding out hope that it was merely being persnickety the night before and would be fine today.

He picked one, mostly because it was relatively close in to downtown, and he was saving the information for it when there was a light knock at his door. The sudden sound made him about jump out of his boxers since he wasn't expecting anyone, and even more fundamentally, didn't *know* anyone in Mobile.

Rett opened the door and was shocked to see Cory standing there on the other side of his screen door, in broad daylight.

Rett gawked for a second wondering why in the world Cory was there. Cory seemed frozen as well, and both stood dumbly until Rett recovered his voice first and said, "Uh, well... hey, Cory."

Finally, Cory seemed to remember where he was and grinned. "Hey, Rett! I, uh, thought I'd swing by and pick you up since you... since your car... you know." Cory's grin slid to the sheepish side of the spectrum.

It was Rett's turn once again to stand there like an idiot for several seconds before what Cory had said really sunk in.

"Yeah. Shit, Cory, that's really nice. You totally didn't have..."

"Oh, no, I wanted to!" piped Cory. "I don't live that far from here and it's no problem for me to swing by and pick you up! Really!"

Rett finally remembered his manners and opened the screen door to let his carpool inside.

Cory was wearing a t-shirt with some kind of roaring lion on the front. Unlike the night before, where the knit polo fit absurdly perfectly, the t-shirt today was definitely a couple of sizes too small. It still showed off the body, though. As Cory stepped in past Rett, he started intently studying the apartment and Rett found himself involuntarily intently studying the amazing landscape of

Cory's back. The words "Lawder Lions Baseball" on the back of the shirt were pulled tight across the muscles underneath. Rett clenched his teeth and muttered "bad hoodoo, bad hoodoo" under his breath.

Cory spun around but continued looking at the almost empty room. He said, "Uh, are you squatting in this apartment?"

It was Rett's turn to grin this time. "Nah..." he said. "Amish, actually."

Cory shot a cocked eyebrow at Rett.

"Ok... not Amish. Would you buy Mennonite?"

Cory cut another glance at Rett before looking back at one of the bare walls. "I didn't realize Mennonites listened to Fleetwood Mac."

"We don't. It's just what was on the stereo when I broke in and started staying here."

Cory cracked up and chose one of the other bare walls to look at. The walls had been freshly painted a light blue when Rett rented the place, and had nice, original crown moldings all around the high ceiling.

"My roomie from college was the one that owned most everything," explained Rett. "It's kind of depressing to find out everything I own in the world could probably fit in the back seat of your truck."

Rett looked at himself and noticed he was still standing around in nothing but a pair of boxer shorts. "Hey, take your pick of any piece of furniture and have a seat. I'll be ready to go in one second."

He trotted off to his bedroom, and while he was getting dressed the rest of the way, he called out, "You want some toast or something for breakfast? Like maybe toast? As in, don't bother asking for anything other than toast? Well, that's not true... You can have sliced bread if you prefer."

He heard the reply from the other room, "Nah, I'm good."

"I bet you eat like a horse," called Rett.

"What are you implying?"

"How tall are you?" asked Rett as he pulled a Joes knit shirt on.

"Six five."

"How much do you weigh?"

"240, give or take."

"What do you *think* I'm implying?"

"That you think I like sugar cubes and you don't have any because they're not toast?" guessed Cory from the other room.

Rett had to stop putting on his sneakers while he gritted his teeth for a moment and thought, *Perfect. Just perfect. He's got a sense of humor.*

When Rett came back into the den, Cory was occupied with browsing through the music on his music player. He held it up at Rett and nodded. "The Pretenders, early Peter Gabriel, Roxy Music... all good stuff!"

Rett grabbed his keys of the kitchen counter and said, "Hey Cory, I know you didn't have to come by this morning to pick me up, but it's really cool of you to do it. Thanks."

"No problemo!" said Cory. He studied Rett a little more seriously before he looked away again, and added, "I meant what I said last night... before I headed home."

They piled into Cory's truck and drove over to the Portyards for the third and final game against the Mariners that evening. Once in the parking lot, Rett and Cory took a look at the ailing Jetta and tried to crank it again, but it was still no use. It seemed just as dead as the night before. Cory's studied assessment was expressed in four words: "Your car's janked, man."

Rett kicked the Jetta's tire again and informed the car that it could easily and more reliably be replaced by a donkey wearing a sombrero. His car seemed unimpressed with the threat.

In the clubhouse, Cory went his own way to fit in a light workout and get ready for practice while Rett called the auto shop and then met them out in the lot to have it towed. The tow truck operator checked for obvious problems, like an empty gas tank or dead battery, but it wasn't anything easy like that, so he loaded it up on the truck to take with him. He promised Rett they'd call him in a while with more information.

Later in the afternoon, as pitching and batting practice was getting ready to start, Dr. Bala asked Rett to go shadow Ryan as he helped the players with stretching and assisted with practice. Rett liked the idea of getting to be outside a little bit. Typical jobs in physical therapy were almost always indoors as he had found out while interning during school, and could get a little monotonous after a while. Now in his third day, Rett was finding the variety and pace of his job was a nice change from that.

JJ was back in the active lineup for that night, and was outside getting ready for batting practice with the rest of the guys. While JJ was explaining to him how the road trips went, Rett noticed out of the corner of his eye that Cory had come out on the field and was looking in his direction. He gave a quick wave to acknowledge Cory, who nodded back and started his own stretching.

Rett continued to watch Cory for a few more seconds before he caught the words "...and that's why we always have a supply of nerve gas on our charter flights" from JJ.

Rett jerked his head back over to face JJ, who had snark smeared all over his expression.

"Man, you aren't even listening to me," said JJ.

"Listening well enough to know you're full of shit, JJ."

JJ laughed. "It looks like you got to meet Cory at some point."

Rett's attention had wandered back over to Cory again. "Huh? Yeah. Yeah, I did. Got to meet him yesterday after the game."

Rett explained about his car dying and how Cory had given him a ride home.

"Bummer, little guy. Let me know if you need a ride after the game tonight," offered JJ. "I can get you home, no problem."

"Awesome! I'm hoping the shop will call and let me know it's fixed, but if it turns out I need a ride, I'll give you a heads-up."

JJ pointed at Gunnar and Cory throwing a few practice pitches and talking, "Gunnar better not use his arm up, but if he can keep that up tonight, he's gonna be playing hot."

They walked over and Gunnar told JJ to head down the foul line so he could pitch to him a few times, almost at full distance. As JJ was trotting along the foul line, Gunnar asked, "Hey, Rett, after I finish a few of these practice pitches, do you mind rubbing my shoulder down a little?"

"Absolutely." Rett was tempted to ask if he could video it just so he could taunt Val.

Gunnar started pitching to JJ and Rett was surprised how different it was to experience a major league pitch this close up. Rett could hear Gunnar huff with the effort, and could even hear the ball leave his hand. The *thwack* of the ball slamming into JJ's glove a split-second later was much louder than he expected.

He looked up in the stands and saw the die-hard fans that came early so they could watch even batting practice, braving the afternoon sun to do so. Rett watched Gunnar fire off another one at JJ and decided he should probably appreciate the privilege he was enjoying — on the field, right in the middle of it, getting to really know the players — since it was something many fans would almost die for the privilege of.

Cory walked over and asked Rett if he had heard anything about his car yet.

"Not yet. I'm hoping they'll call before too long, though."

Before they could chat any more, Topher yelled over to Cory to have him lob some easy balls for batting practice. Cory offered, "If you can get away and want to, come by the bullpen during the game tonight. Sebastion's gonna be the active relief pitcher, but I'm gonna be hanging out there, too, like usual." Rett agreed to come by if he could get away and Cory headed off to pitch to the batters.

Rett considered the offer after Cory had walked away. He usually spent some of the game time catching up on getting his notes and plans into his laptop, but he was getting more adept at that now and it was taking less and less time. There was rarely anyone in the clubhouse once the game started since they all were either in the game or watching. If he wasn't going to be in the way, it might make a nice change to be in the bullpen instead of watching from the upper atmosphere seats as he had the last few nights. The only thing that held him back was just how much he knew he shouldn't be hanging around Cory, even though it was tempting to do so.

Bad hoodoo, he cautioned himself.

On his way back into the clubhouse, Rett passed Skunk, who was showing up late for batting practice. He asked if the shot was starting to help, but Skunk ignored him and walked over to the fence to chat up a few young ladies who were trying everything to get his attention, short of lifting their tube tops up. Rett was tempted to follow him and ask much more explicitly if his gonorrhea was getting any better, right in front of the girls. Ahab beat him to Skunk, though, and was yelling at him that he needed more batting practice than there were hours in the day and to get his ass over with the other batters.

~~~~~

Rett looked up from entering his notes on his laptop and stretched his arms over his head. Up on the TV in his office he could see that they were playing the national anthem out on the field, which meant the game would be starting in a few minutes. He looked down at his scribbled notes and measured how much more he had to enter. It wasn't a lot and he could easily finish it later on, so he decided to take a break. He told Rikky, sitting across from him at his desk and working on his own notes, that he was going to go wander around for a little bit to see how the game shaped up, and to give him a call if anyone needed him to help with anything.

In the hallway outside his office, Rett stopped himself. He had started to go out to the concourse and up to the upper seats that he had come to think of as "his," but he paused. Cory had suggested he come by the bullpen for a little while, and he started to consider that option again. Part of him clung to the decision to be careful around Cory, but aside from a couple of strange incidents that Rett admitted he might be mis-reading (although calling another person a "worthless faggot" seemed hard to misread), Cory had been really great and Rett found that it was really hard not to like him. And it wasn't even "like" because of the smile and his build and the smile and the dimples and the smile, it was "like" because Cory seemed like the kind of guy that Rett could be good friends with. What struck Rett as well was that Cory was one of the hundreds of thousands of boys that had played baseball and dreamed of making it to the majors, with Cory succeeding where so ridiculously few did. But despite what had to be a huge temptation to be arrogant and conceited, he wasn't; there was no hint of ego or attitude that Rett had seen so far, at least. If anything, Cory seemed quiet and perhaps even a little shy, despite a personality and humor that would be hard for anyone to not like. Plus, dimples.

So, Rett wondered why he felt a little different about Cory than he did about, say, Skunk. Skunk seemed like a conceited jerk, probably even a little bigoted. But he had no real problem ignoring that and trying to engage with Skunk anyway. He didn't feel scared of Skunk and he didn't feel cautious around him; but around Cory he still seemed a little wary. Maybe it was because, definitely unlike Skunk, he found Cory genuinely attractive, and Rett didn't totally trust himself around Cory as a result. Maybe it wasn't Cory that he mistrusted at all.

He decided to go to the bullpen anyway. If it got weird, he'd leave. What was so hard about that?

He walked down the stairway in the clubhouse, and then out into the service tunnel that circled the stadium and was used by all the stadium operations staff — grounds crew, concessions, security — everyone except the public. He followed it around to the outfield to a door that led to the Joes' bullpen.

A security guard stationed there checked his ID before he was allowed through the door into the bullpen itself.

Topher, Sebastion, Cory, and Ric were there, along with the catchers Arthur and Bert, and they were all standing around shooting the shit. For a moment, Rett looked at number 72 from behind; Cory was as big as ever in his cream colored uniform, with the teal pinstripes, and his hair sticking out like usual from under his ball cap. Arthur was the one to spot Rett first and waved him over. Mostly they were talking about the pitcher the Mariners had up against them that night; it was someone that they had gotten more hits off of in the past than the Mariners' other pitchers. Rett just listened. He ventured a glance over at Cory one more time, and noticed Cory paying close attention to the conversation.

Finally, Topher broke it up and Sebastion took his position on the simulated mound for some easy warm up pitches to Arthur.

Cory grabbed Rett and they made themselves comfortable in a couple of the chairs along the bullpen wall. Cory adjusted his cap on his head a time or two and said, "I'm glad you could make it out."

"I was pulling my notes from today together, but don't have a whole lot left to do. I needed a break and wanted to see what you guys did out here," said Rett.

Cory started explaining, "Sebastion's the relief pitcher tonight. If Gunnar starts to give out or performing bad, Ahab will replace him with Sebastion. Sebastion throws pitches here in the bullpen just to keep his arm warmed up and his mind focused in case he gets called into the game. A lot of times in pro games, the pitcher gets relieved around the 6th or 7th inning, but it really will depend on how Gunnar and Ahab feel. I like to hang out here and get some pitches in."

Overhead, some of the fans in the stands looking down into the bullpen started yelling "Sebastion, hey Hemphill!" trying to get Sebastion's attention by shouting his last name.

Cory pointed up at them and said, "That's a great way to get ejected from the park. Sebastion really needs to maintain his focus and fans like that are assholes." Sure enough, a stadium security guard came by and cleared the fans away from the bullpen since they couldn't behave.

Cory spent a few minutes explaining how catchers signaled to pitchers what kind of pitch to throw and how they did it through hand signals. Rett had always assumed that the pitcher chose what kind of pitch to throw. Cory said the catcher played a more important role on the field than most people really thought about since he was the one mostly picking what pitch should be thrown, which was a very strategic decision because it resulted in a ball or a strike, maybe a hit or a walked batter, or best of all, an out.

While Cory explained about the game, Rett started to pay close attention to his voice. It wasn't the voice that he expected to hear berating some guy for being a worthless faggot. In fact, it didn't seem to match up with Cory's physical presence quite as expected. It wasn't loud or aggressive or overconfident, but it still managed to demand that you listen to him. Cory's voice was soft-spoken, careful. But rather than make him easy to ignore, it made you pay closer attention. It was like honey. Rett reminded himself about the bad hoodoo yet again.

Cory suddenly sat up and said, "Shit, I forgot to ask about your car! Did they ever call you this afternoon?"

"Yeah, finally," said Rett.

"Did they get it fixed?"

"No, they're looking into multiple problems, which doesn't sound good. They said they'd probably know sometime tomorrow morning for sure what all needed to be fixed. If you know anyone with a late model donkey for sale, now's the time to tell me."

"Ok, well, just let me know what time you're ready to leave after the game tonight."

"You know, Cory, it's been awesome having a major league pitcher chauffeur me around, but you don't have to. You probably have friends or people you want to see after the game."

"It's been good to have the company! And I don't know anybody in Mobile, remember? Gunnar and Topher are good guys, but they've got families they want to get home to, or waiting for them in the clubhouse. I really don't mind, Rett!"

It was hard to say no to the earnest look on Cory's face, so Rett stopped looking for reasons to say no. "Ok, ok. I'd be lying if I said I'd rather take a taxi or a donkey or something."

Sebastion walked over to where they were sitting and without any warning, a baseball sailed past Rett's head and Cory caught it in his bare hand without even really looking at it.

Rett jerked back and gulped, "Shit!"

At the far end of the bullpen, Arthur yelled, "Head's up, Rett, hey!"

"How the *hell* did you catch that?" asked Rett.

The perfect grin and dimples showed up on Cory's face. "Oh, that was just a toss!" said Cory, trying to sound modest. "After a while, it's just reflexes. You don't even think about it anymore. Your body just does it."

Cory stood up to pitch and Sebastion took his place next to Rett. He rotated his pitching shoulder around a few times and asked, "Hey Rett, you mind rubbing on my deltoid a little bit? It's feeling a little warm."

Rett positioned Sebastion in a seat so he could do as requested and started methodically pressing and rubbing the muscles in his shoulder. He glanced over at Cory, who was getting ready to pitch a few to Arthur. Cory was standing still, with his eyes closed and the ball in both hands up at chest level. Rett wondered what he was doing and then noticed that Cory's lips were moving slightly. It was silent, but it looked like Cory was singing a song to himself under his breath. When he finished, Cory exhaled and stared at the ground around his feet for a moment.

"Hey Sebastion, what's Cory singing to himself?"

"Hmm? Oh, that's Cory's thing he does. I don't think he's singing, though, I think maybe he's praying. I've never asked him about it, specifically. Oh shit, yeah, right there, Rett, right... there... right at the bottom of that deltoid. Oh man, that's the spot."

"That's actually getting into the teres major and not the deltoid, but I know what you mean. And hold your back up straight!"

Sebastion groaned and slumped a little further.

Rett pulled him back to straighten his back. "Straighten up!" he said sternly.

Sebastion jerked his back straight and said, "Man, you're like a little Rosemary!"

"Hey! You want a shoulder rub or not?" He focused on the spot that Sebastion had indicated, garnering a fresh groan in the process.

"You know, I know somebody..." said Sebastion, rocking slightly with the force of Rett's hands on his back, "found out her home address one time. He looked it up online, and swears it was a cemetery!"

Rett laughed and said, "That is the biggest pile of bullshit I've ever heard in my life! This bullpen's so deep in it, we're gonna need a ladder to get out!"

"No! I swear! It's true!"

Rett finished with his massage and Sebastion rotated his arm around again, testing it. Rett asked, "Better?"

"Definitely. Thanks. So, what the hell were we talking about before we started telling ghost stories?"

"I was asking what Cory was doing before he started pitching," said Rett.

"Oh yeah. Lots of players have superstitions or rituals that they go through."

Sebastion reached down into the pocket of his uniform pants and pulled a penny out and showed it to Rett. "I won't go set foot on a pitcher's mound without taking my lucky penny out and kissing it one time. Cory prays or recites something, I guess."　　·

Rett watched Cory wind up and pitch to Arthur. It seemed almost casual to Rett, like he wasn't putting much effort into it.

He asked, "Was that a serious pitch?"

Sebastion said, "Nope. He's just keeping warm right now. He could do that pitch in his sleep. When Cory pitches for real, it's way different than that."

Cory caught the ball from Arthur and stepped back for a second, looking over to glance at Rett. Rett yelled, "C'mon, Cory, burn one!" He had no idea if that was a real phrase or not, but it sounded good to him.

Cory grinned and nodded at Arthur. He grabbed a small bag next to where he was standing and squeezed it.

"What's in the bag?" asked Rett.

"That's a rosin bag. Helps to grip the ball," said Sebastion.

Cory paused for a moment and focused, then wound up, and fired the ball off at Arthur. There was a loud, instantaneous *pow* as the ball hit Arthur's glove perfectly.

Rett was confused by what happened afterwards because everyone seemed to react at the same time. Instantly, Sebastion jumped up out of his chair and stared bug-eyed. "Jesus Christ!"

Arthur stood up, too, and took his catcher's mask off and was looking between the ball in his mitt and Cory.

Topher, who had been leaning against the wall of the bullpen and watching, jerked up and exclaimed, "Holy fuck!" He looked over, disbelief in his eyes, to see if Sebastion had seen the same thing he had. He said to Sebastion, "Shit, I wish we had had a gun on that one!"

Cory was grinning again and wiping his chin on the sleeve of his uniform.

Rett asked, "What? What happened?"

Arthur yelled, "Hey boy, Cory! A little warning before you leave me wrist all gammy!"

Sebastion continued to stare at Cory but said to Rett, "That pitch was fast! Not just a run-of-the-mill professional fastball. I mean, that pitch was... *Jesus*, I don't know if I've *ever* seen a pitch that fast."

"So, it was a really fast pitch?" asked Rett, rather stupidly. It certainly looked fast to him, but all of the pitches looked really fast to him.

"Well, we're not pitching at full distance in the bullpen, so it's hard to tell exactly, which is why Topher wishes we had been using a radar gun to measure its speed. But you get a feel for these things when you watch them enough. And that pitch was... something else!"

Rett stayed in the bullpen for the whole game, but Sebastion didn't get called in to play. Gunnar was in great form for the game that night, and for the first time since Rett joined, the Mobile Joes won a game, beating the Mariners 2 to 0. Rett got to see a little of the miniature Mardi Gras parade with a couple of floats that ran along the warning track when the Joes won a home game. The team's "Crewe Girls" shot Joes doubloons and t-shirts up into the stands to celebrate, and the fans that were there seemed ecstatic to have picked one of the nights when the Joes came out on top.

The feeling back in the clubhouse was a lot different than the other nights as well, with a lot more joking, laughing, and horsing around than he had seen previously. Rett still had his job to do, though, and after Gunnar had accepted a lot of back slaps from his teammates for keeping the hits by the Mariners really low, he asked Rett to ice his arm down again.

Rett asked if he wanted to go take his shower first, but Gunnar said he really wanted to get some ice on it and he'd shower at home.

In the treatment room, Gunnar gingerly removed his uniform top, and when Rett took a look at his shoulder, he was a little concerned by what he saw.

Rett asked, "Gunnar, your shoulder looks a little swollen. Is it hurting bad?"

"It's ok. Minor pain. Just the usual when pitching a full nine."

Rett touched Gunnar's shoulder right where the bursa was and Gunnar visibly flinched in pain when he did so.

"That didn't seem so minor there," said Rett. "I barely touched you. Let's get your compression shirt off, too."

Gunnar took his undershirt off as well, and Rett had to help him so he could go easy on his right arm. Just looking at Gunnar's arm and shoulder, Rett could definitely see some swelling.

Rett said, "I think I'd better..."

Gunnar stopped him and said, "Hey Rett, really... it's just the usual for a game like this, ok? Don't make something out of this that it isn't."

It wasn't Rett's place to diagnose... Dr. Bala was the orthopedist and that was his job. But at the same time, Gunnar had been doing this a long time and knew his own arm probably better than anyone.

Rett decided to let it ride. "Ok, Gunnar. Do you maybe want a light massage before the ice?"

Gunnar swallowed and said, "Let's just get the ice on it, if that's ok."

Rett got the ice sleeve out of the freezer and wrapped it on Gunnar's arm. Gunnar flinched once or twice as he put the sleeve on him, but seemed to feel better after the ice started to cool it down.

Rett told him as he was checking to make sure it was secured properly, "You know, Gunnar, you really were amazing tonight." Gunnar smiled at Rett and slapped him on his shoulder with his left hand a few times before heading out of the treatment room.

Rett helped Dr. Bala with a mild grade groin strain that the batter Kevin Ostergaard suffered on his run in the bottom of the 9th inning. It turned out to be very mild and Kevin was already feeling much better even though it was less than an hour after he had strained it.

Rett managed to get the rest of his notes entered and caught up, and the trainers helped him make sure that the supplies and equipment that he would be responsible for on the road were packed and ready to go for their "getaway day" to Boston the next day.

Once finished, Rett had a decision to make. Part of him thought he should still be a little careful of Cory and accept JJ's offer for a ride, but it was already becoming ridiculously easy to ignore that voice. Besides, being careful of Cory didn't necessarily mean avoiding the guy.

Cory it was.

Rett found him and they headed out with a few of the other players on their way home, too. As they emerged from the stadium door out to the employee lot, they were greeted by some screams from girls and a few autograph seekers energized by the win against the Mariners. The fans and groupies were kept outside the lot by security guards, but that didn't stop them from trying to get some of the players to come speak to them.

Frank "Skillet" Rooker, who had scored the home run that night, decided to go sign a couple of autographs and the fans went crazy when he headed their way. Skunk, who still wasn't speaking to Rett, walked over with arms held out like they were all yelling for him.

Rett asked Cory, "Who do you think's more interested in being noticed, the groupies or Skunk?"

"Skunk," said Cory without even pausing to consider the question.

"Have any of them ever yelled at you for an autograph?"

"Ha! No way! These people have no idea who I am. When I was a draft pick, there were a few hard core people that asked me about it, mostly out of curiosity, I think, but that died off after a day or two. It's been crickets ever since," replied Cory.

Once in his truck, Cory paused for a moment before turning on the main road to head back into downtown. "Hey Rett, I'm feeling pretty good tonight, and we don't have to travel to Boston until tomorrow evening... you maybe want to go get a beer to celebrate the win tonight?"

Rett paused to consider his answer long enough for doubt to creep over Cory.

"It's ok, we don't have to," said Cory. "I just thought you'd maybe like to get out, but it's..."

"No, Cory, let's go! I have no idea where to go, but yeah, going and doing something sounds much better than me sitting at home. Celebrating with... uh..."

"Toast?" asked Cory with a grin.

"Fuck you," said Rett. "*Buttered* toast," he muttered.

Cory turned onto the road and steered his truck away from town, like he was going across the bay. "There's a place called Bluegill that's right on the water that's great! George took me there when I first got to town and started talking about the contract."

From the Portyards, it wasn't a far drive at all, and at that time of night, Rett and Cory had no problem getting a table out on the deck right on the water. A few boats remained tied up on the dock next to them where patrons had arrived by water. Another minute later, and after Rett had displayed his ID, they both had mugs of beer in their hands.

Cory said, "Here's to Skillet and his home run tonight."

"And to Kevin's run in the ninth!" added Rett, and they tapped their mugs together.

"Why's he called Skillet, anyway?" asked Rett.

"When he swings, it's like the guy's batting with a cast iron skillet! He has the highest batting average on the team, a .295."

Rett looked at him blankly.

Cory said, "It's just the percentage of hits a player gets out of the times he's at bat."

"Ah. So... if it's just a percentage, why don't they just say it like a percentage?"

"I dunno," said Cory with a shrug of his shoulders. "You wanna call the commissioner of baseball and ask him?" he said, whipping out his phone.

"While you've got him up and out of bed, why don't you ask him why your uniform socks are called sanitaries," suggested Rett, getting a quick laugh from Cory.

The guy playing guitar and singing out on the deck was ending his set, and the crowd was thinning out even more, but Rett found that he was really enjoying himself. Montgomery didn't have a place like this, not even on the riverfront.

He looked up at the strings of flamingo and goldfish lights strung up all over the railing and overhead to create a nice glow, and the fans placed around the deck kept the still June air moving and the bugs at bay. A waitress with a plenty big chest swung by and dropped off the heaping basket of small, fried crab claws they had ordered.

"I guess your parents are beside themselves they're so proud of you, huh?" asked Rett.

"Yeah, my dad is kind of nuts about the whole thing. Actually, a fair number of my friends back in my hometown are a little nuts about all this happening. My mom's proud, too, but she's more worried that the majors are just going to chew me up and spit me out. You know moms."

Rett grunted. He *didn't* know moms, really. Not like that anyway, and not for a long time now. He picked at a couple of the crab claws.

Cory said, "Oh! You'll probably get to meet a couple of my friends while we're in Boston. My best bud from high school, Jason, and Kaitlynn, who I dated for a while in high school and college, are going to come up. They're staying with Kaitlynn's aunt, who lives up there somewhere. They're gonna go to the game Saturday and I'm planning on meeting up with them that night. You can come, too, if you want."

Rett wasn't too keen on the idea. "Uh, maybe. I'm not sure how this whole road show thing is going to work yet."

Cory nodded. "How about you, Rett? Are your parents pretty stoked that you're with the Joes now?"

Rett idly twisted his beer mug around on the table. "So... the thing about my parents... I don't really talk to them."

"Oh! Sorry, Rett. I didn't know. I didn't mean to bring up something that was..."

"Don't worry about it," said Rett. "We had kind of a falling out and I haven't seen them since... well, since high school, I guess."

"You mean you put yourself through Physical Therapy school all by yourself?" asked Cory, rather astonished.

"Yeah. Well, me and a couple of student loan companies. Racked up a nice big pile of student debt in the process, but I did it all on my own."

"That's really great, Rett! That's amazing! I had a full scholarship because of baseball. There's no way I would have managed college trying to do it on my own."

The waitress came by and they ordered another round of beers. Cory plowed through a large portion of the crab claws while Rett watched with a morbid interest.

Cory said with a mouthful, "Sorry. I'm hungry. I didn't eat at the clubhouse."

"Hey, I know you weren't on the team for very long before I showed up, but have you played in a game yet?" asked Rett.

"Oh, God no. I'm still a little green and need to get used to everything first. I'm not even on the active roster. Plus, my parents would flip out if I'd been put in a game and they weren't there to see it. I've got a standing order to let them know anytime I'm supposed to play for real, no matter where the game is. Topher seems to understand and told me Ahab would give me some notice if I was really going to be in a game so I could let the parentals know."

"Hey, speaking of Ahab, is he really a hard-ass all the time like that?" asked Rett.

"His management style is definitely high-volume. It's a lotta bark compared to the bite, though, according to Topher and Gunnar."

Cory glanced a few times back towards the service area out on the deck and said, "Don't look, but that manager dude keeps looking over here at us. I'm getting a little creeped out by him."

Rett had been wondering when this side of Cory would show back up, and had secretly hoped it wouldn't. But right when Rett had least expected it, there it was. Rett cursed himself for letting himself get comfortable around Cory and letting his guard down a little too much. At least none of it was directed at himself.

He managed to say, "He's probably never seen anyone shovel crab claws like you. It's pretty fascinating."

Cory said, "Har har. They're tiny! It takes a lot!"

Cory pushed the basket of crab claws away from him and looked down at the table.

"Aw, look Cory, I was just joking around about the crab claws! Really! I didn't mean anything..."

Cory said, "No, I know you were just shitting around about that."

He paused again and Rett wondered what was going through Cory's mind.

"Rett, can I tell you something a little personal?" he said softly.

"Uh, sure. Yeah."

"I'm kinda scared by all of this," Cory eventually said, his voice quiet and hinting at an almost desperate undercurrent. "This... the majors... has been my dream since as long as I can remember. And I remember having a baseball back when the baseball was bigger than my hand. And, Jesus... here I am. It's really *happening*. But it can... all disappear in a heartbeat. It's so easy for it all to fall apart, and everything could vanish. A few blown pitches and I can be left inactive, or sent down to the minors, or be bought out of my contract and turned loose entirely. Someone else could come along they like better, that would work on the team better, you know?"

Cory hadn't looked at Rett while he spoke. He fidgeted with his beer and said, "I just needed... to admit it to someone. You're new to this, too, so I thought you'd probably be able to understand a little bit what I'm saying. It's pretty fucking scary."

Rett had no idea what to say, how to respond to something like that. What advice could he possibly hope to give to make Cory feel better? Hell, Rett was terrified with nothing more than having Cory open up to him unexpectedly like this.

Rett stammered, "Hey, Cory... uh, shit, Cory, I have no idea... what to say to you."

Before Rett could feel it coming, he was blindsided by something else. Anger rose up in him that he hadn't felt in a long time, and then only in a past he had spent years burying and forgetting. The anger at his father scorched his skin and made him stiffen in his chair.

How many times had he heard his father tell him that "a *real* man *never* shows weakness, Rett?" How many times had the phrase "only strength is respected in a man" been used to make Rett feel weak and inferior? *Be a man, Rett. Be a man.* The times he had heard that from his father were countless.

Well, would his father have the balls to stand and look up at someone like Cory (and he would have had to physically look up at Cory every bit as much as Rett had to) and tell him he wasn't a *man* because he admitted to being scared? Would his father see Cory as being weak for making such a difficult admission? The bullshit he had suffered at the hands of his father made him furious.

Cory frowned a little bit and stared at his beer. "It's ok. I don't expect you to..."

"Well, wait, though," said Rett, no longer content to let his empty comment stand as his only response. "I mean, Ahab and George, they obviously think you've got it in you, or you wouldn't be here, right?"

Cory shrugged.

Rett tried again. "C'mon, they're not going to bring someone directly into the majors under a contract just to fill a seat, right?"

"Uh-huh."

"And you played in college. Is that where they found you?"

"Yeah, at UGA. I stayed an extra year to keep playing."

"And you were good while you played there?"

"Yeah."

"Well... if that was good enough to get you on the Joes, then... then just do what you did there," said Rett.

Rett felt like a complete idiot as soon as the words were out of his mouth. He wondered why he had even let that mush fall out of it.

Cory continued to stare at his beer while he picked at the handle of the mug.

Rett sighed and said, "Worthless advice? I told you I don't know jack shit about any of this, Cory. So, you're probably better off doing the opposite of whatever I think is right."

Still, Cory looked at his mug.

A few seconds later, his mouth opened to speak, but the words stalled out, and it was another second before he started again. "I spend as much time with Topher and Gunnar as I can. Both of these guys are really senior and have been living it for years now. They know it as well as anyone, and know how to do it. I try to soak up everything they say. Like *every* fucking word. And, it's kinda funny..."

Cory paused again and Rett asked, "Why?"

"Because, what they keep telling me is pretty much what you just said."

Rett half closed his eyes and gave thanks that he hadn't been a complete and utter bonehead in front of him.

Rett waited a couple of beats. "Ah, so," he said, "what you're telling me... is that I get to have Topher's job now?"

Cory chuckled. He said, grinning and dimpling all over the place, "Sure, why not."

Rett said, more seriously, "Sebastion was freaked out by your pitch today, the one in the bullpen, you know."

"It was a good pitch," agreed Cory. "Faster than usual for me. Just lucky, though, I think. I was feeling good tonight. Thanks, too, for letting me dump all that on you. It's hard bottling it up, and it's a little intimidating to say something like that to one of the other players. I've only said it really roundabout to Topher and Gunnar."

"Sure, Cory. Anytime."

Their waitress stopped by and leaned over the table conspicuously. "You guys good?"

They decided they were winding down and said they were fine.

The waitress looked at Cory and said, "My manager over there asked me to ask you if you were one of the Joes. He thinks you look like the new draft pick, Cory Pritchart."

Rett started laughing and Cory turned as red as the cocktail sauce that came with the crab claws, but admitted to the waitress that he was, in fact, Cory Pritchart.

The waitress seemed more interested at that point. She leaned over again and said, "Really? Cool! You're a big 'un!" She eyed him up and down before she winked and walked off.

Rett tried to catch his breath and pretended to be Cory, "Ooooh! I'm getting all macked on by a middle-aged restaurant manager dude! I feel so *dirrrrrrty*!"

Cory started laughing, too, and told Rett to shut the fuck up.

The manager came over with one of the t-shirts from the restaurant and a black pen and asked Cory if he'd sign it for them. Cory signed it and added his jersey number underneath. The manager looked at it like it was made of solid gold and insisted on paying for Cory's and Rett's food and beers.

As they walked out into the crushed gravel of the parking lot, Cory said, "That was kind of cool!"

Rett said, "I'll bet you a year of your pay that you'll be sick of that kind of stuff by the end of the season."

Chapter 6

"So what's wrong with it?"

"They said it needs a new ignition switch and something else to do with the fuel injection. Dilithium crystals, flux capacitor, blah blah blah. I don't know. I don't speak car," said Rett, shifting his cell phone from one ear to the other.

"That thing's a piece of shit, Rett. It's a piece of shit with velour upholstery and a cigarette lighter," said Val.

Rett just sighed heavily.

She asked "So how much to get it fixed?"

Rett groaned. "$750!" He grabbed another one of the hotel bed pillows and shoved it under his head to prop himself up a little more.

Val blurted out laughing, "Ha ha ha! That thing's only worth about $800 to begin with!"

"I know!"

"What are you gonna do, Rett? Do you have the money?"

"I guess I'm gonna pay it and get it fixed. Just not this exact moment. I'm still mostly broke until I get my first paycheck at the end of the month. At least I don't need it while on the road."

"How are you getting around in the meantime?"

"Bumming rides. JJ Troyer's offered to carry me around, but I haven't taken him up on it yet. He's really great! You'd love him!"

"So who are you bumming rides off of then? My hottie daddy Gunnar? Please tell me he's making you blow him for rides!"

"No, but he probably would if I asked. Give me a ride, I mean. Have you heard of a guy named Cory Pritchart?"

"Nope. Does he play, or does he have some pathetic support job like you?"

"He's on the team, but on the inactive roster. He's a cool guy, though. You'd probably like him, too. Good sense of humor."

"Well, Rett," said Val, "I know I'm your sugar mama, and I *would* loan you the money... but I can't because mommy needs a Brazilian wax. And mommy comes first, honey."

Rett's breath caught for a second and Val heard it.

"Don't say it, shithead," she threatened.

Rett was biting his tongue, but a tiny little "eep" sound still managed to escape.

"Don't you fucking say it, Rett!"

Rett tried to hold his tongue to keep it in, but it became too much to bear. He gushed in one huge breath, "Oh dear God I can't hold it back even though I'm trying really hard and I'm so sorry Val but *you* did this to me and I'm really the victim here but shit, you're gonna need a *lot* more money than $750 for that wax job!"

Val said, "Wow, that really hurt." She didn't sound very hurt.

"Not as much as that wax job is going to!" sang Rett, finally able to breathe again.

"So *this* is what passes for wit with you now?" asked Val. "You're not even two weeks away from me and these cheap shots are the best you can do?"

"Don't get your, uh... your... Topkapi jewels all in a knot!"

Val said, "My what?"

"Topkapi jewels. Sheesh!" said Rett.

"You moron, those are *Turkish*!"

Rett shook his head. "And? What the hell's the difference?"

"Greeks hate the Turks!"

"Aren't y'all like next-door neighbors?"

"Which is why we hate each other," explained Val.

"I thought you guys hated the Romans," he said.

"Dear God, the Roman empire hasn't existed for like a thousand years or something!"

"You don't hate the Romans? Are you sure?"

"No, asshole!"

"Yeah you do," insisted Rett. "There was that whole thing between Cleopatra and Julius Caesar! There was even a movie!"

Val screamed in frustration and said, "Cleopatra was Egyptian!"

"Are you saying Julius Caesar was Turkish, and not Cleopatra? And that's why you hate them? But you're fine with the Egyptians. You people are fucked up!"

Rett could hear Val's frustrated screams in her room on the other end of the call.

When she came back on, she said lightly, "Oh, that was excellent! Much better! Lordy, I want to have your babies right now!"

Rett was still cross from Val's refusal to understand obvious logic and basic world history. "Are you insane?! I can't afford to support whatever swarthy brood you'd squirt out! I can't even afford to fix my car!"

Val said, "Ahhh, I've needed this. I miss you, Rett. I really, really miss you! You know that, right? Even though you totally don't deserve this jet set lifestyle you've lucked into!"

"I miss you, too. You really are the best, you know?"

"Thanks, sweetie! Anyway, I hope you enjoy Boston, and I'm glad you guys won today! I was rooting for you!"

"Yeah, the afternoon games are kinda good. It's nice to have an evening free."

"Ok. Go have fun! I still want to come visit soon!"

Rett ended the call and glanced at the time as he did so. He went into a panic because he had promised Cory he'd be down in the hotel bar 15 minutes ago to meet his friends that had come to Boston for the Saturday afternoon game. At least the Joes had beaten the Red Sox 1 to 0.

The trip to Boston had been a blast so far. The chartered jet the team took from Mobile to Boston was the best part. He had only been on a plane once before, when his family had been out west to Yellowstone Park. He had been probably 12 or 13 when they went, and it had been one of the few family trips he could remember where he had really enjoyed it, and he and his parents had gotten along really well. He, his parents, and Bo had gone bicycling and ran across a bear in the distance, and his dad was afraid Rett was going to be freaked out afraid. But for once, he seemed pretty pleased that Rett was more curious and enthralled than he was afraid.

On the chartered bus ride over from the airport to their hotel, George Hastings had come and sat with Rett to check in with him to see how he liked his job so far. Rett was able to be totally honest and tell him that he really liked it. They chatted a while and George even commented that Rett seemed to be picking up baseball quite well and that Dr. Bala liked how he was fitting in, too. All of that provided a sense of relief to Rett. He decided he liked this job pretty well, and he was starting to like baseball, too. All those years forcibly maintaining an indifference to it seemed a little stupid now.

Rett rushed down to the bar off the hotel lobby. It was a much fancier kind of bar than he was used to going into; Montgomery didn't really have a hotel as nice as the one they were staying in, and even if it did, he'd never have been able to justify going somewhere like that as a perpetually broke student.

He glanced around and didn't see Cory, and he worried that maybe he was too late and that Cory had given up on him and left with his friends. He spotted Arthur and JJ enjoying a couple of drinks and chatting at the bar, so Rett made his way over to them.

Arthur had finished his drink and was on his way back to his room, so he said goodbye to Rett and JJ and left. JJ insisted on buying one for Rett in honor of their win that day at Fenway.

As the bartender served up the beer Rett ordered, he asked JJ if he had seen Cory and his friends come down to the bar.

"Haven't seen him. Arthur and I have been right here talking for probably the last 30 minutes, too."

At least Rett hadn't missed them.

Rett said, "Arthur got robbed today when he hit that high fly ball and the Sox third baseman didn't catch it. I can't believe the umpire still called him out!"

JJ laughed. "Ahh, baseball virgin! Infield fly rule. And it was on our behalf since we had Josh on first and Skillet on second."

Rett squinted at JJ. "Ok, you're gonna have to Sesame Street that for me."

JJ spent the next few minutes explaining how the Sox were hoping the umpire wouldn't invoke the rule so they could force outs on both Josh and Skillet rather than just getting an out on Arthur alone. It took a few tries, but Rett finally understood. Rett felt like an idiot making someone like JJ explain it, but JJ was totally cool about it as always.

"Don't feel bad about it," said JJ. "It can be a tricky rule. It's at the umpire's discretion and his decision is final. But there was no reason for the umpire today to not invoke it. Can't fault the Sox for trying."

Rett sipped at his beer a little more before he remembered something else he had been meaning to ask JJ for a few days now.

"Hey, do you have any rituals or superstitions you use when catching or hitting?"

JJ put his drink down on the bar so he could fish out a gold cross hanging around his neck on a chain. He showed it to Rett and said, "This cross belonged to my granddaddy. He had it on his bookmark in the bible he always carried around. My dad gave it to me when I was a little boy. When I'm on deck and getting ready to bat, I always touch it to my forehead and think of the granddad I never got to meet."

He sipped his drink again and then remembered, "Oh, also, when I get up to the batter's box, I always say hello to the catcher very politely. It's partly professional courtesy, partly superstition, and partly to psych them out just a little. Some catchers hate it and look at me like I'm crazy or trying to pull something. But some of the others are great and say hello back."

Rett nodded and looked over at the doorway again.

JJ said, "You were expecting something like ground up chicken bones and bat blood, weren't you?"

Rett said "What? No!" but then he saw JJ grinning at him. "But that would be cool as shit if you did!"

Out of the corner of his eye, Rett spotted Cory coming in with his friends. Ever since Cory mentioned they would be in Boston, he was curious to see what his friends were like. The three of them threaded their way through the crowd over to where JJ and Rett were standing and Cory introduced Jason and Kaitlynn to them.

Kaitlynn was very pretty. She was taller than Rett, with dark auburn hair in soft curls and blue eyes. It made Rett feel a little petty, but he wondered if Cory was going to be screwing her later on that evening. Her nose was small and pert and cute and it bugged Rett.

Cory's friend Jason wasn't what he was expecting at all. Rett had really expected Cory's friend from high school to be a jock, too, maybe just not as big. But Jason was a small guy, smaller than Kaitlynn even. He didn't have the body of a jock, either. He didn't look like he played *any* sports, in fact. Rett had always kept his hair really short because Val could manage that with the clippers and that way he didn't have to pay for haircuts, but Jason's dirty blond hair was shaved even closer to his head than Rett's. Jason had beautiful eyes, though — hazel leaning towards green and with long eyelashes.

Rett couldn't avoid taking in Cory as well. He had changed into a yellow dress shirt open at the neck and with the sleeves rolled up to his mid-forearms. He had on a nice fitting pair of new jeans with a dark brown suede belt. Cory looked great and Rett struggled to not stare.

Cory stood behind Kaitlynn and pulled her back against his chest and rested his chin on the top of her head while he described to his friends what JJ and Rett did for the team. Rett couldn't help but notice how comfortable he looked, how relaxed he seemed. For a guy that had admitted to Rett how scared he was, he kept it hidden well.

JJ asked them what they had lined up for their plans that night.

Jason said with a smirk, "Oh, I bet it'll be mostly listening to Cory, and I bet I know what about, too."

Cory reached over and smacked Jason in the head and Kaitlynn said, "My aunt recommended a good seafood restaurant that we're going to, then probably wandering around a little. It'll be good to catch up since we haven't seen Cory in way too long."

Cory said, "You guys wanna come? You're welcome to join us!"

Rett said, "Y'all have fun. Besides, JJ's starting tomorrow, so I've got to go find him a bucket of fried chicken and a fruit bat before the game."

JJ started laughing and Cory stared at them blankly.

Rett laughed, too. "Sorry. It's just a stupid thing we were horsing around about."

JJ said, "Thanks, Cory. But I'm getting something to eat in my room and going to bed. Hotel beds suck, you know?"

Cory nodded and JJ and Rett said goodbye as the three of them walked out the streetside door of the bar to start their evening.

Rett was lost in thought when he heard JJ say, "You need to be careful, Rett."

Rett looked back over at JJ and realized he had a serious look on his face.

"Careful?" he asked.

JJ directed Rett over to a booth that had emptied up and they went and sat down into the navy blue leather seats. JJ studied Rett for a moment, trying to make up his mind, and then said, "I think you've got it kind of bad, Rett."

A queasy knot developed in Rett's stomach. "What? Got what bad?" he asked.

"You're crushing on Cory."

The blood drained out of Rett's face and he felt cold all of a sudden. "I'm not... I'm not... gay, JJ. You think I'm...?"

The look on JJ's face confirmed exactly what he thought.

It had not even been a week. He had been on the job only six days. Was one week all this was going to last before it fell apart on him? The last several days flashed through his mind — Luis getting razzed for picking his nose, helping Gunnar with his arm, Skunk, watching the games from the cheap seats, late dinner with Cory out on the deck by the water, hanging out in the bullpen, riding on the bus with the Joes' general manager. Rett's face slowly fell as he realized what was happening. It had been six measly days, and all of this meant something to him. It wasn't just a paycheck on one side to hold back the debts on the other. It was *all* starting to *mean* something to him. But now the ball was slipping out of his hand just when he thought he had gotten a grip on it.

JJ rapped on the glossy, dark wood table lightly to get Rett's attention.

"Rett, you are gay, right?"

Rett's mouth twitched a little, but he nodded that JJ was right. He was holding onto his drink tightly enough to crack the glass.

"Relax, ok?" said JJ. "It's no big deal. Well, at least not to me. I'm totally down with it, alright?"

JJ smiled to try and reassure Rett. "C'mon, Rett. I'm not so stupid as to think there's never been a gay guy in the MLB. There might be some that think somehow there aren't any, but how shit-brained are those guys? I got no problem at all with gay people."

Rett closed his eyes for a second and wondered if maybe this wasn't going to end in the disaster he was picturing in his head, after all.

Rett asked tentatively, "You're ok with it?"

"Sure. I wouldn't have bothered hanging around you the way I have if I wasn't. Plus, you crack me up."

Rett breathed a deep sigh of relief. "How did you figure me out?"

JJ said, "Well, that's what I was saying. You're making it a little obvious, at least around me, that you're into Cory. I just want you to be careful about that. I don't know how Cory would take it if he picked up on it. And you definitely don't want Ahab or Skunk to catch a whiff of it. Probably some others, too. I'm just trying to help you out, bro."

Rett sat quietly. He had known letting himself get close to Cory was a bad idea. He couldn't quite keep himself in check around the guy. Well, he was going to have to fix that problem. As scary as it was to have this surface, he really owed JJ one for giving him the heads up. Plus, it was a relief to have someone in the clubhouse know.

JJ seemed to sense what Rett was thinking. He leaned over the table slightly to get Rett's attention again. Rett looked up at him, his gold cross was hanging out in front of the tight red v-neck shirt he was wearing. JJ said, "I'm not trying to freak you out, Rett. Cory's a really good guy, and you guys have become friends. Everyone's seen that and no one's thought anything of it. I just noticed how you looked at him at times and picked up on a little something more."

Rett slumped over and put his head down on the table between them. "Fuck! This is so humiliating, JJ! Do you think anyone else has seen me make a complete idiot of myself?" He added hastily when he had another thought, "And I don't want to put Cory in a bad spot. I don't want to embarrass him. He's really been great to me."

JJ shrugged, "I don't think so. No one's said anything at all to me. I just wanna keep it that way. I want you in the clubhouse, man! Even though you're a complete dumbass about baseball!"

JJ grinned again and Rett sat back up and rubbed his hands over his face. "What am I gonna do, JJ?"

"Keep on being friends. Just stop drooling."

Rett rested his head in his hands and groaned, "Fuck! I was drooling now? Great! That's just super! The stupid thing is I normally don't go for jocks, so I thought I'd be fine on this job. And for the most part, I have been. You knuckle-draggers with your brains down in your protective cups hardly ever show up on my radar..."

"Oh, now *I'm* a knuckle-dragger?" said JJ, amused.

"Don't feel so special," said Rett. "You're on a whole team of 'em."

JJ laughed and his dark eyes twinkled now that Rett was relaxing again and his humor was showing back up.

Rett bit at his lip a little in thought. "Cory looked good tonight, though."

JJ looked indifferent and said, "A little too cracker for my taste, but... whatever."

JJ held out his fist so Rett could bump it with his own. He told Rett, "I got your back, Rett. It's all about the team."

JJ stood up from the booth and motioned for Rett to follow him. "Screw the room service... let's go find some dinner, Rett."

Chapter 7

Rett concluded that being without a car really sucked. The only thing that saved him at the time was the fact that he could get as much food as he wanted for lunch and dinner at the Portyards. Breakfasts were still his responsibility and he was starting to run low on breakfast food. He thought about asking Cory to make a stop by a grocery store one evening after a game, if they could find one open, but he was already too dependent on him for transportation as it was. Plus, he was trying, with mixed results, to follow JJ's advice and not let his mild fixation on Cory show.

Cory seemed very happy to have Rett carpooling in the truck with him, and Rett assumed he must be missing his other friends and truly glad to run across someone even newer to the whole thing than he was, someone that felt safe to open up to a little bit. So Rett didn't worry much about it.

What mostly bugged Rett about his car situation was not being independent, even if it was temporary. It bothered him enough that he was going to swallow his pride once he got in to work and see if he could work something out to get his car fixed sooner.

He leaned his head against the window of Cory's truck as they made their way down Government Street towards the Portyards.

Cory glanced over at him and said, "I'm boring you, aren't I?"

That was what killed Rett, right there. That was a perfect example. Cory was totally sincere in his question. The guy was a professional ball player and here he was worried that he wasn't entertaining *Rett* enough. And that was despite the fact that he was already hauling Rett to and from work every day now that they were back from Boston. It made Rett want to jump his bones and squeeze him to death and run his hands through his hair and tell him he was one of the most magnificent people Rett had ever met.

He settled for reaching over and poking Cory in his shoulder, his pitching shoulder, a few times.

Cory laughed and said, "What are you doing?"

"Changing the damn channel. This show sucks. I'm bored," said Rett blandly.

Cory glanced at him where Rett could see both dimples behind the stubble on his cheeks. Rett liked it better when Cory didn't shave because he had noticed Cory did a crappy and uneven job when he did shave.

Rett said more sincerely, "Knock it off! You know better than that, and you're not boring. Not most of the time anyway. All the save-situation-appearances and WHIPs and UZRs and Sabermetrics and the if-you-like-The-Pretenders-why-don't-you-like-Blondie stuff makes me kind of sleepy, but that's not the point. I like riding with you plenty, but I'm frustrated to not have my car, too."

Cory said, "Tell you what, once you get the German jank-vagen out of hock, it'll be your turn to lug my fat ass around and even the score up. I'll even complain that there's not enough legroom and make you play some Blondie. Huh?"

Rett would have told Cory that that sounded great to him, and it did, but his phone rang, interrupting his train of thought.

It was Val. She said, "You're in deep shit, buster."

"Huh?"

"You heard me. You promised, Rett."

Rett wondered what in the world she was talking about. He said, "'Promised' is such a strong word. Do you perhaps have a signed and notarized document to back up your vague and, thus far, unsubstantiated claim? I think..."

Val interrupted him and said calmly, "I ran into Mike last night, Rett. He hasn't talked to you at all. Or, more importantly, *you* haven't talked to *him*."

Rett grimaced. This was bad. Wretchedly bad. This was a dazzlingly bad time for this call, *and* he would have much preferred to have her yelling at him instead of the dry sound of disappointment he was getting.

"Val, I *cannot* talk about this right..." he said.

"You never called him, you never talked to him, you never *anything*, Rett!"

Rett glanced uncomfortably over at Cory, who was listening to Rett's side of the phone call curiously.

Rett tried again, "Val, please, can I call you later? This is not a great time for this conversation."

Val sighed on the phone and he could see her in his mind shaking her head at him the way she sometimes did. "Don't bother, Rett. I love you, but I'm really upset. You let Mike down, but now you've let *me* down, too."

Rett was frozen and had no idea what to say, and for once stayed silent.

Val's voice remained steady and measured. "But you're going to face this, Rett. I know... new job, summer of your youth, no responsibilities, travel, blah, blah, blah... all your usual ass-talking excuses, but you're going to deal with this, Rett, I guarantee you. I'll talk to you later."

Val hung up and Rett sat with the phone to his ear for several more seconds. The thump, thump, thump of the truck's tires on the pavement in the tunnel under the river was all that Rett heard as he sat. Rett hadn't heard her like this in a long time. She would chide him occasionally about being irresponsible or for not following through with something she thought he should, and he could usually make her forget about it sooner or later. But this time seemed more focused and more personal than the others.

"Is everything ok?" asked Cory after a moment, startling Rett.

Rett remembered to put his phone back in his pocket and said, "Yeah, uh, Val and I have known each other for too long. Sometimes she thinks that wanting me to do something is the same thing as me agreeing to do something. And that results in what I just got an earful of."

But Rett *had* agreed to do something, and he knew it.

~~~~~

Rett stood in the hallway trying to screw up his courage. He *hated* doing stuff like this. And this time it was a doubly treacherous task he had to get through. He concentrated first on getting past Rosemary. That was enough to make him feel like he was going to lose the special espresso flavored Moon Pie he had grabbed out of the Clubhouse dining room for breakfast. He hoped he didn't lose it on Rosemary's carpet. She'd probably disembowel him on the spot with her bare hands. Especially since the carpet would already be a mess and all.

Josh Kilfoyle, the Australian guy that played right field and that Val had a crush on, came up behind him. His family had moved to the US right before he went to high school, so he still had just enough of the accent to drive fans crazy. His white teeth and blue eyes and perpetually tan skin didn't hurt, either.

"You waiting on Rosemary?" he asked, with a slight quaver in his voice. He picked at the tuft of a soul patch under his lip nervously.

"Well, I need to talk to George for a minute, but you can go first if you want, Josh, and I'll wait!"

Josh shook his head wildly and backed up a step, "No, mate, you were here first! Just don't piss her, right?"

Rett looked at the open door to her office and Josh added, "Watch your neck! I heard she went on walkabout in the outback, and would steal pups from the dingoes to survive. I mean it, if she goes for you, it'll be the neck she goes for!"

Rett probably would have found that funny if he wasn't about to walk into her office alone. He stepped in and Rosemary looked at him over her reading glasses. Rett started to feel a burning sensation in his chest where she was looking, and it was impossible to convince himself it was only his imagination. Rett wondered how she did that. She probably only weighed 70 pounds.

"Hi, Rosemary," he said, "if George isn't busy, I was wondering if I..."

"No," she said.

George's office door was open, so Rett was pretty sure he was in there.

"Well, I just need to speak to him for..."

Rosemary took her glasses off and stopped Rett. "Why is it that you seem to *speak* English, but don't seem to *understand* even the simplest English words when they are spoken to you?"

Rett swallowed and thought maybe an email would be a better approach.

Before he turned to leave, George called out from his office cheerfully, "Rett, is that you out there? Come on in!"

Rett fearfully watched Rosemary, and he really thought she actually was going to go for his neck for a second. He slid around her desk and into George's office without taking his eyes off of her.

George was puttering around on his laptop and motioned for Rett to have a seat.

"What's up, Rett?" he asked.

Rett was now at the second part that he had a really hard time doing.

He took a deep breath and said, "Morning, George... I wanted to, uh, ask you a favor." Rett could feel his heart beating in his chest.

George leaned back in his chair and said, "Bah! It's no problem, Rett! I already know what you want. I was wondering how long it would take you to get around to asking."

Rett's face puzzled. He asked in disbelief, "You know I was going to ask for a small advance on my paycheck so I could get my car fixed?"

Now it was George's turn to look confused momentarily, then he laughed and leaned way back in his chair, greatly amused. George said, "Sorry, I thought you were going to ask for something else!"

"Uh, no..." said Rett. "Am I *supposed* to be asking for something else?"

"Nah," said George, still chuckling to himself. "You're just the only employee of the Joes that's never asked for free tickets or Owner's Suite access for a game. Even that punk kid — what's his name, Ryan or Brian or whatever, making minimum wage on the grounds crew for the summer — came in here asking if he could have the Owner's Suite for the Friday game against the Blue Jays in a few weeks!"

"Oh, ok," said Rett. "Yeah, I'm good there. If I want to watch, I go up to the general admission seats since there's plenty of room."

"Man, Rett, you're the most laid back guy there is on the Joes when it comes to baseball!" George shook his head and added, as much to himself as Rett, "And we gotta start filling all those empty seats! Hopefully, just a little while longer and we'll turn that corner."

"Uh, sure," said Rett, before turning the conversation back to money. "So, I've got some car repairs that I need to pay for, and the timing has been bad since I'm low on cash until I get my first paycheck. I don't want to put you in an awkward..."

"How much, Rett?"

"Uh, well, $750."

"No problem," said George. "I'll have Rosemary direct deposit it later today."

"Really?" said Rett, greatly relieved. George was becoming one of his favorite people. "Awesome! George, I really appreciate this a lot!"

George saw Rett out, and he called the auto shop to have them go ahead and make the repairs to his car. Since Rett had waited, though, a few other repairs were now in line in front of him, so it was still going to be a couple of days before they could start on it.

~~~~~

On the way home that evening, the Joes had now won one and lost one to the Cleveland Indians, and Rett had mentioned to Cory that the shop was going to go ahead and start work on his car in a few days. Cory replied that he didn't think Rett was able to pay for it yet, and Rett explained to him how he had gotten a little pay advance from George. Cory reacted to that, and Rett was struggling to interpret his reaction. Cory didn't seem upset, exactly, but he wasn't indifferent to it, either.

Cory said, "Rett, if you needed a loan for a couple of weeks, I would have been glad to spot you. You should have just said so. I got a little bit of a signing bonus, and it's not like I'm out spending it on hookers and booze and huge baskets of fried crab claws I can roll around naked in."

Rett's imagination was captivated by that last bit, and while the mental picture had its plusses and minuses, it netted out negative in the end, and so he dismissed the image.

Rett said, "I'm not going to put something like that on you! You've already done something huge for me as it is, Cory! I feel like a big enough leech, knowing I've still got to beg for rides for probably the rest of this week!"

Cory gripped the steering wheel a little more tightly and looked over at Rett. "You've *never* begged, and you don't need to! And if it became any kind of a problem for me, I'd say so and JJ or most of the rest of the Joes would be glad to give you a ride."

There was a silence before Cory said, almost like his feelings were hurt, "This is what buddies do for each other, Rett. We're buddies, right?"

When Rett sensed it in Cory's tone, the idea that Cory seemed to have hurt feelings over this, it was like being stuck with a pin. Was Cory seeing the time they'd spent together as just something Rett was doing only because he needed the rides and otherwise would prefer to not be around him? The truth was almost the exact opposite.

Rett was in agony. He wanted to reach over and touch Cory so bad, it almost hurt. "Of course we are! Definitely! You'll regret making that statement one of these days, but in the meantime, absolutely!" Rett sighed, "Ok, I'll stop shitting around, Cory, for real. Of course, we're buddies. I've just got this pride thing, you know? Ever since I left home, I've done all of it on my own, and so it's hard for me to let myself lean on other people. It's all just my own fucked-upitude, and not any kind of reflection on you."

Rett had started out saying all that as a way of stopping Cory from feeling hurt. But as he said it, he realized that there was a lot of truth in it. He'd never actually thought of it this way, but the unintentional truth had come out of his mouth, and now he could see it a little more clearly than he had before.

Cory continued to drive in silence, considering what Rett had said.

"We're buddies, Cory," said Rett. "But I guess I come with a side item of shit. Sorry, but no substitutions from the menu."

Cory's expression lifted and he laughed a little. He reached over and grabbed Rett by the neck and shook him playfully. Rett closed his eyes and felt like he could die right there.

Cory pulled up to Rett's apartment and said, "Ok, shrimp, here ya go. Tomorrow morning, right?"

Rett hoped he had really cleared that up and made Cory feel better, and he nodded and opened the door to get out. As he did so, one of the baseballs Cory always had down in the floorboard rolled out and started rolling down the street along the gutter.

Rett went to go get it, finally having to trot after it to catch up to it. Cory got out of the truck to see what he was doing and watched him finally grab the ball. As Rett started walking back towards him with it, Cory held up his hand and said, "Chuck it here, Rett!"

Rett walked all the way back to Cory and handed the ball to him.

"What the hell was that?" asked Cory.

"What the hell was what?"

"Did you just walk all the way over here and hand me this baseball?"

"You said to give the ball to you!" said Rett.

Cory grabbed Rett's hand and put the baseball back in it. He said, "Throw this ball to me like a man!"

Rett frowned and grumbled, "Throwing a ball doesn't make you a man."

Cory suddenly realized what was going on. "You don't know how to throw a ball, do you?" he asked.

Rett grew very uncomfortable. "Of course I can throw a ball! Maybe, you know, not well, not like *you*, but I can kinda throw one. Can I just go inside now? It's late."

Cory closed his truck door, grabbed Rett by the arm, and started pulling him out into the empty street. "Come on. We're gonna throw this ball a little."

Rett squirmed, trying to get his arm loose from Cory's grip, and said, "Cory, this is a total waste of your time. You should be resting your arm, anyway. And look at this! It's pitch black out here!"

Cory looked him right in the eye. "I'm not pitching any burners to you and it's just you and me. No one else is around to watch. All we're gonna do is toss the ball back and forth a little. Just you and me, Rett."

Maybe it was the June air, but Rett felt like he was sweating. Normally, he would have wiggled out of this somehow. He didn't want to toss the ball around. The few times he had tried sports or "tossing the ball around" had resulted in some very bad memories. And he didn't want to relive any of those times with his dad. But after their conversation a few minutes earlier, he didn't dare risk telling Cory no. It stressed him out, but he was stuck.

Cory handed the ball to him and positioned him a few feet away. Rett's face was flushing, but under the blue tint of the streetlight, it was hard to see. Cory said, "Just toss it to me. Overhand... underhand... your choice."

Rett rolled his eyes and lobbed the ball to Cory underhanded. It almost went sailing over Cory's head, but he reached up and caught it with no problem.

Cory went to throw it back to him, but Rett said, "I'm *worse* at catching."

"Hold out your hand, palm up," directed Cory.

Rett did as he was told, and Cory gave the ball a light underhanded flick so that it arced over and landed squarely in Rett's open palm. Rett started to say, "Are you kidding..."

Cory shushed him and said, "No talking right now. Just focus on tossing the ball. Talking will screw you up."

They tossed the ball to each other for a few minutes. Rett's tosses were a little uneven, but not unmanageable given Cory was only a few feet away from him. Cory's always landed unerringly in Rett's hand, until he started to vary it just enough to make Rett track the ball a little in order to still catch it.

Once Rett seemed comfortable, Cory backed him up a little further, and they started again. Every time Rett tried to say something, Cory made him be quiet and focus.

To Rett's surprise, he was doing it. He wasn't perfect, and he occasionally sent Cory chasing the ball, but Cory never teased him or made him feel bad about it a single time.

By the time Cory had backed Rett up so he was about ten feet away, he said, "About here you'll probably want to shift to overhand. Take it easy and just practice. All this is is giving your muscles and coordination a chance to judge force and aim without your brain having to think it."

Overhand was a disaster and Cory was running all over the place for the ball, even if he did manage to catch it most of the time. When Cory threw the ball to return it to Rett, it hit its mark every time, at least until Cory intentionally varied it somewhat.

One of the times Rett threw the ball, it sailed just barely over Cory's hands and wound up banging into the tailgate of Cory's truck. Rett cringed and said, "Sorry, Cory!"

Cory said, "Give me a break. It's a twenty year old truck that was used for landscaping most of that time. It misses getting beat up!"

Cory backed Rett up a little further and they resumed tossing the ball again. Rett to Cory, then Cory to Rett. Back and forth. And back and forth again. Every time Rett tried to speak, Cory told him to hush and keep his eyes on him and on the ball.

Cory and Rett stood out in the middle of a deserted street at midnight, under a streetlight and in the still-humid air, and Rett did something he never thought anyone would ever be able to convince him to bother with. Playing catch, tossing the ball around, things like that... they had never figured into Rett's mind as being something that he would do. Or something that he *could* do, even if he wanted to. The crickets and katydids and frogs off in the hedges of azalea and ligustrum were the only sounds up and down the otherwise still street. Rett found it almost hypnotizing after a little while — tossing the ball to Cory and then having it land back in his hand with a light smack a moment later.

Still, Rett knew he was pushing his luck with this. This was the guy that got creeped out when he thought the manager at Bluegill was checking him out. He had turned around and walked out of the shower suspiciously rather than be in there with Rett. Cory had called that guy a "worthless faggot." Baseball players were notoriously like this, and he had seen plenty of it around the clubhouse already. Chumming up with Cory was dangerous, and he ignored the clear warning signs at his own risk.

Cory tossed the ball to Rett so that it landed right in the palm of his hand. Rett threw it back and Cory reached out to grab it. And it went back and forth between them.

Cory kept it easy for Rett to catch the ball, and kept his eyes on Rett the whole time. Rett recalled how his dad reacted with put-downs and disappointment whenever he had made Rett attempt some sport, and then performed badly at it. And it wasn't like his dad was any big sports champion; he had higher standards for Rett than he did for himself. Cory, though, was world-class at exactly this kind of thing. He had every reason in the world to expect a high standard of performance for something like this. Instead, Rett felt like there was no way he could fail at it. He made Rett feel like there was no way he could disappoint him at it. No matter how poorly he threw the ball to Cory, Cory either caught it or chased after it without complaint, or teasing, or disappointment. Rett had a friend that, for the first time in his life, really, he was comfortable trying something that was so straightforward, and yet had always been presented as a test of his manhood. How could Rett ignore that? How could he not appreciate what Cory was doing for him? How could he turn away from this?

Rett caught the ball in his hand and threw it back to Cory. His overhand throw was a far distance from perfect, but he was improving. Cory side-stepped to catch the ball. Back and forth it went.

It was bad enough that Rett was spending more and more time with Cory, even ignoring the warning signs. Worse was the fact that he found himself truly attracted to him. More than the body, it was the smile, the dimples, the humor, and the kindness at odds with the randomly homophobic moments. Rett's attraction to him was adding to what was already a dangerous and volatile mix. It made every minute he spent with Cory more reckless. It gave him too much opportunity to spill his hand in a way that could so easily explode. He'd slip one day and say something. Let a touch linger that would confirm for Cory that what he had feared about Rett was true. Something would happen and it would come out, and where would Rett be then? Definitely in a bad situation, if not the hospital. He knew he shouldn't be there with Cory, even just tossing the ball around.

Back and forth. Back and forth.

But it felt good to be with Cory, even with it being nothing more than it was. It felt good to play like this, to throw a ball around. To spend the time with someone that was fun to be around. With someone that could help him overcome some of his past with his father. And Cory seemed to be glad for someone like Rett, for whatever reason. Cory *felt* like a friend. It felt like it went both ways.

Back and forth. And back and forth.

It was reckless.

It was good to play catch with someone.

It would all end badly.

It gave him the shivers to be there with Cory.

It was dangerous.

It was magic.

He needed to put a stop to it before it blew up in his face.

Rett wished tossing the ball that evening wouldn't end.

Chapter 8

Rett buttered his toast, and this time he had the luxury of using a plastic knife. He had retired the popsicle stick after stealing a few sets of plastic utensils from the dining room at the Portyards. His apartment in the older house had been refurbished pretty well right before he moved in, freshly painted throughout and a recently updated bathroom. The kitchen had been fixed up, too, and even if the appliances weren't high-end, they were recent and in good shape. He looked forward to the day when he'd be able to get real silverware of his very own. Make the place homey and all like nothing but silverware could do.

The rough schedule of working for the Joes was starting to sink in for him. He'd been working there almost two weeks now, and had not had a true, full day off to himself yet. There had been one day before the series at Fenway had started, but even that day was partially taken up with the team's travel to Boston. In the clubhouse, he found himself enjoying what he was doing, so probably, the wear he was feeling was attributable more to not having his car than the schedule itself. But he only had to wait two more days, until Monday, before he finally got his car back. That Monday happened to be the same day they'd be leaving for two different series on the road, one in New York against the Mets, followed by a trip to Toronto against the Blue Jays. But then, *finally*, after that he'd be home and would have his own car back.

He thought about trying to call Val again, but decided not to. He had texted her on Wednesday to see if she wanted to come stay with him for the weekend and meet some of the team. It was a shameless bribe to see if she was still pissed at him or not. Val had texted back later that day that it was a bad weekend for her and she'd have to come down some other time. She was still pissed.

Rett knew that it all boiled down to the fact that he had promised her that he would talk to Mike, and he knew he should, but he couldn't bring himself to do it. To Rett, calling Mike would be stirring something up that was already settled. And on top of that, he didn't really miss Mike, and that made him feel bad, too. He tried to be a little fair to himself and remember that his life was extremely different from the life he had in Montgomery, and Montgomery already seemed like a long time ago in many ways. But there was still that small, constantly flashing beacon of guilt from that part of his life that hadn't fully receded into the distance yet.

Rett ate his toast in silence and wished Val wasn't mad and that she had come down for the weekend. She had been the one constant in his life since he had left his family, and he felt totally adrift when she was giving him the cold shoulder like this.

He dug around in the cushions of his chair and pulled a baseball out. After the first night Cory had made Rett toss the ball around with him, which was already one of his favorite nights of his life, Cory had sent him home with the ball to practice on his own. He had told Rett to bounce the ball off a wall, or throw it up in the air and catch it.

Rett tossed it up in the air and caught it a few times. He and Cory had played catch again just last night, and Rett enjoyed it as much as the first time. Secretly, he thought what he really liked the most was getting to spend time with Cory, one on one. The thought that Cory wanted to do this for him sent a secret thrill through him. Whatever the reason, Rett loved it. Who knew tossing a stupid baseball around could mean something like this to him? He continued to improve, but he'd rate his skill at probably abysmal instead of the outright laughable he had started out at.

While they were tossing the ball around, and after he had beaned Cory's truck with the baseball yet again, he asked Cory why he had such a junker truck. Rett had been a destitute college student for seven years, and he was curious to know what Cory's excuse was.

Cory explained that the truck belonged to one of his best friends back in his hometown. The guy used it for his landscaping business, where Cory had worked part time all through high school. Cory said it reminded him of home and people that meant a lot to him. Maybe one day it would fall apart, but until then, he liked it.

Rett found it strangely funny to think of Cory doing landscaping. But at the same time, he had no trouble seeing it in his mind. He had thought at the time how lucky Cory was to have people in his life, in his hometown, that he was still so close to. It made him think about the one person from his own past that he truly missed — his little brother Bo.

His dad, Newton, had usually ranged from being disappointed in Rett, at best, to downright hostile (a lot of the rest of the time). His mother, Jaye, never seemed anything other than vacant. In Physical Therapy school, he learned enough to realize she probably suffered from untreated depression, which is why she never seemed to have any real interest in anything. She certainly never crossed her husband, not even for Rett's or Bo's sake.

That left Bo, four years younger than Rett. It was a strange sensation to realize his brother was old enough to drink now; when Rett had left, Bo had been only about 14 years old. He wondered what kind of a man Bo had turned into. He didn't doubt that it was one his dad would fully and easily approve of. Bo always succeeded at all the manhood criteria that Rett failed at. But then, Rett was gay, and that was really what was underneath his dad's issues with him the whole time. All the other milestones and qualities Rett failed at or lacked were just ways for his dad to beat around the bush with what he really hated about Rett.

Rett liked guys and could never be a man himself as a result. And his dad hated him for it.

But Bo hadn't picked up on it yet, hadn't sensed that Rett was different or the constant tension between Rett and his father, and he was still able to love Rett for who he was.

He remembered one time when he was about 11 and he had gone to find Bo for dinner like his mom had asked him. He ran across his little brother by the small creek that ran through the neighborhood a few houses over. Bo had found a bunch of tadpoles and was trying to catch them in his hand to bring them home, and failing at it badly. Rett, though, found an old sandwich bag nearby on the bank of the creek and used it to scoop some up long enough to make it home with them where Bo could put them in a jar. Rett remembered the look on Bo's face when he helped him. He remembered feeling ten feet tall during dinner and after. He hoped his dad went easier on Bo than he had on him. He hoped Bo was happy and that he was having a good life.

A knock at the door roused Rett out of his thoughts. He looked at his phone and noticed Cory was a few minutes early picking him up. He yelled for Cory to come on in as he ran to his bedroom to grab his shoes and put them on.

He heard the door open and close as he was grabbing his shoes from the closet and was about to make a smart ass comment when he heard a voice call "Rett?" from the other room. It wasn't Cory's voice.

Rett stood up and crossed to his bedroom door to find Mike standing in his empty den, in the blue shorts and yellow, short-sleeved camp shirt that was his Saturday favorite.

Rett stared blankly for a moment before his guest finally said, "Hi, Rett."

"What are you doing here, Mike?"

Mike's face sharpened slightly with a little anger and he said, "I'm trying to find out what the hell happened, Rett, and I guess it takes a personal appearance since you refuse to answer your phone or call me back!"

Rett was still in a state of shock when he asked, "How did you find me in Mobile?"

As soon as he asked the question, though, he already knew the answer. Both he and Mike said "Val" at the same time.

Rett looked around like he was hoping he had left a window open that he could jump out of since Mike was between him and his front door. He was ashamed to even briefly consider locking himself in his bedroom. He was stuck, though, and now forced to face this. Val had made damn sure of that.

Rett stumbled over his words, "Mike, I, uh... It just didn't seem... I... You... Well, you left that message, which I did get. And it felt like that was all you really had to say about it. I guess I should have called you back, but..."

Rett's explanation hurt more than it helped, and Mike's voice started to rise and his face turned red. "It's not about what *I* had to say, Rett! I wanted to hear *you* say it, whatever it was! Damn it, Rett, I think I deserve some kind of explanation for you just disappearing! But to just get nothing? Not even a 'fuck you?' It pissed me off, and when I ran into Val, she seemed mad, too, when I told her how I had gotten nothing. Jesus, Rett!"

Mike's face was drawn out in anger and hurt, his hands were fidgeting nervously, and Rett had no idea what to do or say.

Mike shouted, "I thought we had something pretty good going! But maybe I felt something you didn't. Or maybe I fucked up. Or maybe the idea of moving out of Val's apartment was too much for you. Who knows? Do you want to explain? *Can* you explain? Can you even give me that little bit? Or am I not even worth that? I had to drive three hours to get a face-to-face answer, so can you at least give me *something?*"

Rett had unconsciously stepped back and bumped into the counter that separated the kitchen from his den.

He said, "I'm sorry Mike, you're right." He grabbed futilely at whatever else he should say, for anything, but he didn't know *what* to say. He hit the same wall he kept on hitting every time he had tried to make himself have this conversation — he didn't know *why* he had let their relationship disintegrate. He just didn't want to get hurt. And so he had moved away as a result.

Mike yelled again, "I don't care about being *right*, Rett! I just want to understand!"

Rett said, "I don't know, Mike. I don't fully understand it, either. It just didn't feel right. And it wasn't right to keep stringing you along, or worse, starting to depend on you if I couldn't find a job."

Rett had found a path now that felt better and so he went with it. "I didn't want to take advantage of you knowing that's how I felt. And then this job popped up, and it's a good job, but there's no way it would work to try and continue what we had. It wouldn't be fair to either of us."

Rett could feel deep down that, while his statements were true, he was still missing something.

Mike calmed down a little, and he and Rett watched each other warily for a second.

He asked Rett, "Did you ever love me, Rett?"

"Yes," said Rett, truthfully.

Mike said, "Then we should have talked about this. Before now. Not like this." But Mike didn't seem to be angry any more. Just sad. Like he wished he had had a chance to repair something that he had no idea was broken until it was too late.

"I'm sorry, Mike. You deserve better."

"I loved you, Rett. I wanted to be there for you. I guess it was already over for a while and I never realized it. I just wish it hadn't taken until now for it to be official."

Rett stared down at his bare feet. He felt genuinely bad for not handling this any better than he had, but he was powerless to stop it, too.

Mike and Rett stood watching each other for several moments, the wreck of their relationship filling up the empty room.

Mike nodded in finality. "Ok, Rett... Good luck with your baseball job and your new life," he said, waving around indistinctly.

Mike turned and walked out the door, and Rett crossed over to close it behind him. He leaned his forehead on the door, trying to understand why he had let what he had with Mike come to this. Why was he afraid of what he could have had with Mike? Why couldn't he tell him about the things Mike had done that had hurt his feelings in small ways? Why hadn't he been able to let Mike support him some? Why couldn't he face Mike and talk about these things? Why couldn't he figure out what he wanted from Mike?

He was going to be a nervous wreck the rest of the day.

He whispered to Mike through the closed door, "I am sorry, Mike. Good luck to you, too." He meant it, too. Rett wrapped his arms around himself, but it was like there was nothing there to hold on to. He was as empty as the den he was standing in.

Ten minutes later, Rett was still sitting in his chair in a daze, replaying what had happened over and over again. It took a second for his mind to pull out of itself just enough to realize there had been a knocking at his door again.

For a flash, he thought it might be Mike coming back to give him another earful, but then he realized that, no, it had to be Cory.

He yelled for Cory to come on in while he ran to the bathroom. He had to splash some water on his face and to get his mind out of what had just happened.

This time, he did hear Cory's voice in the den, "Yo, Rett? You ready?"

Rett looked at his face in the mirror. The day was either going to be hell to get through, or it was going to take his mind off of everything. It was a 50/50 chance of whichever way it would swing, so he'd just have to take the bet.

"Yeah, be right there."

~~~~~

Rett sat at the table in the middle of the team locker room and worked on his plans for the week they'd be on the road. That was the theory, and when Josh came in to change and had asked him what he was up to, that was what he told him. The reality was that he was still hung up on Mike's surprise visit that morning and it was still spinning in his mind like a pinwheel in a thunderstorm.

He decided to send Val a text to at least let her know her plan had worked perfectly. What he actually texted her was:

Mike came by this morning. And yes, we talked. For real. Thx for the heads up that he was coming.

He realized the last sentence was a little dickish, but it was how he felt and he had already sent it.

Skunk walked into the locker room right as Rett was going to knuckle under and get real work done, and he asked Rett to change out the tape on his left knee. Skunk had hyper-extended his knee slightly in the first game against the Yankees and was now using this as an opportunity to boss Rett around as much as possible. Rett longed for the days when Skunk was giving him the silent treatment.

Worse, he insisted Rett do it in the locker room instead of the treatment room so whoever else was around could watch and hear him complaining to Rett about how he was doing it. He also took this as an opportunity to strip down to a jock strap and shove his business in Rett's face to make it all the more humiliating. Rett did as he was asked and ignored Skunk's clappy crotch and the rest of his bullshit attitude.

As he got ready to take the old Kinesio tape off, JJ walked in and saw what was going on. He shook his head and started changing into running shorts and a t-shirt so he could go run some of the steps out in the stadium before practice.

He said to Rett, "When you finish up, Rett, will you have a minute to meet me in the bullpen? You'll, uh, probably need some fresh air, anyway."

Rett stifled a grin at JJ's comment and kept his head down as he removed the old tape off Skunk's leg. "Sure thing, JJ."

Skunk scowled and said to JJ, "Nice shorts. What color is that anyway, boy? Watermelon? Huh?"

Rett froze at the comment. It was one thing for Skunk to be a narcissistic asshole, but this kind of thinly veiled racist comment was too much. Rett stood up and was about to tell Skunk exactly what he thought of him as a baseball player and as a person, but JJ came over and put his hand on Rett's shoulder.

JJ said calmly to Skunk, "Yeah, maybe." Rett could tell JJ didn't want him to react and so he let it go.

JJ squeezed Rett's shoulder and said, "What do you think, Rett? Watermelon?"

"Looks like plain old red to me," grumbled Rett.

"Guess Skunk maybe has a finer sense of color than we do," said JJ and went back to changing his clothes. Rett grabbed the rest of the stuff he needed to finish taping Skunk's leg and put the fresh Kinesio tape on as fast as possible.

A few minutes later and Rett was running down the service tunnel to the bullpen, furious at Skunk and a little upset that JJ seemed willing to tolerate his shit. JJ was there waiting on him.

"Why the *hell* do you let that asshole say racist shit like that?" demanded Rett.

"Calm down, munchkin. Skunk and the crap that comes out of his mouth don't matter." JJ seemed totally unconcerned about the whole thing.

"The hell it doesn't!" yelled Rett.

JJ grabbed his shoulder again to force Rett to look him right in the eye. "It doesn't, Rett. There's racism and then there's petty bullshit like this. I don't let petty bullshit run my life."

"But he's a fucking..."

"Whoa! Down, dog!" laughed JJ. Rett wondered how JJ could be so unconcerned about all of this.

"Take a deep breath, little dude," said JJ. "Skunk's not worth the concern. Let me ask you a question... is there anything really wrong with Skunk's leg?"

Rett was a little confused by the question.

JJ said, "I already know the answer, but tell me if *you* think there's really anything wrong with that skunk's leg two days after he hurt it."

"His knee's fine," said Rett. "It was mild to begin with. A really mild hyper-extension like that would be fine in a half-day at most."

JJ nodded and said, "Yeah. But now he's got an excuse so he can fuck off for a few days. He sucked at fielding last night and he'll probably suck again tonight, you watch. And fielding is the one thing keeping him on this team. The guy's an idiot and he's being lazy and he's giving Ahab and George a reason to trade him or send him down. He's not worth getting upset over, Rett... because he's going to be gone before long. I guarantee it."

Rett calmed down now that he saw JJ's perspective. He wasn't totally convinced, but JJ knew baseball much better than he did. Rett snorted, "Fine, I'll leave it alone. But when he comes and starts burning crosses in your front yard, I'll be there telling you 'I told you so!'"

JJ shook his head, "You know? I got no doubt."

"Ok, so what was it you wanted me to meet you out here for?" asked Rett.

"Nothing. I just was trying to get you out of Skunk's crotch. Unless... you wanted to be there?" said JJ, needling Rett a little more.

"Yeah, cause the oozy ones smell the best," replied Rett sarcastically.

JJ laughed again and said, "But since you're here, you want to give me a foot rub?"

Rett turned to go back to the clubhouse. He yelled over his shoulder, "You want me to whack all the blonde tips off those dreads?"

~~~~~

If nothing else, Skunk's prime example of being unprofessional took Rett's mind off of Mike for quite a while. In fact, he didn't really think about Mike again until right before the game started.

At Ahab's request, everyone had gathered again for one of his infrequent "pep talks" before the game that night. Given the one other of these he had seen, Rett got nervous when Ahab came in and wound up standing right in front of him to address the team.

"What the fuck is wrong with you guys?!" shouted Ahab. Rett tried to back up a little so he didn't get spit on, but Josh Kilfoyle was right behind him and was using him as a human shield.

"This has been the lousiest goddamn game of fielding I've ever seen in the last few nights! It's like a bunch of goddamn bumper cars out there running around and banging into each other! Josh! Do you have a corncob shoved up your ass?"

Behind Rett, Josh said, "Not tonight!"

The comment may have gotten some snickers out of the rest of the team, but it did nothing to calm Ahab down. He shouted, even more loudly, "Funny, Kilfoyle! Almost as fucking hilarious as those two errors in one inning last night! *One fucking inning!*

You know the terms of your contract, Kilfoyle! You want me to remind you of how much you're getting paid per inning?!"

That sobered Josh up.

Ahab continued to yell, but Rett's phone buzzed with a text message and he took it out to see it. It was from Val:

U know y I didnt tell u he was coming? Bcause u wouldnt have been there!

It made the whole scene with Mike that morning flare up in Rett's gut again, like an indigestion. He looked at Val's response and tried to decide if she was still mad or not from the message, but it was hard to tell.

"You, what's your name?"

Rett looked up to see Ahab looking right at him and he flushed pink at getting caught not paying attention.

"Uh, Rett," he stammered, nervous about the painful yell job he was about to get from Ahab.

"Skunk, if your knee's hurt, go on the DL. If it's not, then play ball! But if you fucking keep up that gimp act you've been pulling for the last few nights, I'm putting Brett here in center field instead! You can jack off in the dugout and let Brett do your motherfucking job for you! He *can't possibly* suck ass at fielding any worse than you have lately!"

Great, thought Rett, *yet another reason for Skunk to hate me.*

Ahab shouted as loud as he could, "Get out there and do the fucking impossible! But I'll settle for you shitheads playing ball like you're *not* blindfolded for a goddamn change!"

Josh leaned over and said in Rett's ear with a smirk, "Way to get promoted, Brett!"

Rett sighed and wondered how long he'd have to put up with people calling him Brett.

~~~~~

The loss to the Yankees had been another disappointing one that night, 9 to 2, which Rett had watched from his usual cheap seats. As JJ predicted, Skunk played a half-hearted game and was pulled out by Ahab even before the 3rd inning and replaced with Fred Lipscomb. At least Josh, after being called out in front of the team by Ahab, seemed much more in the game than the previous nights.

Walking out of the clubhouse and on the ride to his apartment, Rett expected Cory to tease him some about the whole Brett thing, but he didn't; Cory was quiet on the way out to the truck and as they began the trip back into downtown. Rett's mind had drifted back to that morning and he decided he needed to call Val when he got home. He'd had the discussion with Mike and he wanted things back to normal with her.

He caught Cory glancing over at him again, and now that Rett thought about it, he had seen Cory doing this several times since getting into the truck. It had happened with enough frequency that he asked, "What?"

"Huh?"

"You keep looking at me."

"No, I'm not."

"Dude, you're doing it right now!"

"You asked me a question and so I'm looking at you while we talk!"

"Fine. What about all the other times?" demanded Rett.

Cory looked straight ahead and set his jaw rather firmly. Now he was studiously *avoiding* looking at him, and Rett could tell something was up.

Cory tapped his steering wheel nervously. His mouth drew tight and he finally said, "You're gay."

There wasn't anything in the world that could have prepared Rett to hear Cory speak those words to him. His heart dropped through his chest, then through the floorboard of the truck where it bounced and skidded on the hot asphalt as they left it behind. In his panic, he even bit his tongue hard enough that he drew a little blood. His hand went to the seat belt release, because if Cory had also figured out how he felt about him, he was going to have to jump from a moving vehicle.

Rett forced a casual laugh, trying to dismiss it and sound like he thought it was a pretty good joke. Rett's insides, though, were busy tying themselves into a nice, tight knot.

Cory repeated, carefully, "You are gay, right?"

Rett shifted to the forceful, insulted approach, "What the hell's wrong with you, man? That takes a lot of nerve to sit over there and make some kind of shit statement like that! And if you're *trying* to be funny, you need to try a fuckload harder than that! I don't know what you think you've seen to make you, uh... you think..."

Rett lost his train of thought and his voice ground to a halt because it sounded like Cory had said the words "I am, too" in the middle of his rant.

Rett blinked a few times. He must be going crazy because it really sounded like Cory had just said he was gay as well. His eye twitched slightly with the confused state he found himself in. Surely, Cory hadn't just said what he thought he heard. Rett wondered if it was possible there was someone else in the truck claiming to be gay that he didn't know about.

"Huh?" was all he could eventually manage.

Cory glanced at him with a pained look on his face. He said, "I'm sorry, Rett. I didn't mean to overhear, and I wasn't trying to eavesdrop, but this morning, I heard you talking to someone... a guy. And, the little bit I heard made it pretty clear that the two of you have... er, had... a relationship. But, in a way, this is..."

"Hold on, hold on... you *heard* all that this morning?" demanded Rett. Rett could not believe the shitty luck he had had with Mike's visit. He might as well have had Mike come duke it out with him on the evening news.

Cory flinched and repeated, "I'm really sorry! I left when I realized what I was hearing. I didn't hear very..."

Rett interrupted yet again, "Ok, never mind that. Back up a second. Because a minute ago, I could have sworn I heard you say, and you're probably gonna belt me back to the Portyards for saying this, but I thought I heard you say that you were, uh, gay, too." Rett drew back expecting to get punched in the face.

Cory swallowed and said, "Yeah."

"Yeah, you're gonna punch me in the face for saying that, or... yeah, you're gay?"

"I'm gay, Rett," said Cory.

There was no mistaking it that time.

It turned out that the only words Rett was less prepared to hear from Cory besides "you're gay" were "I'm gay, too."

"You're six foot five," said Rett.

"Uhhhhh, what's that got to do with anything?"

"You can't be gay."

"I can't be gay because I'm tall?" asked Cory.

"I don't know! I'm not sure what's going on here!" said Rett. His mind was at a total loss trying to pull all this together.

Cory pulled the truck over to the side of the road and turned it off. He looked at Rett with determination. "I'm gay, Rett. I'm a homo. You know... I'm into dudes. I'm a... tall... gay guy."

Rett's mind was still trying to make sense of the reality-distortion field he had somehow entered.

Cory seemed to relax a little more, though, and he even seemed a little excited when he said, "But it's ok, because you are, too! It's better than ok, because now we can be ourselves around each other and, God, that's going to be such a huge relief!"

Rett seemed to be getting it slowly. He said mistily, "You're gay."

Cory grinned, "Come on, Rett, keep up with the conversation here! We're a couple minutes past that now!"

Cory being a smart-aleck seemed to snap Rett back to reality. "Wait a minute! Wait one fucking minute! That night, my first night in the clubhouse, there was that guy I saw you with, the guy in the suit! You called him a worthless faggot!"

Cory looked puzzled for a minute. Then a light bulb went off, "Oh, you mean Jimmy! You heard that?"

"Who's Jimmy?"

"Jimmy's kind of like my business manager. He helped me put together the contract with the Joes."

"But he's a worthless faggot that you pay too much?"

"I didn't know anyone was around to hear that. I was just horsing around with him. And I was giving him a hard time because I don't pay him *anything* at all. He won't let me."

Rett was dipping his toes back into the waters of confusion again. "You have a business manager that accepts no money for his services."

Cory's face lit up. He said excitedly, "I've known Jimmy since I was 13 years old. He was literally the first person to find out I was gay! He's almost more family to me than my actual family!"

"And it just so happens that this guy negotiates Major League Baseball contracts?"

"No, no, no. He owns a landscape company. This truck belonged to Brick, his partner."

Rett put his hands on his head and squeezed it to keep it from exploding. "Your *landscaper* negotiated your Major League Baseball contract with the Joes?"

"He's not my landscaper! I worked for the two of them during high school! Jimmy actually used to do talent management type stuff in New York before I knew him, like with movie stars.

Contracts for sports figures aren't all that different, and he's consulted a specialist when he needed to. You're gonna have to meet them next time they come in town with my parents! They're *definitely* going to want to meet you!"

Finally, it started to come together for Rett. Cory seemed ecstatic to have all this out in the open. Then it got a little fuzzy for Rett again.

"Wait, so these guys know your parents?"

"Yeah, they're two of my parents' best friends."

"We're talking about your dad here, the one you told me was ex-Army Ranger and Chief of Police in your hometown... your small, hickspit hometown?"

"Yeah!"

"Two *gay* guys."

"Yeah!"

"Do you have any idea how ridiculous all that sounds?" said Rett.

Cory shrugged like it all happened every day all around the world.

Rett's mind found something else to seize on, though. "Wait, why did you get offended and walk out of the shower my second night?"

"Offended?"

"Yeah, JJ and I were in the shower. You came in to take one, too, saw me, and turned around and walked out, like you didn't want to be around me," explained Rett.

Cory stammered slightly, "I uh... I don't even remember that. I guess I had just left something in my locker I needed. It had nothing to do with you. Nothing."

Rett said, "You sure? I just assumed you already pegged me as gay and didn't want to be in the shower with a queer. But then you were so great later that evening when my car died... I couldn't figure it out."

Cory shook his head, "Nope. Nothing to do with you."

Rett paused a minute, trying to figure out if there was some other incongruity he needed explained or not.

Cory took advantage, though, and said, "I got questions, too!"

Rett decided that fair was as fair did. "Ok."

"You're really gay, right?"

"Nope. World-class pussy-puncher."

Cory grinned and punched Rett's shoulder.

Rett said, "Ouch! Damn! Yeah, Cory! Fine! You definitely busted me." He rubbed his shoulder where Cory had smacked him. "Guilty as charged! True blue queer, through and through."

Cory said, "You don't know what a relief it is to have someone on the team I can be myself around! All through high school I stayed in the closet just because it was a small town. In college, I stayed mostly in the closet because baseball was more important. I didn't seriously *ever* think I'd be doing what I'm doing right now, but since I am, I've gotta keep quiet about it a little longer."

Rett said, "Well, you and me, both. I need this job and I don't think it'd go over too well with some of the players if they found out that the guy feeling up their hamstring is gay."

"Probably not. Will you do me a favor, Rett? Promise not to tell anyone, please. I don't know what I'd do if it got around that I was gay and it got back to the team. I'd love to finally be open about it, but what's happening right now is such a huge dream for me that I'm willing to stay quiet to not risk it. Are you willing to promise me?" The earnestness of Cory's plea took Rett by surprise.

"Well, sure," promised Rett. "The only other person I'd probably want to tell is Val. But she's got a problem with that big mouth of hers sometimes, so I'll wait until you say it's ok."

Cory breathed a sigh of relief. "Good. Thanks, Rett. I was pretty torn today between getting this out in the open and just keeping quiet about it. I think I would have exploded, though, if I hadn't been honest with you, especially since we've become close friends. You got no idea how fucking awesome I think it is to find out you're gay! So the guy you were talking to today? He's your boyfriend? Your partner?"

"No," said Rett. "Well, not anymore. We dated for a while when I lived in Montgomery. He's a good guy, but we had already drifted apart. And then I got the job and moved here." Rett felt gooey inside from the fact that Cory had used the phrase "close friends" to refer to him.

"And Val... y'all are just friends?" said Cory.

"*Just* friends. Ugh, sharing a bathroom with her was more than I could take most of the time," said Rett. "I'll kill you if you repeat what I'm about to say, but I don't know what I would have done without her. She was always there for me, even when I didn't want her to be. I like to think I did all of it on my own, but I don't think I could have ever gotten all the way through PT school without her. And, I mean what I said about you repeating that... I'll kill you. I'll kill you in a slow way like some brilliant, diabolical serial killer." Rett asked, "What about you and Kaitlynn. Did you really date her?"

Cory said, "Jason and Kaitlynn are close friends of mine, nothing more. They were the only two people in high school that knew about me. Kaitlynn and I have always been close, though. She and I pretended to date for most of high school, and since she went to UGA, too, even in college."

Rett, now that his questions were answered, took a long look at the guy sitting next to him in the truck. Finding this out about Cory changed everything. Everything. It was good that he could be himself totally around Cory. And he felt like they could become even closer friends without having to play it straight. But that was where it got hard again. It was difficult enough to be around Cory when he was straight; now it was going to be torture. Rett had barely started to get himself on an even keel around him, but the news tonight was going to seriously disrupt that. *Everything* had changed.

Cory cranked up the truck and they continued on towards Rett's apartment.

Rett couldn't help but ask, "So you had no idea about me until this morning?"

"None," said Cory. "Did you think I was?"

"Hell no!" replied Rett.

When Cory pulled up in front of Rett's place and he started to get out, Cory said, "I'm really glad we're out in the open with each other now, Rett! Nothing's changed, though, right? We're still buddies, right?"

"Sure, Cory. Nothing's changed," said Rett. He watched Cory pull off from the curb with a big grin on his face. As he walked up the stairs to his apartment, he paused to look back at the disappearing truck one more time. Rett couldn't help but feel disappointed that nothing had changed.

Chapter 9

The very next day was a big test of Rett's ability to handle the unnerving knowledge that Cory had turned out gay. Up until this point, Cory hadn't really needed any specific support from Rett as a physical therapist, save for one day where Rett showed him how to use the SwimEx.

But on Sunday, the last day of the four game series against the Yankees, Cory injured himself slightly during batting practice. It wasn't bad, and Cory didn't even want to deal with getting it checked, but Ahab was adamant about it and sent him in to the treatment room. Normally, Dr. Bala would check it out, probably with Rett assisting, but he was busy giving Satoru Furukawa, the Joes' shortstop, an X-ray on his ankle that he had twisted. Instead, he trusted Rett to do the usual checks on Cory and let him know the results so he could officially issue an opinion.

When Rett walked into the treatment room and saw Cory sitting there, he asked, "What happened?"

Cory shook his head and said, "It's nothing. I'm fine. Ahab insisted."

"Ok, but what did you do?" asked Rett.

"I was batting and practicing sliding a little. My groin pulled a tiny bit and Ahab saw me favoring it. I can barely even feel it now, but he jumped all over me about it."

Rett knew what he'd need to do to check it out, and it made him start to bite at his lip unconsciously. He'd need to touch Cory, there, in his groin area, to understand exactly where the tenderness was. And that made him suddenly itchy and sweaty. He tried hard to quickly figure out a way to not do that because he really didn't trust how his own body would react to touching Cory there.

Rett said, "Oh, uh, mmmm... there's a couple of things I need to do to check this. One is to get you out in the gym and use light weights on the leg adduction machine to test flexibility and pain levels."

"No problem. Let's go," said Cory.

Rett faltered slightly and said, "But first, really... I should check the muscles to make sure that's a safe step to take. I need to feel the adductors, just to make sure it's minor enough to get on the machine."

Cory considered what Rett was saying for a moment. He scratched his head. "Look, I was able to walk in here fine. I really don't think that's necessary. Can't we just skip that part?" He pressed on the inside of this thigh himself and added, "See? Feels almost perfect. No real pain."

Rett wanted that to be enough, but it wasn't. "Cory, I'm supposed to do it myself since I know exactly what muscles need to be checked."

"Oh..." said Cory. "Well... if you say so."

Rett frowned and added, "You need to strip down to your compression shorts."

"Oh, you're kidding me, right?" said Cory. "I'm fine. Really."

Cory seemed uncomfortable with all of this, and Rett was, too. But he stared at Cory, giving him no choice in the matter.

"Oh, ok, fine," said Cory, and Rett helped him take his cleats off and then his uniform pants.

The sight of Cory sitting on the table in nothing but his compression shorts, his strong legs stretched out across the exam table, made Rett's mouth dry up and he froze briefly. He yelled at himself internally to not start getting hard at the sight. He was only able to hold himself in check by remembering the night that he and Val got drunk and Val drew a clown face on her bare left breast using her nipple as the clown nose. Rett had told her later that he had never been afraid of clowns until that moment. But the memory was a big help in the current situation.

He said, "Give me a pain rating, scale of 1 to 10, 10 being unbearable agony."

He paused nervously, then forced himself over the rest of the way. He was really unsure if he'd be able to keep himself from running his hands up and down Cory's legs, to keep himself from touching any part of this beautiful man he could get his hands on. This was exactly the torture he wanted to avoid.

He touched Cory's inner thigh lightly, causing Cory to flinch, which in turn caused Rett to flinch. He found the muscle he was looking for and looked away from Cory.

"Pain?" he asked.

"2, if even that much."

Cory's rock-solid thigh felt so good under Rett's fingertips, even through the compression shorts. The memory of Val with the clown face on her boob wasn't cutting it anymore, and Rett could feel his dick in his pants start waking up. He got drastic and took it up a notch; he started thinking about Rosemary slowly undressing in front of him. That was the thing that finally seemed to do the trick.

Rett tested two other places similarly as fast as he could, trying to not look at Cory or his leg, which proved to be an interesting challenge since he had to look at Cory's leg to make sure he was checking in the right places. And doing it strictly by touch had the potential for being far more disastrous if his hand strayed a few inches too far. Rett desperately wished that they had taught these particular assessment techniques in school blindfolded so he could handle something like this a little better. At least Cory's pain was almost entirely gone at this point anyway, so that was good.

"Ok, that's done. If you want to put your pants back on, I'll meet you out by the adductor machine and we'll test range of motion and get pain readings there."

Rett turned away and wrote some notes down while Cory got dressed. The notes took a lot longer to write because he was spending most of the time willing himself to not get a hard-on from the sensation of Cory's legs still lingering on his fingertips. Any other guy on the team, and this would have been nothing for him to handle. But Cory... Cory was something else. And knowing Cory was gay now made it infinitely worse. He scolded himself that Cory was hurt and the last thing he'd want is Rett getting some cheap thrill out of it.

In the weight room, things got back to normal between them, and Rett was able to work with Cory on the weight machine using light weights to confirm that it was extremely minor, despite Ahab's concern.

As he got to the end of his tests with Cory, Ahab strode into the training room looking for them.

"You checking him out?" Ahab asked brusquely.

"Yeah, just finishing," said Rett. "Dr. Bala will have the final say, but there's really nothing to be worried about. Cory's pain is almost gone and he has full range of motion."

"Good. Thanks, Brett," said Ahab, decisively. He turned his attention to Cory and pointed at him, "No more batting practice unless I say so, you hear?"

"Uh... sure, Ahab."

"I mean it, Cory," said Ahab. He turned and left to get back out on the field for the rest of the team's practice.

Once Ahab was gone, Rett could see the smirk already forming on Cory's face, and he knew exactly what it was about.

"Start it up and die," said Rett. "I'll rip your gimp leg off and beat you unconscious with it. Let's see how well you pitch then."

Cory laughed, shook his head innocently, and crossed his heart in a solemn pledge.

"If you start to feel pain in your groin, stop and let me or Dr. Bala know," instructed Rett.

As Cory was walking out of the training room and out of Rett's reach, he said with that devastating grin of his, "Thanks, Brett!"

~~~~~

In the bottom of the 5th inning that evening, the Yankees were already up 6 to 0 against the Joes. The Joes, though, had managed to load the bases and Skillet was at bat next with two outs, and there was a lot of tension for the home team to get on the board.

Rett, Cory, Sebastion, Ric and Arthur, plus two of the trainers, Ryan and Wally, and the pitching coach, Topher, were sitting up on the stand in the Joes' bullpen looking out over the field and watching the game. Every so often, Sebastion and Arthur would go down in the bullpen to pitch a few in case Gunnar left the game and Sebastion got called in.

Skillet banged it hard, and the ball went high and deep, but the Yankees' left fielder managed to barely catch it by almost climbing up the outfield wall. The boos from the hometown fans overwhelmed the cheers from the few Yankees fans in attendance at the Portyards.

Once he got to the bullpen after the game started, Rett had been glad to see that Cory wasn't favoring his leg at all anymore after the groin pull that afternoon. He was even gladder to see that Cory didn't seem put off or uncomfortable after the exam that he had given him. It had made Rett uncomfortable and he didn't see any way in the world that Cory couldn't have picked up on it.

Rett's phone rang and he was a little happy and a little nervous to see Val's name on the display.

He answered, "So are you..."

Val interrupted, saying, "I just saw you on national TV, you fucker! *National TV!* I hate you now more than I ever have!"

"TV?" asked Rett.

"Yeah. I'm watching the game and at the end of the inning the camera panned over you and some of the players sitting up on some kind of stand before they went to commercial."

"Yeah, I'm hanging out with Cory, Sebastion, Ric and some of the others in the bullpen tonight." Rett stood up and walked around idly while he talked to Val. "So, did I look suave?"

"As much as usual."

"Shit," said Rett, disappointed. He paused a second, then asked tentatively, "Are you still mad at me?"

"I was never mad at you, Rett. You let me down. You're suffering from the dipshit flu and I've got the cure. Ergo, you had to shape up and talk to Mike. Nurse Papadakis knows how to make this shit happen, and don't you forget it! Moral of the story? Douche not and live free!"

Rett watched as the Joes took the defensive positions for the start of the 6th inning. Gunnar was already rubbing his shoulder a little bit before he even threw the first pitch of the inning.

Rett said, "Douche not and live free? You saw that on a bumper sticker, didn't you? Admit it!"

"I did not!" insisted Val. "I pulled that out of my own butt, not someone else's!"

"Ok, in that case, it just officially became my new motto! And just for your information, your 'mad' and your 'disappointed' look a lot alike. And both of those look just like you do after eating too many shrimp. You might want to think about working in some visual distance between those three." He watched Gunnar rotating his shoulder slightly after each pitch, which so far was a straight line of balls to the Yankees' batter.

"Hey Val, I can't talk right now. I'm watching Gunnar, and I'm willing to bet his arm is bothering him and he's gonna give out. Which means, I'll need to meet him inside. I'll call you, ok?"

Rett hung up as Gunnar threw a fourth ball to the batter, giving up a walk to first base. Gunnar requested a timeout from the umpire and Ahab came out to the mound.

Topher was seeing the same thing Rett was and told Sebastion to head on over to the dugout. Rett left with him because he knew he'd need to check Gunnar's arm after he left the game.

In the treatment room, Rett helped Gunnar remove his jersey and began to check his arm out. What he found was the opposite of what he expected — Gunnar's arm was fine. There was no swelling at all, no signs of strain, and there seemed to be no pain anywhere he felt.

Rett went and closed the doors to the treatment room to give them some privacy.

"Gunnar, what's going on?"

"Nothing. Fatigue in my arm. The usual stuff."

Rett watched Gunnar carefully. "You wanna try that again? I've seen your arm when it's worn out, and it looks pretty good to me."

Gunnar didn't answer.

"Just me, Gunnar," said Rett. "No notes, no judgment, no one else listening. You sure you don't want to tell me what's going on?"

Gunnar continued to sit quietly, refusing to look at Rett. Rett gave him a moment, and then gave up. He said, "Ok, you want a rubdown, or heat cream, or even an ice sleeve on it?"

Gunnar shook his head but continued to sit on the exam table, not meeting Rett's eyes. Rett went to open the door to the treatment room when Gunnar said, "It's just..."

Rett closed the door again and said, "Just what?"

"The pressure. You've got no idea what the pressure is like," said Gunnar.

"Yeah, I can only imagine," Rett said quietly.

Gunnar finally looked up at Rett, "I've done this for years now, and it's never bothered me. But now, sometimes it's almost like I'm going to have a panic attack out there or something."

Rett was not expecting and not prepared to have Gunnar open up like this, but all he could do was listen and be sympathetic.

"I've played in the big leagues now for 16 years. The average major leaguer lasts five years plus change. And *now* I feel this pressure to keep it up, to maintain the performance. But I can't. It's not showing in the metrics, but I can feel it. It takes more to maintain than it used to. I can feel it all slipping away even if no one else has said anything. Yet. And it feels like it's crushing me sometimes. Tonight... unless there's a miracle happening out there right now, we'll lose all four games to the Yankees. I just couldn't do it tonight, Rett."

Rett closed his eyes and tried to figure out what the hell he could say. Gunnar was buckling under the weight of the whole team on him, and it wasn't really fair, as far as Rett could tell.

"You know, Gunnar," said Rett, "I know jack dick about baseball compared to you guys. But it's still a team sport, right? I can see how easy it would be for you, and even the rest of the Joes, frankly, to put success or failure on your shoulders. But it's a team sport. You're a huge part of the Joes, practically the face of the Joes, but you're *not* the Joes. Maybe that's a stupid observation, or obvious, or not really the problem at all, but you need to remind yourself of that. If I were in your shoes, the next time I went out to the mound, I'd look around at the guys in the infield and out in the back yard, and I'd look at the dugout, and I'd remind myself... I'm *not* the Joes."

Gunnar continued to look down at his cleats as he listened to Rett, and when Rett was finished, he took a deep breath and nodded.

He said, "Thanks for listening, Rett. I'd appreciate you keeping this between you and me. But tonight was tough, and I had to get that out."

"Yeah, Gunnar. No problem," said Rett. "I'll put down mild fatigue in my notes for Dr. Bala, ok? You want me to go crank up one of the whirlpools for you so you can unwind a little?"

"Sure, Rett. Thanks."

~~~~~

"You really should tell Ahab he's getting your name wrong," said Cory as they drove through the tunnel back into downtown Mobile that night.

Rett shook his head, "I'm not correcting anything that man says. I value my job *and* my paycheck. Both are pretty groovy and I don't want to fuck either of them up."

"It was funny when he was twisting the screws on Skunk the other night, but he's just making himself look stupid if he keeps it up, Rett. It'll be better if you let him know."

"No way. The only person that scares me more than Ahab is Rosemary."

"You're chickenshit. He's not that bad," said Cory. He took a hand off the wheel to adjust the ball cap on his head, the one that had a tree on the front and read "Montgomery Landscaping."

Rett ignored him.

"You know I'm just kidding, Rett. You're not really chickenshit."

Rett sighed. He *knew* Cory was just teasing him, but Cory still had to make sure Rett knew it and that he didn't mean it.

Cory was such a kind person... and that was the *other* kind of torture Rett experienced being around him.

Cory offered, "Ok, I'll do it for you. I don't mind and he needs to know who you are."

"Perfect," said Rett. "I've also got a pile of dirty laundry if you're in the mood to..."

He paused. "Where are we going?" Rett had now realized that they were no longer on the obvious route back to his apartment from the Portyards and were now headed off somewhere else in Mobile.

Cory gave him a knowing grin. "You'll see."

"Are you taking me to a laundromat so I can watch you do my laundry?"

The look on Cory's stubbled face unmistakably communicated the instruction for Rett to eat shit.

Cory said, "We're headed up near my place."

"*Near* your place," repeated Rett.

"Just hang on... we're almost there."

Rett pointed back the other way. "But all my laundry is back over at my..."

"Will you shut your fucking pie-hole about your laundry?" grinned Cory.

A few turns later, and Cory pulled up and stopped alongside the road. He reached into his backseat and pulled out his pitcher's glove and shoved it into Rett's chest.

"You're getting your first lesson in pitching tonight!" said Cory, extremely pleased with himself.

Rett looked at the glove he now held against his chest. Cory was already grabbing a few balls from the floorboard and getting out of the truck.

They had parked alongside a practice field near what looked like a school. In one corner was a backstop fence used for baseball and softball practice. The streetlights shed only a dim light over the dried-out grass of the field itself, but well enough to see alright. Rett took the glove and followed Cory out into the field, unsure about this adventure he was cooking up. Tossing the ball around was one thing, a good thing, but pitching seemed like a colossal waste of time.

Rett almost made a smart-ass comment, but stopped himself. Instead, he asked, "Cory, why are you doing this for me? You still trying to turn me into a man?" Turned out Rett couldn't keep the smart-ass entirely out of his comment.

Cory turned back to him and said, "None of this has anything to do with you being a man or not." Then he added, "You're all the man you need to be already, Rett."

Rett had been prepared to make another snide remark, but the last statement by Cory had taken the smart-ass out of him. He made very sure the sarcasm was turned completely off, and asked again, "Ok, so why?"

Cory had stopped out in the field about twenty feet from the backstop and Rett caught up to him. Cory studied him in the vague yellow light and shadows of the streetlights that made it into the practice field. He said, "Because I get the feeling that, despite you being a little shy about this kind of stuff, you actually have enjoyed it. And I like... I like... I like this, too." Cory adjusted the cap on his head and walked a couple of steps away from Rett.

Rett fidgeted in the field a moment, watching the dust kicked up in the streetlight. He admitted, "You're right, you know? I do like it. Probably more than you realize. Growing up, the few times I ever tried anything like this — baseball, soccer, touch football — I always immediately felt this pressure to get it perfect, right from the get go. Mostly from my dad. It was awful and I was miserable. And I *should* be even *more* nervous around *you* than anybody. But I'm not. You put me at ease, and I'm totally comfortable trying it."

Rett looked at the leather glove in his hand and turned it over, feeling it because it was almost like being able to feel Cory's hand instead. "And I know why, too. It's because you really are a good friend, Cory. You're an amazing friend."

Rett's mind flashed back over the awful pressure his dad put on him as he made him try touch football, baseball, and soccer, trying to find any sport his son could manage well enough to not embarrass himself at, and failing each time. Rett had sometimes even gotten physically ill before practices he felt so much anxiety over it, which only invited more disdain from his father. And he knew that was where Cory was different. Cory did this for Rett, not himself. That's why they were out in some dark junior high school ball field on a Sunday night at almost midnight. Cory chose now because it would be him and Rett only, and Rett could fail until he was comfortable enough to succeed. There would be no contempt and no reproach, no matter how bad Rett was. Aside from Val, Rett didn't think he was ever as close to anyone as Cory.

In the faint streetlight, a small smile touched Cory's face at Rett's comment.

Cory said, "Ok, you ready? Let's start with how to hold the ball."

Cory showed Rett how to grip the ball in his hand for a standard four-seam fastball and had him practice getting the ball into that position a few times. He stood next to Rett to show him the starting position — facing towards third base since they were both right-handed, with feet shoulder width apart. Next was lifting his left leg so his thigh was parallel to the ground. Then he showed Rett how to bring both his arms down and then back up to about shoulder-level while at the same time stepping his left foot out towards home plate without quite touching the ground with it yet. Cory was adamant that Rett keep his eyes on where he wanted the ball to go the whole time.

Rett had trouble with this part, mainly because trying to do it one step at a time caused him to lose his balance and he started laughing at himself. Cory made him practice a few times until he got good enough at it to proceed.

The next part was to get his pitching elbow above his shoulder while he extended his front arm towards home plate to pull himself forward a little. At this point, he showed Rett how to torque his body around towards home plate while throwing the ball with his whole arm, crossing it down and across his body. The last step was to bring his leg around so that he wound up facing home plate.

Once he had the components of a pitch pretty well down, they started going through the motions together without actually throwing the ball. Cory corrected Rett a few times to make sure he didn't start getting sloppy or omitting details. The one thing he had to correct almost every time was Rett's grip on the ball, which he kept forgetting about. Cory would show him each time, thumping his index and middle fingers on the ball to emphasize the correct finger placement.

Cory said, "Ok, this time, pitch it. Take it slow, like we've been doing. We'll pitch together, yeah? You and me, Rett. Don't watch me. Always watch where the ball is gonna go."

For the first time in his life, Rett pitched a baseball. The ball went high and too far to his left, but that's why Cory had put them this close to the backstop. Short of turning around and pitching the other way, Rett couldn't miss it.

Cory grinned at him and said, "That was good! You did a hell of a lot better than I ever did on my first real try."

Rett didn't feel like himself after his first pitch. It was as if he came out of the wind up like a different person. For a second, he almost choked up and thought he was going to cry, but he closed his eyes and forced it down. He asked, "How old were you?"

"Six. No, wait, five. I was five."

That broke the emotion in Rett and he started laughing. "Sweet! I can beat a five year old at pitching a baseball. That feels just awesome!"

The look on Cory's face was positively beatific. He could tell that Cory hadn't lied. Cory really liked doing this for him.

Cory trotted over to the fence and got the balls and brought them all back to Rett. "Ok, now you're going to do that over and over, aiming for me. I'll catch while you practice. We're gonna focus on your aim first."

"Bad idea," warned Rett. "Tossing a ball back and forth is one thing. Having me pitch at you is another. Mr. LeBayonne will send thugs after me if I bang you up and damage his property. Probably thugs with baseball bats."

"Hyuk hyuk! You should do standup!" said Cory sarcastically. "Don't get a big head, chief, you're not good enough to actually hit me."

"Ok, you dared me. When you get a concussion and are lying unconscious in the hospital, don't expect me to wipe the drool off of your face."

"Just pitch."

Cory had Rett back up a few more feet and then took his position in front of the fence. He said, "Eyes on me, Rett. Don't take your eyes off of me."

Rett thought, *no fucking problem there.*

As Rett started the wind up, Cory yelled, "Stop! Grip! Grip the ball right! It's not a bean bag! You gotta hold it right!" Cory held up the ball over his head and thumped his index and middle fingers against the ball to remind Rett of the right grip.

Rett said, "Oh, yeah, right! I forgot!" He made sure he was holding the ball correctly this time.

He pitched just like he had done before and was surprised to see his aim had already improved some. But over the next few practice pitches, it got worse and Cory started to correct him.

"When you wind up, your pitching elbow has got to be higher than your shoulder. And don't forget to reach your forward arm out towards me to pull you towards home plate a little. Keep you right knee bent slightly."

Rett tried again, but it was still no good.

Cory said, "Again."

Rett tried again, but he was still making the same mistakes.

Cory walked over to him and said, "Here."

Rett started to watch Cory show him, but Cory turned Rett away from him and back into pitching position. There was a pause before he heard Cory say, "We're going to do this together."

Cory came up right behind Rett, pressing himself against him, lining his legs up with Rett's and putting his arms over Rett's. He felt surrounded by Cory. Rett froze and suddenly the absolute last thing on his mind was pitching a baseball.

That is, it was the last thing on his mind until Cory bent his right knee into Rett's, causing it to buckle under him. Rett would have fallen, but Cory held onto him and said, "Slightly bent, Rett."

Rett tried a pitch again with Cory holding onto him and leading him through the motions slowly, but his breathing was getting shallow and he knew he was starting to sweat. They went through the motions once, and he heard Cory's breath in his ear, "Like that." But Rett's mind couldn't seem to hold onto the steps he was supposed to go through anymore. The feeling of Cory against his back, his arms over his own, his breath tickling his ear, seemed to have shut his entire brain down.

Cory didn't let go of Rett and moved him back into position. Cory stayed pressed up against him and shadowed him slowly through the motions again — grip, stance, leg up, arms out and up, step, and throw. When they ended, Rett heard Cory say in his ear softly, "Do you understand?"

Rett turned his face barely up towards Cory's, and he felt Cory's cheek against his own. He felt the soft scratch of Cory's stubble against his face. Cory held Rett against him from behind and turned his own face to look down at Rett. Their eyes locked together and Rett knew he was done for. There was no way he could fight this. He had run up to the edge of a cliff and there was no way to stop from falling over now. His knees got weak, but Cory pulled him even tighter in to him, holding him securely. Rett watched as Cory closed his eyes and he exhaled slowly while neither of them moved. He couldn't stop it if he wanted to, and he gently reached his face up to meet Cory's. His own eyes closed, and his lips closed the distance until they finally met Cory's, brushing them lightly, just barely touching. Rett could feel Cory's entire body tense up, and then return the kiss. It was like being hit by lightning out in the middle of the ball field, and every hair on his body stood up on end. The instant he felt Cory's tongue reach out to touch his lips, Rett opened his mouth to allow him in. They kissed harder, pressed their faces together tighter, and Cory's beard stubble ground against Rett's own smooth skin. He could hear Cory breathing heavily through his nose as Cory's tongue pushed deeper into Rett's mouth, desperately exploring him, tasting him for the first time.

Cory's arms pulled tighter around Rett and his hands found Rett's, engulfing them and lacing their fingers together. And even as Rett pushed his tongue into Cory's mouth, learning its way around, he groaned deep in his chest at the rolls of electricity passing through him from head to toe, making every nerve ending in his body hyper-sensitive to every point of contact with Cory's body behind him.

Rett finally broke the kiss between then, unsure of what he had done but completely unable to regret any of it. The expression on Cory's face when he finally opened his eyes, still holding Rett tightly, was what had to be a mixture of pleading for more and abject fear.

Neither said anything for a very long beat, and Rett found himself frozen, desperately wondering if he had really messed up.

Cory finally said in a hoarse whisper, "It was worth it. God, was that worth it."

Rett managed to find his own voice, despite the sparks still firing off deep inside him and wrestling with his own fear. It was barely audible over what was already a still and silent late-June evening. "Oh, God, Cory. I couldn't stop. I couldn't help it. I..."

But Cory smiled and leaned in to kiss Rett deeply again, groaning himself this time. Rett could feel the tension in Cory's body flow out of him as he relaxed into the kiss, and he realized how tensed up he was, too. He finally relaxed with Cory and together, the anxiety and tension drained out so that their kiss became something that felt like they had been doing for years —

relaxed, familiar, deep and comfortable. They did exactly what summer nights were meant for, and it came to both of them naturally.

When their second kiss ended, Cory put his face along Rett's ear, tickling it and tracing it with his lips. Rett could feel Cory's warm, moist breath on the side of his face.

Rett asked softly, "Was worth what, Cory?"

Cory finally loosened his hold and turned Rett around to face him. "The terror. All the terror."

Rett gave a confused grin. "The terror?"

He ran his hands up along Cory's forearms, feeling the tightly corded muscles underneath the skin, and felt like he was being hit by lightning again. Cory must have had a similar reaction as well, because he shivered slightly as Rett did it.

"The terror of wanting this so bad, and being so afraid of what would happen if you knew what I wanted. And it just got worse since yesterday when I found out you were actually gay. I thought I was going to die being around you. But I wouldn't trade it for anything," admitted Cory softly.

Rett had to chuckle softly at the idea. Cory raised an eyebrow at him and Rett said, "You and me both, Bigfoot."

"Bigfoot?" said Cory with a broad grin.

Rett reached up and finally was able to touch the dimples that had so completely fascinated him from the first moment he had seen them. Cory twisted his head so he could kiss Rett's fingertips.

Rett said, "It was sort of how I thought of you before I knew what your name was. Not in a bad way, though. And I was just as afraid of you. So many times I wanted to reach out and touch you like I'm doing right now. God, how many times did I want to do this?"

Cory pulled Rett to him and they kissed again, both of them giddy at not having to be afraid or worried any more. Both of them feeling the sparks all around them, crackling in the night air and at every point where their bodies touched. Both of them relieved at having found each other. Both of them relieved at having each other.

Rett kept his arms around Cory's waist, but looked up at him, "The bad news is that every single thing you taught me tonight about... this, uh, whatever... you know..."

"Pitching?"

"Yeah, that. It's all gone. Every last bit of it. We're gonna have to start over from scratch sometime."

Cory nodded thoughtfully. "Oh, I think I can manage that."

He ran his hands over Rett's golden-blond hair and Rett asked, "So, what now?"

Cory continued to run his hands through Rett's hair while he carefully considered the question.

He said, "I think I take you back to your place so you can get a good night's sleep, and we go get your car from the shop tomorrow."

Rett looked at Cory questioningly.

Cory said, "You and I managed to pitch a perfect game tonight together. You and me. No way I'm going to push my luck and ruin that kind of rare, rare magic. Absolutely perfect. If you're ok with that?"

Rett nodded, "You're right. This has been perfect."

They stood out in the field and kissed again, deeply and with no concern about what might or might not happen next. What should or should not happen next. They simply allowed the kiss, the feel of their bodies pressed together, the relief at having wound up at this point together, to be perfect.

Neither of them had any idea how much time they spent out in that field, but they didn't care, either.

On the way back to the truck, Cory said, "I was so glad when you turned away today after you felt me up. I got the biggest hard-on I think I've ever had. I got no idea how I got my pants back on after that!"

"I had to think about Rosemary to keep from getting one," conceded Rett.

"You know," said Cory, "Skillet told me that if you stand in front of a mirror and say her name three times, she appears behind you and guts you like a fish."

Rett laughed and said, "Thinking about Rosemary didn't work. I got a boner anyway."

Cory said, "Ugh! You got a boner thinking about Rosemary? That's *really* disturbing."

"You know what I mean, fucker!"

"Too late! This *was* a perfect evening until you somehow made it a three-way between you, me and Rosemary," said Cory, but he looked over at Rett and winked at him. It felt so good to still be able to joke around with Cory like this.

As they started off in the truck, Rett reached over and took Cory's hand in his own. The sensation was strange and wonderful. And if he had somehow tried to imagine even that morning that this evening he'd be able to do something like this freely, he would never have believed it. Everything and nothing had changed.

After Cory said goodnight to Rett at his apartment door, and after another lingering kiss goodnight, Rett went in and collapsed on his bed. He felt like he was made of shivers and tingles from the whole evening and he wanted to remember every single detail — Cory holding him from behind and stepping him through a pitch slowly, the warm June air, the clink of the baseball thrown against the chain-link fence, the feel of Cory's cheek against his own, the fresh, clean smell of the clubhouse soap on Cory's skin, that first touch of their lips together, the sound of Cory's breath in his ear, the slight smell of worn leather on Cory's hands from the mitts and baseballs, and finally being able to lay his fingertips on the world's most amazing dimples.

Rett slowly fell asleep with every detail still playing through his mind.

Chapter 10

Cory teased, "No dicking, Rett, you look like you're having a seizure."

Rett walked along the wooden path while the light breeze played through his honey-colored hair. His head turned and twisted constantly and his eyes tried to see in all directions at once, trying to take in everything simultaneously.

"It feels about like that, too!" Rett turned with a wild grin on his face and looked back at Cory, who was walking a step behind him. "This is, no shit, the most amazing thing I've ever done in my life!"

They started walking again when Rett stopped and pointed. "Is that the motherfucking Statue of Liberty?!" he exclaimed.

Cory laughed and looked down the East River and out into the harbor where, sure enough, the Statue of Liberty was brilliantly illuminated against the night sky. Rett stopped and stared at it for a minute, still utterly dazed at where they were and what they were doing.

After their thrilling and rather surprising win against the Mets at Citi Field earlier that evening, Cory had suggested they go here given the limited time they had to really see the city. Rett felt bad for initially being dismissive of the idea, because now that he was there, walking across the Brooklyn Bridge, with all of New York glittering around them, it was all far more impressive than he ever thought a bridge could possibly be. Even after midnight, the entire city was still active and illuminated. Everything was bigger than life and more impressive than it ever seemed on television. Rett would have felt like a gap-toothed, backwoods hick if he weren't so excited to see it in person. And a significant part of all of this excitement for him was the fact that Cory was at his side, sharing it with him. Part of the thrill was knowing that Cory wanted to do this with him. And for him.

Rett had been excited even with a mere cab ride into Manhattan, but this... this was almost beyond anything he thought possible. It almost, but only almost, rivaled the first kiss they shared two nights earlier.

At about the midway point on the bridge, they stopped and an earnest Rett said, "This is the most awesome thing I've ever done. Seriously, Cory. I'm fucking speechless!"

"Yeah? You don't sound too speechless," said Cory. Rett let him have his fun and continued to stare at him in sincere thanks.

"This was probably my favorite thing I did with Jimmy and Brick when they brought me here with them a couple of years ago," Cory added. "But, come over here. It gets even better."

Cory led Rett over to the wide, flat railing of the pedestrian walkway. He patted the railing and said, "Here, jump up and sit here."

Rett looked over the railing into the traffic lanes underneath and said, "What, so you can push me down into the crazy New York traffic below? Fun for *you*, maybe."

"Not on your life," Cory assured Rett.

Rett pushed himself up and sat on the railing. "Bitchin'. And this is better how?"

Cory pushed himself between Rett's legs and put his arms behind him. "Because in New York, no one knows who we are. And no one cares... if we do this." He leaned in and kissed Rett. Once again, the sparklers ignited inside of Rett. The night before, he had so wanted on the plane to be able to kiss Cory, or even just touch him, but he couldn't. But all of the pedestrians and bicyclists this late at night were completely indifferent to what they were doing, and to be over the East River, holding Cory and kissing him, made Rett's head spin. If it weren't for Cory holding onto him, he felt like he would have surely fallen off the railing. As they kissed, feeling the warmth of each other's bodies, Rett found how easy it was to forget about the city swirling around them. The sights and sounds faded into the background. All of Rett's senses tightened in and focused only on the person holding him, kissing him in rapt passion.

Cory broke the kiss, but kept his face close and kept his eyes directly anchored to Rett's. He slowly traced a finger across the features of Rett's face and said, "And if I'm too chicken for us to get together while we're in a hotel with the rest of the team, the very least I can do... is this."

He kissed Rett again. It started as a frantic, urgent kiss. Their lips and mouths moved across each other rapidly, tongues trading places swiftly. But as time ticked by, it slowed and grew more patient. Their lips and tongues touched more delicately and patiently, until finally neither of them moved and their lips barely touched, mouths open but breaths held still.

Rett pulled back and said softly to Cory, "Damn, but you are an amazing kisser." He touched at the ragged and uneven goatee that Cory had left on his face over the last couple of days. Rett picked at it, thrilled at being able to touch Cory. And absolutely overwhelmed about being able to do it here, out in the open.

Cory ran the back of his hand lightly up and down Rett's chest before he leaned in, pushed his face into the side of Rett's neck and bit it playfully. When he stood back up, he took Rett's hands in his and said, "Let's go sit on the bench over here. There's something else I've been saving up to tell you."

Rett jumped down from the railing and they found a bench where they could both sit comfortably and look at the city lights and the boats plying their way up and down the river. Cory was lost in his own thoughts for a moment, so Rett put his arm around his shoulders and pulled him a little closer.

"I met with Ahab and George today," said Cory as he nestled against him. "They're making a few changes in the lineups, and as of tomorrow, I'll be on the active roster."

"Cory, that's great! That's incredible!" Rett reached over and hugged Cory and kissed him quickly on the lips again. "I can't believe you kept that wrapped up without exploding! You must have been freaking out all day!"

"Freaking out... yeah. I'll be relief pitching at first, but I probably won't take the mound until after we get back from Toronto. At least, that's what Ahab told me to expect. My dad knew all this was coming, but when I called him, I think he passed out with the phone in his hand."

"Are you feeling good about it? Are you excited?" asked Rett.

Cory shrugged. "Yeah, I'm definitely excited. This is what I've wanted like crazy."

Rett studied him and could see the other part, lurking there behind Cory's excitement.

"But..." he said, prompting Cory.

"But you're one of the few I've told how nervous I am, too. And I'm *really* nervous. Thank God, I've had enough good people give me the advice to treat it all like college, to do what I've been doing, that I think I can manage that. It's already getting crazier, though. They want to have our publicity people take a few new photos of me tomorrow to get ready, and then a lot more when we get back home to the Portyards."

Rett took Cory's hand and said, "You're gonna be amazing, Bigfoot! You know you are! *I* know you are!"

"Well, here's hoping," said Cory, with a shrug. "I asked Topher what else I needed to be doing in practices to get ready, and he said nothing. He said I've been doing it all along. I feel like I should be doing something different, but Topher and Gunnar, hell, even you, have told me to keep doing what I'm already doing. It's just hard and strange to accept that there's not some additional step, some kind of black magic, I need to take to be ready for this."

"Look, if you can teach me to do... you know... what's it... that thing..."

"Pitching?" asked Cory with a smile.

"Yeah, that. If you can teach *me* how to pitch, you're ready to be the fucking President of the United States," said Rett.

That was when Cory leaned over and put his head on Rett's shoulder. It had been difficult for Rett not to call Val and tell her what was going on between him and Cory, but he had kept his promise to not do so. Rett hoped that when Val came to visit and got to meet Cory, he'd be more comfortable opening up to her. Plus, when it was really important to Rett, he could rely on Val to keep a secret, like she had about his family. She never once gossiped about that to anyone.

A couple of boats passed each other on the river, and Rett decided it was as good a time as any to bring up something he had wondered about.

"Cory," said Rett, "all this brings up a question I've got."

Cory grabbed Rett's hand and laced their fingers together and waited.

"Why am I here with you now?"

"What, like I'd rather be holding hands with Ahab or Skunk in the middle of the Brooklyn Bridge?"

"I'm serious, Cory. You're switching to the active roster tomorrow. Probably any day now, you're going to be pitching for real. It's not like I want to point this out to you, although it's not out of the reach of my self-defeat repertoire... but there isn't a woman or hardly a man for miles and miles that wouldn't give anything to be with you. I always assumed you'd probably want another jock type guy or something. At least not someone you literally had to teach *Ball Tossing for Dummies* to."

Cory pursed his lips and stared off in the distance before glancing over at Rett out of the corners' of his eyes.

He said, "I think I should tell you a story. Going into my freshman year in high school, I already knew I was gay. I'd come to terms with it, and my parents knew about me, and Jimmy and Brick were there to support me. My buddy, Jason, and I had been getting closer and closer as friends, and I realized I liked him more than just as a friend. He was my first crush ever. And it got bad enough to where I let myself fall for the stereotypes about what gay people were like. Jason was small, not any kind of a jock at all, but he had a killer sense of humor once he opened up, and I was totally lost in him. That summer we went to see some movie, and I was so sure that he had to be gay, too, that I put my arm around him."

Rett couldn't stifle a laugh at this point.

"You know what came next," continued Cory. "He thought it was a joke at first and told me to quit it. But I said that it was ok, that I was gay, too. That's when he really wigged. I tried to calm him down, but I kept touching him, which made him even crazier. And then I got flustered by his reaction, and... I told him I loved him."

"Are you fucking kidding me?" asked Rett in total disbelief. He was loving this story.

"It just came out! Jason practically climbed over twenty other people scrambling out of the theater to get away from me!" Cory paused, reliving the memory. He sighed before he continued.

"For at least a couple of weeks, I didn't see or hear from him. He wouldn't answer the phone when I tried to call, wouldn't answer my emails. He wouldn't have anything to do with me. I was devastated. I felt like the biggest chump idiot that ever walked the earth, and I felt like I had blown it with probably my best friend. And then... and then he showed up at my front door one day, and he said we needed to talk."

Cory grinned and continued, "I tried to get him to go back to my bedroom so we could talk, but he said 'no fucking way' and made me go out into the front yard in broad daylight instead. He told me how I had totally mind-fucked him, but that I was his best friend, too. He asked me if I really loved him. And I told him yeah. He said he was straight. Then he said but maybe he should be a little flattered that one of the biggest jocks in school wanted to fuck him, but he was really more just scared of me. And that's when he told me he couldn't be *that* for me, though... that he wasn't that way. But neither did he want to lose me as a best friend. I told him I didn't want to lose my best friend, either, and having him as a friend was better than nothing. So, it took a little time but he got comfortable with it, and I moved past my crush. We wound up better friends than ever."

Cory looked at Rett, his brown eyes sparkling in the city lights. "So, do you understand?"

Rett paused expectantly, but got no further explanation. He guessed, "Your gaydar is defective?"

Cory groaned, "No!"

"Did you keep the receipt? Maybe it's still under warranty."

Cory ran a frustrated hand over his goatee. Rett gave up and said, "I don't get it."

"Does Jason remind you of anyone?" asked Cory. "Someone on the smaller side, slim build, beautiful blond hair? Huh?"

Realization dawned on Rett and his eyes narrowed. "So I'm just a substitute for your straight best friend that you're *still* fawning over? I feel dirty now."

Cory sighed and smacked Rett in the head. "Nooooo, jackass! Jason's fun to give a hard time to, and to grab his ass every once in a while because he goes berserk when I do that, but that's all that is anymore, Rett. He's been a righteous friend for years, but nothing more than a friend."

Cory said, "Physically, yes, you look a little like him. You got the freckles upgrade, though, which cranks me up. And that was what attracted me to you to begin with. But the more I got to know you, your deadly sense of humor, how you genuinely care about others even as you give them hell, *that's* when you became important to me, Rett. *That's* what I care about. *That's* what I *want.*"

Cory pulled Rett practically into his lap. He kept one hand around Rett's waist and slipped the other under the leg of his khaki shorts to stroke his leg tenderly. "I know what I want, Rett, and I'm totally fascinated by you."

The nervousness Rett harbored deep inside about what Cory's answer to his question might be dissolved and floated away on the warm breeze blowing over the river. He thought earlier that maybe what Cory was feeling was just a by-product of identifying with someone else that was new to the Joes, someone harmless that he could confide in a little. The even worse alternative, the idea that maybe Rett was nothing more than a quick fling to Cory, had also surfaced in his mind. But everything about Cory seemed to pull against that particular line of thinking, and Cory's explanation tonight helped to eliminate it entirely; Cory honestly did not seem like the kind of person to be driven by those sorts of motives at all.

"Ok," said Cory, "now it's my turn to hear a story."

"A story? I don't really know that I have any. I can make up shit about Val if you like. I do it all the time," said Rett.

Cory prompted gently, "I was kind of hoping you'd maybe tell me what happened between you and your family."

"Oh. That." Rett sighed and warned Cory, "Your story with Jason had a happier ending."

Cory continued to rub Rett's leg gently and waited patiently.

"Looking back," said Rett. "I think my dad figured out I was gay really early, or at least assumed it. It was really important that I be a man, like him. Not that he was any big example of being a *fucking man*; it's not like he's some macho Navy SEAL or anything. He has a desk job as a scheduling analyst at Alabama Power in Dothan and I'm probably as big and tough as he is, in reality. Like, he complains in restaurants when his French fries aren't served hot enough. Sheesh. Growing up, he pushed me every way he could to turn me into a *man*, but it was all bullshit stuff."

Rett was never very happy to think about these things. He preferred to leave it behind him and he wrinkled his nose up at the memories. "He wanted me to play sports, change tires, even signed me up for karate once. He went completely apeshit when he saw me holding hands with my best friend... when I was *seven*! To make matters worse, my little brother Bo, got it all right. Don't get me wrong, I don't resent Bo at all. He was the one member of the family that seemed to love me the way I was, and I loved him back. Maybe it was just that he looked up to the older brother, though. My mom, man, she never took my side, she never pushed back on him. She was just zoned out most of the time."

"By the time I was 16, I had figured out I was gay; and by the time I was 18 and graduating high school, living in that house had become my own little hell. My dad had long since stopped disguising his contempt for me and constantly insinuated that I was gay, although he never said it outright. I mean, crap like the fact that I liked to have frozen waffles for breakfast on Saturdays was viewed like I was going to church dressed like a Puerto Rican hooker."

Cory interrupted and said, "Wait. Stop. Frozen waffles? Really?"

"Knock it off! I'm talking," warned Rett, not wanting someone else to pile on about the damn waffles.

Cory laughed, "I'm not making fun of you, dummy! I like frozen waffles, too. Maybe it really is a gay thing."

Rett stared at Cory, who cleared his throat and said, "Ok, shutting up."

Rett took a deep breath and continued, "Finally, I decided I had had enough. I came home on a Friday night, right after graduation, when it was just my parents there; Bo was over at a friend's house for the night or something. My dad made some dickheaded comment about me going out with a friend of mine, a girl. 'For all that girl talk you two do,' he said. That was it. That was the comment that broke the gay boy's back and I told him to just say it... to stop beating around the bush and just say it. I didn't think he would, but damn if he didn't. He looked me in the eye and said, 'You're a queer, Rett.' I was so shocked that he had actually said it, I didn't reply. I didn't deny it and he knew he was right. My mom looked at me like I had betrayed her. My dad said,

'I knew you were gonna turn fag on me. Everything about you from day one said I was gonna regret you. Everything I did to make a man out of you was nothing but a fucking waste of time.' He said things that, well... it was clear he didn't even want to think of me as his son. He made it clear I wasn't exactly welcome there anymore."

"I looked at my mom and she asked me, 'why are you doing this to us, Rett?' She wanted to know why *I* was doing this to *them*." Rett stopped and stared vacantly at the city.

"So I left. I walked out of the house. I spent that night in my car. The next morning, I went back. My mom was gone to the store or somewhere and my dad was still passed out asleep. There was an empty bottle of liquor on the kitchen table, so he had drunk himself to sleep the night before. I left a note for Bo in his room telling him that he was the only one in the family that gave a damn for me, and that he was the only one that I gave a damn for back. And I packed up everything I could carry in two arms and left. And I *never* looked back."

Cory sat quietly as Rett finished telling him what had happened, frowning. Without a word, he pulled Rett to him and held him again. He kissed the top of his head over and over and rocked him gently. Rett could hear a sniff every once in a while before Cory was willing to say something.

"It's not fair, you know?" said Cory, his voice cracking. "I've had everything in the world handed to me, almost. And you've had to fight tooth and nail for what you've got."

"You amaze me, Rett. You fucking amaze me!" Cory was squeezing Rett so tight he felt like he might suffocate.

And then it was Rett's turn to try and stop a tear or two from leaking out.

Chapter 11

Cory settled into the passenger seat of Rett's Jetta and immediately said, "There's not enough legroom in here."

Then, "I can't stretch out."

And finally, "Does this seat go back any farther?"

Rett offered as he headed out towards Cory's apartment, "It's got a huge trunk. Why don't I let you get in there? It's a lot quieter, too. For *both* of us."

Cory smiled while he picked at the frayed gray upholstery between his legs. "Nope. Staying up here with you. It's been days since I've been able to touch you, and I plan to be a total lech. I'll just have to put up with the leg cramps." Cory rubbed his legs and added, "I hope I'm not getting blood clots."

Rett rolled his eyes languidly.

Cory started fiddling with the stereo until the Blondie cd he had loaded when they picked up Rett's car from the mechanic started blaring. Rett snarled under his breath, but let him go. "Rapture" started pounding out of the car's nearly-blown speakers.

Cory started rapping along at the top of his lungs, "Rapture, be pure; take a tour, through the sewer!"

Cory stuck his finger in Rett's ear, making him flinch, "Sing! We had a deal, chief! Audience participation is legally mandated for this song, kinda like Rocky Horror."

Rett gave in and they sang along together, "Well now you see what you wanna be, just have your party on TV!"

Rett said, having to shout over Debbie Harry and Cory singing about the man from Mars going back up to space, "Rocky Horror! Now *there's* classical music for you! I've got the soundtrack, so we'll have to load it up and listen to it. And I'll bust your eardrums out I'll sing so loud! Val has a black-belt in playing Columbia, too."

Cory slouched over in the car and put his head in Rett's lap. He looked up at him with a slaphappy grin on his face while he continued to sing.

Rett said, "Bigfoot, you gotta stop that. You gotta sit up."

"Why?"

"Because, Cap'n Tease, you're giving me a hard-on that could reach up and drive the car by itself!"

"So? I got one, too!"

Cory sat up, but then reached over and slipped his hand up under the leg of Rett's shorts and grabbed his dick through his underwear. The Jetta swerved a little and Rett had to put on brakes.

"I shit you not, Cory, I'm gonna wreck and kill both of us before you have a chance to pitch your first game!"

Cory still had the stupid grin on his face, but he pulled his hand out from inside Rett's shorts. "Ok, fine! Then spend the night with me! Waiting that first night was stupid of me. If I had thought about the fact that it would be over a week before we could get together, I *never* would have waited!"

Rett turned Blondie down a little bit and looked at him out of the corners of his eyes. He shook his head and said, "Nah. You and I both know how good that night was. You were right, Cory. It was perfect just the way it was."

Cory took Rett's right hand and rubbed it on his cheek. "Yeah, it was, wasn't it?" he said.

"I don't know if tonight's the right night, Cory. You're lead-in relief tomorrow night, which means you'll probably be pitching. I don't want to distract you or screw up your preparations." The way Cory was now sucking on Rett's thumb was making it extremely difficult to argue against spending the night with him. And his erection had a mind totally its own.

Cory stopped sucking on Rett's fingers long enough to say, "Sounds good in theory, but it doesn't work that way. I'll be way more distracted if I don't get what I want. If you really care about my performance in the game, you'd better do exactly what I say, exactly how I tell you to do it... until I tell you to stop." Cory moved over and started sucking on Rett's index finger.

Rett was starting to feel like he was going to wreck again if Cory kept it up. "Seriously, Cory."

"Ok, ok, bare knuckles honest," said Cory, "I love that you're concerned, but I really am bad wound up here, about you *and* about tomorrow night. I'll be able to relax much better if I get to spend some time with you, just the two of us." He added, "But if you're not ready yet, then we don't have to go far. I just want to spend the time with you, to be able to touch you and hold you if nothing else, Rett. This past week has been frustrating for me. Aside from the Brooklyn Bridge, I mean. That was pretty sweet."

Rett shrugged and said, "Yeah, it was a frustrating week, with a capital 'F', for me, too."

"So you'll stay with me tonight? If you want to keep your distance, you can even have the bed and I'll sleep on the couch!"

Rett couldn't help but cut his head over at Cory. "You have a *couch?!* Well, la dee dah, Mr. Gatsby!"

They arrived at Cory's apartment, and Rett was anxious to understand how his place worked. When he had picked Cory up before the road trip, he had only seen the outside of it, and it didn't look like much of an apartment from the outside.

Cory's place was a single-story, red brick building that looked like it had been used as some kind of warehouse or for light manufacturing or something along those lines. It was situated on the edge of a commercial district in an area northwest of downtown Mobile and, as Cory had pointed out, was not far from the school where he had given Rett his pitching lesson. In the front was a raised loading bay facing the street that now served as covered, off-street parking for Cory's truck. Where the roll-up loading dock doors had once been were now a door and a large bank of windows. Around the corner and along the long side of the building that faced a side street was another bank of metal windows that looked original to the building.

Having only that brief exterior view to go on that day, Rett was curious what kind of place it was inside. He was ready, willing, and able to accuse Cory of squatting in an abandoned building; turnabout was fair play, after all.

Rett parked next to Cory's truck and they got their bags out of the back of his car. Inside, Rett had to throw out the idea of needling Cory about squatting. That ammo was worthless in this place.

The main room was large, with an open, newly installed kitchen off to the left. There was an island with a raised bar and four stools lined up, and the back wall of the kitchen area was floor to ceiling cabinets in a light olive green finish with cream colored countertops. The rest of the front room was all open with dark stained concrete floors. Cory's large sectional couch was placed facing the bank of windows out to the side street. All the exterior walls were the exposed original brick of the building. In the corner, where it could still seen from the couch, was a flat TV on a stand, but all the other equipment was set up on the floor with a mess of cords behind it. There wasn't any other furniture in the room besides the couch and the TV and stereo.

Rett looked around and took it all in, and then he started laughing.

"What?" said Cory, as he turned on a few more lights.

With the additional lights, Rett could see there was a hallway leading to more rooms behind the far wall.

"You've got a couch," said Rett. It somehow made Rett feel better to know that Cory didn't seem to be any more settled in his place than he was in his own.

"Yep. Practically a Ritz-Carlton in here. What with a couch and all," added Rett.

Cory said, "Yeah, I know. I still gotta get some more stuff at some point. Jimmy and my mom will probably come back down in the next few weeks to try and get me a little more settled in. Jimmy was the one that found this place to begin with. They had just converted it to a residential apartment."

Rett realized he was wrong. There was one other thing in the main room besides the couch.

"You have a *pinball machine?*" asked Rett. In the back corner was what looked like a full-blown pinball machine. An actual, full-sized, arcade-quality pinball machine.

Cory smiled and said enthusiastically, "Yeah! Isn't that thing great? It's a Silver Slugger pinball game, with the whole baseball theme and all! Jimmy surprised me with it when I moved in as something of a housewarming gift."

Cory led Rett down the hallway to the back part of the apartment where his bedroom was. It was a good size room, but dominated by a huge king-sized bed that had only hastily been made up the last time Cory was home. There was the same dark-stained concrete floor, but with the addition of a few deep green carpets on either side of the bed. There was a tall, dark wood framed mirror resting on the floor and leaning on a wall next to a large, simple chest of drawers and a large overstuffed chair. Along the window was a series of stands holding a variety of houseplants that helped soften the industrial edge of the apartment. The last purple and blue hues of the day's light were fading in the sky outside the windows.

Cory put his bags down and watched Rett suspiciously for a moment.

Rett said, "What's the stink eye for?"

"You gonna make any more snot comments about my place?"

"Nah, it's a cool place," said Rett. "You think that bed's big enough? You could have twenty refugees flee Cuba on that thing! Plus a couple of goats!"

"See, I knew you wouldn't be able to keep it down!" said Cory. "I'm six five, I kinda need a big bed to be comfortable."

"Yeah, Bigfoot, you're right. You do need something a little bigger than most people," agreed Rett, not wanting to overdo the teasing. He stepped over to Cory and ran his hand down the front of the blue knit shirt he was wearing. He put his hand up behind Cory's neck and pulled him down so they could kiss. Cory obliged and the kiss was a welcome relief after being in both New York and then Toronto and only occasionally being able to steal a touch or a brush of the lips.

When they stopped, Rett reached up and ran his hand through Cory's hair gently, feeling it against his hands, feeling it slip between his fingers. Cory closed his eyes and reveled in being touched this way, groaning and turning his head into Rett's hand. Rett moved down and delicately traced a finger along the edge of Cory's ear, then following along his jaw line. Cory shivered and sighed, "That literally gives me goose bumps."

He wrapped his arms around Rett and pulled him tight against his body and pressed his lips to Rett's, the urgency slowly gaining. Every time Cory's tongue entered his mouth, Rett could feel his feet tingle and tickle. Cory let go of Rett and his fingertips slipped down Rett's arms, barely touching them, setting off slow waves of sparks in the process.

Rett said, "Every single thing about you gives me goose bumps."

Cory took Rett's hand. "Will you take a shower with me?"

Rett looked down at his hand in Cory's. He was always taken by how Cory's hand swallowed his up. He nodded and they stepped into the bathroom together. The bathroom had the same original windows facing out over the street, but the lowest panes of glass had been frosted out for privacy. Jutting out from one wall was a glass-enclosed shower with a bench built up out of the concrete floor at the far end.

Rett started to take his shirt off, but Cory stopped him. "No, let me, please," he whispered.

Cory lifted Rett's shirt up and over his head and tossed it onto the countertop. He sank down to his knees in front of Rett, touching Rett's chest and then stomach with his face and lips, exploring the pale hills and valleys that formed his body with his hands, smelling Rett with his eyes closed. He traced the faint freckles across Rett's lithe body with his lips, giving Rett a fresh jolt of goose bumps. Cory unfastened Rett's belt, unbuttoned his shorts, and allowed them to drop to his ankles. Rett groaned as Cory leaned in and graced his stomach with repeated soft kisses, running his hands along the back of his legs.

"God, I love this body of yours! I love your pure skin." said Cory. "I love the way your abdomen V's down into your groin." Cory traced a finger lightly along the dividing line between the two as it disappeared into his boxers.

Cory looked up into Rett's eyes as he pulled his underwear down so he could step out of them, leaving him fully exposed. Cory laid his head against Rett's stomach again and placed his hands on Rett's ass, pulling him close as he exhaled heavily, enraptured at the feel of Rett's bare body against him.

Cory began to descend even farther, but Rett stopped him. "No way, Mister. My turn now. Stand up."

"Anything you say, chief," said Cory. He stood as instructed and Rett untucked his shirt from his shorts. He ran his hand up under Cory's shirt, kneading and rubbing the muscle and skin underneath, feeling the coat of pecan-colored hair slide against his hand as he explored. He lifted the tail of the shirt up, but Cory had to finish taking it off for him. Rett leaned forward and buried his face in the soft space between Cory's thick pectoral muscles; Cory wrapped his arms around Rett's head, cradling him against his broad chest. There was a rhythmic rise and fall of Cory's torso that Rett felt with each breath and he was able to still faintly pick up the clean scent of soap on him even after a full day of travel. His hands found Cory's shorts and unbuttoned them, then pulled the shorts and underwear down together, leaving nothing to his imagination any more.

Cory led Rett's hand down to his erect penis. His face grazed Rett's ear and whispered, "This is why... this is why I turned around and left the shower that night, Rett. One sight of you naked and toweling off and there was no way I could take my own towel off without embarrassing myself. But now I can embarrass myself around you all I want!"

Rett smiled faintly. All the wondering and anxiety and caution had been for nothing. But here they were now, nothing between them. Nothing holding them back. He found himself utterly lost in the handsome, athletic, towering man in front of him. Lost in the charming, warm, kind, funny, caring man. Lost. As lost as he had ever been.

"It was worth waiting for. Every bit," said Rett. "Every bit."

They reached around each other and kissed again, their bare skin pressed together, sliding their bodies against one another, mimicking the way their tongues twined and slid together, for one moment more before they entered to share the shower and each other.

~~~~~

Rett only became dimly aware of Cory sitting back down on the bed next to him, but even through his closed eyes, he could tell it was already well into the morning hours outside. Rett was typically a heavy sleeper, and usually woke up slowly, especially in a huge and comfortable bed like Cory's. These things became aware to him only vaguely as sleep retreated from him like a slow ocean tide.

Cory had been a gentleman that night, but not too much of a gentleman. They had spent probably two hours after their shower getting sweaty again and earning a second shower, then they had sat in Cory's bed, talking and sharing a quart of ice cream together right out of the container. Cory had opened up about his junior year in college, where he had gone through an extended slump, both in baseball and personally, that he was sure had ended his dreams of the big leagues. But he chose to extend his college career an extra year to continue at baseball and prove to everyone that he was able to get past his slump. And he found he had not ruined his big league chances after all. Rett talked about narrowly getting the loans and financial aid to start Physical Therapy school and of meeting Val and how close they became, even eventually moving in together.

When they had finally put the ice cream away and settled in to actually sleep, Cory insisted that some part of his body remain in constant contact with Rett. Rett normally didn't go for extensive snuggling while sleeping, but having Cory's arm across his stomach, or their legs touching, or Cory's nose against his shoulder where he could feel the steady pace of his breath, turned out to be remarkably reassuring for once.

As he slowly began to wake up, and without realizing he was doing it, Rett put his arm across Cory's midsection. Something about it, though, caused him to wake up a little more. It didn't feel right. Cory was wearing jeans already. Rett lifted his head drowsily out of the thick pillow it had been buried in and saw his arm resting across... someone else.

Rett jolted fully awake when he saw the strange man sitting up in bed next to him. Even more disturbing, the man was at least as big as Cory, but with much grayer hair.

Rett's head jerked up and he yanked his hand away at the same time the man said, "Mornin', Rett. So... you're the one turning my son queer?"

Rett's entire nervous system exploded all at once. He yelled in panic and scrambled to the far side of the bed faster than a meth-addicted ferret. In fact, the bed ended before Rett finished scrambling to get away and he landed with a painful thud on the green carpet next to it.

Rett flew up to his feet and was about to run out of the room to find Cory or a door out, whichever came first, when he realized he was buck naked. He grabbed a pillow and put it in front of himself and prepared to make a break for it. He'd have to take the pillow with him as a souvenir.

The very large man accusing Rett of turning Cory queer had begun to stand up, which immediately ended all of Rett's preparations. He ran for the door, only to crash right into Cory's chest.

Cory let out an "ooof" and grabbed Rett before he could hurt himself. As he turned Rett around so that he was covered by Cory in the rear and the pillow in front, Cory yelled angrily, "Dad! Dammit! I told you to stay out of my room until he woke up!"

At this point, a small, blond woman appeared next to Cory. She immediately took control of the entire situation. "Cory! Language! Jerry, dammit, what the hell were you thinking? Out!"

"I was just...," started Cory's dad.

"Out!" shouted Cory's mom.

Cory's dad slunk out of the room as he was instructed, even as he was suppressing a grin. Cory's mom thumped Cory in the ear and said, "I swear, I don't know what I'm going to do with *either* of you." She turned around and followed Cory's dad out of the bedroom.

Cory was already fully dressed, but he put his arms around Rett, holding him steady, and said, "It's ok, Rett. Sorry about my dad. He gets a little itchy eager sometimes. My mom and I were looking through the cabinets in the kitchen and he got away from us."

Rett finally found his voice and hissed, "Are you people insane?!"

"Certified," said Cory.

"He was going to beat the living daylights out of me, Cory!"

Cory laughed and said, "No, he wasn't. Not by a long shot. Every once in a while, he makes a lame attempt at humor. That's all it was."

From down the hall outside the bedroom, Rett heard, "Hey! It *was* funny!"

Cory reached back with his foot and slammed the door to his bedroom closed.

He said, "They showed up earlier than expected today, and you were dead asleep. You know how beautiful you are when you're sleeping, by the way?"

Rett pulled loose from Cory, but kept the pillow in front of him. He snapped, "I'm beautiful sleeping? *I'm beautiful sleeping?!* You need to help me find my heart, which *lurched out of my chest* and is probably cowering somewhere under that continental shelf you call a bed!"

Cory started snickering and couldn't stop it. "You should've seen the look on your face!"

The look of utter disbelief Rett gave him sobered him up quickly, though.

Cory took Rett by the shoulders and kissed him, which turned out to be the one thing that seemed to do any good at calming Rett down. Cory ran his finger across the freckles on Rett's nose and said, "Put some clothes on, and you can meet them properly. And calmly. We'll remind dad of his manners in the meantime. Just holler when you're dressed and I'll come get you."

Cory went to the door, turned only briefly to admire a naked Rett standing in his bedroom, and left, closing the door gently behind him.

Rett stood frozen, trying to catch the final bits of his breath still not quite under his control. He had no idea he was going to wind up meeting Cory's parents today, and even if had gotten some advance warning, he wasn't sure he'd be ready to do it under even perfect circumstances. And, emphatically, not like this.

He went into the bathroom and splashed some cold water on his face and brushed his teeth. He decided against another shower since he didn't plan on hanging around long at all. He planned to politely say hello and be on his way. And if he could get away with just calling out a terse "hi" as he headed out the front door, then so much the better.

Rett got dressed and made sure his bags were ready to go before he cracked the door to the bedroom and yelled to Cory that he was dressed. He sat on the edge of the bed and waited for Cory to come get him.

The door opened, but it was Cory's mom that entered. Rett's heart began thumping in his chest, and he stood up in case he decided that making a run for it was best for all involved. She had on a white blouse with bright yellow Capri pants. On her arm was a single, thin gold bracelet.

She held out her hand and smiled very sincerely, "Hi, Rett. I'm Carrie Anne, Cory's mom."

Rett shook her hand nervously and said, "Hi, uh, Mrs. Pritchart."

She motioned for Rett to sit back down on the edge of the bed and she sat down next to him. "Oh, no, call me Carrie Anne, please."

Rett nodded and Carrie Anne picked at her hair for a second. She sighed and said, "First off, I have to apologize for Jerry. He doesn't realize how he comes across half the time. And he gets worse and worse at following instructions the older he gets. Neither of us had any intention of startling you, and we have no intention of making you uncomfortable."

"Honestly," she added, "we had no idea we'd be here this early. But Jerry was about to bust and he couldn't wait to get on the road today, so we wound up arriving a lot earlier than we thought we would. I know you're probably a little freaked out to see us here, and I want to apologize again for that. More than that, I want you to know that you can be yourself around us. Cory's told us a lot about you and it's clear how much he likes you."

Rett's nervousness started to abate, while not evaporating totally. He had never, not one time, gotten caught in a guy's bed by the guy's parents, and it was doing a number on his nerves. Accepting a gay son in the abstract was one thing, but showing up and finding a strange man in said son's bed was something else entirely. Rett didn't want to be the strange man, especially when one of the parents was a six foot five ex-Army Ranger. But Cory's mom seemed to be about as nonchalant about the whole thing as a person could be. Rett's nervousness may have ebbed some, but he was still waiting for the other shoe to drop.

"Now, Jerry..." she continued. She sighed once again. "Jerry's a little like a big kid. A very *large* kid." She seemed contemplative for a moment and a wry smile barely played across her face. "So like Cory in many ways," she said. "Anyway, when Cory first started telling us about you, Jerry wanted to make a special trip down here just to meet you, and Cory and I had to hold him off so you guys could get to know each other without Jerry getting in the middle of it. I'd probably still want to wait, but with Cory most likely getting his first crack at pitching tonight, we couldn't avoid it. Jerry feels like he's already known you a while, which is why you got treated to his, uh, sense of humor while you were still half asleep."

"Are you ok, Rett?" she asked.

"Yeah, uh, Carrie Anne," he fibbed. "I'm fine."

She reached over and patted Rett's knee and said quietly, "Jerry's a good man. A good person to have on your side, Rett." She winked at him and added, "And he's already on your side."

She stood up and said, "Ok, sweetie, let me go get Cory. It's very nice to finally meet you!"

Rett remembered his manners and said, "It's nice to meet you, too, Carrie Anne," as she left the room.

Cory came back in the room, followed by his dad. It was disconcerting to see the two of them standing next to each other. Cory was big to begin with, but his dad was equally tall, and even bulkier. His face was sharper and more angular than Cory's, exhibiting none of the softness or kindness that Cory's had.

Where Cory had a dark walnut colored hair with natural highlights, his father had black hair that had turned mostly gray. But at least the senior Pritchart was smiling, minus the dimples. He completely filled both the jeans and the light blue collared shirt he was wearing with the sleeves rolled up. The man looked easily capable of very terrible things.

Cory said, "Rett, this is my dad, Jerry Pritchart. Send up a flare if he gets to be too much to handle, and I'll come run interference."

Cory pointed a warning finger at his dad as he left and Rett found himself alone with the man that had accused him of turning Cory gay. Joke or not, Rett's heart started pounding again.

Jerry came into the room and sat down casually in the overstuffed chair.

He said, "Cory laid down the law and I have to come apologize to you for scaring the crap out of you. I promise to behave a little better from now on."

Before he could stop himself, Rett said, "Ok. Exactly how much better? Can you quantify that? And are you volunteering to deal with the yellow stain I left on the pillow I was holding in front of me?" Rett groaned inwardly and cursed his big mouth.

Jerry laughed and his eyes twinkled. "You're right... I swear I'll be a lot better. It's really great to meet you in person, you know? And I'll let Carrie Anne deal with the pillow. She's gotta be good for something."

From the other room came a harsh, "I heard that! Thin ice!"

"Ouch. Busted!" said Jerry, shrugging his wide shoulders. "Everyone knows she wears the pants in the family. I have to go to work in nothing but boxer shorts, leopard print boxer shorts. Not a great way to earn the respect of a police force," he mused.

Jerry stood up and took a careful step towards Rett, leaning forward deferentially while holding his hand out. His smile was genuine when he said, "It's really, really nice to meet you, Rett."

Rett shook his hand and replied, "It's nice to meet you, too, Mr... uh, I mean Chief Pritchart?" The fact that this man was a cop didn't make any of this any easier on Rett and he wasn't sure what the right way to refer to him was.

Jerry held onto Rett's hand and said, "Wrong on both counts. It's Jerry, Rett. Call me Jerry."

"Sure, Jerry. It's good to meet you, too." Rett would go along with anything to end this conversation. His heart was still beating uncomfortably.

Jerry studied Rett a moment more before he said gently to him, "I can see why he likes you."

As Jerry walked out the door, he called down the hall, "There! The perfect gentleman like always! I don't know what you guys get your panties so twisted up over all the time!"

Rett stood as Cory came back in to the bedroom and closed the door behind him.

"A little better this time around?"

Rett's lip twitched and he said, "Yeah."

Cory shook his head, not being enough of a pushover to believe Rett's lie. He pushed on Rett, making him step back until he fell onto the bed. Cory climbed over him and held himself over Rett, their faces only a few inches apart. Cory said, "You have to relax some, Rett." He kissed Rett's lips lightly. "They both fully approve, and they like you." He kissed Rett again.

Rett didn't realize he'd be this nervous meeting Cory's parents, but he was, and he could tell it had little to do with Cory's dad being too eager.

"Hmmm?" asked Cory.

"Ok, Cory," he said. Looking up into Cory's soft brown eyes was all the reassurance he needed.

Cory's mouth pulled tight as he studied Rett. Rett could tell he was looking for something.

"So, was last night... for you... uh," Cory asked hesitatingly.

Rett saw how unsure Cory was now and understood. If Rett was still doubtful about Cory's parents, at least he was damn sure about the night before.

Rett said, "If you had half as good a time as I had last night, then you're one lucky son-of-a-bitch." He reached up and kissed Cory, who returned it even harder, and happily. "Because I guarantee you I had a hell of a spectacular time!"

Cory melted in relief and said, "Last night was... it was... oh God, it was..." Words failed him at that point. Instead, he lowered himself down on top of Rett and they kissed deeply before Cory lifted back up and lay off to the side so he didn't crush him.

Cory said, "I'm willing to bet you want to get to your apartment to unpack and get ready for today, and I've got to go on into the Portyards early for the publicity shots. Christ, I feel weirder about *that* than I do pitching."

"Last night didn't stress you out or make it worse, did it?" asked Rett.

"No, it's much better that you were with me. I would have laid awake worrying about pitching all night without you here."

Rett ran his hand along Cory's forearm, gently disturbing the hair on it. "Ok, just checking. I'll go ahead and let you have some time with your mom and dad. I need to get some laundry done before going in anyway."

Cory led Rett back out into the den, where Jerry was watching TV and Carrie Anne was still taking an inventory of the kitchen cabinets.

Rett pulled his suitcase behind him and said, "Goodbye, Mr. and Mrs., uh Carrie Anne and Jerry. I'll maybe see you guys at the game tonight."

Rett was about to walk out the front door when Cory stopped him, "Whoa! Hang on!" He put his arm around Rett's waist and leaned in to kiss him, causing Rett to blush furiously and glance nervously over at Jerry.

Cory kissed him anyway, right on the lips. He leaned his forehead against Rett's and whispered, "It's alright, Rett. I promise." Cory kissed him again, lightly.

Rett took his leave, finally able to really breathe freely once he was in his car and driving towards his place.

Chapter 12

The game that evening neared, and Rett sat in the main locker room at the conference table typing up his notes from the players he had worked with that afternoon. He had taken up more and more often to sitting at the conference room table instead of his own desk because it allowed him to interact with the players more, and they seemed to be more willing to ask for his help with any minor physical issues if he was there rather than hidden away in the trainers' office.

From his spot, he could see into the players' lounge area off the locker room, traditionally kept darker and quieter for players that wanted to focus inwardly as they prepared for a game. Cory was there, leaning forward on the couch with his head resting in his hands, mentally steeling himself for the game. Rett hoped he wasn't stressing himself out about it. The little bit of pitching practice that afternoon that he had caught seemed to go well for Cory, and Topher seemed positive, so there was no reason for Cory to get overwrought about the game. Still, Rett let him concentrate and hoped, hoped that he was preparing himself and not tying himself in knots. Rett was nervous and distracted enough for the both of them.

JJ came in and sat down across from Rett, smiling at him as usual. "What's shakin', runt?"

Rett scowled and JJ said defensively, "What?"

"I guess it's better than being called Pikachu. That one's the worst," said Rett.

JJ laughed. "Yeah, Pikachu's my favorite, too."

Rett scowled and flipped JJ a bird. He asked, "JJ, do your parents ever come watch you play?"

"Not really anymore," he replied. "They used to, but they're getting older and their health isn't what it used to be. They watch the games on TV when they can, though."

"I'm sure they're really proud of you."

"I talk to them a couple of times a week, probably. My dad's always been supportive. My mom, though, she's kind of old school and sees baseball as being kind of a cracker sport. She's not seeing it the way it is now, with plenty of blacks and Hispanics. Even Japanese, and we've even got Arthur and Josh on the team, too. I never tell her about Skunk's bullshit because she'd freak out."

"She'd freak out? You seem even more laid back about it than I would be. If it doesn't bother you, why would it bother her?"

JJ nodded. He got contemplative for a moment, then patted the table between him and Rett and said, "Yeah, I'll explain it to you one day." He stroked across his chin with his thumb a few times, then glanced around to see if anyone was paying attention to the two of them.

"So what's changed, Rett?" he asked in a lower voice.

"Hmm?" said Rett.

"What's changed?"

"The seasons? My underwear? The guards outside Buckingham Palace? Take your pick, JJ."

JJ looked at him levelly and said softly, "You and Cory."

Rett shifted in his chair some. Out of everyone on the team, besides Cory, JJ had become the one guy Rett felt the most comfortable and open around. Part of it was that JJ knew he was gay and was unbothered by it, but beyond that, JJ was one of the most easygoing guys on the team.

From the first time JJ had warned Rett to be careful in how he behaved around Cory, Rett had trusted him fully. Except for one thing... he still hadn't said anything about Cory to JJ. That was for Cory to do and not Rett.

Rett wondered if he suspected something and almost panicked, but held himself in check. JJ hadn't brought up his infatuation with Cory in a while and wasn't totally sure what was driving the question.

"What about me and Cory?" asked Rett.

"You guys are hanging out more and more, but you don't seem as caught up on him," said JJ.

Rett internally relaxed a little. "You told me to keep a tighter grip on it."

"Yeah, but I thought it'd be harder for you to do that, given how much more you guys are palling around. Something's changed."

"We're buddies. I'm getting past it," shrugged Rett. It was sort of true, in a very roundabout way. "He made me try to learn to pitch a little one night before we went out of town. That was laughably unsuccessful for both of us." Rett was balancing on a very thin line right now by bringing up that night.

He watched JJ's face to make sure he wasn't getting suspicious of anything.

JJ said, "Ok, just wanted to check. We should all go do something together one day after one of the afternoon games."

Rett nodded over towards Cory sitting silently in the lounge area and asked him, "How's he going to do tonight, you think?"

JJ looked thoughtful but only replied, like he knew something Rett didn't, "You wait and see." He added, "You won't have to wait long."

~~~~~

Rett had taken up his favorite place in the cheap seats to watch the game unfold, his own nerves building with every inning that passed. Rett had stayed away from the bullpen since he wanted Cory to focus on staying warmed up for pitching. Cory had protested a little, but Rett could tell that even Cory was undecided if it would be better or worse for him to be there in the pen. Rett insisted that Cory focus on the game, and he'd be watching.

Through the 6th inning, Gunnar had pitched a good game, and the Orioles and the Joes were tied at one run each. In the 5th and 6th innings, Rett had noticed Gunnar rotating his shoulder a couple of times, but nothing that seemed like it was significant. But in the bottom of the 6th inning, Rett noticed jersey number 72 in the dugout, which meant Ahab had already called Cory in from the bullpen and he was probably going to relieve Gunnar in the 7th.

At the start of the 7th inning, with the score still tied one to one, the announcer boomed out to the stadium that number 72, Cory Pritchart, was going to take the field pitching for the Joes in his first rookie appearance. On the big video board, Rett watched the graphics featuring a clip of Cory winding up for a pitch, one that they had recorded earlier that day in preparation. Rett never felt so proud of anyone in his life, and sent every single wish of good luck he could to Cory as he stepped out of the dugout.

Rett was a little worried that Gunnar would head into the clubhouse and want Rett to ice his arm down or give it a massage, but he could see Gunnar's number 39 jersey remaining in the dugout, standing up at the fence to watch closely what happened. Everyone on the team seemed intent on watching to see how Cory performed.

The home team fans cheered their support as the Joes spread out across the field to their positions, with Cory walking out to the pitcher's mound. Before Cory stepped onto the mound itself, though, he stopped. He held the baseball in both hands up against his chest and stood still, looking down. The big screen showed a brief live close-up of Cory, and Rett could see his lips moving silently with eyes closed, reciting whatever it was he recited to ready himself, his final preparation before pitching.

Cory looked up to make sure everyone was in place and waited for the umpire to signal him that everyone was ready. He stepped onto the mound, grabbed the rosin bag with his right hand briefly, and then he did something Rett hadn't seen him do before. He lifted the ball in his right hand and held it up over his head as high as he could for everyone to see for a moment. The crowd seemed to like it and cheered again.

Cory took his position on the pitcher's plate, wound up, and pitched the ball. There was an audible crack as the ball and the bat connected, sending the ball into a very high fly. It came down in the middle of the infield, and Cory stepped off the mound, tracking a few yards over towards third base where he caught the ball easily for an out. The crowd cheered and yelled loudly, and it was a second before Rett realized he himself was standing and yelling his support along with every other Joes fan in the stadium.

On the next batter, Cory's first pitch was a solid strike, and Rett remembered for the first time to glance up at the screen that displayed the speed of the pitch. It registered 92 mph. The strike was followed by a series of balls, though, that allowed the Orioles' batter to walk to first base.

Rett tried to see if Cory was handling it well, or sweating out his first appearance. It was impossible to tell even from the close-ups shown on the big screen, though.

After a strike and a ball on the next batter, the batter nailed Cory's third pitch, sending it into a clean arc and into Skunk's mitt in center field for the second out. The next batter hit fouls on the first two pitches, but then Cory seemed to pick up on the batter's style a little better and he managed to strike him out three times in a row, ending the first half of the inning with Cory giving up no runs. Rett's muscles were finally able to unwind a little and he was able to lean back and relax in his seat.

No one could argue with Cory's first inning pitching for the Joes. As Cory reached the dugout for the transition from the top to the bottom of the 7th inning, Rett could see everyone on the team slapping him on the back and congratulating him. Gunnar put his arm around Cory's shoulder and pulled him close, Rett assumed, to let him know how well he had done.

Rolly Duvauchelle for the Joes was first up at bat, but struck out. At bat after Rolly was Luis Ojeda. Right as Luis hit a foul right along the third foul line, Rett got a text message on his phone. He looked down and had to laugh and smile when he saw it was from Cory; he had no idea Cory kept his phone with him during a game. It said:

Not bad for a rookie?

It made Rett feel light as air to know Cory was thinking about him. He texted back to Cory:

You are freaking awe-inspiring!

The Joes couldn't manage to score during the remainder of the 7th inning, and the board remained in a tie between the Orioles and the Joes at one run each.

At the top of the 8th, Cory paused for his quiet moment, eyes closed and lips barely moving, before taking the mound. The crowd was warming up to him, and when he held the ball up over his head for all to see, they yelled even louder than the first time.

The 8th inning had Rett sweating bullets. Cory slipped a little and managed to let the batters get a couple of good hits in, allowing runners onto first and second. Rett could tell that JJ and Cory were communicating a little more intensely through signals, trying to strategize. The next batter hit a hard line drive out to Lashawn Myrick in left field, but he was able to throw the ball to Luis on third to get the Orioles' runner out, and then Luis threw to Skillet on first to get the batter out before he could reach base, resulting in a double-play. The next batter managed a walk to first base. Finally, and to Rett's relief, the next batter was an easy three strikes in a row for Cory, and the Joes and Orioles switched places on the field.

During the bottom of the 8th, Skillet managed to bat Rolly in, scoring another run for the Joes. The home crowd was much more active and excited now that the Joes led 2 to 1 on the board.

At the start of the 9th inning, Rett was very worried that the pressure would now get to Cory. Cory paused for his moment, silently moving his lips, then took the mound, and finally held the ball up in the air, driving the crowd crazy. Rett glanced over at Ahab in the dugout, who was pacing up and down like a caged badger.

One of the Orioles' batters managed to get to second because of a bad error on the part of Luis at third base. With two outs, the runner at second got very aggressive in trying to take advantage of Cory's focus on the batter and edged farther and farther away from second base. Before Rett even realized what was happening, Cory had spun and burned a lightning fast ball to the Joes' second baseman, Kevin Ostergaard, at the exact same time the Orioles' runner was returning to his base. There was a pregnant pause across the entire stadium as the umpire decided the fate of the throw, but then called the runner out. The home crowd went nuts since that sealed a win for the Joes.

The manager of the Orioles stormed out to second base to argue the call. He waved his hands around and yelled, but the umpire stood firm on calling the runner out. The crowd went crazy since that call ended the game. Cory trotted over to the dugout where all of the players were jumping on him and high-fiving him and slapping him on the back. The entire team was a big wadded up ball of cream and teal pinstripes all around Cory.

Rett didn't think he'd ever been so caught up in something in his life. He'd never been so proud of anyone in his life. Cory had done an amazing job and Rett's insides were ready to burst he was so happy and excited for him.

Once the game ended and as Rett watched, Cory went back out onto the field and looked up into the stands behind home plate. It took Rett a moment, but he realized Cory was looking for his parents, who he spotted coming down from the stands to meet their son after his exemplary debut. Rett watched transfixed as Jerry came out onto the field and embraced his son tightly, rocking him back and forth, rightfully proud of him and knocking Cory's cap off in the process. Cory grabbed his mother and hugged her too, kissing her on both cheeks.

Behind Cory's parents were three other people that came down as well to congratulate him, two men and a younger girl. Rett couldn't tell for sure who they were, but if he had to guess, he would say one of them was probably Jimmy, the guy Cory considered to be family. Cory lifted the girl up off of her feet and spun her around when he hugged her.

Rett thought how incredible it was for Cory to have his family there for his debut, that they clearly cared for him as much as they did, that they were as unconditionally loving as they were. He thought about how lucky Cory was to be where he was, to have these people around him, supporting him and proud of him. Rett included himself in that group, even if he was having to do it from a distance for the moment.

As he took a few steps down the stands to make his way back to the clubhouse, another text message came in, again from Cory, reading:

Where are you?

Rett smiled again, feeling like warm toast inside. He texted back:

Cheap seats. Headed to the clubhouse now. Enjoy your family and I'll see you there in a minute. You're amazing!

As he walked along the concourse, another text came in, this time from Val:

Yr friend pitched gr8! Cant wait to meet this guy!

Rett texted back to Val:

Don't worry, you will!

As he arrived in the clubhouse and turned down the hall to the locker room, Cory had come up the stairs from the dugout tunnel at the same time. They stopped a few feet apart and stood grinning at each other.

In that moment, Rett experienced something he had never experienced before. He had to hold his feet in place and explicitly restrain himself. Because if he didn't, he would have, without doubt, found himself running forward to Cory, grabbing and holding and kissing him and telling him how incredible he was. Telling him how well he had done. How proud his was of him.

What killed Rett was that he could see it in Cory's face, too. He could see Cory having to hold himself back as well.

Rett couldn't stay there. He couldn't continue this. His will wouldn't hold out forever, and then he and Cory would be in a bad spot. He forced his legs forward, and as he passed Cory in the hallway, he slapped him on the shoulder and said, "You were amazing, Bigfoot!"

Cory beamed and, straining to keep under control, replied, "Thanks, chief!"

They went their separate ways, Cory going to take his shower and Rett going to Dr. Bala's office to see if there was anything he needed to help with.

Gunnar grabbed him first, though, to help with getting the ice sleeve on his arm. Rett was happy to help, but took one look at his arm and became concerned that it was more swollen than usual. Gunnar wanted the ice sleeve and for Rett to not make a big deal out of it, even rotating his arm around several times to prove it was actually fine. It looked to Rett like Gunnar was holding in the pain as he did this, but he gave in and put the sleeve on his arm and hoped Gunnar was right.

Twenty minutes later, while Rett was straightening up and restocking the treatment room, Cory came in, dressed in his street clothes after having showered. His hair was sticking out from under a Joes baseball cap and he was wearing the white knit shirt that Rett loved to see him in so much. In his hand was a baseball that he was tossing around absent-mindedly.

Cory took a seat up on one of the exam tables while Rett continued to dig around in one of the cabinets to keep from throwing himself at Cory. Rett said snidely, "You again? Haven't you been fishing for compliments enough already?"

Rett looked back over his shoulder to see Cory sitting with a smug grin on his face.

"Stop that!" growled Rett.

"Stop what?" said Cory, the smile still plastered across his face.

"All that goddamn 'I'm a big shot pitcher and you're not' bullshit!"

"Am I? Really?" said Cory in mock surprise. "I hadn't noticed, what with pitching three against the Orioles tonight with no runs and all!"

Rett stopped what he was doing, and stopped the teasing, too. He was unable to do it to Cory any more. He said, "You have no idea how proud I am of you, really."

Cory's grin got even bigger and he winked at Rett. Cory looked like he was ready to explode he was so happy.

He said, "We're going to go to Steak 1838 to celebrate. How long before you can get away?"

Rett had anticipated that some sort of offer like this was likely coming, and he had agonized over it since the game ended and he had gotten back into the clubhouse. He really was leaning towards not going, mostly for a couple of reasons. One, he wanted to let Cory have time with his family and friends. And two, he wasn't sure he was ready to be around Cory's parents, even if he knew it needed to happen sooner or later. On the other hand, Rett suspected that it would be important to Cory that he go, and that counted for a lot. Cory deserved whatever he wanted after tonight. And if Rett was honest with himself, he wanted to be near Cory, too.

The fact that Cory had assumed Rett would be going decided it for him, and he didn't even bother deliberating any more.

"Let's go," said Rett, closing up the cabinets.

Walking through the service corridor that led to the parking lot, Rett asked, "Hey, I've been meaning to ask you. The thing you sing or recite or whatever to yourself before you get on the mound. What is that? You do it all the time before pitching."

Cory looked almost apologetic. "That? That's something I do to remind myself. It's kind of personal, though, just for me."

As they got to the service door that led to the parking lot, Rett said, "I get that. You guys have your rituals. So what was that thing you did where you held up the ball in your hand before each inning? That was new tonight."

Cory laughed, and was about to answer, but as soon as they stepped out into the hot night air of the parking lot, there were screams and shouts from a small crowd of fans right outside the parking lot gate waiting for the players to leave the clubhouse. Rett and Cory both stopped dead in their tracks when they realized that, tonight, they were shouting Cory's name once they had spotted him, desperately trying to get his attention.

Cory radiated bright pink in the face, turned away from the crowd, and said to Rett in a low voice, "Shit, this part I don't know if I'm ready for."

"Too late now, big shot!" laughed Rett as he pushed him over towards the crowd. "You made your flatbed-truck-sized bed, now lie in it!"

As they began to walk over to the crowd, which got even louder when they saw him coming their way, Cory said, "And the thing with holding the ball up, asshole? That was for you!"

"What? For me? I don't understand," said Rett.

"I guess you maybe didn't see it well enough from way up in the upper cumulus seats." Cory stopped about ten yards from the waiting fans and held the ball that was still in his hand up in the air, thumping his index and middle fingers against it, reminding Rett again how to properly grip the ball to pitch it. He watched to see the look on Rett's face now that he knew Rett could see what he was doing up close.

Rett stopped dead again when he saw Cory reminding him to hold the ball correctly, Cory reminding him of the night they kissed for the first time. Rett wasn't quite sure if he should laugh at the very public reminder of a very private moment, or roll his eyes at it, or sit down in the middle of the parking lot and cry over one of the most romantic things he had ever heard of.

The crowd waiting had another opinion of it entirely. Seeing Cory hold the ball up like he did in the game drove them nuts and they started yelling and cheering even louder. Cory tossed the ball back to Rett and took a few minutes to sign autographs while the security guard made sure the fans stayed on their side of the fence.

Rett watched the crowd clamor for Cory, all reaching and begging for a little attention from the man he had spent the previous night wrapped up in bed with.

~~~~~

Immediately upon setting foot into Steak 1838, Rett realized how upscale the restaurant was and how nicely the staff and patrons were dressed. He felt certain there was no way they'd let them in, even this late in the evening, given how they were dressed after the game. But the head host for the restaurant greeted them warmly, referred to Cory as Mr. Pritchart, and showed them to the dark, heavily-paneled bar where their companions were waiting. Carrie Anne was sitting on a barstool at the bar with a glass of wine, her husband, Jerry, standing behind her and smoking a cigar. Even for someone in what had to be his fifties, Rett was astounded at the incredible shape Jerry was in. Jerry and Carrie Anne were chatting with the other three people Rett had only seen from a distance that evening, although he already recognized Jimmy from the times he had seen him before with Cory. There were only a few other people sprinkled through the bar area this time of night.

Cory was about to bust he was so glad to finally be able to introduce Rett to his other close friends from his hometown. He first introduced Rett to Brick Taylor, the person whose truck he was still driving around in. Brick was a solid man, with a thick, cropped head of coppered-blond hair and matching goatee. Next, Rett was introduced to Lindsey, or Zee as Cory insisted everyone called her. Zee was a very pretty, thin girl that Rett guessed to be only about 15 or so, with dark, straight hair hanging down her back. Cory mentioned that Zee was Jimmy's little sister, which surprised Rett given the clear age difference. Finally, and only after hugging him tightly again, Cory introduced Rett to Jimmy Montgomery. Jimmy had penetrating, deep eyes and a sharp nose. The other times Rett had seen him, he had seemed very intimidating to Rett in his dark suit, but he seemed a little more approachable tonight in his Joes t-shirt and light blue shorts, but only a little.

Just like Jerry, both Brick and Jimmy had cigars that they were puffing away on while sipping on their drinks. Jerry put his arm around his son and offered him a cigar as well. "For your big night, Cory. You have no idea how much I love you, son," he said, truly moved.

Cory quipped, "And yet you try and kill me with these crap cigars!"

Cory took the cigar anyway and allowed his father to light it. Cory grimaced and choked on the first intake of smoke while Jerry offered one to Rett as well.

Rett said, "Uh, no thanks, Jerry. I've never even had a cigar before."

Jimmy put his arm around Rett's shoulder and said, "They're disgusting and cheap, Rett, exactly like Jerry. And none of us actually like them, except Jerry. But do us all a favor, and take the cigar."

They all laughed and Rett gave in and took the cigar that Jerry was holding out to him. As Jerry lit it for him, Jimmy added in a low voice in Rett's ear, "Just take small puffs and don't really breathe the smoke in. You're better off inhaling directly from a semi's exhaust pipe for a few hours than smoking one of these. Ten years now, and I've never gotten used to these things."

Rett started to relax a little more around Jimmy and did as he was told.

Brick stuck up for Jerry and commented, "I kinda like 'em."

Jerry put a thick arm around Brick's neck and kissed him on the head, "One person! Just one person out of this crowd that's on my side!"

Jimmy ordered drinks for Cory and Rett, and the group spent a few minutes finishing their cigars and chatting about the game. They asked Rett a few questions, but mostly the night was about Cory. That was fine with Rett, who preferred, and was totally content, to let the others carry the conversation.

Once they moved into the dark wood private dining room that Jimmy had arranged for the seven of them to have dinner in, Cory insisted that Rett sit next to him at dinner, with his father on his other side. Rett looked at the prices on the menu and swallowed hard. He was still getting used to the idea that he really did have an income now and could luckily afford something like this every so often.

Dinner progressed amidst a lot of reminiscing, and one of Rett's favorite stories was the one Zee told of how, back when she was eight or nine, she made Cory let her paint his toenails bright blue while he was in high school.

Cory added, "I pitched three playoff games with sparkly blue toenails! I finally got tired of taking showers after the games with my socks on and asked mom how to get the toenail polish off!"

Brick added, "Don't act so special, Cory. Mine wound up hot pink! God, the hell I caught from Roddy when he saw my feet after she did that to me! I finally had to ask Jimmy how to get the stuff off."

Zee was sitting next to Rett, and at one point he leaned over and said, "I have to ask, Zee, how much older is your brother, Jimmy, than you are?"

Zee tossed her hair and laughed. She said, "About 25 years older. I was adopted by our mom when I was real little. But she passed away pretty soon after that. Jimmy and Brick have been more like my parents than my big brothers. It feels like being raised by two old-bitty grandmothers most of time, though. Watch this..."

Zee signaled the waiter that had stopped next to her to pick up a plate and said, "Can I get a glass of white wine, please?"

Immediately, Jimmy corrected the waiter, "White grape juice!" He pointed at Zee and said, "Try that again and next time it'll be grape juice from a sippy cup!"

Zee rolled her eyes over to Rett who had to stifle a laugh.

The one thing Rett noticed was how close the whole group was. It didn't seem to him like Cory's family plus their friends. It felt like one family. Rett even managed to like Jerry once he could observe his sense of humor without being half asleep and in its line of fire. And as silly as Rett originally found the idea that the chief of police for a small, southern town could be close friends with a gay couple, here he saw it firsthand. Jerry did not hesitate to show affection to his friends, or to tease and allow himself to be teased by them. It reminded Rett how lucky Cory was to have these people in his life. And, it was a stark, sad contrast to his own family experience.

As dinner wound down, Rett's phone rang and he excused himself from the table to answer it. He stepped outside to a bench next to the front door to take Val's call.

Val said, "Are you too good to ever call me now?"

"Can I think about that one?" said Rett.

"Can I just say how much I'm still trying to get used to you and this job you've got? It's so weird to watch this Cory Pritchart person up there pitching in a major league game and knowing that he's, like, a personal friend of yours."

If she only knew, thought Rett.

"He's seems like a nice guy, though. At least from what I could tell from the interview on ESPN..."

Rett interrupted, "Wait... what?"

"They had a short interview with him tonight on ESPN. He was still on the field after the game ended."

That was news to Rett. Cory hadn't mentioned it.

"So, I'm coming this weekend. And don't lie to me about being out of town. I know for sure the Joes are playing in Mobile this weekend."

"I've *never* lied to you!" said Rett, offended.

"You told me that Andrew Duttry was in love with me!" retorted Val.

"Oh, yeah. Ha, man, you looked like an idiot throwing yourself at him after I told you that!"

"And there was that time you told me I could get crabs just by handling dollar bills!"

"Well, now see, that was your own fault for believing that one! But... I wonder if maybe you stuffed them down in your underwear..."

Val interrupted, "*And* you told me that Queen Elizabeth and Oprah had a three year affair!"

"Hey! That's what I heard! Don't blame the messenger! And how do you explain those three years she seemed *really* happy?"

"Ugh. You disgust me. Anyway, I've already bought a ticket for the Saturday game against the Brewers."

"Is that who we're playing? Is that actually a baseball team? That's not really a baseball team!" said Rett, unwilling to be a victim of Val's lies.

Val groaned and said, "You're a fucking pinhead. You're like the Grand Poobah Pinhead. Oh! Speaking of pinheads, one of your pinhead subjects, Tony, finally asked me out on a date!"

"You're shitting me!" said Rett. Tony Delgado had always had a little something for Val through school, but had never acted on it. Rett had wondered if that train was *ever* going to leave the station.

"Turns out he really thought you and I were together this whole time!" said Val.

"Why the hell would he think that?" asked Rett.

"I don't know! I told him forever ago that you were the biggest faggot in Montgomery! One time, I even showed him one of my dildos and told him it was yours!"

"Please, not the black one!" begged Rett.

"Noooo, the purple wiggly one. Anyway, you'd think with all that that even *he'd* be able to put two and two together."

"Did you go out? How was it?" asked Rett.

"Better than a wiggly purple dildo. We'll probably go out again."

Rett suddenly felt strange. His and Val's lives were diverging. No matter how close they would remain, it would probably never be the same as it was for the whole time they lived together. He really hoped he'd be able to tell Val the truth about Cory this weekend.

He said, "That's good, Val. I'm sorry I was holding you back all this time."

"Everett, you never held me back from anything, ever. Not one single time."

After seeing Cory and his family together, Rett was able to appreciate what he had in Val that much more. How very much she meant to him washed over him and filled him up.

"I love you, Val. I hope you know that."

She yawned and said, "Super. *Now* you decide you're straight."

"I'm serious, Val."

"Ok, ok. You can fuck me this weekend. Just no anal. Unless I'm pretending to be asleep."

Rett gave up. "Fine, Val. I'll talk to you later this week."

He hung up, but before he could go back inside, he glanced over and saw Brick coming out the front door of the restaurant.

"There ya are," said Brick. He sat down on the bench next to Rett.

"Yeah, just checking in with a friend that's going to come visit this weekend. Is everyone getting ready to leave? I need to make sure I put money in for mine."

Brick laughed, "Good luck with that! Jimmy had that covered a while ago."

Rett loved Brick's laugh. It was deep and natural and comfortable. But he turned pink at the idea that anyone would think he showed up at dinner expecting someone else to pay for his.

"No, I had no intention of letting anyone pay for..."

Brick put his hand on Rett's knee to stop him and said, "Of course not. Now relax. You can go kick up a fuss if you want, but it'll do you dick worth of good, I guarantee you that."

Brick's eyes laughed and he said, "So the story is that you got quite an introduction to Jerry this morning."

"Aw, man... you guys know all about that already?" asked Rett with a pained face.

Brick nodded.

"You guys are really close," said Rett.

"Jimmy, Zee, Cory, and Carrie Anne are the most important people in my life," admitted Brick. "Jerry I just can't seem to shake loose. And I've tried hard."

Rett remarked, "Y'all are super important to Cory, that's for sure."

Brick grinned wryly. "Yeah. Well, not like Jimmy, though."

Rett looked at him questioningly.

Brick mulled it over for a moment thoughtfully, and then said, "Jimmy was there for Cory, and stood by him, when he *really* needed someone. The funny thing is, and I don't know if Jimmy's ever realized this, but I think that Cory happened to Jimmy at a time when *Jimmy* desperately needed *him*, too. I don't even know how to describe what those two share. To call it an abiding friendship is almost an insult to what they have."

Rett nodded that he understood. He and Brick watched the late night traffic along the street for a while. Rett felt very comfortable around Brick, even with a few moments of silence between them.

Brick said, "Cory really likes you, too, though."

"Yeah?"

"He does. He can talk to us and let us know what he's going through and what he's feeling, but it's better that he's got somebody here that he can open up to. He about went nuts when he found out you were gay, too. You heard what happened with his friend, Jason, back in high school?"

"Yeah," said Rett, "he told me that story."

"Well, he no longer assumes anything about anybody unless he's got hard evidence. And since he's stayed pretty closeted to protect his baseball career, it doesn't give him much of a chance to meet other gay guys. I know it's been hard on him in some ways."

Brick smoothed down his goatee with his hand and added, "But you... you were a lucky find for him."

Rett let Brick's words seep into him a little bit, unsure how to respond. Brick put his hand behind Rett's neck to lead him back inside and said, "Come on. Let's go watch Jerry and Jimmy duke it out over who gets to pay."

Chapter 13

Dr. Bala looked at the X-ray and said, "It's hard to tell, but there might be an impact fracture or a stress fracture... I can't see well enough on these pictures. You're not pitching tonight, no matter what, Ric. Rett, let's get one of the finger braces on him until he can go get this checked out for real. Ric, I'm going to go make an appointment for you. I'll put the info on your locker once I've got it set up, ok?"

Ric nodded and Dr. Bala left the treatment room so he could contact the sports medicine practice they used for trickier issues. Rett dug around in the cabinet to find the brace he needed and some tape to hold it in place.

He applied a therapeutic cooling spray to Ric's swollen and bruised finger, then carefully put the brace on it, trying not to hurt it any more than he had to. Ric said, "This is what I get for trying to catch one of Lashawn's wild throws with my pitching hand instead of my mitt. Ouch! Shit, that hurts, Rett!"

"Sorry! Sorry! I'm trying to move it as little as possible. Almost done," said Rett.

When he had finished, Rett gave him the tape and said, "Here's some extra if you need to re-tape the brace, or you can just find me or Dr. Bala and we'll do it for you, ok?"

Ric nodded and thanked Rett and left the treatment room while holding his injured hand gingerly. Rett hadn't been there, but apparently Ric had tried to catch a rough ball thrown by

Lashawn during hitting practice and crunched his finger in the process.

Rett cleaned up and was about to take the X-rays down to Dr. Bala's office for filing when Cory appeared in the doorway.

Cory looked worried. "How's Ric's finger?"

"He's gonna have to have it looked at better than we can do here. We put a brace on it until then. Nothing obvious showed up in the X-ray, though, so we might get lucky and it won't be fractured at all."

Rett noticed that Cory seemed a little pale in the face.

He asked, "You ok? You look muy, muy pasty, amigo."

Cory cleared his throat nervously. "Ahab wants me to be the starter tonight."

~~~~~

From what Rett understood, there had been quite an argument between Ahab, George, and Topher regarding who should be the Joes' starting pitcher that night since Ric had injured his finger. One of the relief pitchers, like Sebastion or Ernie, would be the obvious choice, especially since Cory had already pitched three innings the night before. But Ahab had made up his mind and decided he wanted Cory up front.

Rett was mostly concerned if Cory's arm could take two nights in a row pitching and if he was mentally prepared for it, but Cory had replied his arm was fine for another night. And as for being mentally prepared, maybe having it sprung on him like this was better than having too much time to worry about it. Mostly, Cory was shocked that he was being asked to start after just one single night of relief pitching. He had expected, at best, to spend another month or so relief pitching before he was ever *considered* to start. It was Ahab's decision in the end, as long as Cory felt up to it, and so Cory was starting. Once the decision was made, the news spread like wildfire through the rest of the team.

His parents had already left to drive back home when Cory had called to let them know what was going on, and they turned around and came right back to town. While Jerry was driving them back to Mobile, Carrie Anne had gotten on the phone and bought the best seats they could get at the last minute. Jimmy, Brick, and Zee were sick that they couldn't come back for his first night starting, but they had to get back to Lawder for some reason.

Rett had settled into his usual spot in the cheap seats to watch as much as he could. When Cory had first taken the mound, after reciting his reminder routine to himself, and had held up the ball in his hand, Rett about burst. To know that the gesture, seen and cheered by the entire stadium, was meant specifically for him and no one else made him feel both huge and small at the same time. It both took his breath away and made him want to yell at the top of his lungs. It was the most intimate of statements written in front of a crowd of thousands and thousands.

Cory exceeded expectations, though. Every inning he pitched was handled even better than the night before and he showed no signs of slowing down.

Rett may still have been pretty ignorant of baseball, despite learning quickly in the weeks since starting with the Joes, but by the 5th inning, even he couldn't ignore what he started to see play out on the field. By the 5th inning, Rett realized that Cory was putting in more than just a good performance. What finally inserted itself into Rett's consciousness was that not only had Cory not allowed a single run by the Orioles, but he had not even allowed a single hit. In the middle of the 5th inning, the score was 0 to 0. It wasn't that there weren't runners getting on base; the Joes had gotten a few base hits in and walked a couple of times, but with no resulting runs. The Orioles had gotten on base a couple of times, too, but that was because of a few walks and one case where Luis, on third, and the shortstop, Satoru, had coordinated poorly on an easy out between them and let the batter get to first. But the Orioles hadn't been able to get a clean hit in against Cory. It was the 5th inning when Rett finally realized this and started to wonder just exactly how unusual this was. Even more, he wondered how unusual it was for a rookie pitcher like Cory.

Rett had watched the pitch speed sign when he remembered to, and was seeing numbers ranging from 78 or so, which he knew were probably intentionally not fastballs, up to the mid-90's. There had even been one particularly savage pitch from Cory that hit 98 mph. He knew enough now to know that those numbers were totally in line with even very accomplished pitchers.

The other thing that Rett began to pick up on, too, was that the stadium as a whole seemed to have gotten quieter. The usual cheers and shouts seemed to be dying down while Cory was pitching.

Something was definitely happening; Rett could feel it and sense it in the whole of the stadium, but he wasn't sure what it was or exactly what it meant.

He looked over across the stadium to where he knew Cory's parents were seated, about twenty rows up from the field and to the left of home plate slightly. He had only been able to spot them earlier because Jerry was so big and was wearing a Joes knit shirt that was a bright teal. Carrie Anne and Jerry were sitting quietly, intent on watching the game. It was hard to tell from the distance what they were thinking or experiencing, though.

Finally, Rett couldn't stand it anymore. He hated leaving and perhaps missing something, but he had to understand if what he thought was going on was what was actually going on. He ran down the concourse and around the plaza behind the outfield, then down into the service area to get to the bullpen as fast as he could.

When he got into the bullpen, JJ, Sebastion, Ernie, Ric, Topher, and several others were all up on the stand watching the game keenly. JJ saw Rett coming up the steps and motioned him over.

Rett started to ask JJ what it meant if Cory managed to go the entire game without allowing the Orioles to get a single real hit, but JJ planted his hand over Rett's mouth before he could say anything.

JJ said, "No, Rett, no, no, no! I know what you're about to ask, but don't! Talking about it is a jinx. A bad one. So just let it go, minnow. You don't want to be the one that jinxed this!" JJ held his hand in place and made sure Rett could see how serious he was.

Rett nodded and JJ removed his hand from his mouth.

Instead of asking what he wanted, Rett said, "Your hand tastes like popcorn. Have you been eating popcorn?"

JJ grinned and nodded. He said, "I know what you want to know, Rett. What's happening is definitely not usual. If this goes the entire game, shit, I don't even know how rare that is. A rookie pitcher in his first start doing this? It's gotta be less than a handful of times."

Topher said seriously, "A rookie in his first start? Three times. That's it. Just three fucking times."

Rett didn't quite understand. "Three times? Since when?"

"What do you mean, 'since when?'" said Topher. "Since the beginning, in all of professional baseball!"

Rett grabbed an extra chair as the 6th inning was starting. The Orioles were obviously concerned about what was happening, too, because they had now substituted in a pinch hitter to try and break Cory's spell and get on the board.

Rett sat on the edge of his seat and bit at his finger he was so nervous. Cory took his moment reciting before taking the mound, then held the ball up in the air before his pitch, which seemed like the only thing that could get an audible response from the crowd at this point, and who were otherwise cowed to silence by what they were witnessing. Except for the small crowd of Orioles fans in attendance, which were making as much noise as possible to try and break Cory's concentration.

It didn't work. In fact, Cory seemed to be getting smoother and smoother. One of Cory's pitches this time registered 99 mph on the board.

Ric was one of the few to venture a comment during the entire top of the inning. He said, partly joking, partly in awe, and partly worried, "I'm out of a fucking job."

The 6th inning ended like the others for Cory. He simply was not going to let them get a hit in. The Joes couldn't manage to score while they were at bat, either, so the game remained tied at nothing.

In the 7th inning, the Orioles tried substituting yet another hitter. After a series of balls allowed the first Oriole to get to base, Ahab requested at timeout, and he and Arthur met Cory at the mound to confer for a minute.

Rett and the others couldn't hear what the three of them were saying on the mound, but what they saw made them start laughing nervously. They watched Cory point Ahab back over to the dugout rather emphatically.

"That boy's got some cojones to do that," said JJ to Ric and Topher, "but if he's gonna tell Ahab to waddle his ass back to the dugout, this is the one time in history he's gonna be able to get away with it!"

Once Ahab left the field and Arthur went back to the catcher's box, Topher phoned Ahab in the dugout. When he finished talking, he looked at Sebastion and shook his head, which Rett interpreted as there was no intention of taking Cory out of the game with the streak he was on.

The 7th inning ended, again with no hits for the Orioles. Rett had given up entirely on keeping his leg from bouncing up and down nervously. He had found himself looking up into the stands at Jerry's bright teal shirt, and decided he couldn't stand it or sit still any more. Rett told the guys in the bullpen he'd see them later and left.

He made his way around to the more expensive seats and walked down the steps to where Jerry and Carrie Anne were seated along the aisle. They were so wrapped up they didn't even notice Rett squatting down next to them in the aisle.

Carrie Anne almost jumped out of her seat when Rett said, "How are you guys holding up?"

She grabbed Rett's arm and said, "Rett, thank God you're here! Jerry and I are about to pass out from anticipation!"

Jerry leaned over to Rett and said, "Do you know what they were talking about on the mound a little while ago? Do you know?"

Rett said, "I don't know what they said, but I just came from the bullpen, and it doesn't look like Ahab has any intention of messing with what Cory's doing. Sebastion's not even keeping warm. No one will talk about it because they don't want to jinx it."

Jerry said, "I've been on the phone with Jimmy, and he and Brick and Zee are about to pass out they're so nervous."

"You ok otherwise?" asked Rett. "I can't stay here since the security guys get worked up about people hanging out in the aisles, but I wanted to come check on y'all."

Carrie Anne and Jerry thanked him and said they were good. Rett left them and found a place to perch back in the concourse where he could watch the rest of the game.

The 8th inning remained scoreless, but with Cory's streak still going strong. The crowd was almost dead silent now, and everyone seemed to pick up on the fact they were seeing something very remarkable in baseball happening.

When Cory went to take the mound for the 9th, Rett could tell he was taking noticeably longer to complete his ritual, taking his time. When Cory finished, he looked up and slowly turned around one full time while looking up in the stands at all of the people in silence. Rett was about to die and couldn't understand how Cory could possibly handle this kind of pressure when his own heart was beating him to madness in his chest. Cory stopped looking at the crowd and instead looked down at his feet and appeared to recite his reminder again. Even the umpires, who could get impatient if they felt a pitcher was unnecessarily delaying a game, gave Cory leeway tonight. When he took the mound and lifted his hand with the ball up in the air, Rett could barely make out his fingers thumping on it as his reminder. Rett wasn't sure if it helped Cory or not, but it calmed him down to see it. That was when Rett looked down at the railing he was standing at and realized his fingers were digging into it so hard he was scraping the paint off of it.

Cory pitched two balls to the batter. On the third pitch, the batter managed a bunt, but the ball had enough power that Cory got to it fast and threw to first to get him out. The second batter hit a foul, followed by a couple of balls, followed by a high foul that went back into the stands behind home plate, not too far from Jerry and Carrie Anne, followed by a couple more balls that let him walk to first. The third Oriole hit two fouls, but then hit a high fly that Kevin Ostergaard at second base caught for an easy second out.

Rett looked over in the dugout and saw Ahab pacing back and forth so furiously he looked like he might cause the dugout to catch fire. The other players in the dugout were motionless and transfixed.

The fourth at-bat got a ball and two strikes. When Cory pitched to him again, he tried another bunt, but the angle was wrong and it popped up behind them into foul territory. The umpire called the batter out creating a storm of protests from the Orioles fans in attendance, but the top of the inning was over.

Rett decided that Ahab was on to something, so he took to pacing back and forth in the concourse as he watched. He also began running through his usual list of gods to see if any of them would please give the Joes a run so the game would end before he or Cory had a heart attack. There were no takers, though, and at the end of the 9th, the score was still zero all. It was killing him that they were now going to have to go into extra innings with Cory still on the mound.

In the 10th inning, the first batter got enough balls to where he walked. The second batter managed to get in a good hit along the ground that slipped past Cory, but Kevin recovered the ball to get the runner out at second base, then threw to Skillet at first, tagging the batter out there just in time. With two outs, the

Orioles called a timeout, and then the manager requested a substitution of the next hitter. When they announced the hitter, there seemed to be quite a reaction from the Orioles crowd at the stadium, one even greater than for the other substitutions that night. It was a player named Devin Templeton, which meant nothing to Rett. In the next section, Rett saw a few Orioles fans go nuts and hold up a sign saying "Go, Reaper, Go!" That didn't sound good to him.

The first pitch to Templeton was an obvious ball. Once again, Rett noticed that Arthur and Cory seemed to be communicating more extensively through signals for the batter. The second pitch was also a ball, but closer in to the strike zone as Cory tried to tempt the batter into a swing. On the third pitch, Devin Templeton connected cleanly with the ball and it went sailing out over the outfield. Skunk tracked back with it as it went farther and farther, Rett praying it would finally drop into Skunk's mitt. But the ball continued and landed out past the outfield wall. Rett stared, his mouth hanging in disbelief as it fell into the scrambling crowd, all vying for the trophy baseball. Cory had given up a home run to this Devin Templeton and the Orioles finally had managed to squeeze both a hit and a run out of Cory.

Rett stopped pacing and could sense all the energy in his body evaporate. It felt like time stopped once the ball had fallen into the crowd in the outfield stands. He finally got the courage to look at Cory, who was standing on the mound with his hands limp at his side, eyes on the ground. Everyone else seemed to be watching Devin Templeton make his rather arrogant circle of the bases for the home run.

Rett still had trouble believing it, but just looking at Cory on the mound told him it was true. Cory had given up his first hit of the entire game, and it was a hit that may very well lose the game.

But the game wasn't over yet. The next batter for the Orioles came up to the plate with as much noise and fanfare as the visiting fans could generate. Cory took a moment on the plate to gather himself and ignore what had just happened. Rett glanced over at the dugout and saw Topher and Ahab having an intense discussion as Cory pitched. Cory, though, seemed determined to punish the next batter. His pitches were furiously fast and barely in the strike zone. He managed to strike the batter out quickly and finally.

Rett's nervousness didn't end there, though. If the Joes didn't get a run, they'd lose. If they tied, the game would go into more innings. Rett prayed again for multiple runs. Over in the dugout, Topher and Ahab both took Cory aside and were both talking with him. Rett wished he knew what they were saying to him, but everything about Cory's body posture said he was dejected.

The bottom of the 10th inning proceeded for the Joes like every other, though, and on the third out, they remained scoreless. The Orioles won, 1 to 0.

As soon as the game was over, Cory slowly shuffled back out of the dugout onto the field, his head hanging. Even with the loss, as soon as Cory set foot back out on the field, the crowd cheered for him, and loudly. He looked around and nodded weakly, at least acknowledging the crowds' response. Carrie Anne and Jerry pushed their way down to the field through the fans that were beginning to exit the stadium, trying to get down to their son. Rett wanted so bad to go with them, but decided to let Cory be with his mom and dad instead. Once on the field, Cory hugged his dad and they rocked back and forth, clinging to each other for a long time. Carrie Anne went to lift her son's chin up when it was her turn to hug her son.

Rett watched and wondered. What was it like to see your father like that? As a source of comfort and refuge? Someone that you were so sure of, when things went bad, he was the first person you could turn to, and not feel worse for doing so?

As Rett watched Cory with his parents, he got a text message, this time from Dr. Bala, telling him that Ahab wanted the entire team in the locker room for a quick conference as soon as possible. Back down on the field, Ahab had personally crossed the field to get Cory and take him back to the locker room. Carrie Anne and Jerry didn't know quite what to do, so Rett weaved through the exiting crowd down to where they were on the field.

Before he could even ask how they were doing, Jerry had grabbed Rett, too, and hugged him, followed by Carrie Anne. Rett said, "Cory didn't look like he was taking it well. Is he ok?"

Carrie Anne shook her head, "He feels pretty bad."

Rett told them, "Ahab wants a team-only conference in the locker room, but I'll take y'all into the family lounge until we're done, then I'll make sure Cory gets back with you guys, ok?"

They followed Rett through the dugout and up into the clubhouse where he showed them into the family lounge and made sure they were comfortable.

He just made it into the locker room when Ahab stood up on his stepstool and started to address the team. Cory spotted Rett come in and gave him a weak, defeated smile. It cut through Rett to see him look like that after a spectacular night of pitching that still managed to end badly for the team.

The room went completely silent and Ahab looked seriously out over the entire room for a long time before he gathered his thoughts enough to speak.

"Everyone in here saw what happened tonight," said Ahab, shaking his head sadly. "We lost a game tonight. But... we've lost plenty of games before."

Without looking at Cory, he said, "The pitching on the Joes is shining right now. It's shining brightly. But that bright light is showing the weakness on our offensive side, guys."

He paused again, then resumed, "A member of this team, this team itself, got robbed of something very rare in baseball because we couldn't get on the board during nine regular innings, and we all have to live with that. It's on the rest of us to step up our game now. It's on the rest of us to measure up to the kind of performance we saw tonight. And if we *don't* pull it together better than what I saw from the rest of you tonight? Then we don't deserve the kind of pitching that was exhibited out on our own front yard this evening."

Rett almost preferred the yelling from Ahab to this kind of talk. It made Rett feel like he, personally, had let Cory down in the game tonight.

Finally, Ahab looked directly at Cory and said to the entire room, "Now having said that, I'd like to personally tell you, Cory, we owe you far more than what you got from the rest of us this evening. You held up for a full nine innings in a way that deserves a place in baseball history. No matter what the rule says, you pitched nine innings with no hits in your first rookie start. And that... that right there... what you did is the kind of magic that makes baseball special. And every person on this planet that is a fan of baseball will be talking about the Mobile Joes and Cory Pritchart come tomorrow morning."

Ahab reached out to Cory to shake his hand, something Rett couldn't remember ever seeing Ahab do. "Cory Pritchart, you deserve a hell of a lot more than a round of applause tonight." Ahab started clapping and was immediately joined by the applause, cheers and yelling from everyone else in the locker room, not the least of which was Rett's.

Ahab told Cory to go to the media room because ESPN, Fox Sports and a bunch of the other media outlets were screaming to get time with him for interviews. Cory tried to leave, but couldn't get away because every member of the team wanted to congratulate him on an amazing night.

Rett watched the stream of people file past Cory to give him encouragement or congratulate him. He felt caught up in it. A game that Rett had spent a lifetime ignoring and caring nothing for meant more to him than he could stand in that moment. He had gone from indifference when he joined the Joes, to not wanting the night to end the first time Cory had made him toss the ball with him on a deserted street, to the pure agony and overwhelming pride he felt at that moment for what Cory had done during the game.

Rett finally caught him before he left to go do the interviews.

Cory gave him a broken smile and Rett said, "I've never known anyone like you."

Cory didn't seem to know what to say. "I probably smell terrible right now."

"You always do, like a dirty musk ox. I've almost gotten used to it. But you're right, tonight you're exceeding even those expectations," said Rett, trying to lighten his and Cory's mood, but finding it very hard to do so.

A tired chuckle escaped Cory, and Rett winked at him to let him know he was kidding.

"I brought your parents into the family lounge, so they're waiting for you. I'll probably wait with them for you to finish your big media tour in there."

Cory sighed in relief, "Thanks, Rett. Ahab yanked me off the field so fast and I had no idea what was happening." Cory stared at Rett, not willing to let any other emotion he might be feeling show on his face.

Rett asked, "How's your arm feeling? I can ice it or give it a rubdown if you need it. You put in a lot of innings tonight."

Cory shrugged and said, "A little tired, but ok, really."

Rett turned him around and pushed him towards the door of the locker room. "Ok, Cinderella... go meet the media."

~~~~~

Rett made sure Cory's parents sat in the back of the media room while he gave the interviews to ESPN, Fox Sports, AP News, and a few local stations. Cory was worn down and ready to get in the shower and go home, and so he sent his parents on back over to his place.

On their way out, Rett asked Cory if he wanted to deal with any fans that might be waiting outside the team parking lot. Cory felt like he should, but really didn't think he could face them right then. So instead of walking out together, Rett sent him around to the stadium's loading dock and drove his car around there to pick him up. It was probably a good thing, too, because while there had been between 15 and 20 people waiting for players the night before, Rett was shocked to see well over a hundred waiting out there this evening.

Cory spent most of the ride back to his apartment on the phone with Jimmy. When he finally hung up, Rett asked him, "Cory, your parents are there waiting on you, and I guess you want to spend the time with them tonight..."

Rett stopped what he was saying when Cory reached over and grabbed his hand and said, "Please, Rett. I'll beg if I have to. I need you nearby tonight."

"If that's you begging, you suck at it," said Rett, gently teasing Cory and pulling a laugh out of him.

"Of course I want to stay with you, but I don't want to crowd you, either," added Rett.

Cory rubbed Rett's hand against his face. "Thank you for joking around with me, Rett. It makes me feel... I don't know... normal. Tonight has been a whirlwind of so many emotions I can't even count them all. It's good to have you pulling me back down to earth."

"Always happy to drag others down to my level, Bigfoot," said Rett.

Inside Cory's apartment, Jerry had ESPN turned on and was watching the highlights, which was focused heavily on Cory's pitching that night.

Rett and Jerry both got extremely frustrated with Devin "Reaper" Templeton, who came across as a conceited asshole, trivializing Cory's performance every chance he got during his interviews. Cory, though, when asked how he felt about the

Reaper's home run, said it was a solid hit, the kind any batter would want to get.

The analysts on ESPN picked apart every aspect of the game. The MLB rule defining a no-hitter was very specific; it had to be the complete game, not just nine innings. But the feeling was that, after what happened, there would be considerable pressure on the MLB to reconsider that rule. The assessment of Cory's performance was glowing, with the analysts saying he looked like he had been playing in the majors for years. They decided that if tonight's pitching wasn't just a fluke, then the Joes would suddenly be a force to be reckoned with. That was the question, though, that only time would answer... how much of tonight would Cory Pritchart be able to maintain going into future games. There was no doubt, though, that Cory Pritchart, and Cory Pritchart alone, now owned the gesture of holding the ball aloft for the fans before pitching an inning.

After watching the highlights and discussion, Rett felt nothing except pissed at that Reaper jerk for being so dickish about the whole thing and literally referring to Cory as a "little leaguer." He glanced over at Cory, who was next to him on the sofa, but Cory had his eyes closed and was ignoring the television.

Carrie Anne had already noticed Cory like this as well, and decided it was time for her and Jerry to go on back to their hotel room. Jerry resisted, wanting to keep watching all the coverage of Cory and the game, but Carrie Anne's motherly instinct and final authority kicked in, and she yanked him out of there.

As they were saying goodbye, Rett was both surprised and touched to have Jerry hug him tightly again and whisper in his ear, "Thank you for taking such good care of him." Rett nodded, and considered once again how lucky Cory was to have parents like that.

After they had left, Cory turned the TV off and Rett asked him, "How are you feeling about tonight, Cory?" He wasn't quite sure how to approach it, or even if he should.

Cory sighed and said, "I honestly don't know how I feel. Part of me feels like I let the team down for letting Templeton get a hit

216

like that, and I feel like I was the one that lost the game, but I'm not stupid enough to think this wouldn't happen. It's baseball. It's a fundamental part of the game. Maybe it's better I got this reality check out of the way since it's gonna happen one way or another. Now it'll be easier to handle."

Cory stretched out on the large sofa and put his head in Rett's lap. Rett started running his hand through his hair. "How did it feel out on the mound? For what had to be a stressful night, you looked really comfortable out there."

Cory sighed and said, "I did what Topher told me to do. I picked the hardest college team I pitched against, and did what I would do playing against them. It was good, Rett. It felt good out there. As long as I thought about it as just plain old baseball and not the majors, I did ok."

"Do you feel cheated that tonight won't be counted as a no-hitter?"

It was several seconds before Cory responded to the question. "The pressure's enough as it is," was all he said.

Rett continued to brush through Cory's hair with his fingers and stroke his face and shoulder and arm, trying to sooth away the pressure from the game and from the night. He wanted to help however he could, and if this small comfort did any good, he was more than happy to do it. Cory lay there quietly, letting Rett touch him, letting him run his hand up and down the arm that had performed a miracle in front of a stadium full of people, no matter what the official rule said. Rett studied the arm as he ran his fingers over it, tracing the heavily-developed brachioradialis and extensor and flexor carpi ulnaris muscles. Even the abductor and extensor digitorums were pronounced in his arm. Rett sat, quietly amazed at what this truly beautiful example of an arm had accomplished that night. Quietly amazed that he could touch it and hold it the way he was. In the silence and the dim light of the apartment, minutes passed like this, Rett gently running his hand over Cory.

Without warning, Rett felt a hitch in Cory's chest, and Cory grabbed onto his lap a little more tightly. It broke Rett's heart to hear Cory begin to cry while laying there in his lap, but he continued to touch and hold him so Cory could finally let it out. Cory sobbed softly for several minutes and clung tightly to him, finally able to let all of the pent up feelings and emotions from the night seep out of him. Rett whispered to the man who was feeling so much he couldn't hold it in anymore, "Let it out, Cory. It's ok to let it out." Rett stroked Cory and cradled the man that had held up through an excruciating night, and only now, with the two of them all alone, was able to let go of it all.

Chapter 14

Rett wondered how Val did it. Here he was bleary eyed and struggling, but Val seemed perfectly awake while she tried one of the Coca-Cola flavored Moon Pies that the Portyards was famous for. She had come in late the night before from Montgomery, after the first game in the series against the Brewers had ended, and then the two of them had stayed up even later talking and drinking and catching up while sprawled out on Rett's bed. Val had a ticket for the game against the Brewers that afternoon, so Rett had let her follow him in to work to give her a tour of the clubhouse and meet a few of the players early that morning before practice began.

No one was really there yet, so they had gone to get something to eat in the clubhouse dining room for breakfast before walking around again. Rett had eaten a banana and a bowl of cereal, but Val was now on her fourth Moon Pie, and she was determined to try all the weird flavors.

"How do you manage to keep that down? Those Coca-Cola ones are disgusting. I want to horph my cereal just watching you," said Rett.

"It's exotic! It really tastes like Coca-Cola," she said, far too enthusiastically for Rett's ability to handle it.

"So would a cat turd with a Coke poured over it." Rett had tried one of the Coca-Cola Moon Pies once, and had sworn never to again. His favorites were the classic chocolate and banana flavored ones, but the espresso one wasn't bad in a pinch for breakfast.

"But that wouldn't be exotic," said Val.

"It could be a Scottish Fold cat turd."

"Oooh! Wrap that motherfucker in bacon and deep fry it and you'd have people lined up around the corner! Deep sautéed Scottish Fold log enrobed in pancetta with a Coca-Cola reduction!"

Rett was definitely going to hurl now. Where the hell did she get this kind of energy this early in the morning?

He spotted JJ coming into the dining room and grabbing a granola bar, dressed for his usual run before practice, so he motioned him over. Val's eyes got huge when she saw JJ Troyer, an honest-to-God MLB player, live and in person, coming over to say hello to them.

Rett leaned his head on his arm and said with effort, "Val, this is JJ Troyer, our catcher. JJ, this is Val. Keep back four feet if you know what's good for you."

JJ sat down next to Val, who said in awe, "Oh my God! It really is you!"

JJ had to laugh and commented, "Rett's told me all about you, Val. It's good to finally meet you!"

Val's face exploded in delight and she slapped Rett's shoulder. She said excitedly, "Did you hear that, Rett?! He said it's good to meet me!"

Rett sunk down a little farther on his arm and mumbled, "He'd probably be even more impressed if you gave him your autograph. He may even save the Moon Pie crumbs you're spitting all over him as a souvenir."

"What's up, Tic Tac? You look a little whiter than usual today," said JJ, brushing the crumbs off of the skin-tight compression shirt he wore when running.

Val squeaked, "No way! Did you just call him Tic Tac?" She shook her head in helpless adoration. "You are now my new best friend! That's so awesome! I used to call him lily white, but Tic Tac's way better!"

JJ and Val gave each other a fist bump. JJ said, "Yeah, I had to learn to stay away from Pikachu. He gets real grumpy over that one."

Val asked Rett, "So, JJ's the one that knows you're gay, right?"

Rett banged his head on the table a couple of times and grumped, "If he didn't, he would now, Val. Today's going to be just super swell."

JJ laughed again and said, "Careful, Val. Some of the guys probably won't appreciate your sense of humor."

They, or rather Val and JJ, chatted for a few more minutes before JJ left to go get his run in. Rett made Val stop with the Moon Pies so he could take her out and show her the ball field.

As they were putting their trash away, Val asked, "So when do I get to meet your friend, Cory?"

"He'll be around, probably pretty soon," said Rett.

He hadn't stayed with Cory the night before since he was with Val. Sleeping in the bed with Val was a far cry from sleeping in the bed with Cory. When he had gotten up that morning, it had hit him how quickly he'd become attached to having Cory next to him in bed. The road trips, since they wouldn't be able to do that, were suddenly looking less attractive. Before she had shown up late Friday night, Rett had promised Cory that he hadn't said anything to Val, and that he was going to let him tell her if and when he wanted to.

He added, "Go a little easy on him, Val. He's still a little keyed up about what happened in the game the other night, and he's starting this afternoon again."

As they left the dining room, they ran into Josh coming into the clubhouse. Val stopped short when she saw him, immediately recognizing who he was. She froze like a small animal caught in headlights and her breath snagged in her throat in anticipation.

Rett rolled his eyes and introduced them, "Josh, this is Val, my friend I warned... I mean, my friend I told you about. Val, this is Josh Kilfoyle, but I think you already know who he is."

Josh held out his hand for Val to shake, but she just stood there biting her fingers on both hands, waiting.

Rett said, "She wants to hear it, Josh. Lay it on thick and let's get this over with."

Josh grinned and nodded, understanding what he needed to do. He said in his deepest Australian accent, "G'day, Val! Good to meet you! You up for the game today? It's gonna be a corker, too right!"

Rett laughed and said, "Yeah, now you just sound fake."

"Too much?" asked Josh, his blue eyes sparkling while he scratched at the soul patch under his lip.

Rett confirmed it was with a "yeah" at the same time Val insisted, "Hell no!"

"Bah, ignore him, Val! He's got kangaroos loose in the top paddock!" said Josh with a sly grin, pointing to his head.

"That's even worse!" said Rett. "Now you're just stringing Australianish words together. That's not even a real saying, is it?"

Josh shrugged innocently before shaking Val's hand. "Nice to meet you, Val. Enjoy the game today!"

Rett and Val left to continue their tour of the clubhouse. She glanced back at Josh one more time and said, "God, I have *got* to get me one of those!"

They went downstairs and out onto the field itself where the grounds crew was starting to bring out the practice equipment. He showed her where the team mascot, Old Slac, was usually stationed during the games to drum up the fans, and where the miniature Mardi Gras parade ran to celebrate a home game win.

Rett took her around through the service corridor to show her the Joes bullpen, too. They were the only ones there, so Rett decided to show her how to pitch a ball, or at least as best as he could remember. He stationed her where she could watch, grabbed a spare ball, and positioned himself on the practice mound. This time, he remembered to check how he was gripping the ball before going any further. He wound up and pitched the ball at the backstop fence, almost managing to miss it his aim was so far off. Rett looked over at Val, rather pleased with himself for showing off.

Val, though, was standing there with her mouth hanging open slightly. She pointed behind him and Rett turned around to see Cory standing there in his uniform pants and a tight white compression shirt that accentuated every muscle in his upper body.

Cory was grinning and said enthusiastically, "Holy shit! That one must have burned in at around 7 mph, Rett! I could hear the sonic boom all the way over here!"

Rett scowled at him and said, "Oh, fuck you, Cory. I'm trying, right?"

Cory walked over and Rett introduced him. "Val, this is Cory. Cory, this is Val."

Val continued to eye Cory, almost shyly and shook his hand. She said, "You're, uh... a... *lot* bigger than you look on TV."

Cory said, "Ok. I don't know if that's good or bad."

Val snapped out of her reverie and said, "You're freaking amazing, you know? You were even on the national news! Not just ESPN, but like NBC and CNN and stuff!"

The day after Cory's debut start, the story of his nine full no-hitter innings followed by a heartbreaking 10th had indeed gotten extensive coverage, and Cory's face seemed to be everywhere. The media especially loved clips of Cory holding the ball up in the air before he pitched.

Cory winced and said, "Man, all that stuff's been its own special brand of nerve-wracking."

Val looked horrified, sure she had totally said the wrong thing unintentionally to arguably the most famous baseball player in the world at the moment. "I'm so sorry, Cory! I didn't mean to say anything to upset you!"

"No, no! Not at all, Val!" Cory put his hand on her shoulder. "I'm just ready for all that to die down. The interviews have been kind of a pain."

Rett said casually, "You're here early today. I didn't think I'd see you for a little while longer."

Cory managed to keep a totally straight face and said, "Yeah, turns out I didn't have any good reasons to stay in bed this morning, so I came on in."

Rett had to bite his tongue to keep the stupid grin off his face at the comment. If Cory was expecting to hide what they had together, he was going to have to stop pulling shit like that.

Cory turned back to Val, "Rett's talked about you a ton, Val. I feel like I've known you forever already."

Val relaxed. "Oh, thank God. So it won't be a shock if I lift my shirt up and ask you to autograph my boobs, then? And then I will never wash them!"

Rett whined at her, "*Val.*"

"How about my ass?"

"You don't wash that enough as it is," explained Rett. "And I thought you already had an autograph on your ass. A Gene Simmons one from that KISS concert you went to a few years ago in New Orleans. What about that?"

"Oh, that thing was fake," said Val.

"So, who signed his name on your ass, for crying out loud?"

"Gene Simmons!"

"You said it was fake!"

"It *was* fake! There's more than one Gene Simmons in the world!" explained Val impatiently.

"So you found some *other* Gene Simmons at a KISS concert and had *him* sign your ass?"

"Yes! Jesus, Rett, it's not complicated!"

"Why would you let some random dude sign your ass at a KISS concert?"

"I like to show my ass!"

"Christ, that explains a lot! I spent *years* wondering if there was maybe such a thing as Ass Tourette's that you suffered from," said Rett.

Val rolled her eyes. "Great! And now the Mobile Joes gets to take advantage of that superior medical mind you have. Lucky them!"

Val shifted her attention back to Cory, whose mouth was hanging open slightly after the interplay he had just witnessed.

She said, "So, Rett said you may go to dinner with us tonight after the game?"

"Uhh... will your shorts stay on in the restaurant?" asked Cory cautiously.

Val's eyes twinkled. "God, if I had a nickel every time someone asked me that!"

~~~~~

"Could you at least pretend to be listening to me, Val?"

"What?"

Rett reached across the table to physically move the basket of crab claws out of her reach, but she growled throatily at him.

"You touch that fucking basket," she snarled, "and you'll need a tourniquet for the stump you pull back!"

After the game against the Brewers, which the Joes had won 5 to 4, Rett had taken Val out to Bluegill. Cory was going to join them, but had gotten caught up signing autographs on the field right after the game ended, and Rett knew there'd be even more waiting outside the parking lot. Cory had told them to go on and he'd meet them there.

Val said through a mouth full of crab claws, "These things are sooooo good! I wish we had something like this in Montgomery!"

She pointed out at the water where the moon was reflecting. In the background, the guitarist was covering some John Mellencamp tunes. She said, "This would almost be romantic, if you were anybody other than you, maybe."

"I know! I kept thinking the same thing!" said Rett.

"Can you FedEx me a box of these every week? I'll finally love you if you do," said Val sweetly, picking up another crab claw.

"You already love me."

"There's a difference between 'love' and 'tolerate,' Tic Tac. And I don't even tolerate you... I just watch you make a spectacle of yourself."

Rett said, "Remind me again who added a love note on the end of her Prosthetics/Orthotics final exam because she thought the teaching assistant was adorable? And then found out the 80-year-old horn-dog professor graded those personally?"

"Remind me again," countered Val, "who was the one that answered the door totally naked for the pizza delivery guy on the off chance that it would be the hot one with the red hair and tattoos? On *three* different occasions?"

"Touché," said Rett, with a frown. He grabbed a crab claw and ate it in silence.

After the tour that morning, Rett had given Val a credit card, a budget, and sent her out to buy whatever she felt like his apartment needed the most. When she showed up later for the game, Rett watched it with her, and it was a tight one. Cory pitched well, but the Brewers managed to score four runs in the first six innings, most of which were due to errors on the part of the Joes' fielders. But in the bottom of the 8th, Skillet got a grand slam home run, tying the score up. It was JJ that managed a home run in the 9th that won the game for the Joes.

"Do you think he's really going to come?" asked Val.

"Of course he is! Cory and I are pretty tight." Rett took a swig out of his bottle of beer.

"That tight?" asked Val.

"Shit, yeah," said Rett.

"I don't know," said Val while chomping into two more of the small crab claws at one time. "There were a lot of screaming girls begging for his autograph after the game. There might be something better that comes up tonight."

Rett let out a sudden belly laugh and then stopped immediately when Val's eyes darted up to him. He got nervous that he may have overplayed his hand with the laugh. She had many years of learning all of his tells, after all.

It was a minute later when Cory showed up, and none of that mattered anyway. It only took one instantaneous look at Cory for Rett to realize the gig was up for the two of them and he groaned in defeat. Val glanced briefly at Cory walking towards them and her eyes exploded to the size of dinner plates.

She hissed violently at Rett under her breath, "This is insane, Rett! You two are fucking?! Are you out of your goddamned mind?"

By the time Cory sat down, Rett was as red in the face as a screaming, angry Ahab. Any possibility of doubt on Val's part was already gone when she saw Rett's face.

Cory sat down next to Val, noticed the uncomfortably high tension, and said, "What?"

Before anyone could answer, the waiter came by and stammered, "Hi, uh... you, uh... oh shit... you're... you're Cory Pritchart, aren't you?"

Cory tried to be nice, but was confused by Rett's and Val's strained expressions in front of him. He glanced at the waiter, smiled thinly, and said, "Yeah."

"Oh, dude! Holy sh... You were just pitching tonight! Jesus! You were on that TV right over there a little while ago! This is awesome!"

By now a few of the people still hanging out on the deck by the water had realized who had showed up and were craning their necks and staring.

Cory wrinkled his nose and said, "I don't know if I'd call giving the Brewers four runs 'awesome.'"

The waiter finally pulled himself together a little more and said, "What can I get you, man? Anything! You name it!!"

Cory pointed at Rett's beer and said, "One of what he's got, and another basket of the crab claws. And a house salad."

The waiter nodded violently and walked off. Cory said to Rett and Val, "What the hell did I walk into the middle of here?"

Rett laid his head down on the table in defeat and mumbled, "I swear I didn't tell her."

Val whispered to Cory in astonishment, "You two are *doing* it!"

Cory's lips pulled tight in the fear of what he thought she meant by that statement. He said slowly, "Doing what?"

"Fucking!" said Val much more loudly than she intended and drawing attention from several nearby tables.

The waiter showed up with Cory's beer, salad and crab claws, looked at the strained faces on the three of them, set it all down carefully and backed off slowly like they might attack him at the slightest provocation.

Cory turned white and Rett grabbed Val's hand. "Val, no shit here! You *cannot* tell anyone! *Any*one! At *all*! And you've got to keep your voice down!"

Val nodded and turned a little pale herself now that she had heard explicit confirmation from Rett.

"How did she know?" asked Cory, glancing between the two rapidly. "How did you know, Val?"

Rett sighed and said, "Where did you get the t-shirt, Cory?"

Cory looked at Rett in confusion.

"It's Rett's Pretenders t-shirt," said Val. "It's about his most prized possession. I borrowed it one time and you'd have thought I was a Hamas terrorist all of a sudden. There's no way, absolutely no way, you'd have it if there wasn't something going on. I know Rett well enough to know that."

Cory looked at the shirt pulled tight across his chest. He asked, "Does anyone else know about it?"

Rett shook his head. "Relax, Val's the only one that would see the significance."

"You were doing your laundry over at my place," said Cory, "and I kind of stole it."

Val said, "It looks way hotter on you than it ever did on Rett. He looks... I don't know... *frumpy* in it." That managed to get a minor grin out of Cory.

"It's alright, though, right?" asked Cory. "I was going to tell you tonight anyway, Val. But yeah, please God, don't tell anyone, ok? You're ok with it, aren't you, Val?"

With the initial shock finally wearing off a little, Val said, "Do I look stupid? Of course I'm fine with it! It's just... Holy Jesus in a hairnet, it's shocking! Besides, as long as Josh is still straight, I'm good." She poked Rett in the side and added, "But you *have* to get me some of that, Rett! You *owe* me!"

"Why do you want Josh? You're dating *Tony* now!" said Rett.

"Tony's a pinhead."

"You said he had a big dick," said Rett.

"I don't mean he literally has the head of a pin, dickwad! I meant mentally!"

"What? When did you start caring about a guy's mental capacity?" said Rett, like the girl seated next to him had been hit on the head and was talking crazy.

"Just because *you* think Voltaire is a brand of heating and air conditioning units doesn't mean I don't want brains in another guy!"

"And so you date Tony? Wasn't he the one that still thought I was straight despite you showing him one of your dildos and claiming it was mine?"

Val sighed in exasperation, "*He's got a big dick!* Which makes up for... Oh never fucking mind! Don't you ever hear a single word that comes out of my mouth? Besides, one man will *never* be enough to satisfy me!"

Rett guffed in laughter, "You barely ever dated at all while I was living with you!"

"That's because you're exhausting to be around, just like right now! Just watching TV with you in the room made me want to crawl back into bed!"

Cory laughed and said, "Man! You too?"

Rett pointed his finger at Cory and warned, "No ganging up! No ganging up!"

Val high-fived Cory, and Rett complained, "This sucks ass."

Cory laughed loudly and rubbed Rett's head roughly. His eyes twinkled and he said, "You know I'm just kidding, chief!"

"Oooh," said Val, "those dimples are gonna be the death of me before... hold on... Did you eat *all* of those crab claws? The *entire* basket?"

Cory looked down at the empty basket like a scolded child. "Y'all were busy. I pitched nine innings."

Val shook her head, took Cory's hand in hers, and said, "I can't do it. I can't stay mad at those dimples."

The waiter came back over and pointed at the empty basket, "Would your girlfriend like another round of the crab claws?"

Cory put his arm around Val and pulled her closer. He kissed the top of her head and said, "She goes through 'em, doesn't she? Yeah, bring the lady another."

Val watched Cory for a moment, then had to unequivocally confirm it, "This isn't some elaborate joke? You're really gay? You and this one, y'all are for real?" She pointed indistinctly at Rett.

Cory nodded.

The conversation turned earnest, and Val wanted to know how it all came about, so Rett and Cory told her the story. How Cory overheard Mike and Rett's discussion. Their first kiss when Cory was trying to teach Rett to pitch. Making out on the Brooklyn Bridge. How Rett met Cory's dad the first time they spent the night together.

Rett also tried to apologize for not telling Val earlier, but then Cory took over and insisted that he was the one that should apologize. He had asked Rett to please keep it quiet until he had at least met her. To get to know her a little before opening up that way. He explained that he really didn't want to risk his MLB career now that it was barely getting underway.

Cory eventually asked, "Val, if you and Rett want the time together, that's fine, but if you'd rather spend the night on my couch, you're more than welcome to. It's a pretty big couch and I can be a little selfish and have Rett with me that way."

Rett acknowledged, "It's a huge couch, Val."

Before Val could answer, Rett's phone rang. He didn't recognize the number, but answered it anyway.

"Rett?" said the voice on the other end.

Val and Cory both watched as Rett's face turned very strange, distant and confused, like he was suddenly a thousand miles from there. That one word in his ear took him back into a life that felt like it had happened to someone else in some other distant time.

"Mom?" said Rett quietly. He stared down at the worn wooden table they were sitting at. Without even realizing he was doing it, Rett stood up, leaving Val and Cory at the table, and walked around to the dock where a couple of boats were tied up while their owners had their late drinks or dinner. He moved like he was sleepwalking and in a strange dream.

"Everett? Son, is it really you?" the soft, quaking voice asked again.

Rett didn't doubt who it was this time. For a flash, Rett considered hanging up. The life that he felt unexpectedly and violently dragged back into wasn't one he wanted to see again. Strangely, the image that popped into his mind was that of Cory after the game, after giving up the home run in the 10th inning, and seeking comfort from both of his parents on the field afterwards.

Rett came back to himself, but his heart had hardened in defense at the same time. Something in her voice, though, kept him from hanging up.

"Yeah, mom, it's me."

There was a long silence.

Rett's mother eventually said, "It's been so long, Rett. I almost didn't know whether I should call you or not, even after I managed to track down this number."

Rett waited, but there was another pause. He was on the verge of telling her she probably shouldn't have, but his mother resumed, "But I shouldn't make this decision for you."

Rett squinted. This was different. For the first time he could ever recall, that one sentence almost came across like she was treating him like an adult, even if he had no idea what it was about.

She said, "I... uh... It's your father, Rett. He's had a heart attack. A bad one."

Rett's first thought was *I'm not surprised.* Maybe it was a bad thought to have, and maybe he'd regret it. But it was what popped into his mind.

"How is he?" Rett asked.

"It's been touch-and-go for the last few days. But a little better today. I couldn't..."

She paused again, and Rett thought he might have heard a choked sob from her end of the phone.

"I didn't think it would be right, Rett, if something bad had happened, or still happens... I had... I know things aren't great between you and your father, or between you and us, even. I know the night you left, some... things were said. But this is different, Rett."

He listened quietly, unmoving and stone-like, while standing on the dock. The water around him glimmered in the lights from the restaurant and the moon overhead.

He heard his mother exhale from the effort of making this call and she said, "I thought you deserved to know, no matter what's happened in the past. I thought you deserved to decide for yourself if... if you wanted to come see him."

Rett recoiled and he blurted out "Come see him?" before he realized he was saying it.

There was another long pause on the phone. His mother finally said, "After seven long years of no contact at all, I didn't have much hope, but you deserved to know, son. You deserve the opportunity. I'm sorry, Rett. He's in the hospital here in Dothan if you change your mind."

And with that, his mother hung up.

Rett let his hand with the phone fall limply to his side and he stared transfixed at the water under the dock. His mind was blank for a full minute, and then without realizing he was remembering it, the picture in his mind was his dad yelling at him, sneering at him, on that Friday night. He saw his dad looming and saying, "Everything about you from day one said I was gonna regret you!"

Rett wondered how a man with a cold granite heart like that managed to have a heart attack.

"Rett?" he heard from behind.

Cory and Val were standing there, the worry furrowed deeply in their faces. For a moment, Rett had been dragged so far away from his present life that he felt like he didn't know who they were.

Still in a fog, he said, "My dad has... he's had a heart attack."

Chapter 15

The uniform practically hung off of him, and he adjusted it every so often trying to get it comfortable, but it still would slip back down artlessly a moment later despite his efforts. Rett stood in the field and tried to get it to wear right again, but the catcher was beating his fist in his mitt to let him know he needed to hurry up.

As Rett took his stance, the hair on his arm stood up on end. He could feel it in the air and looked up in the black night sky. He had barely jumped away and off to the side when a powerful crack of lightning landed right where he was standing a split-second before, with a peal of thunder that felt like it would burst his eardrums.

He wiped at the sweat on his forehead, which was pouring off of him now, and moved to a different location on the field. He glanced up at the sky but could see nothing beyond the hillsides of empty seats rising up all around and the bright stadium lights of the Portyards shining down on him. He checked the catcher to make sure he was ready, but as he was about to attempt the pitch again, he sensed the building electricity in the air. He jumped back as another crack of lightning landed right in front of him, blinding him and blowing dirt and grass up out of the field all over him.

This repeated two or three more times, Rett trying to pitch, and having to dodge lightning and ear-splitting thunder and the increasing number of holes blown into the field where he had been standing. His heart was beating faster and faster each time, pounding at him from the inside and the sweat was coming off of him in sheets and stinging his eyes.

He stood and looked helplessly at the catcher, who stood up in frustration. Rett could tell he was glaring at him, even though he couldn't see the catcher's face.

The catcher yelled at Rett from behind his mask fiercely, "Stand your ground, Rett! *Be a man!*"

Rett felt the air charge again and he jumped out of the way right as the lightning struck. He had to brush all the dirt off of his uniform once again. He didn't understand how he was supposed to stand his ground with lightning hitting all the spots he was trying to pitch from. How was he supposed to do that? He'd get hurt before he could throw the ball.

The catcher yelled at him, "I've done nothing but regret you, Rett!! You're just a *fucking* waste of time!"

Rett heard his name being called again, this time from far off the field. Not in scorn, like the catcher had called to him, but in worry and concern. Then he heard it yet again.

The catcher became furious now, and right as he went to yank his mask off and yell some more, Rett's eyes popped open and he felt big hands shaking him gently.

He jerked up in the bed, panting rapidly in shallow, dry breaths, right as another crash of thunder hit his ears. He thrashed wildly for a second, fighting to get away from the lightning trying to hit him, but was held back. It took him a moment to separate the dream from reality, but he finally realized Cory had his arms around him and was saying his name to him.

"You were dreaming, Rett, just dreaming. It's ok," said Cory softly, rocking Rett and holding him against his bare chest.

Outside, lightning flashed in the sky and was followed by the boom of thunder, making Rett flinch again. Cory pushed Rett flat down into the bed and climbed over him, pressing his body down onto him. He rubbed his face against Rett's and kissed him on his cheeks and lips, comforting him. Outside, wild rains pelted against the windows, driven by the winds of the storm. Another bright flash and boom caused Rett to jerk under Cory's weight again.

"Shhh, Rett, shhh. Just relax. Everything's ok. I'm here," whispered Cory, kissing Rett again. The reassuring weight on top of him, the feel of Cory's bare body against his, their warm skin touching eventually brought his heart rate down to near normal despite the storm's fury on the other side of the windows.

Cory slowly ran his hand across Rett's face and hair, caressing him, and Rett caught the familiar scent of the worn glove leather that never seemed to leave Cory's left hand, no matter how much he showered. It was a smell that he hoped Cory would never find a way to get rid of.

"Better?" asked Cory, his dark eyes worried.

Rett nodded in the faint light of the room, the only illumination provided by the distant streetlight down on the corner.

He said, "Yeah, better," and reached up and kissed Cory again on the lips. It was probably six years now since he had had one of the thunderstorm nightmares. The baseball theme was a new twist on it, though.

Cory rolled off to Rett's side and pulled him close. He nuzzled into his neck and whispered to him, "You scared me there for a while. I thought you were going to leap right out of the bed!"

Rett mumbled, "I fucking hate thunderstorms in the middle of the night."

"Something to do with your dad?"

Rett pulled free from Cory and propped his pillow up behind him. He sat up in bed and sighed.

Cory followed suit and sat up next to him. He took Rett's hand in his and played with his fingers. "You scared Val to death while you were on the phone with your mother tonight. Which in turn scared me. She knows you a lot better than I do."

"When I was little, storms like this terrified me. I wanted nothing more than to get in bed with my parents, but my father would never let me. He'd tell me to go back to my bed. He'd close their door and lock it so I couldn't come back in. When I was really little, I'd sit outside their door and cry, but it didn't make any difference, he'd let me sit there and bawl my eyes out. Sometimes, my dad would tell me he was going to drag my ass out into the storm and lock me out in it if I didn't shut up. Other times, I'd go get in bed with Bo. God bless him, he loved it... he loved protecting his big brother. That was humiliating, the big brother getting scared and getting in bed with the younger brother. Eventually, when I got a little older, that felt wrong and awkward, but I still hated the storms. I had to ride them out on my own."

Rett pushed the sheets down off of him a little farther because he felt damp from the dream, and added, "God, it seemed like there was a hundred million ways to disappoint my dad. To do every little thing wrong in his eyes. To turn into the queer little faggot cocksucker despite his best efforts."

Cory continued to play with Rett's hand. "Are you going to go see him?"

Rett breathed deeply. "I don't know. I don't see what good can realistically come out of it. And if he's had a heart attack, then me showing up may make things worse. For him *and* me."

"Maybe he had the heart attack because everything that happened between you guys built up and had nowhere to go," said Cory. "Maybe you need to go. Maybe it would make things better."

Rett said, "I don't even have the vaguest idea what I'd say to him."

"So... don't say anything. Just go see him. Let him talk if he wants to. Or just tell him you hope he gets better and does ok and don't say anything else."

"I don't want to take a day away. I'm supposed to be checking on Ric's finger again tomorrow and Josh has complained about his Achilles' tendon a couple of times, and I want to make him stop long enough for me to check it before he does something bad."

Cory said, "Go Monday. We'll be on the All-Star break and we've got four days off. I'll go with you if you want."

Rett stared off into Cory's room. The light from outside played shifting patterns on the walls and on the bed while the rain came down in sheets.

"It's your decision, Rett, and I'll respect it either way," said Cory. "But he's your father. I know I can't begin to understand what it was like for you and what you dealt with in his house. But maybe some things transcend even that. Avoiding him now, under these circumstances, feels almost as bad as what he did to you. What if he had died and you never got this chance?"

Rett thought, *then I wouldn't have to make this fucking decision. I wouldn't have to deal with this.*

Rett still didn't say anything and Cory decided to change the subject.

"So this poor Tony guy that wasn't here to defend himself tonight... is he really as dumb as you guys make out?" he asked.

Rett chuckled slightly and shook his head, "Nah, that's just me and Val doing our thing. Tony's a really good guy. He's had a thing for Val a while now, and Val's always liked him. I, uh... I was just always in the way, I guess. They should have gotten together a long time ago."

Val was right then asleep on Cory's couch, but he felt farther and farther away from her now. He said thoughtfully, "Maybe it was best I got out of Montgomery no matter what. To give her a little space so she'd stop clinging to my side like a fucking remora."

"Tony's a lucky guy then. She's a really beautiful girl," said Cory.

"I love her, Cory. I don't know what I would have done without her."

"You're *still* lucky to have each other," corrected Cory.

Cory played with the fingers on Rett's hand. "So... since you have her... can I keep the Pretenders t-shirt?" he asked innocently.

Rett looked at him snidely. "Did you know that your left hand always smells a little bit like your glove leather? No matter how many times you shower?"

Cory looked at Rett for a second. Then he said, "Really?"

"Mmm hmmm."

Cory put his left hand up to his nose to smell it. When he did so, Rett smacked his hand, forcing Cory to pop himself in the face.

Cory yelped and then started laughing and Rett said coolly, "*That's* what you get for stealing my t-shirt, Bigfoot."

Cory ripped the sheets away from Rett and pulled him down onto the bed before he knew what was happening. Rett laughed and tried to scramble away, but Cory threw himself on top of him, instantly ending any hope of escape.

Rett gave up and let Cory have his way. He could think of worse things to happen than having Cory's chest grinding into him and his thick arms pinning him down on both sides. Cory kissed his ear and nibbled at it until Rett turned his head and their lips could meet. Rett opened his mouth and let Cory's tongue in, their breaths turning deeper and heavier the more their kiss kindled the fire. Cory lifted up off of Rett barely enough so that his entire body could rub across him, the heat and friction building quickly between them. Rett could feel Cory's dick fully erect and grinding against his own, teasing and pushing against him. He lifted up, pushing himself up against Cory, doing his own teasing in return. Cory pushed his legs between Rett's and forced them a little further apart, giving himself a tiny bit more access. He reached under and pushed his dick down between Rett's legs so that it could slide up towards his ass. Cory began to grind and push a little harder, letting his cock slide against the trough of Rett's ass-crack while he took Rett's tongue into his own mouth, pulling and sucking on it, trying to swallow as much of Rett as he could get.

Rett groaned, feeling his own hard dick pressing and rubbing against Cory's furry abdomen, demanding more of the gentle bulk of the big man on top of him. He lifted his legs up and wrapped them around Cory's waist, giving him even better leverage. He wanted the teasing to end and to feel the warmth of Cory inside him, to feel the security of having him all around him. He wanted Cory to consume him so he didn't have to face the storm that was haunting him, trying to catch him.

Cory whispered hoarsely into Rett's ear, "You can keep the t-shirt. I'd rather have you."

Rett was surrounded and engulfed by Cory, warmed and excited by him, and the thunderstorm raging outside the bedroom windows no longer mattered.

Chapter 16

Rett grumbled to himself and wondered how he had wound up here.

That morning, as he and Cory were getting ready to go in to the Portyards for the Sunday afternoon game against the Brewers, and as Val was getting ready to go back to Montgomery, the pressure was applied.

Val agreed with Cory that Rett needed to go. He could go to patch things up with his dad. He could go just to wish him a good recovery and nothing else. He could go to see if his mom maybe was finally getting the depression treatment Val agreed she needed. He could go to ignore both of them and see Bo. He could go to see if his dad's nurse was a cute guy and then hit on him in front of them. He could go and flaunt his education and his job as a final "fuck you" to his dad. Val wasn't picky about the reason, but she thought it was a mistake to pass up the opportunity since his mother had reached out to him.

Rett had tried to trot out the same excuses he had given to Cory in the middle of the night, but Val was even less inclined to listen to them than Cory was. In fact, she seemed to get irate at the fact that he was looking for excuses to not go. Val had enough history with Rett to where she didn't stand on ceremony or subtlety or deference at all. She told him point blank to get his freckled ass to Dothan and see them.

Cory was more gently encouraging.

They all still seemed to be at a stalemate when Val left and Rett and Cory carpooled in to the Portyards.

Right as they arrived at the stadium, Rett received the text from Val:

I kno yr not gonna go, so I am. On my way to Dothan!

What irritated Rett was that he knew she might very well do it. After some of the other stunts she had pulled over the years, this would be cake for her. Even if she didn't go, Rett could tell she'd be on him about it from then on.

So he had caved.

He sent a text back to Val saying he was going. He let Dr. Bala know what was going on, and Dr. Bala was very understanding and fine with him taking off for the day. He gave the trainers Rikky and Ryan some notes for things to do on his behalf while he was away. And finally, he made sure Cory would be able to get a ride home after the game, which was the least of Cory's worries. Since he wasn't pitching that day, Cory offered again to go with him, even if he just sat in the car, but Rett insisted he needed to do this alone if he was going to do it.

He had kept his resolve to see it through, to pull some kind of good out of the situation, during the entire drive from Mobile to Dothan. But as soon as he set foot in the front door of the Southeast Alabama Medical Center, he wondered what the hell he was doing there.

He stood in the lobby of the hospital and told himself, *sixty seconds. Give yourself sixty seconds and if nothing's changed, then you can walk out of there a free man once and for all knowing you did what you could.*

And then he added, *and at least you'll get to see Bo, even for a moment.*

He walked over to the front information desk and asked what room Newton Dougherty was in.

The lady at the computer took a moment to look it up before glancing back over at Rett. She asked, "Are you related to him?"

Rett never anticipated exactly how hard it would be to force the three words out of his mouth.

"I'm his son."

He wondered, *am I? Or did that stop being true years ago?*

She answered, "He's in room 211," and pointed him towards the elevator.

When he got out of the elevator, his feet developed a mind of their own and started dragging as he passed the doors.

His mind chose the moment to drag him back to one of those times in his past, one that didn't seem so terrible at the time, but through the magnifying lens of age, had felt worse and worse.

Rett pushed as far away from his father as the seat belt and the car door would allow, and he stared out the window at the shrubs and houses passing by. Even with his eyes and face turned away, he could feel his father looking over at him every so often, even though he had not said much since they got in the car. His knee still stung and bled where Derrick Odom had kicked him getting the ball away from him. And Derrick was on his own team.

"You've just made up your mind to not be good at this, you know." his father finally said, angrily. Rett ignored his dad and sulked into the car door further. All he wanted was to get home, go to his room, and crawl under his bed and hide.

It was bad enough to have everyone on his own team not want him there, but to have his dad at practice telling him everything he was doing wrong and that he wasn't trying hard enough was unbearable.

"Are you listening to me, boy?"

"Yes, dad," said Rett, sarcastically.

"I don't understand why you don't try a little harder."

"I hate this game! I hate all of them!"

Soccer was no different than Pee-Wee football had been. Rett leaned over and started taking his sneakers and socks off so he could be barefoot by the time he got home.

"Sports are good for you, Rett! They build teamwork. They help you make friends. Men like sports. You like sports, don't you?"

He wanted to scream at hearing that question again. "No, I hate sports! Especially soccer!"

When it had been Pee-Wee Football, that was the game he especially hated. Now it was soccer. He wasn't any good at any of them. And every time he tried, he got teased more, and his dad got more upset. Everyone hated him a little more with every attempt at this.

"Guys love sports, Rett!" His voice was emphatic, like he was demanding Rett like them, rather than trying to explain something to him. Rett was back to looking out the window of the car and pretending to ignore him. They were on the corner of their street and he wanted to get home before he started crying.

Even before the car came to a complete stop in the driveway, Rett had unbuckled and was bolting inside as fast as he could. He ran past his mom, who was watering a plant on the table behind the sofa in the den. She tried to say something to him as he ran past, but he didn't hear it, and when he got to his room, he slammed his door as hard as he could.

He stood for a few minutes looking at the now-dried blood on his knee where Derrick had kicked him intentionally, wishing there was anything he could do to not ever have to go to soccer practice again, to hear his father shouting at him from the sidelines.

Rett heard the knob to his room turn, and he wanted to hide so his father wouldn't come in and complain to him even more about practice, but all his father did was open the door enough to throw his shoes and socks into the room.

"You forgot these in the car, Rett," was all he said before closing the door again.

He heard his mother ask a question from the den and his father walk back down the hall. He had a sudden urge to know what his mother had asked. Rett opened his door quietly, and crept down the hallway on silent, bare feet until he could hear them talking, but not be seen.

His father was saying, "The other boys don't even want him there."

His mom started to say, "Well, maybe..."

"I'm not having the one son in this town like this, Jaye. I'm his father and what I'm doing is for his own good, even if I have to drag the little twerp through this kicking and screaming, which is obviously what it's gonna take!"

There was silence for a while. Rett wished he could see what his mother was doing, but she was probably not doing anything except looking out the window.

He had a hard time hearing what his father said next, because he was stomping off to the kitchen, but it sounded like "gonna turn pansy." He didn't know what it meant, but his dad definitely didn't like it.

He jumped when Bo pulled at his shirt behind him. Bo was completely oblivious to anything going on and insisted, "Rett, come help me with my Lego's."

"Go away, Bo!" he hissed. But when he saw the look on his brother's face, he turned and sank down to his knees in front of him. He whispered, "Gimme a minute, ok? I'll come help." Bo seemed satisfied with that and ran back to his room.

Rett snuck into the den, scared to death. His mother stopped staring out the window when she saw her son out of the corner of her eye.

Rett was frowning, a tear forming in the corner of his eye, but he asked, "What does it mean to be a pansy, mom?"

His mother's frown now matched his. "Oh, honey... you heard that?" she asked, pain in her voice.

Rett nodded.

"Sweetie... it doesn't mean anything. Your dad was... you know... it just means you're a late bloomer. A little later than some of the other kids, darling."

Rett sniffed, but that didn't sound like the kind of thing his father would say.

Even at nine years old, his dad had already pigeon-holed him. But that wasn't even the worst his father would think of Rett before it was all over.

The bullshit pissed him off. And then he got mad at himself that getting through this visit, getting it over with, seemed to be so motherfucking hard. Was it only because, for years now, he never expected to see them again that this was affecting him so much? Was it because, now that he had built a life he felt good about, he resented his family inserting itself back into it? Or was it that even now, the thought of being in his father's presence made him feel like a contemptible loser, a worthless pansy?

He forced himself to practically start running down the hall the rest of the way, and went right into room 211 without stopping or hesitating or knocking or giving himself any chance to back out of this with only a measly ten feet left to go. Even as he stepped into the room, he had a burning, hostile look on his face. He was pissed that it took this kind of effort and resolve to do this instead of running back out to his car and driving all the way back to Mobile for nothing. Why was it always so much easier to run away than to face people?

As soon as he stepped into the room, he saw his dad, lying in the hospital bed. The antiseptic smell of the hospital was almost comforting to him from his days interning in school. The fluourescent lights in the room were off and the midday sunlight from outside filtered in through the sheer curtains over the window. His dad was napping, eyes closed. His father, who had always felt twice Rett's size even though he hardly ever was, looked pale and small and gray; his skin looked thin and like it was hanging off of him. He looked drawn and weak; even his hair looked thinner and grayer. It took Rett completely by surprise to see him like this, a way he had never appeared to Rett before. It shouldn't. Rett knew what the aftermath of a heart attack looked like. He had seen it before when he had interned, and here it was again. But there was something about the shock of seeing his own father that way, so different from how he remembered him, that he wasn't prepared for.

He had to wonder for a moment how someone like this, small and feeble, could have caused all the fear and pain he had gone through. But even seeing his father lying there, eyes closed, he could feel it deep inside himself still. Never really gone. Just buried, minimized as much as possible, and ignored the rest of the way. But still there.

A motion in the far corner of the room drew Rett's attention away and he saw his mother look up from a magazine. At least she looked a little better than he remembered. She still had her reddish-blond hair in short, soft curls and her hazel eyes. There were a few more wrinkles in her face than he remembered. But she also looked a little rounder in the middle than she usually did. Maybe it was just the years, or maybe it was that she was finally eating a little more.

As soon as she saw her eldest son standing in the room, saw him for the first time in more than seven years, she gasped audibly. She looked like she might cry and she started to get out of her chair.

The hard edge remained on Rett's face and he stepped back a fraction. The message to his mother was unmistakable. His showing up did *not* mean things were ok and they were *not* a family again all of a sudden. And whatever she thought she was about to do was strictly off limits.

His mother froze, and then sat back down in the chair and said nothing. But she didn't take her eyes off of her son, either. She took in every detail she could given whatever small opportunity she might have.

Rett scanned the rest of the room, but Bo wasn't there. He was disappointed, but had to check that feeling. It was definitely best that Bo wasn't there. He'd have a hard time not going to Bo if he had been there, focusing on him and ignoring his parents in the process.

But he couldn't hold the question back. He asked his mother, "Where's Bo?"

She smiled feebly, nervously. "He ran back by the house to get a few things for your father now that he's out of ICU."

She asked carefully, like it might cause Rett to vanish if she put the wrong inflection on it, "How are you, Rett?"

"I'm fine." Seven years away from them, and that's all he felt like sharing.

The voices in the room caused his father to stir slightly. He shifted in his hospital bed and tugged at the sheets covering him, but he didn't open his eyes immediately. His mouth opened, and he smacked at his lips a little, like his mouth was dry, and only then did his eyes open.

He reached out to his wife shakily, but then realized someone else was in the room. He looked over and stared, expressionless, for a long time. Rett couldn't tell if he recognized him or not.

After what seemed like forever, Rett could see the recognition dawn in his eyes. He knew exactly who was in the room with him now.

His father said, "You're here."

But it wasn't spoken like it was a relief or a comfort. It was spoken like it was an accusation.

Rett was there, but why was he there? His dad hadn't changed. Two words and the expression on his father's face proved that.

And all of this was just ripping open wounds inside Rett that had taken years to heal. Years to get over. And now he was just starting them fresh again so he could feel like he was bleeding to death in front of his parents. Maybe that's what they wanted. Maybe that's why they convinced him to come. But his father didn't deserve that victory, not at Rett's expense.

Rett stared at him — a chalky shadow of the man he had known, lying in a hospital bed. But not even a heart attack, not even near-death had changed his mind or his heart.

Rett wasn't worth anything to him, and it wasn't going to change. His dad had had a major heart attack, and yet, standing there, Rett felt like it was his own heart that was trying to shut down. Felt like critical muscle tissue was dying from lack of blood supply. It felt like the night he had fled his own family had happened merely hours ago.

Rett forced himself to remember who he was since that night, what he had done. Seven years of busting his ass and living in near poverty to be where he was today. To have a life of his own that no one had handed to him. To have people in his life that actually fucking wanted him there.

At least this time, when he walked out the door, he'd have that life to go back to. He wouldn't be walking out into nothingness.

Rett's expression had not changed in the slightest, and when he opened his mouth, he had no idea how he was able to keep it calm and steady because, inside, it was like a bomb had gone off in his chest. And everything that he had become was splattered all over the room in a million pieces. But he managed it anyway — a calm, firm tone.

Rett dipped his head towards his father a tiny fraction and said, "That's right. I'm here."

They held each other's gaze for a moment, unblinking and with fixed expressions.

Rett said, fighting the overwhelming urge to drop his eyes from his father's stare, "I'm sorry you had a heart attack. I hope you get better."

And before his father could have a chance to see that he was lying, Rett turned around and walked out of the hospital room. He heard his father call his name hoarsely one time, but he didn't turn around or even slow down as he left.

When he got back in his car, Rett sat for a while. He didn't feel like crying, though. He remembered the look on his father's face, as cold and sterile as the hospital room he was lying in. It hurt, and yet it didn't hurt, either. It was the way things were, and things were unchanged. He had the confirmation of where things really stood that he had come to get.

But even as he cranked his car and left the hospital behind, he had to repeatedly tell himself he wasn't allowed to cry over that man. Not anymore.

Chapter 17

The trip to Dothan took more out of Rett than he realized it would. When he had gotten home afterwards, Cory was beside himself to be with him and to support him, but Rett really wanted to be alone. He spent that Sunday night at his own place to sort through how he felt over the whole thing. And in the end, all that sorting turned out to be a lot of wasted effort. The whole trip had amounted to revisiting something that Rett already knew — he was better off on his own. The biggest conclusion that he came to was that his initial reaction was right; he could have not even bothered going and had the same result.

The next four days were the MLB All-Star break, which was a welcome relief to Rett after not having hardly a real day off since he had started the job, and even more of a relief after the sour visit with his family in the hospital.

Cory wouldn't be kept away for long, and was there to pick Rett up first thing Monday morning so they could go get a big breakfast. Rett also found a used, dark taupe sofa on the internet that was in good condition, so they went and picked that up. The guy selling the sofa almost wet his pants when he saw Cory Pritchart there helping Rett get it, and took another $50 off the price of it if Cory gave him an autograph. Rett offered his own autograph for another $50 off, but the guy politely refused.

When they got the sofa up the stairs into Rett's apartment, Cory pulled his shorts down and said that, because of the discount, Rett now owed him $50 worth of head. This led to a back-and-forth negotiation over how much head amounted to $50 worth, which in turn led to five minutes or so of playful arguing over who gave head better. This turned into back-and-forth teasing about who gave head worse. And *that* took the form of smack talk along the lines of "you give head so bad all your tricks just want to go back to the phone sex," "Islam forbids giving head as bad as you do," "you give head so shitty I can finish five or six Sudoku puzzles in the time it takes you to get me off," and "well, you blow so bad I have to think about more erotic things like paying bills so I can shoot." This was followed by rigorous scientific sampling to see exactly who, empirically, gave the worst head. For over an hour. The results were inconclusive. But they both enjoyed the time trying to figure it out anyway.

The next day, Rett grumbled at having to watch the All-Star game with Cory. They only had a few days away from baseball and here they were, watching motherfucking baseball. But Cory insisted, and Rett hung out with him during the whole game. Cory tried to make a game out of figuring out which All-Star players he thought Rett would find good looking, but Rett didn't seem interested in any of them. When Cory asked Rett what he saw in him since he didn't seem to find ball players attractive, he was honest and said he didn't know, that he didn't have a type and just went with his gut. Guys were either attractive or they weren't.

As they watched the game, it got Rett wondering what attracted him to Cory. There was definitely something about his body that he liked, but Rett decided that Cory's face what the biggest physical draw. He was handsome, and while Cory's dad, Jerry, was very handsome, too, for someone his age, Cory's handsome was different. Cory had a boyish aspect to his face — a very gentle, true face — one that fit his personality. Rett realized that was what really attracted him; it was Cory's personality. For someone so large and imposing, Cory almost seemed small in some ways. Quiet, without being a wallflower. He was kind and thoughtful, but could joke around and tease easily, without ever being malicious. It was all the things that made *everyone* seem to like Cory.

On Wednesday, they drove down to Dauphin Island in the Gulf and spent some time goofing off in the water and on the beach. Rett scored a major victory while there when a couple of girls found him "too cute for his own good," but barely even noticed Cory. Cory consoled himself by trying to sell Rett to the girls for twenty bucks and then giving Rett a hard time when he couldn't even bring in a couple of sawbucks on the open market. In reality, Cory was relieved that he went the whole day without being recognized.

On the way back from the island, Cory got a call, but Rett, who only heard one side of it, couldn't tell what it was about, other than figuring out it was probably Jimmy on the phone.

When he hung up, Cory looked distant.

Rett asked, "What was that, Bigfoot? You look like your dog died."

Cory looked down at his lap sadly and said, "He did, kinda."

~~~~~

It wasn't until they showed up in Lawder that Rett found out the dog's name wasn't just Kicker, but Shit-Kicker. Rett was curious about why anyone in their right mind would name their dog Shit-Kicker, but knew better than to ask that particular question at the dog's memorial service. His job was to support Cory, who seemed genuinely upset over the loss of someone else's pet, and not to ask what was bound to be seen as a stupid and insensitive question. Rett wasn't quite able to identify with any of this since he had never had a pet growing up. Instead, he quietly assumed it must have been a very good dog.

He and Cory had gotten up early Thursday morning and had driven to Lawder. There, Jimmy and Brick were having a backyard memorial service so everyone could pay final respects to the yellow lab named Shit-Kicker. Rett had asked Cory if he needed to take a suit or anything, which only made Cory laugh at him. Cory got a punch in the arm for that since Rett had no idea how over the top Jimmy and Brick were going to go with this whole doggy memorial service.

If nothing else, Rett was fascinated to see the town where Cory grew up and the people he knew so well.

The memorial service, as it was, was held in the backyard of Jimmy and Brick's house. Their house was a nice two story one, slate blue in color with dark trim and a big porch across the front. The front yard was immaculately maintained without being overdone. In fact, Rett noticed a trellis of plain old honeysuckle on the side of the house facing the corner street. Cory had mentioned that it was the same house that Jimmy had grown up in, and now that he saw it, Rett wondered what Jimmy's parents were like. He remembered Zee mentioning their mom, but nothing about Rett's dad. He wondered if they knew Jimmy was gay and how they handled it if they did.

Besides Jimmy and Brick, Zee was there as well, along with another five or six people that apparently worked for the landscaping company that Jimmy and Brick owned. And Carrie Anne, Cory's mom, was there, but not Jerry. Cory's presence was almost cause for a celebration, though. All of these people knew him well, but hadn't seen him since he before had signed on with the Joes. Even for a somber occasion, they were happy to have Cory home. Rett was introduced around as being with the team and a good friend of Cory's, so he left it at that and didn't volunteer any more details about his relationship with Cory.

In the back yard, which was larger than Rett expected it to be, there was a hole dug for Kicker's remains near a Japanese maple and an ornamental fish pond. Everyone gathered around it informally to say goodbye to the dog they all knew so well.

Brick took a few moments to tell the story of how he had first gotten Kicker. He had been driving from Albany up to Lawder when he saw someone by the side of the road with car trouble. He stopped to see if there was any way he could help since they weren't near anything. He found an old man looking under the hood of his car, scratching his head at what was wrong and was giving him problems. Brick spent a few minutes poking around and found what he thought was the problem and asked the old man to try starting the car. It cranked up fine, and as the old man waved his hand in appreciation out his window to Brick, he told him he had left him payment on the seat of his truck. Brick walked over and looked into the cab, where there was a yellow puppy looking back up at him with his tail wagging. He yelled at the man before he drove too far away that he didn't want a puppy, and the old man had yelled back "You're welcome! His name's Shit-Kicker!"

Everyone laughed and Rett wondered how many times they had all heard that story. Brick got reflective and he said more seriously as he wiped at his eyes and then took Jimmy's hand in his, "People, and I include dogs in that category, come into your life sometimes and you got no idea how they got there or what it means. But it sneaks up on you one day, and you know... you know for damn certain, just how much emptier your life would have been without them. What can you do but thank God for what you were given? And remember what you had once they're gone."

Back inside, the others visited for a few moments while Brick, and Brick alone, filled in his dog's grave and said his final good-bye. Everyone else went back to their day, but Jimmy insisted that Cory, Rett and Carrie Anne stay for lunch with them.

Rett was expecting a sandwich or something, but Jimmy had fixed homemade meatloaf, mashed potatoes and a salad. When Cory saw what they were having, he grabbed Jimmy and gave him a big kiss and said, "My favorite!" He told Rett, "Jimmy's an awesome cook and his meatloaf is the fucking best!"

Carrie Anne smacked her son in the back of his head and warned him, "Language, Cory! How many times do I have to tell you?"

Cory replied, "A fucking shitload!" and had to tear off running through the house to escape his mom. Rett stood by and watched with strange wonder the sight of a huge, laughing Cory being chased by such a small Carrie Anne through the house.

They settled in at a big, rough-wood farmhouse-style table for lunch in the kitchen, and Rett had to agree that it was some of the best meatloaf he had ever had. Brick brought up the last game Cory pitched in and his chances against the Oakland A's in the upcoming series. He seemed glad to have the distraction from the loss of his dog. Carrie Anne picked at Cory's hair some and wondered when was the last time he had gotten a haircut. Zee offered to cut it for him, but Cory said, "I'll let you cut mine if you let me cut yours. And I get to go first." That rapidly dampened Zee's enthusiasm for the idea and she huffed at his proposal.

After lunch, back in the den, Cory stretched out on the sofa, his head in Brick's lap and his legs across Jimmy's lap. It made Rett feel good to see how comfortable Cory was with both Jimmy and Brick. Watching them this way made Rett understand better where Cory got his penchant for being very tactile with people he cared about. He also admired Carrie Anne and how completely comfortable she was with her son in the hands of these two men.

Cory lay across Jimmy and Brick and told them about the day before on Dauphin Island, Rett getting hit on while he was ignored, and then about helping Rett get a sofa. Rett started to worry, and wondered if he was going to tell them all about his visit to his father and all of the history behind that. He hadn't thought to tell Cory to not go into that with any of them. He didn't need to worry, though, because Cory stayed away from it all on his own.

Jimmy shook his head and glanced over at Carrie Anne, "Your mom and I need to still come back down at some point to finish getting some things for you. I need to come down anyway because there've been a few questions coming to George about sponsorship possibilities for you now that you got everyone's attention. Rett, I know how tight time is for you guys; if there's anything you need, too, just put it on a list and we'll get it."

It was a very nice offer and Rett appreciated it. "I think I'm pretty good. My friend Val picked up some stuff that I was still missing while she was in town over the weekend. And I feel right proper now that I have my very own sofa instead of having to be jealous of Cory's."

"Cory told us about Val. He said she was a really pretty girl. Very exotic looking," said Jimmy.

"Her family is Greek," replied Rett. "Soooo... if you consider hairy legs to be exotic, then, sure, exotic is a great way to describe her."

Cory looked over from Brick's lap and leaped to Val's defense, "She doesn't have hairy legs! God, they go round and round with each other like that non-stop! It's pretty scary to see it firsthand."

Brick had remained very quiet all during lunch and afterwards, but Rett supposed it was appropriate given what he had just gone through with the loss of his dog. Every once in a while Jimmy would reach over and put his hand behind Brick's neck to comfort him. Rett wondered how they got together; the two of them seemed, in some ways, like a mismatched couple. He decided to ask Cory about how they met one day.

Carrie Anne glanced at her watch and said, "Cory, there's a little league practice starting at 2:30. You ought to go by there for it. Coach Belton would love to see you and the kids would be thrilled if you showed up. And call your father and tell him you're going there... he may be able to meet you and say hello."

Cory pulled his phone out, called Jerry, and told him that he and Rett were going by the Little League practice. Rett heard Cory say, "Huh? Right now? Just laying across Brick and Jimmy's laps, letting lunch settle."

There was a pause and then Cory held the phone up into the air for Jimmy and Brick and said, "Dad says to stay put. He wants a turn in your lap."

Brick and Jimmy shouted "No!" in unison at the phone. Rett glanced at Carrie Anne to see how she would react to something like that, but she only rolled her eyes, apparently used to these antics from her husband, Jimmy, and Brick.

Cory said goodbye to his dad and went to sit up. He wound up sitting in Jimmy's lap, which was something to behold. Jimmy grunted loudly and said, "Jesus, Cory! What the hell have you been eating in Mobile? You feel like you've put on thirty pounds!"

Cory answered, "Nothing," at the same time Rett called out, "Crab claws!"

Cory shot Rett a dirty look for telling on him and then admitted, "Yeah, ok. Those crab claws are *everywhere* in Mobile."

Rett agreed this time, "He's not lying. They even put 'em in maple syrup and pour 'em over pancakes for breakfast."

Cory and Rett took a long time to say goodbye to their hosts, and offered again their sympathies for the loss of Kicker. Carrie Anne hugged and fussed over her son for a long time, both of them lingering over their goodbyes, which would have to hold Carrie Anne over until she could see her son in person again rather than on TV.

Before they got in Cory's truck, Carrie Anne reached up to place her hand on the side of her son's face and told him, "I'm so proud of you, Cory." She added in a whisper, "Even on your worst day, I'm more proud of you than you'll ever know."

Little League practice was in a dusty field set up for baseball and softball in one of the city parks near downtown. It reminded Rett a lot of the field by the junior high school in Mobile where they had kissed the first time, except this one had a few worn bleachers set up behind the backstop fence.

Coach Belton recognized Cory right away and embraced him warmly. The little kids weren't sure who he was at first, but when Coach Belton explained, they turned awestruck. When Cory said he was going to spend practice with them, they all went nuts.

After Cory introduced Rett to Coach Belton, Rett settled in to the bleacher seats to watch the practice for the next hour. He found it fascinating to watch Cory with the kids. They seemed a little leery of him at first, but after a few minutes, they were all over him. They started out with some hitting practice, with Cory making sure the kids held the bat right, watched the ball, and followed through on their swing.

Sitting in the stands under the south Georgia sun also reminded Rett of his own turn in baseball, probably when he was only a little older than the kids he was watching right then. It had been one of the very brief attempts by his dad to get Rett involved in sports. But after the coach had come to have a one-on-one chat with his father about how Rett wasn't cut out for it, Rett didn't have to go to baseball practice anymore. He wondered if any of the kids out there was a small version of him, forced into Little League to satisfy a father that would likely never be satisfied. He watched the kids to see if there were any that obviously didn't want to be there, off to the side or hanging back, but these little guys seemed all for it.

About halfway through practice, a dark SUV drove up and parked next to Cory's truck. Jerry got out, dressed in a full police uniform, and walked towards the bleachers. Rett tried to picture that same man lying in Brick's and Jimmy's laps and simply couldn't do it. He had a hard time even picturing this man joking about it, but knew that it was just like him at the same time.

Jerry waved to his son out on the ball field in a crowd of kids that were barely half Cory's height, like a big scarecrow sticking up out of an excited, raucous field of young corn plants. Cory started to come over to see his dad as he climbed up in the stands to where Rett was, but Jerry waved him back out onto the field with the kids.

Even with all the space in the stands around them, Jerry insisted on sitting right up against Rett.

Jerry said, "Thanks for coming with him, Rett. I know it means a lot to Jimmy and Brick as well."

Rett replied that he was glad to be there.

"I used to accuse them of treating Kicker better than they treated Zee," said Jerry. "That got me nowhere but in deep hot water, let me tell you." He grinned at the memory.

"Then I accused them of treating Kicker better than they treated me. They all nodded in agreement for that one, Cory and Carrie Anne included. If respect had calories, Rett, I'd be starving to death in this group."

Rett surprised himself and he said, "You know, Jerry, I don't think I believe that for even one second."

Jerry smiled at him and shrugged maybe, maybe-not. Out on the field, the team had switched from hitting practice to pitching, Cory's specialty, and he was showing them a few real-live MLB pitches with Coach Belton catching. Even so, Rett could tell that Cory was seriously holding back on his pitches for Coach Belton's benefit. He thought back to Sebastion saying how he could tell just by watching, and Rett got it now. He was rather proud to find he had developed some of that sense without even realizing it.

Jerry said, "I'm glad you're with Cory, Rett."

"A little road trip was good," replied Rett. "Plus, I was interested to see Cory's hometown."

Jerry looked over at him more seriously and said, "No. More than just today. I'm glad you're with Cory."

Rett never expected to have this kind of conversation with a Chief of Police about screwing around with his son, even if it wasn't *just* screwing around. But Jerry had been one surprise after another for Rett. He looked at man next to him curiously.

"I worry about Cory, of course. I worry about him being too single-minded on baseball a lot of the time," said Jerry. "He's given up a fair amount of his life to focus on and succeed at baseball, and I know he loves it. But I don't want him to miss out on other important things, either. I don't want him to eventually look back and regret missing out on other important parts of life."

Jerry studied the field with his dark eyes. "Having you around has been good for him, Rett. You get his mind out of the glove some, and he needs that."

Rett's mind drifted for a moment to his father lying in the hospital bed. He asked, "Would you have been disappointed in Cory if he hadn't made it as far in baseball as he has?"

Jerry took a deep breath and continued to watch his son, who was now on his knees showing the kids how grip the ball for various pitches and helping them get it right. He said, "Once upon a time, Cory was afraid to death of what I would think of him, what Carrie Anne and I *might* think of him, that he was going to disappoint us. And it pulled him away."

Jerry started to bite at his thumbnail with the memory. "I can't even begin to tell you the pain that caused me. And I had no idea what was happening, what was causing it, what was going on. That fear of what I would think of him, of disappointing us, of not measuring up to some standard he imagined we had, caused him to drift away from us. All I saw was this ever-widening gap between us and I felt like I was dying because I didn't understand it and didn't know what to do to fix it. I was helpless and Cory got farther and farther away every day, it felt like."

Jerry frowned and had to pause for a moment to keep his voice steady. He looked down at his feet.

"I thank God every day that Jimmy was there to bring him back to us. To show all of us what we needed to see. Jimmy was the one that showed all of us how expectations, real or imagined, can ruin a family so easily. How even the idea of conditional love can tear people apart. Do you know what I mean, Rett?"

Rett knew it all too well. "Yeah, I do. My own dad was kind of a ball-buster." He said it off-handed, trying to minimize it.

Jerry looked at Rett out of the corner of his eye, questioning him.

Rett sighed and said, "My own dad had lots of expectations for me. All *very* explicit. And pretty much none of which I met." He really didn't want to get into this with Jerry, but he was the one that originally brought it all up.

"I get the feeling," said Jerry, "that there's a lot more to this than what you're saying. But I won't make you go into it. I think that, now, maybe I do understand the little bit of mistrust vibe I get from you, though."

Rett didn't want him thinking that and he reacted, "It's not that I don't trust..."

"It's ok, Rett." said Jerry, matter-of-factly, "When I've fully earned it, I'll have it."

Cory had taken a catcher's position not far from the kids and they were taking turns pitching to him.

"I look out there at Cory, now a man as big as I am," continued Jerry. "Not nearly as good-looking, of course... but probably a lot smarter and definitely much kinder. I see Cory out there right now, or I watch him on the mound pitching against the Orioles, throwing a ball a hundred miles an hour, and all I see is my tiny son. I see him as a tiny baby still small enough to fit in my hands at the hospital, or crying with both knees scraped when learning to ride a bike, or grinning when hitting the ball off a T for the first time, helping out at a car wash for the high school baseball team just so he can be around the big guys. Or... or telling me he's gay and his eyes... *begging* me to still love him. As if... I... as if I could ever do anything else."

Jerry had to stop again, close his eyes, and wipe at them to pull himself back under control.

"He's a big man now, Rett, but all I see is that tiny little boy. My son. I just want him to be happy. However that comes to him. I just... want to see him happy."

They sat in silence and watched Cory with the kids. It was starting to look less like practice and more like a lot of horsing around out on the field.

Rett cleared his throat and said, "You're not... You're just not what I expected at all, Jerry. Not anything like my own dad. I expected you to be pushing him harder than anyone."

Jerry shrugged. "I won't say I haven't made my mistakes. I want him to succeed, but on his own terms."

Jerry grinned and looked at Rett, "When Cory was small, I used to sing 'Itsy Bitsy Spider' to him. You know the song?"

Before Rett had a chance to answer, Jerry was singing the song, accompanying it with the hand motions and all:

The itsy-bitsy spider
climbed up the water spout
Down came the rain
and washed the spider out
Out came the sun
and dried up all the rain
And the itsy-bitsy spider
Climbed up the spout again

When he finished, Rett laughed loudly at the sight of Jerry, in full police uniform, singing "Itsy Bitsy Spider" horribly off-key. He told him, "Yeah, Jerry, with that voice, if anyone offers you a recording contract? It's a dirty trick. A cruel, dirty trick."

Jerry and Rett laughed together and Cory looked their way to see what was so funny before being tackled by two or three of the boys again. He was dragged back down into the dirty, dusty wrestling match the practice had degenerated into while Coach Belton stood aside and let them all have their fun.

Jerry said, his eyes still watching his son closely, "I sang that to him to remind him, to teach him, that it's ok to mess up, to have setbacks. But maybe it was more to remind myself that it's ok to mess up, that it's ok to fail. You just pick yourself up and try again. Sure, I probably screwed up plenty of times or pushed him in ways I shouldn't have. Mostly I just needed the chance to fix it. We all fuck it up some. It's what we do *after* that that matters. Part of being a man is knowing when you're wrong, admitting it, and fixing it. As long as Cory gives me a chance, I'll figure out I'm wrong and fix it. He gets his patience from his mom, thankfully. Well, his mom and Brick, both, I think."

Jerry squinted and said distantly, "People always seem to think of parent-child relationships as being one-way streets, and maybe they start out that way. But somewhere in there, they turn into two-way streets. There has to be give and take both ways. And both sides have to figure that out at some point for it to really work."

If Jerry was waiting for the point when he had earned Rett's trust, he earned it sitting on those bleachers at Little League practice. He earned both Rett's trust and respect. Cory had been so lucky and so blessed with so much in his life, and Rett felt like he had had so little in comparison. It made Rett feel like he had grown up in dire poverty, not material or financial, but emotional. Seeing how rich it was for Cory growing up made him understand how lacking it was for himself. It made the pain of the Sunday before all the sharper.

All that Jerry had said now weighed even heavier against the words from Rett's own father — "Everything I did to make a man out of you was nothing but a fucking waste of time."

Coach Belton rallied his troops and pulled them off of Cory, making them all thank their guest coach for the day before thanking Cory personally himself.

Cory walked over to the bleachers, shaking dirt off of himself on the way, and hugged his father, getting a layer of sweat and dust all over Jerry's pristine uniform. The grin on Cory's face indicated that he knew exactly what he was doing when he hugged his dad, but it didn't seem to bother Jerry in the least.

They sat back down on the bleachers, with Rett somehow winding up stuck in the middle of the two oversized men. Cory wiped at the sweaty dirt on his face and said happily, "Well, that was awesome! I'll have to do that again next time I'm back home!"

Rett let Cory and his father talk for a while without interrupting. He sat squished in-between the two of them, intentionally he was sure, and felt deep inside himself the lack of that kind of relationship with his own family in his own life. And it hurt.

Chapter 18

Cory wrinkled his nose and said, "You call this toast? It's barely warm! And what the hell kind of marmalade is this?"

Rett went to take the trash-talked breakfast away from Cory and grabbed at the plate, but Cory kept it out of Rett's reach and continued to eat.

Rett said, "This, from the guy that, after I made a crack about crab claws on pancakes, sincerely wondered if maybe that might be a good thing to try. And don't say 'marmalade.' That's gotta be the gayest word in the world."

"Some places serve fried chicken and waffles. Would crab claws on pancakes be all that different? I like the plates that Val picked out for you, by the way," said Cory with his mouth full. He added, "'Marmalade's' not gay!"

Rett said, "It is when *you* say it!"

"You wanna know what's even gayer no matter who says it?"

Rett looked at him disinterestedly.

"Everett Dougherty," said Cory insolently, stuffing the last piece of his toast into his mouth.

Rett ignored Cory's silly, satisfied grin and took their plates into his kitchen.

"When's Val getting here? I don't want to miss her before I have to go in," asked Cory.

"Any minute I assume. She was turning off the highway when you were finishing up in the bathroom."

Rett's door burst open and Val came in with a large cardboard box in her arms.

"Not just any minute! But this exact minute! Lucky you!" she said cheerfully, setting the box on the floor and kicking it over into the corner indiscriminately. "And man, Cory was right when he overheard you and Mike. You can hear everything outside that door. Anyway, here's the rest of your crap that you forgot. I kept the incriminating stuff because, you know, I'm gonna blackmail you one of these days. Sooooo... hurry up and make some money."

Val threw herself onto the sofa next to Cory and gave him a kiss on the cheek.

"I like the beard," she told him, touching it. "Rett said you were favoring one with no mustache lately. I like how it creeps up the corners of your mouth a little, though. It looks great!"

"I have to do it for him," said Rett. "If he does it himself, he looks like he glued razor blades to a schizophrenic cat and rubbed it around on his face."

Val ran her hands over the sofa seats. "I like the sofa, too. 'Bout time you got one!"

Cory got a dirty grin and said, "We broke it in real good last week over the break."

"Oh, thank God!" said Val, visibly relieved. "Because if you bought it with all this crusty stuff already on the cushions, I was going to be seriously heebie-jeebied."

"Any of it that feels fresh and sticky," said Cory, "is probably just spilled marmalade from the toast this morning."

Val pursed her lips and instructed him, "Don't say that word. Wayyyyy too gay for you to be saying."

Cory leaned his head back and held his arms out wide, like an opera singer at the climax of an aria. "Maaaaahmahlade!" he sang, letting the word roll off of his tongue luxuriously, majestically.

"And, wow!" exclaimed Val, "You've managed to make the gayest word in the English language one hundred percent faggier! Congratulations! Your dad would be so proud!"

"You haven't met his dad," said Rett. "He probably would."

"Ok, I've got to go on and drive in to the Portyards. Val, I'm sorry you're not staying tonight for the game." Cory got up and grabbed Rett while he was finishing cleaning up in the kitchen. He held Rett from behind and kissed him several times on the neck. Rett was ornery and fought him for a moment before giving in and kissing him back on the lips more seriously.

"Don't push me away, Rett. You're all I've got," whispered Cory in his ear, teasing him gently.

"You've got no idea how much you've got," said Rett, a little miffed.

Cory held onto Rett for a moment, doing nothing more than keeping his arms tight around him and looking at him with a smile on his face, before he forced himself to let go so he could leave.

"Aww, why do you have to leave already?" said Val, disappointed.

"New publicity shots. They want to switch over to video clips of him holding the ball up in the air like has become his signature," said Rett. "I'll see you in a little bit, Cory."

Cory headed out the apartment door and Val called after him, "Go get 'em, Chunk Style!"

"Don't call me that!" called Cory as his feet pounded down the stairs outside the apartment.

"I can think up something worse!" yelled Val.

"Chunk Style is fine!"

Val said to Rett, "Can I just say again how you totally don't deserve him? I do, though. I should have Cory! He *will* be mine! Him and Josh. And I'll keep Tony around to clean the bathroom."

Rett barely grunted in reply.

Val closed the apartment door and studied Rett, who was leaning against the kitchen counter with his arms folded across his chest.

"You have the Moon Pies I demanded in exchange for your stuff? Unmarked and with non-sequential serial numbers?" asked Val.

Rett pointed to a bag at the end of the counter with the five or six Moon Pies that Val was referring to. She watched Rett's body language closely for a moment.

"What?" she said, ignoring the Moon Pies. "What's got your butt so puckered?"

"Nothing."

Rett crossed over to the doorway to the bedroom where Cory had forgotten his overnight bag and moved it over to the front door so he'd remember to take it in to work with him.

Val heaved a sigh and said, "Fine, I admit it. I didn't wear any panties today. I didn't think it would hurt for Cory to get a tiny glimpse of what he was missing out on!"

"You mean trailer trash?" asked Rett. Trash talk was better than getting into what was really on his mind.

Val sucked on her finger and nodded at Rett with a seductive grin. She slapped each ass-cheek once and said, "Everybody loves a double-wide!"

Rett frowned even further and ignored her behavior. He said, "I was really looking forward to you spending at least *one* night down here. Instead, you swing by just long enough to dump my crap off, grab your Moon Pies and run."

Val said, "Tony had to..."

Rett blurted, "Tony's already putting a leash on you."

Val's brow knitted. "Are you fucking kidding me?! Tony's *dying* to come down here! He's chomping at the chance to meet *your* best friend, Cory! He just couldn't come this weekend because he was backed up with a lot of work stuff. And he and I are starting something good. What the hell are you even talking about?"

"I don't think this Tony thing is going to work out, Val. I don't think he's right for you," he said.

Val said, "Why are you dumping on Tony now? You like Tony!"

Rett plopped down in the chair across from the sofa and sulked. He had no idea what to say. He didn't like the way Val was changing everything between them.

"I miss you."

"You're jealous!" exclaimed Val, finally understanding. "*You're* the one that moved, remember? I didn't run out on you, Rett!" she charged.

"I didn't run out on you, Val!" said Rett.

"You know what I mean! You almost act like I'm supposed to keep our relationship *exactly* like it was, even after *you* moved 200 miles away!"

He may have been the one that opened this conversation, but he couldn't deal with it anymore. He got up, grabbed the bag of Moon Pies and shoved them at Val. *Was* he jealous? Was that what was going on in his mind? He didn't like this feeling like he was slowly losing Val. He wished he hadn't brought it up; these kinds of conversations always went badly for him.

"I can't get into this now, I've got to go on in to work. Why don't you go ahead and leave?"

"Bullshit!" barked Val. "You don't have to be there for at least another hour. You got a problem with me, Rett? Spit it out! Don't run and hide now! *I* don't have a problem with *your* life here. Cory and his friends and family. I'm *glad* you've got them."

"You don't know anything about what it's like being around them," snorted Rett. Then he wondered why he had said that. They had been really great to him, all of them. Why had he said that like he resented being around them?

"Then tell me! God, you do this all the time, Rett, right when things get a little too thick or rough..."

Both of them stopped talking because there was a knock at the door.

Rett rolled his eyes. Why was Cory knocking just so he could come back in and grab his overnight bag? Rett yelled, "Come on in! I put it right by the door for you!" Secretly, he was glad Cory had come back to interrupt this whole conversation. Anything to drop it now.

There was a pause before the door opened slowly.

Rett froze, every drop of blood in his face draining out, and Val turned around to look.

"Oh my God..." said Val in total shock. "It's like there's two of you!"

The person in the door, Rett, and Val stayed rooted in place for several seconds. No motion. Hardly even a drawn breath stirring the air.

"Rett?" said the visitor.

"Bo?" said Rett, utter disbelief in his voice.

The things that went through Rett's mind when he saw his younger brother standing cautiously in his doorway were staggering. It overwhelmed him and he had to sit back down in the chair, not taking his eyes off the face of the person standing in his apartment. He was older and bigger now, the same size as Rett. They looked remarkably alike, even if Bo's golden hair was cut longer than Rett's. But the eyes, nose, mouth, even the chin, were almost identical. Even the black knit shirt and long tan shorts looked like something Rett would wear. But where Rett still had some freckles on his face, the ones Bo had when he was younger had faded away.

Ever since Rett had gotten a call from his mother about his dad's heart attack, he had wondered what it would be like to see his brother again. He'd wondered what he'd say to him. He had gone through a million things he wanted to say, none of it really quite getting to the heart of what Rett felt. He had missed him, but that was a simplification of it. To say a part of him was missing was closer to the truth. But with Bo suddenly in front of him, all the words and thoughts escaped him — wisps of smoke out the chimney and disappearing into the sky.

The last time he had seen him, Bo had still been a child, 14 years old and as small as Rett had been at that age. Now his brother had grown into a man. Rett felt proud, and fascinated, to see him this way, but also like he no longer knew anything about him. The kid was gone and in his place was a young man. Rett wanted to grab him and hold him and tell him how good he looked, how much he missed him, how he had thought about him more than anyone. He wanted to erase the last seven years away from his brother as fast as possible.

But he couldn't. There, in Bo's face, there was a defensiveness. Rett could see it because he knew he had the same look in his own face when he had walked into the hospital room to see his father.

Rett finally found his voice and whispered, "Bo... Jesus, Bo! It's good to see you!"

Bo flinched but stepped into the room a little further and closed the door behind him. "Is it?" he asked.

The question stung Rett, but he said, "Yeah, Bo. Of course it is!"

Val sat unmoving on the sofa, watching this unfold. Mesmerized by how much the two brothers looked alike. Captivated at being able to see Rett's brother in person for the first time.

Bo's face still expressed significant doubt.

"You mean more to me than anyone else in that family!" said Rett.

He stood up, no longer able to sit still with his brother a few mere feet away from him after all the years. He wanted to have a brother again so bad he couldn't remain in the chair.

But Rett stopped when he saw Bo draw back a step, keeping the distance between them. It was like an ice pick in the chest. It cut Rett to see him doing the same thing he had done to his mother in the hospital room. Had his mother felt the same way when he did it to her?

"You came to the hospital. To see dad," said his brother.

Rett glanced at Val for a split second knowing the pressure that she had put on him to go. Bo seemed to take no notice of Val being in the room at all.

"I thought I needed to. I thought it was the right thing to do. I thought... that... maybe things had changed some," he said. He looked down at his feet. "But it didn't feel like anything was different, Bo. I couldn't be there with him. I couldn't even stay in the same room with him."

Rett gave a pained grin, pleading with Bo for him to understand.

Bo stood up a little straighter. "You think I don't know what he's like?" he asked sharply.

That stung Rett again, and he gritted his teeth at the pain of that question.

"You left a note, se..." Bo paused, his chest starting to heave as the emotion rose up in him and he had to start over. "You left a note, seven years ago, saying you gave a damn about me. But you left, Rett! You left me behind with that man! You think I don't know what he's like? I know better than you do! You left me to deal with the two of them alone! Yeah, I always could manage him better than you and you caught it worse from him than I did."

Bo's voice rose and his eyes were boring into him, narrowed in pain. "But that doesn't mean I didn't put up with a lot of his shit or that it was easy!"

Bo wiped across his eyes nervously. Rett was unable to even move, unable to even blink. Every accusation of Bo's felt like a slash across his body with a razor blade.

"You left a note saying I was the only one you gave a damn about, Rett!" shouted Bo, now crying. "If you gave such a *fucking damn* about me, why did I never hear from you? Why was I left behind in the fucking dust you kicked up getting out of that house as fast as you could go? Huh? The one person that was always there for me just... disappeared!"

A cold sweat began to form all over Rett's face and hands. He never expected Bo to feel like this. He never expected Bo to put up with their father the way he had. How could he possibly answer that question?

"I, uh..." stammered Rett. "I couldn't stay, Bo. Once it came out. Once *I* came out. I couldn't be gay and stay in that house. I wasn't wanted!"

"*I wanted you there, Rett!*"

The tears were flowing freely out of Bo's eyes. Rett put his hand to his face and realized he was crying, too. He never understood how deeply Bo felt about him, until now.

Even though his voice was cracking and it was broken by sobs, Bo cried, "All I know is I wanted my brother there. Every day I wanted my brother back! I loved you! I *still* want my brother back. Even all these years later, I miss my brother! I don't give a fuck about gay or straight! *I miss my brother!*"

Bo looked at his feet and the tears falling on them from his eyes. "But you never wanted me! That's how it felt, Rett. From that day forward, all I knew was that I wasn't worth hanging around for!"

Val interjected and said, "Your dad kicked him out! He *couldn't* stay!"

Rett held up his hand at Val to tell her to stay out of it, but Bo shouted, "*No one kicked him out!* He just left! You just disappeared and left me there by myself! You left a note like I meant something to you. But seven years and I never heard anything from you. Nothing!"

"Bo," said Rett, "I thought it was better to stay away. I thought it would be easier on you, on all of you, if I was really gone. You guys... you didn't contact me, either."

Bo shouted, "*Not when you fucking hid from us so well!* From me! Mom tried to. I tried to. But there were no utility records, no phone account, nothing! Once mom finally got on some medication, she looked for you! I did, too! You made damn sure we couldn't find you, and you want to blame *me* for not contacting you?"

Rett choked on the realization. He *had* hidden from them. Everything had been in Val's name until he moved to Mobile.

"I'm sorry, Bo. I didn't... I wasn't... I, uh... uh..." Rett fell over himself trying to figure out why he hadn't tried to reach Bo in seven years. At least Bo if not anyone else. But anything he tried to say just backed up in his throat, caught there and stopped his voice, until there was nothing but a jumbled, nonsensical clog of meaningless words.

Bo sniffed a few times loudly, trying to regain his control. He said, "When dad had his heart attack and mom tried again and finally managed to find a cell number for you, she said you would consider coming by. I was happy. I was *so happy* at the thought that maybe I'd get to see you. My big brother. I'd maybe get to see my big brother." Bo smiled under his damp, red eyes at the thought.

"But I missed you by just a few minutes. Just a few minutes. You couldn't stay just a few minutes for me. I wasn't worth a few minutes of your time."

"No," said Rett, shaking his head. "That's not true, Bo! I should have, yes. You're right. But after seeing dad, hearing that same tone in his voice even years later... You don't know what it felt like."

"You could have told me," said Bo weakly. "And I would have listened."

Bo stared off vacantly and Rett tried to figure out what to say. Tried to put words together that would make Bo understand, but he felt so ruined, and empty, and helpless that he couldn't do anything.

Bo held his arms out and gestured around the apartment limply. "You're ok, though. That's good. I can at least let mom know that."

Bo turned and put his hand on the doorknob and Rett let him. Rett still had no idea how to make amends for what he had done wrong. To make Bo see his point of view. To bridge a crevasse that was now seven years too wide.

"You look great, Bo," said Rett, grasping at any straw he could lay his hands on. And the only one he could find was as pathetic and ridiculous as that.

Bo opened the door and stepped out. He said emptily, "So do you, Rett. You look... like you don't need us. I guess you never did." There was a deep sadness in his voice as he spoke the words.

Bo closed the door behind him. Rett was unable to move, pinned down by the crushing weight of Bo's words and the sadness in his voice. It wasn't until there was a slight motion from Val, freeing him, that he sprang for the door and threw it open. He called after Bo a few times, trying to get him to come back, but his brother was already in his truck.

Rett stood on the landing outside his apartment door as his brother's small, red pickup drove off down the street.

Val cleared her throat softly inside the den and Rett looked over at her.

"Are you ok?" she asked.

"I don't know."

What Rett did know was that he didn't feel like he deserved Bo.

~~~~~

The day would have been painful for Rett, but he was in such a stupor from that morning that the day barely even registered with him. It was bad enough to have Val mad at him because he expressed his opinion that she was drawing away from him, but that had been vastly overshadowed by what had happened with Bo.

Cory was pitching that night, and so Rett avoided him as much as possible during the day and didn't say anything about the events of that morning.

He was in such a fog, he hardly even noticed when Skunk insisted he tape his leg again, despite there being nothing wrong with it whatsoever. Rett couldn't even manage to be annoyed by Skunk's childish behavior. He went to work taping Skunk's leg the way he had been asked, in the meantime thinking about Bo and how much it had hurt to see him again, only to watch his brother turn around, walk out the door, and drive away.

He didn't even realize Skunk was talking to him until Luis and Satoru came into the locker room arguing with each other, again. Rett, and the whole team, had to occasionally listen to those two get into it over nothing. But that was when he realized Skunk had been talking to him.

He managed to hear Skunk say, "...not that you'd be able to get pussy like that. But I'll do you a solid, you can have some secondhand." Skunk pulled the pouch on his jockstrap down so his dick and balls flopped out right in front of Rett's face. He pulled on his dick once for Rett's benefit.

Skunk said, "I fucked her just a little while ago in the downstairs equipment room. I bet even a pocket fag like you can smell her pussy on my dick!"

Rett didn't flinch. He didn't draw back. He didn't roll his eyes. He continued putting the Kinesio tape on Skunk's leg and ignored the rest of him. He said calmly, "Did she douche right before you fucked her? Because the only thing I smell is douchebag."

Skunk pulled his jockstrap back up and pulled away from Rett. He shouted at him, "You goddamn faggot! You're just a fucking queer! I get more pussy in one week than you'll get in your whole lifetime! Are you even man enough to know what to do with a pussy if you got one?"

Rett didn't care about Skunk or his shouting. He collected his tape and scissors, turned his back on Skunk and walked away, unfazed by the rest of Skunk's shouts and curses. Arthur, who had been changing, walked over to Skunk and shouted at him to knock it off or he was going to go to Ahab and George with how he had treated Rett. Rett didn't stay around to see how it turned out. He didn't care how it turned out.

JJ found Rett a few minutes later working with Brian Thorn, who was still on the Disabled List, in the training room. He was gently putting Brian's shoulder through some passive motion therapy. JJ was pretty burned up about Skunk, and Rett asked Brian to hang out for a minute while he talked to JJ. He took JJ into his office while none of the other trainers were in there and they had some privacy.

JJ started pacing and said, "That shithead's gotta go, Rett. He can't do this shit!"

Rett pushed his laptop off to the side and leaned against his desk. He didn't want to talk about it, didn't want to think about it, and had already forgotten about it entirely. But he couldn't leave JJ worked up like this, either.

He said, "JJ, you can ignore it when he spews his racist bile at you. I can ignore it when he tries to dig into me. Believe me, he is the last thing on my mind today. Let it go, man."

JJ watched Rett carefully to try to gauge if he was really ok, or just hiding it. He must have decided Rett was really ok, because he asked with a sly grin, "Did you really ask him if his girl had douched because all you smelled was douchebag?"

Rett said distantly, "It just came out."

"You ok? You seem a little out of it compared to your usual self."

"Just some stuff going on. That's partly why I don't give a fuzzy rat's ass about Skunk's bullshit today."

"You know, little man, you can talk to me about anything. You just let me know."

Rett nodded, feeling a little more encouraged for the first time that day. He slapped JJ on the shoulder a few times, tired and worn down from the day that was still a weight around his neck and said, "Let me get back to Brian, JJ. I'll see you later."

The hardest part was after practice, right before the game. Cory tracked Rett down in the trainers' office before he went into the player's lounge to focus himself. Rett had to put on more of a happy face for him and he didn't look forward to the effort.

Cory said, "Am I the last one to hear about Skunk screaming at you today in the locker room? Why haven't you said anything to me, Rett?"

Rett shook his head and said, "He's the same asshole to me that he is to everybody. It'll take a hell of a lot more than his school-girl tantrums before I feel the need to call in the big guns. You psyched up for the A's tonight?" He wanted to change the subject as soon as possible.

"As ready as I'll ever be, I guess. You gonna watch from the bullpen or your cheap seats tonight?"

"Cheap seats, probably. I may have to find somewhere even cheaper to sit, though. For some strange reason, games sell more when you're pitching, Bigfoot."

Cory grinned like he always did when Rett called him Bigfoot.

Rett wished him luck and pushed him out the door to go meditate before the game. He did it more for himself than for Cory, though. Just that tiny amount of acting normal had been a huge struggle for him and he knew he wouldn't be able to keep it up for much longer. He sat down in his chair and stared vacantly at his desk for a long time.

In his mind, he heard Bo telling him, "You could have told me. And I would have listened." If he had waited only a few more minutes in the hospital, he would have had Bo's full forgiveness.

If he had just waited a few more minutes.

~~~~~

Cory pitched all nine innings that night and did a spectacular job against the Oakland A's. He gave up only three hits in the entire game, but it was a walk to base that wound up turning into a run for Oakland. Still, the Joes beat the A's 3 to 1 that evening.

Back at Cory's apartment after the game, Rett almost still didn't tell him what had happened because Cory was in such a good mood. He hated being the anchor dragging down his high, but he knew Cory would want to know about it, too. When he said the words, "My brother Bo showed up at my apartment today," it was like a bomb had gone off.

Cory didn't say a word. He stretched out across the navy blue leather of his sofa, leaning up against one end. He pulled Rett onto his chest, wrapped his arms around him and held him tightly, stroking Rett's forearms.

"Tell me exactly what happened," said Cory seriously, his nose and lips buried in Rett's light amber hair.

Rett recounted the entire conversation, starting with Val getting upset with him, through Bo showing up and then leaving. Cory listened patiently, not interrupting him or prompting him.

When he finished, Cory said, "Why didn't you tell me this, Rett? Why did you wait until now?"

Rett sat up on the sofa. He wound up leaning against one of Cory's legs and with the other one stretched across his lap. He was about to answer when Cory asked, "Don't you trust me with this?"

Rett took a deep breath. First Val, then Bo, and now Cory seemed pissed off as well. Rett thought to himself, *throw Skunk on the pile and I'm batting oh-fer today.*

"It's definitely *not* that I don't trust you, Cory. You were pitching tonight, and I didn't want any of this distracting you. What you're doing is hard enough."

Cory pulled his leg out from behind Rett and sat up next to him. He said, "That's crap! I'd rather you not make that decision for me, Rett."

Rett sighed. He could hardly remember a day he wanted to be over more than this one. "I needed time to sort through it myself, too, you know. I needed time to deal with my own... family... in my own way. It's nothing about you. Really." Why did it feel to Rett like he was using the word "family" where it no longer applied? That made him feel even more gummed up inside. He leaned forward on the couch and rested his chin in his hand, wondering if he had really lost his one chance at having Bo back in his life.

Cory rubbed Rett's back with his strong hand. "You're right, Rett. I'm sorry. You've been through a lot today. But you gotta know... if it's important to *you*, it's important to *me*."

"I'm just worn down," said Rett. "I'm worn down from everyone being mad at me today. And the truth is, I can't say that they don't deserve to be. Val left still kind of mad at me this morning, I probably fucked up my one chance to have a brother again, and you're unhappy because I held this back from you. It's just been a bad day."

Cory grabbed Rett's hand and stood up, pulling Rett up with him, and led him across the dark concrete towards the door.

"Where are we going?" asked Rett, tiredly. He didn't feel like going out anywhere.

"You and I are gonna go out to the field and we're gonna toss the ball around a little. You and me, chief. Just the two of us."

Cory put Rett in his truck and drove them down to the field next to the junior high school. He put a baseball in Rett's hand and they walked out onto the field. The streets were quiet for a Saturday night, save for an occasional car driving by and paying them no attention. A quarter moon hung in the sky and Rett could smell the dust and grass of the field.

Rett threw the ball to Cory and started to say, "I don't know if I should try..."

"Shhhh, Rett. Just toss the ball and forget about everything else for a while. It's just you and me and the ball. Let go of everything else."

Once again, Rett found himself throwing the ball easily, back and forth, with Cory. Back and forth. It was quiet on the field, broken only by the regular sound of the ball landing in their hands when they caught it. Back and forth. And with the steady, repeated motion, Rett felt the day slide off of him some.

He allowed himself to concentrate solely on Cory, standing twenty feet away, illuminated by the moon and the faint streetlight on the corner. He watched him torque lightly on his sneakers to gently toss the ball to Rett, his chest and arms barely even registering the effort, even after nine innings that night. He smelled the dry grass of summer, felt the warm air around him, and kept his eyes on Cory. Back and forth. Both of them letting the ball focus themselves on each other and nothing else.

Val, Bo, his family... none of that would change drastically in the next half hour or so, so Rett allowed it to slip from his mind. He and Cory held each other's gaze while the ball passed between them. Until it was just them and a ball. And nothing else.

Rett caught the ball and held it. He walked over to Cory, and without a word, wrapped his arms around him, embracing him tightly, clinging to him. He closed his eyes and gripped Cory, allowing his head to fall and rest on Cory's shoulder. Cory put his arms around Rett and held him back. They held onto each other and rocked slightly in place.

Back and forth.

Just the two of them.

Chapter 19

The view in Los Angeles wasn't as cool as what Rett hoped it would be. Well, it wasn't even actually Los Angeles. They were in Anaheim for the series against the Angels instead of Los Angeles proper. He wasn't even sure how much different LA would look from the view he had now, except none of it looked like the LA they showed on TV. Which was another way of saying he couldn't see the Hollywood sign or the beach from his hotel room window. What he did see when he looked out his window was a sprawling series of big box stores, gas stations, hotels, and strip malls as far as his eye could reach. Disneyland was supposed to be somewhere nearby, but he couldn't see it.

He wasn't focused much on the bland view, though, anyway. Like the last seven days, he saw Bo again in his head, now grown up. In some ways, he was proud that Bo looked as much like him as he did; his brother had turned out very handsome. Ironically, his little brother was probably the most "authentic" man in the family. But in some ways it made him feel worse; he didn't feel worthy of looking like his younger brother. And these days, after his brother's surprise visit the preceding Saturday, just how much he had let his younger brother down bored into him every day. He felt no particular remorse over walking out on his parents a second time, but hearing how much he had hurt Bo in his own rush to leave the house and abandon his parents felt like the air being sucked out of his lungs. It felt like that every time he thought about it.

Part of him wanted to try to contact Bo again, to apologize again, to maybe help him see *his* point of view, the same way Bo had made him see his. That idea made his palms sweat and his heart race, and instead, he tried hoping that maybe giving Bo some space and letting him decide for himself, especially now that he had gotten it out of his system some, would lead him back. That might be better. It was a slim and convenient hope, but he was comfortable with it. Besides, contacting him would be hard since he didn't have Bo's number. He could call his mother back and ask for it, but the idea of hearing her voice or his father's again *really* made him feel queasy.

He hadn't talked to Cory a whole lot about it, instead choosing to deal with it internally. Being on the road for several series meant that Cory was a lot more arm's-length around Rett, anyway. Since they were around the whole team all day every day, it was out of necessity, and Rett's head understood that. But his heart wasn't quite as quick to fly that flag. Cory had all kinds of family in his life, biological and otherwise, who had always been there for him and who he could be there for. Rett didn't have that, and knowing what Cory had, and Cory's necessary reticence while on the road, made the void in his own life painfully acute. He was feeling a little isolated, and being on the road, with all it entailed, made it worse.

Maybe he had blown it for good with Bo. And now there was nothing to do but let time scar over the wounds again so that he didn't have to think about them.

The second game in the series against the Angels was later that day, and he grabbed his shoes to put on before going downstairs to catch the team motorcoach to the stadium, but he glanced at his phone before he started putting them on. There was a message from Cory on the screen that he had completely missed somehow:

Where are you?

He glanced at the time and all thoughts of everything else disintegrated immediately in his panic; he grabbed his shoes and ran out of his room as fast as he could, hoping to catch the bus before it left him stranded at the hotel.

Out in front of the hotel, one of the two black motorcoaches was already gone, but the second one was still there. Rett prayed he wasn't the last one holding it up; he'd never hear the end of it if he was. He stepped up into the bus with his shoes still in his hands, hoping to arrive unnoticed, but immediately all the players and team members started shouting and razzing him for being late. Arthur, Sebastion, Ernie, Rolly, and others started yelling to not let him on the bus. Ryan shouted through a smile that Rett should get out and push. A couple of the guys even threw towels at him.

Since his attempt to board the bus inconspicuously was blown to hell, he walked back to where Josh, Cory and JJ were sitting and took a seat next to JJ. Unlike what they had in most cities, this one was a very deluxe motorcoach, one with groups of seating facing around small tables, more like a nice train car than a bus. Josh, JJ, and Cory were sitting in a group talking, mostly getting their digs in about Rett making the entire team late.

Rett sat down as Josh resumed their earlier conversation, "So when does D'Angelo start?"

Rett interrupted as he finally got to put his sneakers on and tie the laces, "D'Angelo's flipping to active?"

"Yeah, he's replacing Satoru as shortstop. You were, *ahem*, late to the bus and Ahab mentioned that Satoru's been traded to the Rays," said JJ. "I think D'Angelo will be starting when we get to Chicago in a few days."

"I got nothing against Satoru, but it was about time Ahab did something about the whole Luis—Satoru thing," said Josh.

This was all news to Rett. Sure, he knew that Satoru and Luis never seemed to get along, even on the field, but he didn't realize Satoru was on the verge of being traded off the team. On the plus side, D'Angelo Cheatham was a good guy, but had been on the inactive roster since Rett had started his job with the Joes. It made him think about yet another one of Skunk's racist potshots the day before while they were in the visiting team's clubhouse at Angel Stadium. Ever since his last run-in with Skunk, he had gone back to ignoring Rett completely, which was fine with him. But JJ hadn't been so lucky.

Rett said, "Great, Skunk will probably stop ignoring him since he's been inactive and start treating him to the same classy banter you get the benefit of, JJ."

Josh looked at Rett and at JJ. "What, has Skunk been at it again? I mean besides you, Rett. I heard he got you up last weekend. Glad you gave him a gobful back, by the way."

Rett said, "It's not just me. JJ has to put up with his shit, too. He called him the 'eight ball in the corner pocket' before the game yesterday. What about you, Josh? Has he ever laid into you? Maybe called you a roo-fucker?"

Josh and Cory laughed, and Josh replied through his grin, "Not yet!"

Then he added, "Besides, I prefer koalas. They don't kick like roos. And they're tighter, too. You should give 'em a burl if you make it down under sometime! JJ, forget about Skunk. Everyone knows he's a figjam anyway."

Cory looked puzzled and asked, "A what?"

"Aussie slang. Stand's for 'Fuck I'm good! Just ask me!'"

JJ laughed out loud at this and leaned back in his seat, pushing his blond-tipped dreadlocks back behind him, "Man, that's Skunk all right!"

Cory shook his head and said, "Why do you put up with him, JJ?"

"It may have been Satoru that got traded today, but Skunk's turn is coming up. Cory, you and Gunnar are starting to show the weaknesses in the hitting and the rest of the fielding, and Skunk's leading that list. We all know he's all talk and barely can back it up most nights. He can't cash all the checks his ego keeps writing. Either that or he's gonna get busted for screwing some underage girl at some point. One or the other."

"Probably both," said Rett.

287

Josh said, "Ahab's a piece all right. He looks the other way when he sees Skunk plowing through groupies, but was whinging to Topher about the poofters asking for autographs outside the stadium yesterday."

Cory looked lost again, "Josh, dude, you gotta speak English."

"Ahab was complaining to Topher about the gay guys asking for autographs. You know how you can always tell the guys that are baseball fans from the ones that have a more *personal* interest in the players?"

Rett got quiet and Cory looked down at his lap with Josh's explanation.

JJ laughed, "Ahab's got a high opinion of himself if he thinks even a fraction of those guys were trying to get into his pants last evening!"

"So those guys, the gay ones, you give 'em your autograph when they come around?" asked Josh.

"I'm giving out an autograph, not my room key," said JJ. "A fan's a fan out in public."

Josh agreed, "Yeah, same here. You think Ahab's a closet case? Usually those yelling the loudest, you know..."

They all laughed at that. JJ said, "I'll ask him and tell him you were wondering, Josh."

Josh jerked back and exclaimed, "Hell you will!"

"Now, Skunk... I'm less sure about him..." said JJ.

"What about you, Cory?" asked Josh.

Cory flinched just barely and froze for a second. The question came at him so casually he was totally caught off guard. Rett almost panicked at the directness of Josh's question.

"What about me?" repeated Cory, carefully, as the blush started to appear on his face.

"Yeah, with the autographs. You give gay guys autographs? You're gettin' hounded more than any of us these days."

Cory relaxed a little and said, "I don't know. I never even thought about it. I mean, it doesn't make any difference to me. I'd give an ugly girl an autograph, why not a gay guy? Rett, how about you?"

"When I get a guy asking for my autograph, I'll let you know. I'll probably add Skunk's phone number and the word 'anytime' next to it." Rett watched JJ as he replied, and JJ seemed to especially like the answer he gave. JJ held out his hand for Rett to give him a fist bump for a perfect response.

They rode in silence for a moment before Rett asked a sincere question. "Any of y'all ever know an MLB player that was gay and out? I've never heard of one. But, you know, what the hell do I know and all that." He glanced at Cory and could tell he was uncomfortable with Rett continuing this conversation.

JJ and Josh both shook their heads and agreed that they weren't aware of one.

"There's gotta be one. Hell, more than one. They're just keeping quiet about it and not coming out," said Josh. "Kevin McClatchy is probably the closest I'm aware of."

"Who?" said Rett.

"He owned the Pirates for a while. But he came out years after he stepped down as the owner," said JJ.

"It's different for someone like him, though," said Josh. "For a player, while active, it'd be a shit sandwich, that's for sure. Even if the team was fine with it, the fans wouldn't be. And then the owner and the GM would have a business liability on their hands. They probably wouldn't be able to trade the guy fast enough. And that's if they could find a team that would take him. I don't care that sexual orientation is part of the players' collective bargaining agreement now, at the club level it's still a business decision, and that's gonna be mostly driven by ticket sales and fans."

JJ agreed that that was probably the case.

"It's not the MLB or the team that would really cause the biggest problem," repeated Josh. "It's the fans."

JJ frowned and said, "Just like the early days for blacks in baseball. The fans were the hardest hurdle to get past."

~~~~~

Cory and Rett were some of the last ones getting off the bus when they returned to the hotel that evening after the game. In the lobby, Rett sat in a chair while he waited for Cory, who had stopped to tie one of his sneakers again. By the time they got on the elevator, all the other players and team members had gone their own ways, and they were alone. Rett held out a little hope that maybe he'd get to spend some time with Cory that evening since he rarely did on the road and had hardly been able to say two words to him all day once they arrived at the stadium for the game. It was Rett that had been tied up all day, though, and not Cory.

In the elevator, Rett said, "Out with it, Bigfoot. I can tell you're a little funky."

"I'm fine," said Cory, which worried Rett even more.

Rett stared at him, unconvinced.

"You just freaked me out a little bit on the bus to the game today," said Cory, "I was uncomfortable with the conversation to begin with and then you kept it going by asking if there had been any out players."

Rett said, "It's not like I was winking at Josh and pointing at you. We'd look more suspicious sitting around whistling, avoiding the conversation and looking up at the ceiling."

Cory grumbled under his breath a little. Rett wondered if Cory really thought that he had pushed their luck by participating in the conversation that morning.

Rett added, "Besides, you know JJ already knows about me and is totally cool about it and hasn't said a word to anyone about it. I get the feeling that Josh would be exactly the same way."

Cory's face set in stubbornness. The elevator door opened on Cory's floor and they stepped out and down the hallway towards his room.

Rett understood Cory's concern about people finding out about him. He knew how important playing in the majors was to him, and he wasn't about to play fast and loose with it, risking it, for anything in the world. But today, despite trying to do exactly the right thing, it felt like he had done exactly the wrong thing. This on top of the fact that Cory would never risk Rett staying with him in his room while on the road, and the time apart that resulted in, made him feel worse.

"I'm not saying you need to come out. It's your decision and you'll do it when you're comfortable and only with the people you're comfortable telling, Cory. I was just trying to not obviously be terrified of the conversation we were having."

Ever since Bo had come by his place, Rett felt like he couldn't do anything right. But he knew this was ridiculous.

He said, "Look, I'll even out myself to Josh. I'll test the waters with him to see how he reacts."

Cory stopped in front of his hotel room door and jerked his head at Rett. He wasn't angry, but Rett could tell he didn't like anything about that idea.

"No, Rett," said Cory, pleading. "I *don't* want you to do that. Not for yourself or for me. Let me have things the way they are, please."

Cory went into his hotel room and the door closed behind him, leaving Rett standing in the hallway.

Rett stood there for a minute looking vacantly down at the glaring gold and blue and ruby pattern in the hotel carpet.

He blinked slowly a few times with his head hung down and said quietly to the door that Cory had walked through, "I'm not trying to change things, Cory. Really."

Chapter 20

Rett took his phone out of his coat pocket and looked at it. Forty-five minutes late, but he didn't really care this time. He didn't want to be there and doubted anybody would notice if he wasn't.

He stepped the rest of the way through the entrance hall into the hotel lobby and stopped short. He had never been in a place like this in all his life. He looked around the lobby of the Battle House and tried to describe what he was seeing. Opulent. That was the only word that really came to mind. The place was opulent.

The entrance hall of the Battle House Hotel opened up into the main lobby, which was cavernous. His eyes rolled around, gawking at all of it in slack-jawed wonder. Dominating over the massive space, high up in the ceiling, was the most amazing stained glass dome he had ever seen. Well, it was the only stained glass dome he had ever seen. When had he ever had a chance to be in a place like this before?

The Battle House Hotel, probably the most historic hotel in downtown Mobile, had been magnificently restored at some point, and it was the most luxurious one he had ever set foot in. The hotel where he had stayed the last few days for the series in Chicago was pretty amazing, but not like this. The lobby area was circled by ornate, double-height archways, with incredibly detailed plasterwork filling in between the arches. A few people sat chatting in the couches and chairs placed in groups around the lobby, and others were passing through, crossing the patterned marble floor and thick carpet while going to or from their rooms.

Rett swallowed hard and stood, bug-eyed, trying to take it all in. His eyes drifted down and he looked at the suit he was wearing. Now he felt even more uncomfortable than he did when he had gotten dressed earlier that evening. Off to the side, hanging over a heavy, carved-wood console table, was a tall mirror in a gilded frame. He walked across to it and looked himself over yet again. His hair looked fine, but he picked at it anyway, as if attempting to shift a few hairs around would make some sort of difference in his appearance. He held his arms out in the ill-fitting suit he was wearing, which was the real problem.

He had bought the suit four years earlier while still in school and it was the only one he owned. Unfortunately, since he had bought it, he had managed to grow a little more, and now it fit too snugly on him. Plus, it had been cheap when he bought it, and time had not done the cut, color, or fabric any favors. While he had been interviewing, it didn't really bother him. But tonight, wearing it really, really bothered him. He felt uncomfortable and foolish in it, and didn't want anyone seeing him this way. Not Cory, not JJ or Josh or Arthur. Not even Ahab. Definitely not Jimmy, and he was probably going to be around tonight.

Rett frowned and growled under his breath and wished he hadn't even found out that he was supposed to be here. Until Dr. Bala caught him on the plane ride back from the series against the White Sox the day before, he had assumed that the Make-A-Wish Charity Ball was for the players only. But Dr. Bala had made sure he knew, at the last minute, that it was for the whole team, not just the players, and that he was expected to attend along with everyone else. That left him the afternoon yesterday, after they got back from Chicago, and this afternoon, after Cory had held the Arizona Diamondbacks down in their afternoon game for a 6–2 win, to get ready for the event that evening.

He debated simply leaving. No one was coming to this charity ball to see him. No one would even notice his absence. What harm would it be to simply disappear?

Well, Cory would probably notice. Although part of him wondered about that after this last road trip. Three cities nonstop had been rough.

He scratched at his nose in irritation and looked back longingly at the glass doors that lead outside. Rett sighed and walked further into the lobby, looking for something that told him where the ball was being held.

He found a sign that directed him out the far side of the lobby and into a newer convention-type space in the back. He checked in at a desk for the charity ball, and showed his team ID for access. They handed him a name sticker that read "Rett Dougherty — Medical Services" next to the Mobile Joes logo, the one that had Old Slac's feather crown hanging off of the "J". He slapped it on his suit and walked through the doors into the party.

The party made him stop in his tracks just as the hotel lobby had. It wasn't anything like the few college parties he had been to, not by a damn shot. It was huge for one thing. There was a live band at the far end of the room playing diabetes-inducing rock, the kind so inoffensive that it became offensive, with a crowd of people in front dancing along with watered-down moves to match the song. Along one wall, a decadent buffet was splayed out across a series of long tables in white linen, massive ice sculptures and towering flower arrangements centering each one. Along the wall closest to Rett was a series of bars set up to lubricate the crowd.

And the people. So many people. There had to be well over a thousand people in the room. Talking, laughing, taking pictures. Dancing, hugging, drinking. All of them dressed very well, all suits and ties and evening gowns and cufflinks and glittering necklaces. Rett gritted his teeth and tugged at the suit he was wearing once again.

He walked over to the bar and pushed his way up front. He was going to need alcohol to get through the night. Lots of it. No way was he going to spend the night being the one piece of grit in this greased up crowd.

He downed half of his beer before he pulled it away from his lips, and then turned to survey the room again. The crowd tended to be older, forties and up mostly, and clearly with money. Country club bait. Rett guessed this was what Mobile high-society looked like. Finally, on the far side of the room, up closer to where the band was playing, he spotted a denser crowd. He spied Arthur O'Creaghan standing on the edge of it talking to several people and was relieved to find a familiar face.

He started making his way towards them, threading through businessmen and trophy wives, through aging society ladies with their trophy husbands. Before he got halfway there, he stopped in his tracks for the third time that evening, his eyes locking onto a small group standing a little ahead of him. He was suddenly a hundred times more self-conscious about how he looked and how he was dressed. Cory, though, looked amazing. He was wearing a warm gray suit, which fit him perfectly despite his size, over a crisp white shirt with cufflinks. Cory hadn't worn a tie, instead leaving his shirt discreetly open at the neck a button or two. He towered over Kaitlynn and had his arm around her waist, and was smiling and chatting with Jimmy. Kaitlynn was wearing a close-fitting sequined dress of pale green that brought out the soft curls of her auburn hair even more than usual. Jimmy had on a dark pinstripe suit with sharp lapels and an aggressively bright tie.

Rett had no idea how Jimmy had managed it. In the time since they had gotten back from Chicago, he had taken Cory out to get a new suit and had it altered and ready to go for the party tonight. And it was perfect. Cory looked perfect in it.

Jimmy had come to Mobile for a few days to discuss sponsorships that had been surfacing since Cory had made such a huge splash his first night starting. Kaitlynn had come to town specifically for the charity ball to be Cory's date. In fact, because of Jimmy and Cory's shopping trip, and then with Kaitlynn arriving in town, Rett had not pushed to stay with Cory the night before, even though after being out of town for three different series, it had been a while since they had been together.

Rett kept his distance from them, instead preferring to hang back, unnoticed, while he watched Cory for a few minutes.

It was hard to miss Cory, even in the crowded room, and there was a steady stream of people that wanted to come up and meet him. He invariably introduced all of them to his business manager, Jimmy, and then Kaitlynn, who was the perfect, pretty date to have on his arm. There was a doddering, older man that had trouble walking, but had no trouble keeping a blond wife at least half his age, and they chatted with Cory for a few moments. Amusingly enough, the old man seemed more interested in Kaitlynn than Cory. Then there was a cocky businessman who looked like he was doing Cory a favor by having his picture taken with him. There was an aging socialite who had no qualms about already having too much to drink at the party, no qualms about having too much plastic surgery before the party, and who had no qualms about touching Cory's chest repeatedly while she talked to him, even with Kaitlynn standing right there. Rett decided to spill a beer on her later on if he could find her again. Then there was a middle-aged guy, with a bald spot, a gut and a wife, talking animatedly to Cory and making pitching motions, no doubt giving Cory the benefit of his pointers on how to improve his game. Cory scratched his head and looked around briefly before trying to nod politely at the man.

Rett spent at least twenty minutes doing nothing more than watching Cory from this safe distance. The stream of people, all wanting a piece of him, never seemed to end. All of these people wanting their little bit of Cory that they could take home.

When his first beer ran out, Rett went to get a fresh one. He felt weird about going up to Cory now. At this party and with all these people around, so many of whom wanted to see Cory with his pretty girlfriend, Rett would have been out of place. Rett started counting down the minutes until he could leave the party and be free of the whole situation.

When he got back from the bar, there was a break in the stream of people that had been meeting Cory, and Jimmy had disappeared. Jimmy re-appeared soon enough, fresh drinks for himself and Cory in his hands. Cory grinned, and while both of Jimmy's hands were helplessly occupied with the drinks, he reached over and rubbed his hand around on Jimmy's head, thoroughly ruining his carefully-styled hair. Jimmy tried to pull away and gave him a searing look that was probably only a few degrees shy of causing Cory's new suit to burst into flames. He handed Cory his drink and reached up to return the favor by messing Cory's hair up as well. But Cory ducked back, laughing and staying just out of Jimmy's reach. Kaitlynn was there, though, and she did what Jimmy couldn't. She stood up on her tiptoes and reached up behind Cory's head and ruffled his hair, much to Jimmy's satisfaction.

But as Rett had learned a while ago, with Cory's hair, it didn't matter. His hair always had a natural, sloppy look that was impossible to mess up. Dry, or sweaty after a game, or right out of the shower, it didn't matter. Freshly brushed, or right after waking up, or after having been under a ball cap all day, it didn't matter. It was just as hard to argue with how it looked on him; he looked good. Casual, good-natured, amiably handsome. He looked as good in an old t-shirt and shorts as he did in a suit and cufflinks. Even after sabotaging his hair, Cory pulled Kaitlynn in front of him and put one arm around her.

Rett thought to himself and listed them off. Tonight, here, it was Kaitlynn and Jimmy. There were also Brick and Zee. And then there were Cory's parents, Carrie Anne and Jerry. And he shouldn't forget Jason, too. Plus there were all of the people that had worked at Montgomery Landscaping back in Lawder. All of them had been so happy to see him when they made the trip there for the day, even on a sad occasion. Kaitlynn and Jimmy were just the tip of the iceberg for Cory. He had so many people behind him, supporting him. Loving him.

Rett polished off the rest of his beer and turned away so he wouldn't have to see Cory standing with Kaitlynn pulled affectionately against his chest. He turned to go get another beer, almost bumping into a gentleman trying to snake through the crowd. The man started to excuse himself, but glanced at Rett's nametag and smiled broadly.

"So, you're on the team, too?" the gentleman asked.

Rett nodded. "I'm Rett. I'm the physical therapist for the team."

The man introduced himself and his wife, shaking Rett's hand vigorously in the process. "Wonderful! I have to ask, though... how's Gunnar's arm holding up? Before Cory came along, he seemed to be struggling with it."

Rett remembered Dr. Bala explicitly warning him about this. And worse, Rett was probably the only one that knew that Gunnar was hiding strain and damage to it, despite his claims that his arm was fine. Gunnar tried to avoid having Dr. Bala really examine him, but seemed ok with letting Rett handle it after having opened up to him about the stress of pitching. Rett still worried about it, but things seemed to weigh less on Gunnar the last few weeks.

He told the gentleman, "Gunnar's doing great. And Ric's back off the 15-day DL after he sprained his proximal IP, so we're looking good on pitching."

Rett really wanted another beer, but the man seemed fascinated to be able to talk baseball with someone, anyone, actually on the team. Rett indulged him since his whole purpose in attending the charity event was to engage the public this way.

They chatted a few minutes, the poor man's wife looking quietly bored the whole time, until the man's face suddenly gaped. He said to his wife, "Look, honey! There's Cory Pritchart, the star of the show these days! Let's see if we can go talk to him!"

The man dipped his chin and said, "Thanks, Rett, for the chat! It was great talking to you!" Before Rett could say anything in return, the man was rushing his wife away to meet the Joes' newest pitcher.

He twisted through the crowd back to the bar, where he saw that Skunk had taken up residence to one side. It was very strange to see him standing with his lime green mohawk starkly contrasting against the dark blue suit he was wearing, his arms around a couple of younger women in revealing dresses. Of course, he had no tie on and his shirt was open way down his chest showing off several of the tattoos he had plastered across it.

Even worse, he noticed that tonight Skunk was trying even harder for some style cred by wearing a pair of fake Buddy Holly eyeglasses.

When one of the girls he was wrapped around snaked her hand inside his shirt and pursed her lips at Skunk lasciviously, Rett turned away. He'd had enough of that. It was past time for another beer.

He tried to judge which bartender had the shortest line when he felt a hand on his back. He swung around to find JJ behind him, smiling broadly. He had his dreadlocks pulled back behind his head, and wore one of his trademark black compression shirts under a black sports coat. Rett grinned at him.

JJ put his arm around Rett's shoulder and said, "Pikachu, I want you to meet Jada, my girlfriend. Jada, this is Rett, who I've told you about."

Jada was striking. She was as tall as JJ and had short, cropped hair, highlighted by large gold hoops dangling from her ears. Her dress was a hot red sleeveless one that hugged her figure down to right above the knee.

Rett shook her hand and said, "Hi, Jada. Good to meet you."

She leaned over and said, "JJ's told me a lot about you. It's good to finally meet you in person."

They made small talk for a few moments before JJ nodded his head over towards the corner of the bar. "Well, well, look at Skunk over there."

Rett followed JJ's gaze and saw Skunk having his picture taken with several girls.

"No, no, no," said Rett drily. "That's some Russian pimp that crashed the..." He stopped and squinted for a moment before exclaiming, "No! It *is* Skunk! Didn't recognize him all Clark-Kented up in those glasses!"

They got in line to get their drinks and Jada asked, "You two don't care much for Patrick?"

"Patrick?" asked Rett. "Does anybody call him that? All I've ever heard is Skunk, which fits metaphorically as much as it does literally."

Jada's perfect white teeth blazed out from her smile.

Rett asked JJ, "You haven't told her about Skunk?" Rett assumed that she'd have to know all about him.

JJ shook his head, "No, I leave all that at the Portyards."

Rett wasn't sure how JJ stayed so cool about all of it. He looked back at Jada and said, "I'll be polite... he's a dick. JJ? How long before he's gone? You keep promising and promising, but there he is, right there, in his hipster glasses and look-at-me mohawk. If he's not gone in two weeks, you owe me $100, asshole!"

JJ laughed, shaking Rett by the neck. "Fine! $100 if he's not gone in two weeks!"

"And you gave me a good idea, Jada," said Rett. "I think I'm going to start calling him Pat. I can't *imagine* him getting pissed about that one bit!"

They got their drinks and talked together for a few minutes before the interruptions from people wanting to meet JJ or have their picture taken with him became too much. Rett wandered off again, walking back over to where Cory had been so he could finally admit to having shown up.

Cory wasn't there, though. Kaitlynn and Jimmy were there, talking to a very elegant older man and his wife. Kaitlynn was waving her arms around and talking animatedly, her face glowing. Rett imagined her telling stories of Cory in college or perhaps even ones from high school to the older couple.

A voice from behind Rett said, "She looks great tonight, doesn't she?"

He turned to see Cory standing right behind him. He had to hold himself back so that he didn't throw himself on Cory right there in front of everyone. The road trip across three cities had been hard to take. And deep down, Rett still hurt a tiny bit by Cory panicking over the "gay" conversation on the bus in LA.

"Not nearly as good as..." said Rett before he stopped abruptly.

Someone had approached Cory and wanted to shake his hand and congratulate him on his pitching that afternoon against the Diamondbacks. Rett stood aside while Cory talked with the man for a moment before they could resume their conversation.

Cory asked, "Did you just get here? Where have you been?"

"Nah, I've been here about an hour now."

"Why didn't you come over?" Cory seemed confused.

Rett shrugged and Cory waited to see if he would want to fill in more of an answer than that.

Why hadn't he gone over? Why had he stood around for a long time watching them from a distance? Rett wasn't sure of the answer to that question.

He looked down, "You and Kaitlynn and Jimmy needed some time, and there's a constant stream of people who want to talk to you." He tugged at his suit before he told himself to stop drawing attention to it.

Cory continued to look at him curiously, as if he wasn't sure if that really was the reason or not. Rett felt like there were a thousand pairs of eyes on them. He opened his mouth to say something else to Cory, but stopped when a very pretty girl in a silver beaded gown gasped and came running up to Cory's side.

She said, breathlessly, "Oh my God! I have to have a picture! Do you mind? I just have to have a picture!" She handed her phone to Rett and said, "Will you take it? Do you mind?"

She looked back up at Cory's face in starry-eyed wonder, biting at her lip. "Mr. Pritchart! Cory, I mean, Mr. Pritchart! Can I call you Cory? I was at the game this afternoon! You were just fantastic today!" She squealed and stomped her high-heeled foot a few times in excitement.

Cory laughed and said while putting his arm around her waist, "Yeah, thanks! What's your name, by the way?"

The girl literally had to stop and think for a second she had gotten so flustered. "Oh, God, I can't even think! It's Meredith! Of course that's my name!" She gave a silly grimace in embarrassment.

"Alright, you guys ready? I'll take a couple, ok?" Rett counted off and took two or three pictures before handing the phone back to the girl. She thanked them profusely and glided away on a cloud of giddy excitement.

Cory made a nauseated face and told Rett, "I've had two women slip me their phone numbers tonight. I'm used to that outside the Portyards parking lot after a game, but it seems sleazier here than it does there."

Rett didn't reply and looked down at his shoes instead.

Cory wrinkled up his face after the girl had left and nodded his head towards the band. "Are they actually playing ABBA songs over there?"

Rett finally huffed a weak laugh and nodded, "I was hoping it was ironic, but I don't think it is."

"Jimmy loves this crap. Worthless faggot," sneered Cory with a slight grin while his eyes held Rett's as tightly as they could. "I wonder if I could bribe the band into playing some Roxy Music. I wonder if they've ever even *heard* of Roxy Music."

Rett shook his head in doubt.

"You disappeared today after the game," said Cory.

"I had to do some laundry so I'd have a clean shirt, and I had to iron it and get ready. I needed all the time I could get and I was still pretty late."

Cory smirked and said, "You're *always* late."

Before Rett could say anything in return, Ahab had appeared and put his arm around Cory's shoulder. He briefly acknowledged Rett with a "Hey, Rett," before focusing entirely on Cory.

"Cory, I wanted you to meet Allen Messner, the MLB's VP for Community Affairs. He definitely wanted to meet you this evening," said Ahab while introducing the silver-haired man at his side. Cory shook his hand while the man congratulated him on his win that afternoon.

Rett waited for a moment, downing the rest of his beer in one long swallow before it became apparent that Ahab was done with the introductions. Cory was tied up with the MLB hotshot, so Rett backed away discreetly to go get another beer.

He added himself to the end of the shortest line at the bar, but then wished he had picked a different line. Skunk had picked up a couple of mixed drinks from the front of the bar and was coming back in his direction.

Before Rett could avoid him, Skunk said, across all the people in-between them, "Couldn't get a date to the hottest party of the year, I see."

Rett was about to comment that he didn't hire his dates like Skunk did, but said nothing instead. Skunk came up to him and said, "What's wrong with you, man? Even the biggest loser can pick up a bitch for this party. Except you, I guess. Hell, I've got more snatch here than I know what to do with. You know... I'd offer you some, but... I won't."

Skunk laughed at him and walked off. Rett scowled and pulled at the collar of his shirt, trying to get it to loosen up a fraction.

He grabbed another bottle of beer from the bartender, but when he turned to walk away, his head swooned a little. He stopped to steady himself and realized he had probably drunk the other beers a little faster than he should have. He pushed through the crowd until he could see that Cory was still fully engrossed in his conversation with the MLB executive.

He stood for a moment, uncomfortable in the tight suit, wishing he had not realized the band was now playing a Lionel Richie song. He tried to decide between going over to the crowd where the rest of the players were, to find Arthur or Sebastion or Josh, and going ahead and leaving. He struggled with the decision for a moment before he looked down at the bottle of beer in his hand, which was still full. His head spun gently and he decided he needed to slow down and let the beer work its way out of his system before trying to leave and drive home.

He threaded through the crowd until he was out of the party and found the restroom. Once finished and exiting the men's room, he noticed a sign pointing out the pool area for the hotel. His head was still a little buzzy and going outside and getting some fresh air was the perfect idea, so he followed the signs. It was a little further than he expected and he had to cross a sky-bridge to the top of a large parking deck across the street from the hotel. The pool, sundeck, and tennis courts were there, with a great view of the surrounding city from seven floors up.

Out in the fresh air of the evening and far from the crowd, he felt better. He walked around to the far side of the pool and was surprised to see how close to the waterfront the hotel was. From seven floors up, he could see the industrial port across the street, and to the right and across the river he could see the lights of the Portyards itself.

There wasn't anyone else there this time of the evening and Rett finally felt more relaxed to be outside and away from the teeming country-club throng. He leaned against the heavy half wall running around the circumference of the pool deck and enjoyed the warm breeze while he watched the ships still loading and unloading, coming and going out of the port.

He pulled out his phone and tried to call Val, but she didn't answer. Maybe that was a blessing. She could always tell when he was buzzed and would taunt him that she could have drunk him under the table when she was nine years old.

He wished she had picked up so she could make fun of him. She must be out somewhere with Tony, having a blast. Now that he thought about it, he hadn't really talked to her since the morning that Bo had come to his apartment. They had traded a few short text messages, but nothing of real substance. His head swam slightly again and everything felt distant. Nothing felt like it was solidly in his grasp anymore.

JF SMITH

He wondered what Bo was doing. Was he still in college? Did he even go to college? He wondered if Bo was even living in Dothan or not. He regretted that he had not had enough of a conversation with his brother to find out even that little bit about him. Now that he was back from the games out of town, Rett wondered what he should do about him. He tried to weigh the pros and cons of his options, but his mind kept showing him pictures of Cory and Kaitlynn down at the party. And all those people having their pictures taken with him.

Rett didn't even have a picture of him and Cory together.

A voice next to Rett said, "Pretty good view from up here."

Rett turned, surprised to see Jimmy standing next to him, cocktail glass in hand. Jimmy had corrected the damage Cory had done to his hair while horsing around with him earlier.

Rett nodded silently, taking a few long swallows out of his beer. He had barely touched it so far, but now decided it was a good time to speed up. He glanced behind Jimmy to see if Cory or Kaitlynn were with him, but didn't see anyone else.

"Sometimes I stay here at the Battle House when I come in town. The pool area is really great." said Jimmy.

Rett nodded again. He was sure he didn't want to talk to Jimmy right then. That was because Jimmy always made him uncomfortable. Brick didn't, but Jimmy did. Rett pulled at his suit, trying to get it to loosen up some because it suddenly felt like it was constricting around him again. He felt like he couldn't get a solid lungful of air in that suit.

Jimmy said, "You know, I realized tonight that you and I haven't had much of a chance to actually talk, one on one. I think you and Brick have. But not you and me."

This was a bad time for any talking. Rett couldn't breathe.

Rett's head throbbed once and he realized he was going to have to make some kind of small talk whether he wanted to or not.

He pointed over across the water. "You can actually see a little bit of the Portyards from here."

Jimmy nodded without looking where Rett was pointing. He kept his eyes on Rett and took a slow sip of his drink.

Rett tried something else. "What kind of sponsorship deals are you signing Cory up for?"

It took a moment for Jimmy to answer. "There's a shoe one, but it's not a very good deal. They want to lock him in for a long time for not much money. They want all the options and flexibility while giving none to Cory in return. There's another for athletic shirts, which I think would be better. I think the one I like the most for him is for baseball gloves, though."

"He's lucky he's got you to handle all this for him," said Rett. He wondered if Cory was in the ballroom dancing to a Lionel Ritchie song with Kaitlynn.

"Honestly, I don't want to do this kind of stuff."

"Why don't you want to do it? You're supposed to be really good at it."

"I have my reasons," said Jimmy. "But I can't say no to Cory. Never could."

Rett took another long swallow from his beer. The faster he finished it, the faster he could excuse himself and go back inside.

Jimmy rattled the ice in his drink and stared off across the port. He asked, "Why do you love him, Rett?"

Rett stood up straight. Where the hell had that question come from? What happened to the meaningless small talk? How was he supposed to answer a question like that? Could Jimmy at least give him a little heads up so he could put on his seat belt before he took a turn like that?

"Who said I loved him?"

"You don't love him?" asked Jimmy.

Rett was tempted now to walk away and end this conversation whether his beer was finished or not.

"I didn't say that, either," he said emphatically. "I've never told Cory that I love him. He's never told me."

"Do you love him, though, between you and me?"

Jimmy's questions didn't sound like he was trying to corner Rett. If Rett believed the tone in Jimmy's voice, the questions were sincere — *if* he believed the tone in Jimmy's voice. Rett closed his eyes and consciously breathed a few times. "Yeah, I do," he admitted.

"Ok. So why?"

What was the point of this conversation? Why did it have to happen right now? Did Jimmy follow him up here just to grill him about this?

Jimmy watched him, calmly, while he patiently waited for a reply.

Rett felt the familiar sensation of not knowing how to reply to something like that. Why was it even any of Jimmy's business to begin with?

"I don't know," he said into his bottle of beer, pathetically.

Jimmy didn't react to his answer. He continued to stand, leaning against the railing, but with his eyes fixed on Rett. There was silence and Rett hoped that maybe Jimmy was done with this conversation and would hopefully go away.

Rett took another swallow of his beer nervously.

Without warning, Jimmy said, "I'll give you a hundred thousand dollars to leave him."

Jimmy's voice had been calm and steady when he said it, but Rett felt like he had been punched in the face abruptly.

He squinted at Jimmy. Was this all some kind of horrible joke?

Jimmy's eyes were still locked onto Rett, steady and level. It didn't look like a joke to Rett. Was that what all this was about? Jimmy wanted to get rid of Rett and this was how it finally all played out?

Rett wanted to tell the son-of-a-bitch to go fuck himself. He opened his mouth and said, "Ok."

Jimmy's lips tightened across his face, but he didn't say anything. He stared at Rett, expressionless and unmoving for a long time. For the life of him, Rett wasn't sure why he had said ok.

After another extended silence, Jimmy's eyes dropped down to his drink and he asked carefully, "Are you sure?"

Hardly aware he was doing so, Rett nodded that he was.

Oddly, what Rett thought of wasn't Cory. What he thought of was Jerry. He thought of Jerry the day they sat together, watched Cory with the Little Leaguers, and talked. He thought of Carrie Anne. Of Jason and Kaitlynn. Of the fans outside the clubhouse parking lot screaming for him. Media clamoring for interviews. A thousand people in the ballroom right at that moment. He thought of all of them.

Then Rett thought of the day he stood in the hospital room and saw his dad's reaction to him. "You're here" coming from his father's pale lips as his face hardened. When he walked out, he had had the illusion that it wouldn't be into *nothing* like when he left the first time. But had that been the case? Right now he wasn't so sure. Right now, what he did have felt like a sand castle on the beach, and the tide was coming in, pulling it all away from him no matter how much he wanted to keep it. He knew fighting a tide could only end one way.

And if he was going to be given a choice between nothing, and nothing plus a hundred thousand dollars, he knew which he'd take.

Rett asked "So how does this work?"

Jimmy didn't look at Rett. He stared off into the distance, but didn't seem to be looking at the port or the night sky or anything in particular. His face set hard and he said, "Walk away. Do Cory a favor and cut it all off completely, right now. No contact at all. I'll handle him and let him know. I'll be back in town in a week when the team gets back from Dallas. I'll have your money then."

He added, "You realize you'll have to quit your job, right?"

Rett's lips twisted into almost a snarl. He snapped, "Yeah, I get it, Jimmy. First thing in the morning."

Jimmy frowned and said, "I gotta have your word, Rett, that you won't come back on Cory. That you won't use your relationship against him."

Rett had already tuned Jimmy out at this point. But that last point forced its way into his conscious attention like a knife cut. He kept looking over at the Portyards. From here, he could make out the lit up "Le" in the LeBayonne Portyards sign.

Rett said, "No. You don't need to worry about that. That wouldn't ever happen. Ever."

They stood silently for a few more minutes. Both looked out across the water in the direction of the Portyards in the distance. Both lost in their thoughts.

Jimmy tapped on the top of the parapet wall and said, "Ok. We know what has to happen, then. I'll be in touch, Rett."

He turned and left Rett standing against the wall, still staring at the lights of the stadium in the distance.

Inside, a thousand people were all gathered around Cory, all wanting a piece of him.

And Rett had nothing.

Chapter 21

Rett stretched out from where he was sitting on the floor and leaning against the wall so he could shove his phone back in his pocket after checking the time. He blinked slowly and resumed turning the baseball over and over in his hands.

In a few minutes it would be 10am. He continued absently playing with the ball and staring at the cream colored wall with spaced out teal pinstripes across from him. He yawned once, but still didn't feel sleepy. From the point of his conversation with Jimmy outside the charity ball the night before, he had not slept a wink. There had been too much on his mind the whole time, all bunched up in the air like gnats on a humid summer afternoon. He had tossed and turned in his bed, then paced around in his den, then sat on the landing outside his apartment door looking out at the empty street in the middle of the night, and then futilely tried to get in his bed again and sleep. He had been sitting on the floor since 8am, in exactly the spot he was in, waiting.

He wondered if Jimmy had talked to Cory yet. He hadn't heard anything from Cory, so he wanted to think that Jimmy must have said something by now. But he wasn't sure. Maybe Jimmy had told a lie last night, told him that Rett wasn't feeling well and had left to go home early, just so he could wait until sometime today to tell Cory what was *really* going on, that Rett wasn't up to their relationship after all. That would be the nice, gentle way for him to frame it — "Rett isn't up to y'all's relationship, Cory." Rett doubted if Jimmy would be that nice, though.

He tried to picture how Cory would react to what was going on. What would Cory think of Rett once he heard? Would he be upset? Would he cry? Would he be furious? Would he feel betrayed? The strange, sad sensation deep inside Rett was that, after the last few weeks, he wasn't sure how Cory would react. Would Cory shrug his shoulders, chalk it up to a short, insignificant fling, and be ready for pitching practice a few hours later? That one stung, but Rett also felt like maybe it would be best for Cory if that was how he did react. Since he wouldn't ever know how Cory took the news, he hoped it would have minimal impact on him. He hoped Cory recovered and moved on quickly, if it even bothered him at all.

Rett had promised not to contact Cory, and had no intention of doing so, but what happened if Cory contacted him? A call or a text was easy to ignore, of course. But what if he showed up at his apartment? What would Rett do in that situation? What would he say to Cory? Even chewing on that all night long, he still had no good answer for it. When things had ended between him and Mike, he had left town to avoid that kind of conversation.

Rett sighed and closed his eyes, the baseball now sitting idle in his hands.

Maybe he'd have to do that again.

He may have to do it to survive, anyway. He was sitting outside the door to George's office, and as soon as he showed up in the clubhouse, Rett would once again be back out on the job market. The idea of having to look for another job was depressing.

He traced his fingers along the seams of the baseball in his hands. Cory was going to wind up hating him for this. Who wouldn't?

Why had he accepted this offer from Jimmy? What had led him to say "ok" when Jimmy suggested he go away? Rett wished he knew. At least, he wished he knew clearly. Instead, he had bits and pieces. Jimmy didn't want him there. And so many people wanted Cory. Who was he in all of that? Looking out into the future, he wasn't sure where he stood and didn't see how he would fit in with Cory's life. He felt lost among all the noise of people clamoring for Cory, and this was just the beginning.

He wondered, indifferently, if Jimmy would cheat him and not bring the money as agreed. He couldn't fight someone like him if Jimmy decided not to honor the deal. Jimmy was too smart and had everyone that was close to Cory on his side. Not that it really mattered. Rett honestly didn't care if he got any money or not. He might not know exactly why he *had* taken the offer, but he knew well enough that it wasn't for the money.

Rett set the baseball down on the carpeted hallway floor next to him and spun it around like a top a few times.

Why did things turn out like this?

A noise down the hallway caught his attention and a moment later, Rosemary appeared walking around the curve in the hall towards her and George's offices. She was wearing a dark red top and skirt, just like the blood of her victims, with her reading glasses on the silver chain around her neck. As soon as Rosemary spotted Rett, she stopped and studied him for a minute, like a smelly homeless person had somehow managed to camp out next to her office door.

"Why are you sitting outside of my office?" she asked contemptuously. "What did you do to it?"

Rett barely even looked up at her. He said, "I haven't been in your office, Rosemary. I'm waiting for George to show up."

"Go wait somewhere else," she ordered caustically.

"No."

She frowned mightily while she tried to decide how to categorize and then react to this audacity. Rosemary tried to get past Rett, but he didn't bother to move his legs to accommodate her. Her attitude had no power over him today.

Rosemary finally stepped over his legs and snapped, "Stop trying to look up under my skirt."

He didn't bother to respond to that at all.

She unlocked her office door and said as she went in, "You can't wait in here. George isn't here yet."

Rett had made no attempt to follow her into the office. "Ok," he said.

He sat outside the office for another hour waiting on George. Rosemary left her office a few times during that period, always stepping over Rett's legs and pulling her skirt tight against her, but never saying anything else.

A little after 11am, George showed up.

"Hi, Rett! What are you doing out here?" he said, his usual friendly self. If he had partied too much at the charity ball the night before, Rett couldn't tell it.

Rosemary hurried from her desk to the door of the office, practically shouting at George, "He's been here since before I got here. I think he's unstable. I think he has a gun and is going to try to kill all of us."

George looked down at Rett in confusion, trying to gauge if the look in Rett's eyes was murderous or not.

"Don't be ridiculous, Rose!"

"I'm calling security," insisted Rosemary.

George shifted his briefcase to his other hand and scratched at his balding head.

"Relax, Rose," he said. "Rett, are you here to kill all of us?"

"No."

"*Any* of us?" challenged Rosemary, knowing George's question was a little too vague for her taste.

"No."

George smiled, happy that the outburst of violence had been fully put to bed. He said, "See, Rose! You need to talk about something, Rett?"

Rett said, "Yeah, I do," and stood up from where he was sitting.

George showed him into his office and put his briefcase down by the side of his desk because there were too many delicate piles of paper covering the desktop itself.

He sat down and smiled at Rett again. His eyes twinkled and he said, "I bet I know why you're here this time!"

Rett twitched. He said uneasily, "Oh, no... I really bet you don't."

Before he continued, Rett had to stop and make sure he was in control of himself. This was suddenly much harder to do than he ever thought it would be. His clothes felt like they were tight around him, choking him, like he was still wearing the suit he had worn the night before. His eyes found the pictures of the baseball players and teams up on George's wall and he looked at them. He stopped and dropped his eyes when he panicked that there might be a picture of Cory up on one of George's walls now. Rett wouldn't be able to do this if he saw Cory, even if it was merely a picture. He glanced down at the mess of papers and folders on the desk and saw the placard George always had sitting there.

"This is the test of your manhood: How much is there left in you after you have lost everything outside of yourself?"

Rett had to clear his throat to get the words to come out as anything more than a dry scratch. "I have to quit my job with the Joes, George." His face turned as red as Rosemary's dress as he spoke the words, and his eyes avoided George's gaze.

George's smile faltered and he tried to make sure he had heard Rett correctly.

"And it has to be today, George," continued Rett. "I'm sorry for how sudden this is, really, but I can't help it. I've left my laptop on my desk, and I've already sent Dr. Bala and Ryan and Rikky some notes on some things that they'll need to..."

The smile disappeared from George's face entirely and he said forcefully while he held up his hands at Rett, "Stop, Rett. Please."

George got up and closed the door to his office.

"What do you mean, Rett? Quit?"

It was hard enough to say it once. Rett didn't want to have to convince George of what he was doing.

He continued avoiding George's eyes as he repeated it. "I'm quitting, George."

Rett stayed quiet to let his words sink in while George resumed his seat behind his desk.

George finally said, "Is this because of Skunk?"

Rett wiped his hand across his mouth and shook his head feebly. "No, George. I don't know what you think this has to do with Skunk, but it has nothing to do with him."

"I've had a few of the guys complain about how Skunk has treated you. I'm surprised you haven't been in here before to say something about it yourself."

Rett shook his head again, "No, Skunk is the least of my... This isn't because of Skunk."

George still looked bewildered. "Well, help me understand, Rett. What's going on? Don't you like your job? Is there something I can maybe change for you?"

Rett bit at the inside of his lip. George, God bless him, was making this as hard as possible for him to get through.

"I *love* my job. I *never* thought..." Rett stopped again from going too far down that path. He might not be able to get back and finish what he was doing.

He tried again, "This has nothing to do with the Joes or my job. I have some personal things going on that I can't avoid and I can't be in this job as a result. That's all."

Rett knew he shouldn't say it, but he said it anyway. "You guys have been great to work with."

Rett took out his ID and put it on George's desk, his hand shaking slightly as he did so. The full depth of what he was doing finally hit him, now that it was too late. He was walking away from a job that he didn't realize exactly how much he had grown to love until right then. Baseball had meant nothing to him the day he started, and now it felt like it was everything.

George said, "Rett, I don't know what to say. I want to do something to change your mind. But... it doesn't sound like that's really an option for me. Is it?"

Rett frowned and shook his head sadly.

"Ok," said George with a sigh. "I'll make it happen, effective today. If there's anything I can do to help with whatever's going on, Rett, let me know."

Rett looked up at the ceiling. Would he ever again have a boss that measured up to how incredibly great it was to work for George?

He thanked George again for everything and walked out of his office.

He only barely caught the satisfied grin that spread across Rosemary's face as he was leaving since she had obviously heard everything. He half expected to see vampire fangs in her mouth.

Before he left, he walked down to the locker room one last time. No one was in yet because it was still early. He walked over to the conference table in the middle and touched the seat he so often sat at while working on his notes or talking with the guys. He stood alone in the center of the locker room and slowly looked around him. He didn't belong here anymore. He wasn't a part of this anymore.

He stopped when he got to where Cory's locker station was, with the nameplate reading "Cory Pritchart #72" up over the top of it and Cory's uniform hanging there. He tried to understand what he felt looking at it, but it all felt foreign. Sorting through it was pointless, and it was too late to worry about how he'd feel about this now.

He heard a throat clear behind him and Rett turned to see Rosemary standing in the doorway to the locker room.

"You are no longer employed here. You need to leave now or I *will* call security," she said with an almost demonic glee.

Rett nodded and managed to say in a hoarse whisper, "Ok, Rosemary, I'm leaving."

He walked out past Rosemary with his head hanging, and she followed him down the hall to the main door to the clubhouse. When he left, he stopped as he felt the door close behind him for the last time, Rosemary making sure it shut securely.

As he drove away from the stadium, he spotted the big LeBayonne Portyards sign across the top of the outfield stands in his rearview mirror. Rett felt hollowed-out and sick to his stomach; he felt like he must have left most of his insides back in the clubhouse he had just left.

Chapter 22

The late July heat was stifling, even with all of his car windows completely open. Rett flapped at his t-shirt a few times hoping to generate a little air movement that would evaporate some of the sweat and cool him off. Montgomery never seemed to have any wind at all in the middle of summer, but always had a bumper crop of humidity. This was the kind of situation when he was glad his Jetta had the threadbare velour interior instead of hot and sticky leather, even if his upholstery did smell bad.

He heard a car approach and he sat up in his car seat, which he had leaned all the way back since he had been sitting there for two hours, but it wasn't Val. He curled back up into an almost fetal position on his side to resume waiting.

Since quitting his job that morning, and feeling gutted in the process, Rett left the stadium, drove down Government Street past the street with his apartment, got on the highway and drove all the way to Montgomery. Part of it was that he was afraid to be in his apartment. Afraid of what would happen if Cory showed up. But secretly also a little afraid that Cory *wouldn't* show up. That it wouldn't matter enough to him. But it was also partly that Rett needed to talk about it. He needed some friendly support. Everything felt like it was falling apart around him with his parents, with Bo, and now with Cory, and he needed to talk. A three hour drive was a small price to pay since he had nowhere else he needed to be. And not really anyone else he could turn to.

Until Val showed up at her place, he'd have to face feeling dismembered on his own.

The consequences of the prior night and this morning, though, finally did start to show up. His phone buzzed with a text message in his pocket. He was afraid to look at it for a few minutes in case it happened to be from Cory. When he finally did, he found instead a message from JJ:

What the hell? You quit? What happened? Why didn't you say anything to me?

Rett sighed and felt the emptiness again. He waited a few minutes before replying:

Something very personal. Happened at the last minute. Sorry JJ.

He thought for a second before sending another text:

I'll really miss working with you.

JJ replied almost instantly:

Was it Skunk? I'll kill him if he did something to you.

Rett replied back: *No. Not work related at all. Sorry I didn't get to say goodbye.*

JJ said: *Tell me what I can do to help.*

Nothing. Thanks, though.

A few minutes passed with no other message, relieving Rett that he was done with that conversation.

But it wasn't long after that before he wound up getting messages from a whole series of other people — Dr. Bala, Sebastion, Arthur, Josh, Gunnar, Topher, and probably ten others — all saying they were sorry he had to leave without a proper goodbye and that they would miss him. Rett supposed it should have made him feel good, but it made him feel much worse; the emptiness and sadness at the path he had taken, at what he had given up when he handed in his ID that morning, welled up in him again. He put his arm over his eyes, breathing deeply while a few salty tears slipped from him.

After the messages stopped, he laid back in his car seat and closed his eyes again, trying to get rid of all the text messages and sick feelings knotting up inside him. Eventually, the lack of sleep from the night before and the boredom of waiting caught up to him and he dozed off.

"Get up, Rett."

Rett blinked and realized he had fallen asleep. He shaded his eyes with a hand and looked up to see Val frowning at him through his car window.

He pulled his seat back upright as Val said, "Why are you here, Rett? Aren't you supposed to be at the game?" She sounded more annoyed than anything.

"I need to talk to you."

Val stared at him for a moment before she sighed and nodded for him to come inside with her. He had expected Val to be glad to see him, or at least concerned; now he felt like this was a bad idea.

It felt odd to Rett to be back in the apartment for the first time since he had moved away. It hadn't been that long since he had moved out, but it felt like it had been years ago already. His whole life in Montgomery felt like it had been years ago instead of only a few months. It didn't help his emotional state given the upheaval in his life in Mobile, either. He was adrift and dislocated in every way possible, and desperately looking for a rock to cling to.

Val sat down in a new gray club chair she must have bought recently and watched Rett patiently until he was ready to talk.

Rett said, "I... uh..." Now that he was there, with Val looking at him like that, he had no idea where to start. He didn't know how to say it.

Val leaned forward and observed bluntly, "Let me guess... you broke up with Cory."

It burned, the way she said it. It felt like she had thrown scalding hot water on him. The moment she had seen him in his car outside her apartment, Rett knew that she already knew what the whole thing was about. He turned red in the face, but nodded plaintively.

Val rolled her eyes and ran both hands through her long, black hair in frustration.

"What happened, Rett?" Her voice wasn't sympathetic; it was downright irritated. Rett didn't want to talk about it if she was going to be like this. If she didn't care, then there wasn't any point in going into it.

"Why are you acting like all this is nothing but a burden to you, Val? We've always been there for each other," pleaded Rett.

"You know I love you, but this is so old. You burned through every available gay guy in Montgomery, and now you've cranked up in Mobile. Summer reruns bum me out, Rett."

"Ouch!" said Rett, getting a little angry now.

"Seven years I've known you and five years of us living together... I've heard all this before, Rett! God, the number of times I've sat and had this conversation with you! I've tried to get you to stick with it a little bit, to man up, but you never do!"

Rett's mouth hung open hearing these words from Val.

"You broke up with Tyler because he reminded you too much of your dad. You ditched Ethan because he was too much of a druggy, although I totally agree with you bailing on him. He was a cokehead and he deserved it. You broke it off with Brian because he reminded you too much of your mom. You left Ted in your dust because he got too clingy. And then Christopher because of his name!"

Rett pouted, "The fact that he insisted on being called Christopher was just the tip of the iceberg. He was a really pretentious guy, and you know it! You made fun of him constantly!"

"And then the best one, Mike... no one knows why you left him, not even Mike. But, hell, you even moved out of town to get away from him! I think I know what it is, though, what's at the bottom of all these," said Val, ignoring Rett. "Every time anyone gets close to you, you bail out."

"What? That's ridiculous! Every one of those situations was diff..."

Val interrupted, "Ok, so what was it with Cory? What *specific* thing did he do that was so bad that warranted you breaking up with him, huh? I'd *love* to hear what exact brand of an asshole he is. On you mark, get set, go!" Val sat back in her chair with her arms crossed, daring Rett to give a legitimate reason to her.

"I can't fight everybody, Val!"

Val threw her head against the back of the chair and groaned. "God! No one's asking you to fight everybody! You don't ever fight *anybody*, though! That's the fucking problem!"

"His friend Jimmy wanted me out of the picture! And Jimmy's got everybody that's anybody in Cory's life on his side! And Cory's so fucking famous now, I can't... I don't..." Rett's face flushed again and he didn't know what to say. He hated when Val got like this.

Val continued, "Fuck Jimmy! Does this Jimmy dickhead have veto power over Cory's love life? That sounds like total bullshit to me!"

"You don't understand," tried Rett. She didn't. She didn't know how close Jimmy was to Cory. How much Cory trusted and listened to him.

"I understand fine, Rett! I've had years to finally figure it out!"

Rett grasped for anything, anything at all. "You're just pissed because Cory's a major league ball player!"

Val rolled her eyes and she jumped out of her chair, totally inflamed. "*FUCK YOU!* That's one hundred percent bullshit, Rett! *Fuck you* for even *thinking* that that's what I care about. I don't care if Cory digs ditches, or is some kind of... of... genetically engineered florist! Cory is one of the best people I've ever met.

He's the best guy you've *ever* gone out with! And he's *fucking crazy* about you! I saw it every time he looked at you, or got that dimpled-ass grin because you were giving him a hard time! Mike and some of the others you dated were good guys, Rett, but Cory's really special. And you're a brain dead fucktard for walking away from that! Jesus!"

Val was pacing back and forth now and Rett sat stunned, his hands squeezing at his head.

Rett shouted, "Thanks! That's great! Some friend you are! All of this... all of this is my fault. Always has been." He wanted to crawl through the back of the sofa to make this stop.

Val pointed her finger at him, "Some of those guys weren't worth your time, but I finally understand the pattern now! If I listen to you, there's always some paper-thin excuse. But I finally figured out I shouldn't always believe what's coming out of your mouth, Rett."

She might as well have slapped Rett in the face with that comment for what it felt like. "What are you talking about? Are you saying I'm *lying* about this?"

Val paused for a second, scowling at him, the hurt in her eyes deeper than just the conversation they were having at this moment.

"I didn't say anything, Rett, because Bo was there," said Val more calmly, holding her temper and her own pain in check. "But I always thought your dad *kicked* you out of the house. But that's not what happened. Bo said you just left. Things got thick and you just walked out on them!"

Rett was speechless.

"All of it makes sense now, knowing that," spat Val. "You run when it gets tough with people close to you. But you lied to me all this time about your dad kicking you out!"

Rett stammered, "I never said he kicked me out! Not once!"

"You never corrected me, though! You *knew* that's what I thought and you let me believe it!" shouted Val.

"You don't understand! There's no difference in the end! You don't understand what happened that night!" yelled Rett. He shook his head and felt like he had been beaten up. He wiped at the tears in his eyes. She didn't know what happened that night, not really. No one did.

"You *never* corrected me, and it's *NOT* the same thing!" shouted Val again.

It didn't matter. Val wanted him to argue all the time, with everyone, about everything. Rett knew the truth about doing that, though. It had never done him any good. His father had shown him that.

"What you want me to do doesn't work, Val! It doesn't! Arguing a point never changes someone! It never changes their mind! It just gets them pissed at you! All anyone cares about is their perspective... how they see it! Why do it when it's not going to get anywhere?"

Val cried, "That's your excuse for never trying? Really? Making a stand for yourself is hard, so you just walk away and start over with other people? Of course it's never going to work if you never really *try* to make it work, shithead! Because if you don't, you wind up right where you are right now. And is that what you want, Rett? Because it's what you've got! It's what *you've* done to *yourself!*"

Rett looked down and put his face in his hands, wiping at the tears pouring down his face. He choked back the sobs and couldn't say anything.

Val calmed down some and wiped at her own eyes, smearing her makeup across her face in the process. "I don't like saying it, but it's *you* with the problem! Every time you get close, every time there's a rough spot. Rather than do the right thing and stand up for yourself and work it out, you just ditch and move on!"

Rett looked down between his feet, the drops of tears falling from his eyes onto the ratty carpet. She didn't understand. He came very close to getting up and walking out on her to end the conversation.

"You're so worried about what someone might do to you, you never think about what *you're* doing to *them*," said Val. "Summer's over, Rett, and you're not a child anymore! Be a man, for once! Finally! Be a man and stand up for yourself and *face* people. Be one for yourself!"

Val walked over towards the door and said more firmly, "How long, Rett? How long before you do this to me? Rather than face me and work a problem out, you'll just walk away from me? When's my turn coming? I'll bet you feel like running away from me right now!"

Val's face was twisted in pain again. "Well, you know what? Maybe you deserve a taste of your own medicine."

She opened the door. "Goodbye, Rett. I don't think we're really friends anymore."

The shock of the last sentence was like taking a shotgun blast in the heart. Val was the only person that had stood by him.

Rett stood up and tried to look at her, but he couldn't. He opened his mouth to say something, but Val repeated, "Goodbye, Rett," through her own tears.

He stepped out through her door and he heard it shut behind him. Every step he took back to his car made him feel more and more like he was filled with wet concrete, every step heavier and slower. Every step took more and more effort.

And if he stopped, he felt like he'd freeze in place and never be able to move again.

Chapter 23

"Ok, chief, I think I need to cut you off after this one."

Rett blanched at her use of the word "chief." She needed to find her own damn name for him besides that one. "Chief" was taken. He gave the red-headed demon bartender girl the best glare he could manage through his foggy eyes, which only managed to come across looking like his stomach was bothering him. She set his beer down in front of him on the wooden bar and gave him a firm look.

"It's only my second one!" groused Rett to her. That was an outright lie. It was his second one at the sports bar, sure, but he'd had three others already in his apartment over the course of the afternoon and early evening. Maybe five. Maybe a six pack and maybe he had actually started drinking that morning. They were spread out so he wasn't really drunk, but close enough to maintain the welcome, numbing buzz that was getting him through another day. When did this bitch become his AA sponsor?

"What you're seeing is just me tired. I've barely slept in days, *sweetheart*, which is why I'm having a few drinks before I go home and crash and hopefully get some actual sleep," explained Rett, trying hard to not slur his words too much and give himself away. Instead, his voice had a patronizing edge to it that he would have realized was doing more harm than good if he hadn't been too buzzed up to notice.

He may have lied about the number of drinks he'd had, but at least the part about the sleep was the truth. In five days since the charity ball, he'd barely slept. He was in a constant trance at this point from the lack of sleep, but it took alcohol to numb the stinging hollowness inside after Val ripped him a new one and turned him out of her apartment.

The bartender eyed him with a studied dissent, so Rett tried a different tactic. "I just need something to eat. Bring me some wings or something. Wings, maybe. Or I can just take my tip money and go drink somewhere else, Red. You're not the only game in town. Where are those wings?"

She wiped her hands on her black vest over her white shirt insolently before walking over to the register terminal to enter an order for the wings.

With her gone, Rett tried to ignore the two straight boys yammering on next to him. The place had been empty enough for a Thursday night, but then these numbnuts had come in a few minutes earlier and had to park it right next to him where he was trying to drink in peace.

He wasn't even sure why he had come to this place, whatever the hell it was named. It was a typical sports bar, old brick and rough wood and TV's everywhere. Token sports schlock splattered here and there. Rett corrected himself... it was a *nice* sports bar. He knew this because the chicks working there had white shirts and black vests with fake boobs stuffed into them instead of tight t-shirts with fake boobs stuffed in them. He wondered why he hadn't taken the effort to find a typical gay bar instead. Then he remembered... it was the music. He never could stand faggot music with the pounding disco beat. Stupid faggots. Who wanted music that sounded like drum machines, synthesizers and drag queens having an ecstasy-fueled three-way? Listening to that would have been much worse than sitting in his apartment for another day, drinking and rapidly going insane. Then he had seriously considered going and buying another case of beer and a new vacuum cleaner, and then wondered if there was somewhere he could buy both at the same place so he wouldn't have to make two stops. That was the thing that finally sounded raging warning klaxons in his head as to his state of mind. He had decided he had to stop counting the four blue walls of his apartment or he was going to go crazier than a lesbian cat-hoarder off her anti-depressants.

When he had come in, he had had the misfortune to spot someone wearing one of those stupid Joes jerseys they bought at the stadium store. This one was even worse... it said "Pritchart" and had a big 72 on the back of it; for some reason, he wanted to punch the guy for wearing it. He had sat down at the bar, the TV nearest him playing something that he could easily ignore, and began to drink in peace. But when the two loud-mouthed straight guys, Xavier J. Dickwad and his sidekick, Chester Fuckface III, showed up, they set up right next to Rett and insisted the bartender change the channel to the Joes game, currently in progress out in Rangers Ballpark in Dallas. Rett turned away from it, tried to ignore it, did his best to tune Dickwad and Fuckface out, and finally failed miserably and gave up on it.

Dickwad was saying "I don't know what the hell they were thinking trading Furukawa and bringing Cheatham in as shortstop."

Christ, thought Rett angrily, *here we go with the whole Satoru and D'Angelo thing again.* Maybe he should have gone to listen to audio equipment anally raping a drag queen over a back-room bar while a rainbow disco ball swirled around overhead after all.

Fuckface echoed his buddy's thoughts. "And Cheatham's fielding percentage is actually *lower* than Furukawa's. You gotta wonder who's running that team."

Oh, God dammit, thought Rett. Even he got why Ahab and George had done it. It wasn't that hard.

"Hey, you," he called at them obnoxiously. "Yeah, you," he repeated when they looked over at him. Rett could see the game playing out on the TV just past them. The TV seemed a little blurry, but then he realized it wasn't just the TV that was blurry; it was everything.

"D'Angelo's range is bigger, and that's why he's gotta slightly lower fielding percentage," he explained. "That's not D'Angelo's fault; fielding percentage doesn't take range into account. Satoru gives up a few more hits because he doesn't have the range that D'Angelo has, but that doesn't figure into fielding percentage. But I'm sure you already knew that, huh?" He blinked his eyes hard a couple of times trying to get the focus to firm up a little more. He felt like someone had smeared Vaseline on his eyeballs.

Fuckface obviously felt like his baseball gonads had been challenged. He looked at Rett and said, "It's not just fielding percentage, buddy. Furukawa's UZR is even higher than Cheatham's."

Rett sighed and ran his hand across his mouth. Then he surprised himself and wondered when he had managed to grow a beard. Had he really not noticed that in the last five days? Then he got preoccupied with how much facial hair he had grown in that time. Maybe if he went to the bathroom he could examine this whole natural phenomenon a little more closely and get a better scientific understanding of it. Perhaps take a measurement.

"It's bad management," insisted Fuckface while Rett continued to be distracted by the appearance of a beard on his face. He had never grown a beard before.

Rett tried to decide where to start. He hoped Dickwad and Fuckface could understand him so they'd shut the fuck up. "UZR assumes individual behavior only. And it assumes players stick to their zones only. Both of those assumptions suck cock. And not good cock. They suck, like, tiny little worthless cocks. Probably like Xavier's and Chester's cocks." His words were starting to slur even more, but Rett no longer particularly cared.

Dickwad and Fuckface looked at him strangely. "Luis and Satoru never got along with each other," continued Rett, his speech smearing together significantly. "All their yap-yap-yap crap spilled out onto the field and they didn't coordinate for low-grade donkey shit. D'Angelo and Luis get along great, and they'll coordinate a lot better when there's balls that go into the left field hole. And, defensively, we get an assload of hits into the left field hole. Right? You do know that, right? Baseball's still a team sport, and the fucking metrics don't take this shit into account. Ahab and George? *They* take it into account. You watch, D'Angelo will wind up being better out there next door to Luis than Satoru ever was."

Rett stared off into space a little bit trying to focus his eyes again. Was that harsh? He felt like he was being harsh. "Not that Satoru's a bad guy. He's alright," he added, woozily.

The two guys weren't quite sure how to respond to what Rett had said. And Rett was already ignoring them again at this point. He was chugging on his beer and lamenting a bunch of Saturday-afternoon managers that didn't know how the lives of the players figured into their performance. These guys had lives, and those lives affected how they played. Rett wanted to see the fucking metric that took *that* into account.

Rett suddenly spouted, more *at* them than *to* them, "*And* D'Angelo's a better hitter, too!"

Chumps, thought Rett as he tilted his beer back again.

The bartender brought out a stack of chicken wings with blue cheese and celery on the side and placed it all in front of Rett. He looked down at the wings in front of him and, with one whiff of the hot sauce on them, almost lost the beers he had been drinking all over the bar. The red-headed bartender stood there judgmentally, arms crossed across her overly-boobed chest, watching Rett turn pale at the sight of the food.

"Eat up," she prodded, maliciously enough for even Rett to pick up on. "We're famous for those wings!"

Rett picked up one of the wings and looked at it for a minute. He thought he really probably should try to eat something. He barely could remember eating hardly anything at all over the last few days. But he wasn't hungry, either. Toast would have been better than the nasty chicken wing he was examining. Why hadn't he ordered toast?

Rett's ears perked up at a sound, though, and he put the hot wing back down. Dickwad and Fuckface had changed their conversation.

Dickwad had said something about Cory to Fuckface.

"The guy can pitch," continued Dickwad, "but there's no way that dude's not taking steroids. The MLB's gonna catch his ass and kick him out."

Fuckface nodded in agreement.

"He's even got the mood swings," added Dickwad. "His pitching has been shit the last two games he's started. Like totally different all of a sudden. How do you explain that?"

"Steroids," said Fuckface, sure of the answer. He made a face and said, "The Joes are back to being the Mystic Crewe of the Perpetual Oh-Fer again. Shoulda known the winning streak wasn't gonna last."

Rett stared down at the thick, dark wood of the bar in front of him. Cory had pitched poorly in the last two games? He wanted to know *how* poorly, but didn't dare ask. He wished he hadn't overheard these two guys now.

He glanced over at the TV, something he had avoided ever since the bartender had put the game against the Texas Rangers on. It was the bottom of the 6th inning; Gunnar was pitching and JJ was behind home plate. The score was 2–5 with the Rangers leading. At least Cory wasn't pitching. He wouldn't have been able to handle it if he had seen a "72" out on the mound.

Rett grumbled and moved down to the far end of the bar to get away from the game and as far away from Dickwad and Fuckface as possible.

He propped his elbows on the bar and rested his chin in the palm of his hand. He'd spent four days now since Val had reamed him out with no idea what to do. He hadn't slept and couldn't remember eating. He was hungry, but looking at the syrupy chicken parts in front of him made him want to horph all over the bar. He had tried to apply for a few new jobs that afternoon, but since he was a little out of it, he wasn't sure if he had been successful or had only imagined it.

He tried to remember the phrase that Fuckface had just used. The Mystic Something of the Something Oh-Fer. That was it.

Who else had used that phrase with Rett that one time? Rett remembered someone using "oh-fer" and he had no idea what it meant at the time. It seemed like it was a long time ago, but who knew for sure with his mind in its current state? They had said something about Rett pulling an oh-fer; but he wasn't able to remember the specifics right now. Not with his brain riding high on beer and sleeplessness. And he had had no idea what that person meant when they said it, but he knew now.

He was living it with every day and with everything that had ever meant anything to him.

How much is there left in you after you have lost everything outside of yourself?

Oh-fer.

He sat, looking at nothing, barely remembering to breathe.

His eyes fluttered shut since it was too hard to hold them open. In his mind, he saw Val pacing back and forth in her apartment, shouting at him. She'd gotten pissed at him before, but never like that. She was yelling. Yelling at him because he had lied about the night he had left. Yelling at him because he had let her believe something that didn't actually happen. Letting her believe it for the entire time he had known her. Letting her believe he had been kicked out by his parents instead of sneaking out and leaving. But she didn't know all of it. The truth wasn't that easy. It wasn't for other people. Even now, it wasn't for others. Even if it cost him Val.

Rett tried to stop thinking about it. People just didn't understand. They only saw their own point of view. He called Red over and ordered another beer and put up with the pissy look she gave him. He tried to listen to the murmuring noise of the crowd in the bar with him. He tried to drown out his own thoughts and memories with it. White noise was the answer to thinking about all this. Avoiding the thoughts was better than the beating he took by constantly playing them in his head, over and over.

But after a minute, he wondered if Val was right. Was that how he always handled it? For the first time in days he stopped thinking about the claws she had dug into him and the bleeding and hurt it had caused, and he thought about what she had said instead.

You never fight anybody, Rett. That's the problem! You just run when it gets tough with people close to you.

It's what you've done to yourself.

Was that really true? Is that what he had learned? Just run away rather than stand up, push back a little, demand his place? Was it that important? Was every failed relationship within his life nothing but a repeat of his failed relationship with his father? Isn't that what Val implied in the end?

Would he have walked away even from her like she claimed? If things got too tough, would he have done that to her as well?

He remembered feeling it even then, as he had sat in her den, right as she said it. He wanted to walk away from her. He wanted to leave her behind and avoid the pain of dealing with her.

But she beat him to it.

And it had felt like battery acid coursing through his veins. It burned from the inside out. That's what it felt like to be on the receiving end of it.

She had accused Rett of cutting and running without ever thinking about the effect it had on the other person. She wanted to force Rett to understand what it was like to be that other person. To understand the impact on him.

His mouth pulled down into a frown. It was always easy to ignore the impact to the other person if he never really saw them again. But Cory... Cory... with Cory... he could turn on fucking ESPN and see the effect it had had on him. There'd be a goddamn highlight reel of the effect, Cory slumping and pitching like a drugged tree sloth. There'd be on-air analysts wondering what the hell happened. Clucking about his current situation. Like they knew *anything* about his current situation.

Oh-fer.

Rett had nothing in him. Everything was gone and nothing was left in him. He was a void.

His eyes stung and he saw the void that he was in his mind. Everything else around him disappeared and he saw the empty space that he was. He was a hole suspended in empty air, and not alcohol, not one relationship after another, not the Joes, not Val, not his family could fill it. Not even Cory could fill it.

The only thing that could fill it was Rett.

He ground his teeth together because not even the Rett as he was would fill it. The Rett sitting drunk at that bar at that moment would never fill it. It had to be a *different* Rett. He had to grow up and stop running away from every tough situation, from every relationship once it got too tight for comfort. He had to fill the void with himself first. Val, as heavy-handed as always, was right.

Rett squinted when it hit him. Even his dad, in every wrong way possible, had been sort of right all along at the core of it.

In his mind, he saw Cory standing in the dim light, tossing a ball up in his hand as he looked back at Rett right before their first pitching lesson. Just before their first kiss. Cory had assured him that Rett was all the man he needed to be.

But Cory was wrong. As wrong as anybody could be. Rett wasn't a man. He never had been. He had failed his dad at a bunch of bullshit superficial signs of manhood, but he had failed himself where it really counted. That was why he was hollow. That was why he had lost everything.

Rett's head turned towards the far end of the bar, Dickwad and Fuckface still there. He stared vacantly at the game playing out on the large television next to them. It was just shapes and colors and motion, though. All he could really sense was the yawning sinkhole where he was supposed to be.

It was overwhelming, the idea of fixing himself. How could he snap his fingers and decide to finally be totally different? Especially when he had fucked so much up as badly as he had? Would he deserve the chance? Would anyone even give him the chance if he tried?

Without hardly noticing it, he saw an image of a cloud of dust and Cory wrestling with a bunch of kids on a field. But in his ear he heard a song:

The itsy-bitsy spider
climbed up the water spout
Down came the rain
and washed the spider out
Out came the sun
and dried up all the rain
And the itsy-bitsy spider
Climbed up the spout again

He remembered Jerry saying, "We all fuck it up some. It's what we do *after* that that matters."

That was comforting. That helped. It didn't matter if he succeeded or not. It didn't matter if anyone gave him the chance or not. All that mattered was that he try.

Rett heard a noise and looked up to see Red talking to him, her face pissed off too much this time. He put his hand to his face and realized he was crying. He glanced around weakly and saw people all around looking at him, including Fuckface and Dickwad.

He cried out at no one, at everyone, "What's the matter with you people?!" He wiped his sleeve across his running nose. He slurred at them, "Haven't you people ever seen a grown man drip snot onto his hot wings before?" Rett felt the icy stares of a hundred eyes on him from every direction.

The bartender stepped forward. "Alright, chief, you gotta pay and get out. Now. You can't stay here like this," she said, brooking no more of Rett's sad state. She pointed at his check that she had already placed in front of him.

Rett nodded and put some money out on the counter, his head throbbed and he hardly noticed the people watching him as he stumbled out of the bar, knocking into chairs and tables as he tried to find the exit.

Once he stepped outside into the stifling summer night, he took a deep breath and forced his head to finally clear, if only insignificantly. He took a few more deep breaths and steadied himself.

He knew what he needed to do. Sort of. He hoped.

First things first.

Chapter 24

The biggest difference Rett immediately noticed was that the two river birch trees in the front yard were gone. It gave him a bitter satisfaction to see this since he hated those trees; they were a bitch to mow around and their leaves made a mess that he had to rake up all the time. The big camellia bush out by the street was still there, which was good. He parked along the curb so that the camellia bush blocked anyone in the house from noticing his car out on the street.

The roof looked new, too. Otherwise, it was still the same house he had grown up in. Same single-story ranch house of beige brick and dark brown shutters. The grass out front needed mowing, but Rett supposed that could be excused since his dad had had a bad heart attack.

He settled in to wait. There were two cars in the carport, and neither of them were Bo's red truck, so he assumed his dad was home from the hospital and that he and his mom were inside. With both of them there, he wouldn't be caught by them driving up unexpectedly and seeing him out on the street.

The big question was whether Bo would show up. He wasn't sure if Bo still lived at home or not, or would even be there anytime soon since it was Friday evening. But he was going to wait.

This was how he began to fill the empty spot that was bigger than he was. This was how he grew so that he could fill that hole.

This was how he repaired the damage. This was how he started. Back to the beginning. The one he had wronged the most. It started with waiting.

The years since he had walked out the door of the house he was in front of now felt like only hours instead. There had been so much that happened behind those beige bricks. Pain, and anger, and disappointment. And fear, too. He could still see himself hauling out the few possessions he could get in his car the morning after his father had made it clear he didn't belong in the family anymore. It made him uneasy to know he was this close to his parents again and he still felt unwelcome, but this was how he had to fix things. Doing this, facing this, was how he forced himself to grow up. Today would be the beginning of the end for the old Rett.

He settled in to wait, however long he had to. He was glad the hangover from the day before was mostly gone now. He doubted he'd go back to that sports bar again, even if they'd let him in after the spectacle he made of himself the night before.

He waited patiently, keeping alert, and the daylight began to segue from late afternoon to early evening; the sun softened, the heat lessened, other people arrived home down the street, the workweek shifted slowly into the weekend. The sky had a thin, gauzy white cloud cover that made him feel closed in.

Rett's phone buzzed and he looked at it. He had been expecting the message at some point, but still he read the text from Jimmy grimly.

I have the money for you. Let's meet Sunday morning.

That was it. Rett sighed and hoped he could work this out, or nothing would follow correctly after. He ignored the message for the time being, instead focusing solely on what he was there to do. *First things first,* he reminded himself.

Well over an hour later, Rett was almost ready to pack it in and go home. The light was fading to twilight and he didn't expect Bo to show up if he hadn't already. He made the decision to wait a little bit longer, just in case, when he saw the little red truck turn the corner a half a block away. He shifted nervously in his seat when the truck pulled into his parents' driveway, oblivious to Rett's black Jetta parked out on the street. In the fading light of the day, Rett could see Bo behind the wheel.

He was almost too nervous to even try. It was still so easy to hide away from everything. It would be so easy to let Bo walk inside the house while he turned his car around and drove back to Mobile. It was always so easy to run the other way. It would be so easy to stay empty. But he had to make this work or nothing ever would. He listened for the truck door to close and then tapped his horn quickly to get Bo's attention and before he lost his nerve. Rett's hands were wet with sweat, and his car door handle slipped out of his fingers before he could open his door. He kept the camellia bush between him and the house, but called Bo's name right as Bo walked to the end of the driveway to see who had honked the horn.

Bo's face changed from curious to hard. His expression tightened and he folded his arms over his chest while he stood next to the camellia looking at Rett, not speaking.

Rett took a deep breath and said, trying to sound much more confident than he was feeling, "Bo, we need to talk." The fear wanted to swallow him. It was so easy to be swallowed by it.

Bo looked back towards the house with a tired effort and said, "We already talked, Rett. Not much seemed to change."

"It will this time," insisted Rett.

Bo shrugged his indifference, "What do you want to say, Rett?"

"Not here. Not this close to their house. I can't see them right now. This is between you and me."

Bo looked at his watch impatiently. "I can't, Rett. They're expecting me."

Rett stepped forward and then held the ground he stood on. "No, Bo. We're gonna talk, damn it. Give me somewhere that we can go. They won't care if you're late."

Bo stood motionless, trying to decide. "Ok, follow me back over to my apartment. But I have to be back here before long."

Rett nodded, and Bo got back in his truck and backed out of the driveway. On the way over to Bo's apartment, Rett still was awed at the man his brother had become; he was the same person, but yet seemed so different from what Rett remembered. Older, yes, but something else, too. More sure of himself, less in awe of his big brother. It made what he was doing harder. He worried that there was too much time and space between them. That he had messed up too badly with Bo. But... that was the Rett he had to bury. He had to be bigger than that. He had to be big enough to fill the void. Time couldn't stand still forever and things had to change. Rett had to change, and he had to make Bo see it.

Rett was absorbed in his thoughts, and hardly paid attention to where his brother was leading him. When they arrived, Bo's apartment was in a complex that Rett remembered — a smaller, older one, in a half-hearted faux Mediterranean style, with probably only four buildings and not far from their high school.

Bo was silent as he let Rett in. Rett smiled wryly to himself when he saw the inside. It could have easily been Rett and Val's apartment when they first moved in — cheap, worn, and under-furnished. But it had been their own and not student housing, and that was all that mattered. Rett was sure it was the same for Bo.

Inside the den, Rett turned back to his brother, who was standing with his arms crossed over his chest again, waiting. Bo didn't offer him a seat or take one for himself.

Rett had thought about what to say all day and had come up oh-fer, and even now wasn't sure what the right approach was. He said, "I'm not happy with how we left things last time, when you came by."

Bo said nothing.

"I know you're pissed at me," said Rett, dropping his gaze from Bo's. "And you have every right to be. I should have gotten in touch with you somehow, and I didn't. I let you down."

Bo's forehead furrowed and he said, "I'm not pissed, Rett. I just thought you didn't love me, that you didn't care. I thought the note was bullshit in the end. You want to cut the ties with mom and dad? I can actually understand that. But what hurt was that I got lumped in with them. Even seeing you a few weeks ago after all these years, I still wasn't sure where I stood with you. I wasn't sure if I was pushing my way into your life where you still didn't want me, that I wasn't welcome in. I was hurt, and I still had my doubts. I *still* have those doubts."

Rett knew he had to lay it on the line. He had to put himself out there and let Bo decide if he would accept it or not. Rett had to be man enough to accept the answer, whichever way it went. That was how the void started to fill.

"It was never you, Bo. I was chicken, and scared, and I was wrong to be that way. No more will I evade it and try to excuse it. I was wrong to hurt you that way. And if there's a way for me to make it up to you, I will. I want my brother back, Bo. Tell me what I have to do to earn you back as my brother."

Rett could see Bo's expression shift. The wall he had put up, the hardness he had put in place to keep Rett from hurting him again, gave way slightly. But just barely.

"I just want to understand," said Bo. "And I want to know that you're not going to disappear like that again. It hurt when you left, and then I got mad at you. I hated you for a while because I thought you had lied to me. I thought you hated me like you hated mom and dad, and I hated you back. But that faded away. The longer I was around dad, the more I understood and I couldn't hate you for leaving. I could feel hurt, but I couldn't hate you."

Rett shook his head, "I meant what was in the note, Bo. But my fear of everything, my fear of dad, was greater than keeping my brother. It shouldn't have been, but it was. I'm sorry, Bo, for hurting you that way."

Rett watched to see if the words were getting through to him, but Bo stood still. He frowned as Bo remained there, unmoved. This wasn't working. Words weren't working. Rett felt his resolve slipping away. He didn't know what to do. He held his arms out without knowing what else to say, a plea for Bo to please understand.

And then it flashed into Rett. It was harder than words, what he had to do. But it was how he would become more than he was. He saw how this would be so much harder than words.

Rett stepped forward, causing Bo to step back away from him. He refused to accept the flinch from his brother this time, refused to let Bo step back, and Rett embraced his brother, pulled him close, and hugged him. Rett physically erased the seven years of separation by pulling his brother to him and holding him. He buried his face in his younger brother's shoulder.

He wasn't sure if Bo would push him away or not. All he could do was try, and leave the rest to his brother.

And then Rett felt Bo's arms reach around him and embrace him back. He heard Bo sniff, and Rett couldn't hold the emotion back, either. It was the first time in far too many years he had touched his family. Rett had family again.

They stood holding each other, Rett's chin on his brother's shoulder. He whispered, "I swear, Bo, I'll never do that to you again. You'll never lose your brother ever again."

Bo grabbed him even tighter at the words. The physical contact serving as a covenant not to repeat the mistakes of the past again. The embrace re-forging the bond of family between them. All the words in the world wouldn't fix this. Rett saw now that it was deeper. He had to do the thing that was hardest for him to regain his brother; he had to be the one to take that first step. He had to give Bo the option to accept or reject it. Being a man meant making himself vulnerable and giving the final decision to Bo.

When they separated, Bo smiled despite the dampness on his face. "I have my brother back." His mouth quivered with the words and he wiped at his eyes.

Rett said, "You never really lost me, Bo; I just had to get my head out of my ass."

Bo chuckled and studied his brother again, "So you really turned out gay after all? It wasn't just that dad drove you away?"

"I'm gay, alright," said Rett, "but dad drove me away anyway. Does it bother you?"

Bo sneered, "Jesus! Don't try and make me the same as dad, Rett. I love him, but I know he's a jerk about a lot of things." Bo's eyes were still glistening and he brushed at them again with his hand.

"Do you remember," asked Bo, "when I was around 12 and dad was in his phase where he was trying to teach you to change the oil in the car?"

"Oh, yeah," said Rett. "Wish I could forget."

"You wanted nothing to do with it, but I was more than happy to learn. I thought it was cool to work on the cars. But then I tried it one time when he wasn't around and I fucked it up and drained oil all over the driveway and then put new oil in while it was still pouring out underneath. He got furious at me. And, he said I was turning out just like you."

Rett nodded with a pained smile. He remembered all of that happening. As much as it hurt for his dad to treat him like that, like he was a pariah in the family, it was a hundred times worse when he used him to make Bo feel that way.

Bo said, "When he said that, I could tell he meant it to be something mean, but I couldn't understand why being like you would be a bad thing. That made him yell at me even more and he sent me to my room. I remember you coming into my bedroom later that night, and I had been crying because I didn't understand. You told me I wasn't anything like you and that was good because dad would be happier that way. You told me that I was better than you. You gave me a hug and cheered me up, and told me to always remember that. I remember thinking that I *still* wanted to be like you."

Bo nodded and said, "Gay or straight doesn't matter to me. It never did. I'm just glad to have my big brother back."

Rett closed his eyes and let the words wash over him. He couldn't possibly describe what it felt like. To have family again. To have his brother back. He'd never let go of him again, no matter what.

Bo looked thoughtful and continued, "After you left, he wouldn't talk about it. He never said a word about the night you left. But I already had picked up enough by then to know what the friction was between the two of you. I knew you'd left because you'd had enough. I just wasn't sure if you actually were gay or simply fed up with dad. It's not like you're obvious, and dad has some pretty fucked up standards. He refused to talk about you, but he changed after you left, too. He seemed angry all the time. He never laughed any more. For a while, he doubled up on riding my ass, I guess to make up for you being gone, but you know I always went along with him. You pushed back and tried to fight him, until he crushed that in you and you couldn't anymore, but I'd go along. Then, eventually, he got quiet and spent more time by himself. He talked less to me and mom. And he never talked about you. He absolutely refused to talk about you and got mad at me or mom if we brought you up. You had left, but, in a way, you were still there. All that time. None of us were allowed to talk about the hole that was left behind, but we all tiptoed around it every day."

Bo's shoulders fell and he admitted, "It hurt twice. Once when you left, and then again when Dad would get pissed if we mentioned you."

It felt strange to know how his leaving impacted his father. Rett had always assumed that his dad would be glad he had left, happier. Hearing how Rett's disappearance hit the whole family made him uncomfortable.

Rett saw that Bo's sofa was the one that had been in the house when he left, and he decided to change the subject. "But you got your own place now!" he said, trying to cheer his brother up.

"Yeah, I feel a little guilty, especially after dad's heart attack. But it's good to be out of that house," said Bo. "The deal was, once I got done with school and got a job, I got my own place."

"So you went to college? What are you doing?"

"Just went to the community college, learned how to build software. I'm doing that now. Web stuff, mostly."

Bo seemed timid for a moment, but then asked, "What about you? What did you do after you left?"

"I lived in Montgomery for seven years, until just recently. I went to physical therapy school at Alabama State, and have sort of been doing that after graduating." Rett didn't feel like going into the specifics given his current job situation.

"Shit! Seven years? How the hell did you afford that?"

"I got some tuition assistance since I was on my own. But mostly I did it like any red-blooded American... a *lot* of debt."

Bo laughed, "But still, that's a lot of school to go through. But you've got something solid now you can do! I'm proud of you, Rett!"

Rett wondered how proud he'd really be if he knew his current situation.

"Do you want to go with me, over to mom and dad's?" Bo asked cautiously.

Rett's face twisted.

"I didn't think so," said Bo.

"I don't know if I can see the look in dad's face again. Like the night I left, and then again in the hospital. Or hear the bitterness in his words."

Bo nodded sadly at him.

"I don't think I'll ever be able to face them again, Bo."

"Ever? Really?" asked Bo.

"Mom, maybe. She seems to have pulled herself together a little, and you said she was getting her depression treated, which is good. But dad? I don't think so. But for me, the two of them still feel like too much of a set."

Bo shook his head, trying to sort it out. "I don't know, Rett. That sounds a little weird to me. Dad knew mom was trying to contact you. I think he wanted her to. It might have even been his idea, but that's me making a guess. It's strange that he would still treat you like before."

Rett thought about it for a few seconds. He wasn't sure what to make of it, though. It didn't make much sense to him, either. While Rett was thinking about it, he felt Bo's hand reach out and touch his face.

He might have otherwise jerked away at this, but it was good to know his brother felt comfortable touching him. Bo was studying him very intently.

"What?" he asked Bo.

"You look weird with a beard."

"It looks like shit? I probably look like shit."

"No, I didn't say that. Just different. Older," said Bo, lost in his examination of his brother. "You're so old now. It's strange because I remember you being 18 for so long and now you look so different."

"Same for you, Bo," said Rett. "You're a man now. My memories of you were a frozen version of you at 14."

They studied each other in silence for a minute. "I'm sorry, Bo," said Rett. "Sorry for the lost time. For leaving you on your own. I really did miss you, but I was just too big a chickenshit to do what was right..."

Bo stepped over and hugged Rett again. "Doesn't matter. I've got my big brother back now. Better late than never, you know?"

"Yeah." Rett knew exactly what Bo was saying.

Bo looked at his watch and frowned. "Rett, I gotta get back over there. I want to stay here and talk to you. Man, I could stay up all night talking to you. But they'll get worried pretty soon."

Rett said, "How is dad, by the way?"

"He's getting better. Still weak. But he's been home about two weeks now. The doctors told him to take it slow, but he's been getting up and taking short walks lately."

Bo's eyes lit up. "Hey, you can stay here if you want! If you don't want to drive back to Mobile, you can spend the night. I'll be back later this evening."

Rett nodded and smiled. "That would be awesome, little brother. But I've got some things I really have to take care of." It honestly did sound great to Rett.

They walked back outside, and in the parking lot, Rett said, "Before I go, I have to say something."

He glanced up at the faint stars gaining ground in the twilight sky. "No matter what, I swear to you that I will never leave you behind like that again. And if I have a problem, or if you have a problem, I will *not* walk away from you. We'll work through it. Family, Bo. You're all the family I've got, and I won't let go of that ever again."

They hugged again and Rett watched his brother drive off to go back over to their parents' house. When Rett got in his car and pointed it back in the direction of Mobile, he felt good for the first time in weeks. He had family again. He had a brother that he loved.

As he was about to pull out of the parking lot, he got a text message. It was another one from Jimmy:

You there, Rett? Did you get my last message?

Rett stopped his car. It was time for him to stand up, take back control, and he was ready to reply to Jimmy's message this time.

I want to meet at the Portyards tomorrow night. We need to talk.

He smiled to himself because it gave him a great deal of pleasure to send an additional note to Jimmy:

And you can keep your fucking money.

He pulled out of the parking lot still smiling, ready for the drive back to Mobile.

He was ready.

Chapter 25

Devin Templeton, the Reaper of the Baltimore Orioles, laughed casually at his off-camera interviewer.

He said, barely bothering to consider the question he had been asked, "I'm not sure what the roar was about him. It was easy enough on our first encounter. Tonight's game was trivial. The Joes might seriously consider replacing him with a T-ball stand for all the good he's done."

The off-camera interviewer tried to moderate Templeton's statement, saying, "Well, he's had a slump the last few games, but he's still a very promising pitcher. Surely you have to agree with that."

"No, I don't," said Templeton with a condescending smirk. "Giving up 14 hits in tonight's game and 8 runs before Ahab Delrossi has the good sense to yank him off the mound? You can sit behind your desk and philosophize about him all you want... but when I want an easy win without having to work for it, I want Pritchart pitching. I guess the MLB needed some comic relief, so God bless the Joes for that!"

Rett stared at the TV screen and felt the life drain out of him upon hearing these comments. He groaned out loud and wished so much that he had stayed in bed looking up at the ceiling in his bedroom rather than breaking down and turning ESPN on. The initial surge of confidence, downright giddiness, he had felt at winning his brother back a few hours earlier, at having family

350

again, had already faltered when he got home to his apartment and went to bed. He had started thinking about what he had heard the two guys at the sports bar say about Cory's performance. Then he started obsessing about it. After getting home from Bo's apartment, he couldn't sleep because of it. He laid awake in his bed for hours worrying about what needed to happen next; what he was meeting Jimmy the next day to do. Against his better judgment, he finally got up about 2am and turned the TV on when he couldn't stand it anymore.

And God, how he had wished he hadn't.

The game earlier that evening had gone very badly for Cory, and Templeton alone had scored two runs and 2 RBI's against him. Not content with winning, the Reaper was more than happy to twist the knife in the wound as hard as he could. On national TV. Rett really hated that guy.

He had started realizing what he was up against, not just Jimmy, who wanted him gone, but also the hurt he had definitely put Cory through as well. And then there was the debacle he was watching on TV at the moment. It was all far worse than he could have imagined. Trying to make things right was one thing. Trying to make all of *this* right was beyond him. How could he possibly expect Jimmy or Cory to give him a chance? He might as well fly to the moon with a few feathers in his hands and holding his breath.

Outside his window, Friday night slowly turned into Saturday morning, and every minute brought him closer to the disaster he had scheduled with Jimmy. But he couldn't deny he deserved it. No one had created this situation except him, and no matter how badly it ended, he deserved it.

Still, he'd try. He had to, because it wasn't just about getting Cory back.

He wrapped his arms around his knees and watched as they cut away from the interview with the Reaper and back to the ESPN analysts. As much as he knew he should, he couldn't turn it off now if his life depended on it.

The analysts began discussing what had happened to Cory lately. All agreed that, despite Devin Templeton's assessment, Cory had been off to a very promising start. The Joes, with Cory in the starting rotation, had gone from being at the bottom of the AL rankings to being just barely in the bottom half; their win ratio had gone from a dismal 25% to upwards of 40% since Cory came on. But Cory's last three starts weren't a good sign. He'd lost all three. All the games he started prior to that, he'd given up an average of only 3 runs per game; in the last three, he had suddenly given up an average of 8 runs per game, a huge difference.

There was a lot of hand wringing among the analysts as to the cause. Was it just a particularly deep rookie slump? Or had his earlier performance been just an adrenaline-fueled good luck streak? No matter what, the slump had rippled through to the rest of the team, just like his earlier good performance had as well. One analyst made a comment that caused Rett to wince and feel physically sick — he had said, "It seems, as Pritchart goes, so goes the Joes." Before they cut to commercial break, Rett heard the analyst remark with a patronizing shake of his head, "Pritchart had better pull out of his slump fast, or the Joes will have to seriously consider their options with him."

Rett felt the whole damn world on him, suffocating him. He had never felt more hopeless than he did at that moment. How could he possibly put all this right? How could he realistically demand a second chance after this?

Rett closed his eyes. He saw Cory standing in the dark of night in the middle of the junior high school field, saying "You're all the man you need to be already, Rett."

He would have given anything for that to have been true.

~~~~~

Rett didn't even show up until into the 3rd inning of the game. And then he stood outside the gate of the Portyards for twenty minutes trying to screw up his courage to go inside. Even without Cory pitching tonight, it was killing him to think about what he was about to try to do. It took him reminding himself that no matter how bad it went, he deserved it. And that none of that gave him the privilege of walking away from the attempt. There was too much at stake to walk away from whatever the result was.

Rett settled into his seat in the emptiest section they had when he had bought his ticket. He was in the very worst seats in the stadium, and he had the section entirely to himself. He sat down and kept his eyes off the field for a moment, trying to calm his shaking hands.

Naturally, the very first thing that jumped into his vision the instant he allowed himself to look down on the field was jersey 72 sitting up on the Joes' bullpen stands across the outfield from where he sat. The entirety of the stadium seemed to press in on Rett, the weight of everything crushing him. He wondered what the hell he had been thinking? What the hell was he thinking that night at the charity ball? What the hell was he thinking showing up now? Rett was glad he hadn't eaten any food or he would have thrown it up right then. He could close his eyes to shut the game out, but he had to listen to it whether he wanted to or not.

The Joes were ahead, 1 to 0, at least. He opened his eyes again, forcing himself to focus on the field itself. It took everything he had to not stare at the "72" on the other side of the field.

He waited for Jimmy to finally show, but over the next five innings he alternated his time between lingering and painful glances at Cory sitting motionless in the bullpen, watching Gunnar straining like crazy as he pitched his heart out to prevent the Orioles from getting on the board, and worrying about what the hell he was going to say to Jimmy when he did show up.

The more Rett watched Gunnar, the more concerned he got. He could tell how hard Gunnar was pushing himself and straining his arm, putting the weight of the entire team on his back once again. Gunnar was going to kill himself trying to win this game.

By the bottom of the 8th inning, the score hadn't changed and Rett noticed that the bullpen was now empty. Cory and Sebastion had moved over to the dugout, which meant that Ahab was planning to let Gunnar finish out the game.

Rett had almost chewed his thumbnail off at that point, and Jimmy still had not shown up. Rett was so stressed out he began to consider leaving, but before that thought could take root he saw Jimmy emerge out into the stands and look around for him.

In a split second, what little resolve Rett had brought into the stadium with him evaporated, and he understood there was no way he could face this man. Jimmy alone was too much for Rett to handle.

He had already lost before even the first word was spoken. Lost at everything he was trying to accomplish there.

He stared down at his hands, and he felt rather than saw Jimmy sit down a couple of seats over; it was impossible to look at him.

There was a moment or two of only the sounds of the game, but Rett wasn't paying much attention as the 8th inning was winding down.

Eventually, Rett heard Jimmy say, "So, I'm here, Rett. What was it you wanted to talk about?"

The calm, even tone in Jimmy's voice irritated the hell out of Rett. But even so, Rett felt lost. There was no way he could do what he was here to do. Jimmy wasn't the one that had fucked up, and he could hear it in his voice that Jimmy knew that as well as he did.

Rett stared at the back of the seat in front of him. Somewhere in the distance he could tell the 8th inning had just ended.

"I... uh..." attempted Rett. He stopped.

And he gave up entirely.

"I don't even know where to start," he said, still refusing to look at Jimmy.

"Why don't you start with the money. You don't want the money?"

Rett snarled at how Jimmy wanted to make this about the goddamn money. It infuriated him.

"Fuck your shitty money! Fuck you and your fucking money!" he shouted at Jimmy.

Jimmy didn't respond and Rett's anger at him boiled over even more. "And fuck you for thinking you *own* Cory!"

"I definitely don't own Cory," said Jimmy.

Rett continued to refuse to look at him. He shouted, "Yeah? You're trying to control his life! His decisions! All you care about is getting rid of me to protect his career!"

Rett found out what would be worse than Jimmy's calm, unflappable tone. Jimmy laughed out loud at Rett, and *that* was much worse. Rett was torn between running away, and physically assaulting Jimmy right there in the stands. He forced himself to hold his ground. And he decided the Portyards was more his than it was Jimmy's.

Despite the laughter, when Jimmy spoke, it wasn't patronizing or bitter. It was patient. And something else. Rett picked up on it and found that there was something a little sad in it, too.

Jimmy said, "I care about Cory, Rett. Not his career. Believe me, if there is one person on this earth that understands that distinction, it's me. There's no way in heaven or hell I'll ever make that mistake again."

Rett didn't know how to react to that. This was some kind of trick. Why had he orchestrated this if not for Cory's career? Did he simply hate Rett that much? Did he think he was that bad of a match for Cory?

Jimmy prodded again, "Come on, Rett. What's this about?"

"Who the fuck are you to decide who gets to be with Cory and not?" Rett could feel his face turning red.

"I didn't know that I was doing that."

Rett bellowed, "You made me leave him!" It was a good thing there weren't any other spectators anywhere near the two of them because Rett couldn't contain his anger and fear any longer.

"Calm down. You do realize that *you* made that decision. Not me. Right?" Jimmy's tone was still even and patronizing and wildly infuriating.

Rett hated Jimmy so much. He hated how calm and smug he was. And right. God, he hated that Jimmy was right.

"What's this really about, Rett?" asked Jimmy again.

Rett exploded without even knowing what he was saying, "*Fuck you* for making me *compete* with you for him!"

There was dead silence from Jimmy and Rett finally looked him in the face for the first time. Jimmy's face was drawn out and he stared off across the field as he considered what Rett had said.

Rett realized Jimmy had prodded him to the heart of it. Rett realized why it had been so easy to give up, and why there was no hope of making this work. He looked again at the back of the seat in front of him. "You're everything to him. I can't... I'll never..."

Rett closed his eyes entirely. "I'll never be to him what you are."

Jimmy said softly, "No. You won't be what I am to him."

Even Jimmy understood. Even Jimmy knew.

"Why do you love him?" asked Jimmy.

Rett sighed. "I don't know."

"It's not a trick question. Why do you want to be with him?"

"I don't know! I just do." Rett rubbed his eyes to keep them from stinging. Then, "He's handsome, but he's not the kind of guy I normally go for. He's kind, and funny. And he cares. And he's freaking amazing, and he has no idea that he is. He's... he's the most beautiful person I know, and it has nothing to do with his dimples."

Rett leaned forward and rested his head on his arms on the seatback in front of him hopelessly. "Because every minute I spend around him, I become a better person."

Jimmy waited a moment before prompting, "Is that it?"

Rett asked crossly, "Yeah. Should there be something else? Am I failing your test?"

"No. I just wanted to make sure that was it."

Jimmy added, "The night we went to the steak restaurant for dinner, Rett, you sat next to Cory. I don't think anyone else there noticed, and I certainly didn't say anything... but that was the first time in the ten years I've known Cory that he didn't want me sitting next to him."

Rett said, "You just said I won't be what you are to him, asshole."

Jimmy ignored Rett. He asked, "Why does Cory like to be with you?"

"I don't *know*."

"Take a guess."

"*I don't know, Jimmy!* We didn't write out lists to compare like 13-year old girls!"

Jimmy sighed. "You never talked about it at all..."

Rett sat back up and shook his head in frustration, "I'm his Jason stand-in. I'm the Jason whose pants he can actually get in."

Jimmy laughed again. "Man, you really don't get it."

Rett looked at him angrily again, "What the fuck do you want, Jimmy? I can't fight you! I can't fight you and win this. If you want me gone, which you obviously do, then what the hell chance do I stand? Huh?"

Jimmy locked his eyes on Rett and said harshly, "So what the fuck do you want, Rett? You said you didn't care about the money. What is it you *do* want?"

"I want Cory back. I want *Cory*, damn it!" Rett shouted, "Cory's the best thing that ever happened to me and I want *you* to stop fucking pushing me away from him!"

"Why, Rett? *Why* should you have Cory?" demanded Jimmy.

Rett ran his hands through his hair furiously, "Because a week ago I finally realized what he was to me! I have a baseball sitting on my counter at home. It's the one that Cory and I tossed around together the first time I *ever* did that with *anybody* and actually enjoyed it! He smells like the soap from the clubhouse shower, but his left hand smells like the leather of his glove. Because I secretly love how he makes me sing along with him to Blondie songs! He calls me 'chief!' He's every god damn thing to me! He's every god damn atom in the universe to me!" Rett was practically screaming by the time he finished.

Jimmy watched him intently. Rett slowed down and said, hopelessly, "But you're *more* to him. And if you want me out of the picture, I can't win him back."

Jimmy said very carefully, "What makes you think I want you out of the picture?"

"Because you offered me money to leave him! Jesus Christ, Jimmy! You were there!" shouted Rett.

Rett looked out at the field. His eyes were burning and he hated crying in front of Jimmy. He hated being reduced to this kind of an emotional disaster in front of this asshole.

Jimmy continued to speak slowly to Rett. "You *assume* that I *wanted* you to go along with that offer."

Rett sat dumbly, tears leaking out of his eyes.

"You've been watching too many soap operas, Rett," said Jimmy. "I was *hoping* that you'd tell me to shove that offer up my ass until it squirted out my ears. I think both of us were surprised when you took it."

Rett shook his head. This couldn't be happening. This couldn't be true. There was no way he had gone through all of this because he had misunderstood Jimmy's intention all along.

"I can't believe you don't see it," continued Jimmy, "but you're *more* than I am, than Jason is, or Kaitlynn, or Brick, or anybody, to Cory. I care about Cory, more than just about anybody else in the world, and it's hard for me to let go of him, but I knew the day would come. As much as I tried to ignore it, I always understood that I was a placeholder until Cory found someone that was all his own, someone that made everything in his life more worthwhile." Jimmy paused before continuing, "I think that my reluctance to let go, and bad judgment on my part, and wanting to make damn sure he was in good hands, led me to make that offer at the charity ball. But once you had accepted, I couldn't go back on it; I couldn't risk you being the wrong person for him."

Rett tried to work his way through what Jimmy was saying, but it was so hard. There had been so much pain because of it. He wanted to hit something. Or someone. He wanted to hit Jimmy. He wiped his sleeves across his eyes to try to dry them. But Jimmy wasn't the one that had accepted the offer; he had. He had chosen to run because of his own insecurity of who he was to Cory. He hadn't stood up for Cory. Or even himself.

Jimmy asked, "What changed, Rett? What changed your mind?"

Rett looked out at the field in front of him. Gunnar was delaying and rotating his arm repeatedly, obviously bothered by it. The Reaper was now on second base and another player from Baltimore was on first, and there was only one out.

The honest answer came to Rett more easily now. "Because... for the first time, I lost everything around me, and I saw how little there was inside me. It took losing Cory... more than Cory, actually, to see how little of *me* there really was. How I ran from everything I was close to out of fear of getting hurt."

Rett wiped at his face again. He said, terrified of the statement, "I want so bad to be the man that Cory seems to think I am."

Jimmy managed a pale smile at Rett. He shocked him when he eventually said, "Tonight's a good start."

Rett was so exhausted from this and he felt like he had just crawled out of a car wreck. But had this been what Jimmy really wanted all along? The same thing that Rett himself wanted? He looked down onto the green of the field, to the brown circle in the middle of the infield. Gunnar threw a rough changeup at the batter in the box, and managed to get a third strike, gaining the second out in the top of the 9th inning.

Jimmy said, "Up until now, Cory's trusted me more than anyone else in his life, with everything. But even though I'll always be there for him, I can't be that person forever, not without hurting him. As much as this kills me, I've got to let go of him. You'll never be me, Rett. And you shouldn't be. Cory may love me dearly, but he's not *in love* with me. You have to be *more than me* for him. But in return you'll get one of the biggest hearts you'll ever run across. A lot like his dad's, I think."

Rett felt terrible. He had fucked this up so bad, in a way he had no idea he was doing. He gave up trying to stop the tears.

"Why, Jimmy? Why are you giving me this second chance? I made such a huge mess of this."

Jimmy said, "Maybe one day, I'll explain. But we all deserve a second chance, Rett." Jimmy's own face was drawn and a little haggard looking now.

Rett had no idea how he was supposed to feel. He was happy, but still suspicious of Jimmy. He was relieved, but ashamed. He was leery of how Cory would feel about all of this, but anxious to try, and terrified of what might happen. And he was so exhausted. But he had managed to get past Jimmy somehow, and that was all that mattered.

Rett's eyes traveled over to the Joes' dugout. He could see Cory sitting in the back.

Rett said, "So what do I do? How do I face him?"

"Let's call him," said Jimmy.

Rett gave Jimmy a confused look. Jimmy was already taking his cell phone out.

Rett asked in disbelief, "*Now?* Are you talking about calling him right now?"

"Sure."

"They're in the *middle of a game!*" Rett pointed out at the field like Jimmy had somehow neglected to realize what was going on out there.

"So?"

Rett stood up, shocked that Jimmy was doing this. He moved a little away from him like he didn't want to be associated with something this unorthodox, like Jimmy was going to be struck by lightning from the baseball gods.

Jimmy punched the speed dial and put the phone up to his ear. Rett couldn't stand it. He climbed over the seat in front of him and started pacing. Why did Jimmy have to do this right this minute? Right in the middle of a game?

He couldn't listen to this. Rett moved out into the aisle. He squinted over into the dugout and thought he could see Cory answering his phone. He hoped he was seeing wrong. He prayed he wasn't actually seeing Cory answer his phone.

On the field, Rett's attention was pulled away by Gunnar firing a ruthless fastball at the batter in the box. The ball connected and went deep into center field. Skunk stumbled slightly backing up after the ball and errored, which meant the batter made it to first and now all the bases were loaded. And worst of all, that meant the son-of-a-bitch, Reaper, was now on third base.

Back on the mound, he realized Gunnar had sunk to his knees and was doubled over, gripping his shoulder with his left arm in pain. Already, Dr. Bala and Rikky were running out to the mound to check on him. Rett normally would have already been running inside to be ready to check on Gunnar and help, but he wasn't a part of that. Not anymore. He was only able to watch helplessly from the stands.

Everyone watched intently to see how hurt Gunnar was, to see if he'd be ok. Dr. Bala and Rikky helped him up and started to lead him off the field.

Rett thought there had to be some mistake. He heard the announcer say that number 72, Cory Pritchart, would take over pitching for the Joes. Rett wheeled back and looked at Jimmy while the color drained out of his face. Jimmy was talking on the phone to Cory right then. Rett's mouth hung slack in total disbelief that any of this was actually happening.

He whipped back around to look in the dugout again and could see Ahab yelling at Cory to get out on the field. Cory started to set foot out onto the field with the phone still at his ear and his glove under his other arm.

Rett felt something behind him and turned to see Jimmy holding out the cell phone to him. Rett shook his head.

Jimmy said, still absurdly indifferent to the game on the field, "Talk to him, Rett. Just for a moment."

Rett hissed, "Are you out of your fucking mind?! He's *walking out* to take the mound right now!"

Jimmy's eyes held Rett's in an iron grip. He put the phone in Rett's hand and demanded, "*Talk to him, Rett!*"

Rett took the phone and had no idea how to reach out to Cory for the second chance he so desperately wanted. He closed his eyes and put the phone to his ear. He said, "Cory... I'm sorry."

There was silence on the other end.

Rett wanted his second chance. He frantically needed it, but this wasn't going to get it for him, and he had no idea how to get through to Cory. He had only seconds before Cory would be at the mound. How could he fix this before Cory... before... In the back of his mind, he heard something. He heard that it was ok to fail.

That all that mattered was picking up again and trying. And it all suddenly made sense.

He looked out at Cory, now a few steps onto the field and walking towards the mound, the phone still at his ear.

Rett said quickly, "Sing it with me, Cory. Sing it like you always do out there. Just you and me..."

Rett continued to watch Cory cross the field, one leaden step at a time, and he started singing into the phone, "The itsy bitsy spider, climbed up the water spout..."

Cory stopped in his tracks on the field and started looking wildly around when he heard these words, like he was trying to find where in the stands the song was coming from.

Rett continued singing, only to hear the horrible, off-key, beautiful, magical sound of Cory joining in with him, even if only tentatively:

Down came the rain
and washed the spider out
Out came the sun
and dried up all the rain
And the itsy-bitsy spider
Climbed up the spout again

Rett watched as they finished singing, but his relief quickly turned to panic. The Orioles' manager was running out on the field and yelling, and the head umpire was, too. Both were running at Cory, who had slowly resumed his walk towards the mound, totally unaware of the uproar he was causing. Everyone in the stands was shouting at the unprecedented sight of a pitcher walking out to the mound while on a phone call.

But none of that mattered to Rett as much as the fact that he had gotten to Cory.

Cory's voice came small and still unsure on the other end, "How did you know, Rett? How did you know that I always sang that as my ritual?"

Rett could see Ahab running out towards the umpire and the Orioles' manager as well.

"Your dad. But I only realized it just now. Forgive me, Cory. If you give me a second chance, I won't let you down again."

Cory stopped out on the field again, oblivious to the two managers and umpire about to reach him. He said, "Anything, as long as you're really back. That's all I want."

"I swear to you, Cory, I'll never do this again. I... I love you."

Rett thought he heard a small sigh of relief, and then Cory's voice was small and unsure as he said, "Thanks, Rett. The last few games have hurt. Thanks for reminding me it's ok to mess up, as long as I keep trying."

Rett hastily added, "Bigfoot, you're about to get yelled at. Just do me a favor... take that baseball and burn that motherfucker Reaper another asshole with it! Ok?"

Cory said, suddenly more spirited, "Anything for you!"

Rett heard the smile in his voice even as the umpire yanked the phone out of Cory's hand. A shouting match began between the Orioles' manager, Ahab, and the lead umpire, but Cory backed up a step and seemed to ignore all of it. The Orioles fans were incensed and were screaming to have Cory ejected from the game and to have his head on a platter. In either order.

The yelling and finger pointing played out for several minutes near the mound, but Cory stayed calm and indifferent to all of it. The manager for the Orioles looked like his head was going to explode he was so furious. The umpire finally gave Cory his phone back and spent a few seconds loudly lecturing him. Ahab started to walk back to the Joes' dugout and the umpire had to yell at the Orioles' manager to make him go back to the visitors' dugout.

The announcer in the stadium came on and said, "It's a little unusual, folks, but the umpire is going to allow play to continue with Pritchart on the mound. Even after, uh, a phone call, apparently."

The Orioles fans started booing wildly.

Rett turned to Jimmy and handed his phone back to him. He said, "Man, you know how to start some shit storms."

Jimmy had already sat back down in his seat casually and shrugged his shoulders. "It's just a game," was all he offered as an explanation.

He told Rett, "You got through to him, I can tell." There was a trace of a smile playing across his face.

Rett turned back to watch. The umpire turned and tossed a ball to Cory, and right as he reached home plate, he gave the "play ball" signal, offhandedly and before he was really even fully back in position behind JJ.

What happened next was so fast that not one single person in the stadium was prepared, especially after the confusion of the argument over the cell phone on the field.

Cory wheeled around and threw to Kevin Ostergaard at second base so fast that no one was paying close attention and no one was ready for it, including Kevin or the Orioles' runner that had drifted off of the base towards third a short distance. Kevin slid out trying to catch the rocket Cory had thrown, fumbled it and grabbed around under his legs and feet, looking around crazily, frantically trying to find the ball that had gotten away from him as he had slid. The runner on second had already made it back to base safely.

Rett's attention shifted to third base. The Reaper, and the third base coach, along with everyone else in the stadium, had been caught off guard with all the confusion of the phone call and the rapid throw to second. When the Reaper saw that Kevin had lost the ball somehow, he didn't need any additional prompting to run for home, and he took off at top speed.

In the stands, Rett could see Templeton glance triumphantly over his shoulder in Cory's direction as he ran, only to see Cory standing calmly. To even more shock and confusion, Rett watched as Cory took the ball out of his glove where everyone could see it, the glove it had never actually left. And as Templeton began his slide into home, Cory fired it at JJ as hard as he could.

The moment hung there in Rett's eyes, the entire stadium's eyes, the ball flying towards JJ's glove while the Reaper slid towards home. JJ snagged the ball just as Templeton's feet touched home plate. He watched for what seemed forever, unable to tell if the ball had beaten the Reaper to the plate or not.

The entire stadium held its breath and then the umpire hammered his closed fist to indicate that Templeton had been called out.

The announcer verified the umpire's call. Cory's throw had made Templeton the third out, ending the game so suddenly no one realized for a long moment what the hell had just happened. The Joes won 1 to nothing.

The entire stadium sat in paralyzed silence. Every player and the thousands of spectators were frozen in mute confusion as they tried to figure out where the ball had come from and what had just played out in front of them. And then the stadium erupted into nothing Rett had ever heard at a ball game before. He watched as everyone in the Joes' dugout emptied out onto the field and ran to Cory on the mound, mobbing him completely. The Orioles' manager was back on the field and, along with Templeton, both were screaming at the umpire, who kept shaking his head that his decision was final.

Rett turned back to Jimmy, who was sitting quietly, a foot up on the seat in front of him and ignoring everything happening in the rest of the stadium. Jimmy stood up and said placidly, "It's kind of funny... I know of exactly *one* person on this planet that could have pushed Cory into making a play like that."

"Talk to him, Rett," he added, encouraging him. "You both really need to talk to each other and open up a little more. Tell him the things you told me. He needs to hear them. And there's some things I bet he'll tell you that you had no idea about. But you have to talk."

He stepped out into the aisle and said to Rett after a deep breath, "You know, I think you and I both screwed up a little bit here with all of this. You're getting your second chance. Maybe you'll see fit to give me a second chance, too."

Rett had no idea what to say to that, and stood transfixed while the rest of the stadium and the field below them were in utter chaos. But Jimmy wandered off before Rett had a chance to say anything, anyway.

Chapter 26

It always started with waiting.

Rett leaned back against the chain-link fence and waited. As much as he was worried about facing Cory, in person, and that was *if* Cory even actually showed, he couldn't help but smile at what Cory had done in the game. Even if Rett hadn't literally been in the middle of it, on the phone with Cory while he was walking out to the mound, he would have had to take a certain pride in what Cory managed to do in the game. And it was all the sweeter knowing Cory had played the Reaper for a fool and given him what was coming to him. Even the most jaded baseball fan in the world would have to sit up and take notice at the trick play that had occurred that night. These kinds of plays were rare in the majors, because the pros never fell for them. They paid close attention and they had coaches on first and third base whose whole job was to pay attention to this kind of stuff and tell the runners what to do. And Cory had managed to pull one over on everyone in the stadium that night. But especially the Reaper.

Rett would have loved to think that maybe his request for Cory to tear the Reaper a new asshole was what drove the play. God, Rett would have loved to know he had played a part in taking the Reaper down a notch. But realistically, Cory had merely spotted the confusion on the field, and took advantage of an opportunity to end the game quickly without risking any more hits. It felt really good to watch Cory play the game like a master.

After the game was over, and amidst all the chaos, Rett had tried to call him again. Cory hadn't answered, which Rett half expected since the media would be all over him afterwards, clamoring for interviews, and so Rett had left a message. He had left it entirely in Cory's hands. His message said, "I'll be in the field if you want to join me." He hadn't heard anything back.

And so, now he waited.

Jimmy... Rett still wasn't sure about him. He was less skittish about him than he had started out that evening, but he still wasn't sure. He still wasn't sure how much he trusted him. But then again, Jimmy *had* said he hoped Rett would give him a second chance. And then he left that in Rett's hands to think over.

Had this entire disaster been caused by nothing more than a collision of selfishness, bad judgment and insecurity across both of them? And with poor Cory being the innocent victim of all of it? That didn't make Rett feel any better. And it made facing Cory all the more difficult yet again. Rett knew he had to accept responsibility; no one but him had accepted the offer and walked away. Rett still had his hopes, though; Cory's voice on the phone encouraged him. It had taken a moment, but it sounded like Rett really had managed to connect with Cory again on the phone.

So, all he could do was wait.

The same as he had done with Bo. And just like he had done with Jimmy. It always started with waiting.

It was peaceful and quiet in the practice field, contrasting deeply with the loud pandemonium at the Portyards earlier. A late night light breeze slipped through the trees across the street and brushed across Rett's face. He wished he had brought a baseball with him to keep him company while he waited.

A set of headlights swept across the field and came barreling down the street, and a familiar, large, blue and white truck slammed on brakes along the edge of the road, sliding a few feet in the dust before coming to a stop. Cory leaped out of the truck and started running towards the field in a frenzied dash. As he passed the streetlight, Rett noticed he was still wearing his uniform from the game that night. He hadn't even bothered to change.

As Cory got to the edge of the backstop fence that Rett was sitting against, Cory stopped and paused, then walked slowly, carefully. He walked around the fence until he stood a few feet in front of Rett, his face pulled down. Rett's heart ripped inside him when he saw the pain and hurt on Cory's face. Maybe Cory had rethought the connection they had made on the phone earlier. Maybe he hadn't connected the way he hoped at all.

Cory stood frozen in his cleats and cream and teal pinstripe uniform, his face pulling down farther. Hanging limply at his side was his pitching glove he didn't seem to realize he had carried with him. It was like watching him break into a hundred pieces right in front of him. Cory didn't even try to wipe the tear that fell from his eye, dropping to the dry dirt of the field at his feet.

Rett waited for Cory, but he knew what was coming. Even now, the pain he had caused Cory was too much. It was leaking out of him.

A groan escaped from Cory's throat, agonizing for Rett to hear in the quiet night. Rett watched as the tears fell from Cory's eyes and his legs buckled and he fell slowly to his knees in front of Rett.

Cory finally tried to speak, but only managed a broken squawk of a word.

"Anything," he tried to say.

Rett wasn't sure what that meant, but it was hurting him to see Cory like this — twisted up in a heartbreaking frown of pain and regret. He was fighting his own tears back, too, now, even as he didn't understand why Cory was like this.

Cory's face contorted in agony and Rett couldn't hold back any more, not with Cory in this much pain. Rett's own face pulled up into the anguish he himself now felt and his throat drew tight, at not understanding, at Cory's suffering. Why was Cory feeling like this after one of the most beautiful thirty seconds of professional baseball ever?

Cory sobbed, "Anything, Rett. I don't... it doesn't... matter what you want. Just tell me. I'll do anything."

Cory smeared his sleeve across his face to wipe away the tears.

He tried again, "I'm sorry, Rett. I'll give you anything... you ask. Just take me back." The words were broken and hoarse through Cory's sobs, and Rett was having a hard time understanding them.

He looked at Cory in confusion.

Cory inched forward closer to Rett, still on his knees. He held his hands out, "Whatever I did, I'm sorry, Rett. I'm sorry for all of it. Just tell me anything... anything you want to come back."

Rett croaked, "What... what are you talking about, Cory?"

"I'm sorry I drove you away. God, I'm so sorry! Give me another chance! Please!"

Rett had to shake his head. Was Cory really taking the blame for everything that had happened? Did he really think this was his fault in some way? Had he done *that* to Cory by leaving? Rett found it inconceivable, but those were the words coming out of Cory's mouth.

Rett sobbed at the thought, at the inconsolable and shaking Cory at his feet, at what Cory had been feeling the last week over all of this. He said, "No, Cory. Not you. You did nothing!"

Rett sniffed and looked up at the moon for a second. "It was me, Cory. I was afraid. And weak. It was *me*. It's always been me fucking up, since... well, since too long. It was nothing you did, Cory. I fucked up. I fucked up so bad! You're the... the best thing that's ever happened to me. I love you, Cory! I should be begging *you* to take *me* back!"

Cory inched forward again and groaned out loud. He fell forward onto Rett, pushing him down into the dirt and resting on top of him.

"I love you, too, chief! Dear God in heaven, you have no idea!" cried Cory.

Rett lifted his head up and kissed Cory. Their lips met. Their tears mingled together on their cheeks. The heat and anguish and anxiety mixed between them before draining away from them like runoff from a summer shower. Cory squeezed him so tightly as they kissed that Rett couldn't breathe. So tightly that Rett would never be able to separate from him.

Rett finally had to wheeze, "Bigfoot... spine! My spine! Need... spine for... work!"

Cory managed a small laugh and rolled off so they could face each other. They lay together in the dirt of the ball field, and Cory reached up and brushed his hand through Rett's hair. Rett had wondered if Cory would ever touch him like that again, and feeling it was like a tightly wound spring being suddenly released. His insides felt like they exploded in a huge tangle of relief. He never wanted to leave the dirt of that ball field.

They kissed again, deeper, relaxing into each other for the first time in weeks and weeks.

Cory said, "I can't help but think how I treated you in LA, what it must have felt like for you at the charity thing to see me with Kaitlynn. I drove you away, Rett, and it was more than I could bear. And when Jimmy told me about his offer and how you accepted it, I knew I had driven you away. I wanted to go to you, to beg you to come back, but Jimmy told me to stay away, to give you some time, and he reminded me how many times he fucked up around Brick before they finally came together. I didn't mean to do any of that, Rett. But I can't do this without you!"

Rett traced his finger over Cory's ear. "None of that stuff mattered, Cory. The truth is..." Rett paused, but knew he needed to say it. "But the truth is, I would have chickened out sooner or later. I've done it every other time. I had to lose everything to finally see what the real problem has been all along. And it's *me*. All that's happened is *squarely* on me."

Rett ran his finger down the front of Cory's uniform. "And you did amazing tonight without me! You're so *fucking* amazing!"

Cory shook his head violently and looked like he was going to cry again. "That was you, Rett! You have no idea what happened inside of me when you sang 'Itsy Bitsy Spider' to me. To know that there was someone, one single person, who knew me like that. That's what I've wanted so bad for as long as I can remember! I've wanted what Jimmy and Brick have so badly. And tonight, when I was at my lowest point, I found out I've got it. It's *you*, Rett! I suddenly felt like I could do anything in the world. I love you, and I'll do absolutely *anything* to keep you. You just name it!"

Rett remained silent while he let the impact of what Cory was saying sink in. How Jimmy had tried to get him to see all of this earlier that evening. How Val had tried to get him to see it as well. How stupid and scared he had been all along.

Cory wiped his arm across his eyes again, smudging dirt and dust from the ground they were lying on all over his face. He sniffed and said, "I'll quit the MLB, Rett. If that's what it takes for us to stay together. I don't care anymore. If I lose you, I lose the MLB anyway. This past week showed me that. If you want me to, say the word, and I'll hand in my glove tomorrow." He took his glove from the ground next to him and folded it carefully in Rett's hands, against his breast.

"What?" cried Rett. He couldn't believe what he was hearing. He stared at Cory's glove, now in his hands.

"I mean it, Rett." Cory's lips quivered.

Rett would never have thought he'd hear Cory say those words. They took his breath away and paralyzed him at the same time. They paralyzed him with the same fear that always gripped him when he got close to people. The fear he had to overcome. This fear was the emptiness he had to fill.

Cory said, "The night I started for the first time and pitched a no-hitter for nine innings, only to wreck it in the 10th. Everyone told me how it didn't matter what the rules said, I had done something amazing. But I had lost the game. All these empty words from people, none of it making the hurt any better. All I wanted, the only thing that made it better, was to put my head in your lap and let you touch me. No words, no other people, just you letting me let it out. You mentioned once about all these people wanting their part of me, wanting their little pieces of me.

You're right. They do. But they can't have it, Rett. You've got all of it already. I have nothing to give any of those people, not one of them, because it's already all yours. I love you so much, Rett. So much! And to have you sing with me tonight, to hear you say those words back to me... I felt like I could see every single star in the sky. Just tell me what you want. Anything. Just don't leave me again."

Rett closed his eyes and tried to understand how fundamentally different this whole conversation was from what he thought all of it was about. How could he have misjudged Cory this badly?

Everything Rett had learned about being a man was so wrong. So completely wrong. Sometimes, being a man was surrendering everything to another, giving them absolute power over you, putting your fate entirely in their hands. And then accepting whatever decision came of it. The coward, the boy, would shy from that and run away from it. The boy would be selfish and want to always make the decision, to control it, to be in the lead. Rett now saw himself doing that at every critical point in his life. He could play back every time he had done that in the past, but now he could see it through different eyes, and it was shameful to him.

The man knew when to surrender, to yield.

That was what Cory was doing right now, even with no cause to do so. That was what was playing out in the pain in Cory's face in front of Rett at that very moment. Cory was more man in the last few minutes than Rett had been in his entire life.

Rett felt the light of dawn hit him, and he never felt fuller. Because also part of being a man was recognizing the responsibility being placed in his hands, and respecting it, not carelessly tossing it aside or dismissing it. He needed to comfort him, to reassure him; he owed Cory that. He couldn't let his own past and his own fear pull him away. This was how he filled the emptiness. And Cory deserved it more than anyone he knew.

"Nothing, Cory. I want nothing more than what you've already given me, and shown to me. And don't you even think about leaving the MLB," said Rett. "There's nothing more that I want than this," he said as he put the glove back in Cory's hands where it belonged.

Rett touched his forehead to Cory's. "It's you and me, Bigfoot, just you and me. Just to know you love me back is more than I deserve," he finished.

Cory's eyes were still damp and Rett could see through his brown eyes to where Cory had laid himself bare to Rett, and willing to accept whatever happened for doing so. Cory said, "All of this... this stuff, it's all insane. Before I started with the Joes, I thought about what it might be like, but it's way beyond my imagination. It's all like some... crazy machine — the money, sponsorships, the games, the fans, the groupies, the negotiations, the travel, the pressure, all of it — it's beautiful and tempting from the outside, but scary as all shit when you're in the machine, and I'm in a constant panic to not get chewed up by it. *You're* my link to the real world. Knowing you're there means I don't have to get chewed up by this machine, Rett. A week without you, and I almost lost myself. It almost destroyed me. I *cannot* do this without you!"

How selfish he had been, and how much he meant to Cory... Rett finally saw it. He saw what he had walked away from. What they really did have together was already far deeper than he understood, and walking away from it had almost been the end of both of them. Rett thought how Cory was willing to sacrifice anything to keep him, but it was he that needed to sacrifice, not Cory, and it wasn't even that much. He just needed to give Cory the space he needed to maintain his career. Just that little bit. All he had to do was let Cory have an evening of dancing with Kaitlynn every so often. To let other people have their picture taken with him. To be secure in his knowledge that he held more of Cory in his hands than anyone could possibly imagine.

He could easily be selfish about it; he could keep Cory to himself, and Cory would surely let him. Or, he could sacrifice so little, be a bigger man in such a small way, be secure in what he held in his hands, know that it really was his entirely, and give so much more back to Cory by doing so. He'd give Cory a hundred times more than what he was giving up by doing so. And wasn't that the measure of a man?

Rett whispered, "I'm there. I'm there with you, Cory. Always. You and me. Just you and me."

Cory leaned over into Rett and buried his face in Rett's chest. He pulled Rett close again and held onto him. Rett kissed the top of Cory's head gently. He'd do anything now to keep Cory safe from the machine.

Cory held onto Rett tightly again, both laying next to each other in silence. They had both almost fallen over a cliff, only to pull each other back at the last moment. Finally, Cory sat up and leaned against the backstop fence, and Rett sat up next to him.

"You're gonna go ask for your job back, right? You're gonna come back to the Joes, aren't you, Rett?" asked Cory worriedly.

Rett honestly hadn't thought that far ahead. He'd been so preoccupied with getting past Jimmy, he hadn't thought that through.

"I guess. Maybe George'll take me back."

Cory grabbed his hand and insisted, "Tomorrow! You gotta come in early tomorrow! You gotta be on the road with us tomorrow evening when we go to Minnesota!"

Rett said, "You're kinda counting eggs that aren't chickens yet, you know."

Cory looked at him, unvarnished pleading in his eyes. And if had any doubt remaining about how much Cory belonged to him, about the responsibility he now shouldered as a result of that, it disappeared with that glance from him.

Rett nodded, "Ok, ok. I don't know what George will say, but of course I'm going to ask."

Cory closed his eyes and leaned his head back against the fence. He took Rett's hand in his. Rett loved feeling having his hand wrapped entirely by Cory's. He loved feeling surrounded by Cory, by his hands, by his arms, by his body. He loved the man next to him in ways he couldn't even count. He pulled Cory's left hand, his glove hand, up to his face and smelled the faint scent of the leather that was always there. It made him feel home.

"I hit bottom, too, Cory," said Rett. "Val was on your side about the whole thing, and rightfully so. Still, it hurt like hell for her to kick me when I was already so down. She dumped me as a friend because I ran away from you."

Cory took Rett's hand and pressed his mouth to it quietly, in sympathy.

"And I hit bottom. But I needed to. It made me see what was really missing in my life, that I needed a dose of growing up."

Rett wondered what he would have to do to get Val back. He wondered if there was a chance it would be too late, that he had screwed up around her one too many times. She had put up with a lot of his shit for a lot of years; that much was certain.

"I'm sorry, Rett," offered Cory.

"No, you have her to thank for the fact that I'm here. We both owe her, big time."

And then Rett remembered. "But I got Bo back!" he said.

"You did?"

"Yeah, I went to Dothan last night and stood up to Bo and made us work through it, despite being scared shitless." Rett added, "I have a brother again, Cory! I have family!"

Rett spent a few minutes telling Cory the story of waiting for Bo outside his parents' home and winning his brother back. When he finished, Rett leaned over against Cory's shoulder. He was feeling exhausted again, and the stress of the past week and the lack of sleep was rapidly catching up to him.

Rett said, "Wait! There *is* something I want."

"Absolutely, positively anything," said Cory, happy to finally be able to *do* something.

"I want a key to your place, Cory."

Cory was silent for a moment, then asked, "That's it?"

"It's a bigger deal to me than you might think. I want you to have a key to mine as well."

"Ok. Done. That was... suspiciously easy," said Cory, unsure if it really could be that simple.

"And I want a picture of you," said Rett.

Cory said dryly, "Uh... you want it autographed? I can have the Joes' PR person send you one."

Rett turned and thumped Cory's ear hard. "Asshole! I want a picture of us, *together.*" It felt very good to have some smart-ass creeping back into their conversations.

Cory laughed and said, "Gimme your phone."

Rett handed his phone over to Cory. Cory pulled Rett close to him and held the phone out to take a picture of the two of them together right then and there. He snapped the picture and gave the phone back to Rett.

He said, "You can have as many more of those as you want."

Cory nuzzled again into Rett's neck. He whispered, "You can have anything you want, Rett. Just ask."

Rett looked at the picture. They both looked like last week's shit. Cory was dirty from the field and his hair, for once, was standing up at awkward angles. Rett had bloodshot eyes and dust smeared on his left cheek. It was instantly one of his most prized possessions.

Cory continued to rub his face against Rett's neck and chin, kissing him lightly. "I like the beard," he said.

"The beard was me hitting bottom," said Rett.

Cory snuggled into it even more. "You hitting bottom makes me horny."

Rett laughed, which made Cory laugh. Rett reached over and pawed roughly at Cory's crotch. "I'll be damned... it *does* make you horny!"

Rett stood up and stared at Cory, sitting against the fence in his uniform. What the hell had he been thinking when he took

Jimmy's offer? How could anybody walk away from someone like Cory? All that mattered was that he had enough in him to fix the biggest mistake of his life. It felt good.

He said, "C'mon, Bigfoot, let's go hit bottom together," and held out his hand to pull Cory up.

~~~~~

In the dark of the bedroom, Rett sat up and watched the shifting lights from outside. The streetlight filtered in lightly and onto the bed and concrete floor, creating spots of light and shadow, like a camouflage pattern. Cory's arm was in his lap, and Rett slowly traced a finger up and down the thick forearm, feeling the chamois-soft, brown hair sliding under his fingertip as he did so.

Cory was fast asleep next to him in the huge bed, and Rett wished he was, too. But now he was thinking about the next day. He was going to have to face George and ask for his job back. In a way, it should be one of the easiest tests of all for the new Rett, the bigger Rett. But it didn't feel that way. Now that it was no longer masked by everything that went along with quitting his job, he was seeing how much he really loved his job with the Joes, how much he missed it. How much he missed baseball. What a strange thought, to know he actually missed baseball. He worried what would happen to him if he didn't get it back.

Only because he could, Rett stuck his finger in Cory's ear.

Cory stirred slightly and mumbled at Rett, almost intelligibly, "Finger outta ear." He pulled away a little, but not even enough to pull his arm out of Rett's lap.

"You said I could have whatever I wanted," insisted Rett.

There was a pause, and Cory muffled something into his pillow that sounded like, "Oh yeah, I did."

"Ok," Cory heaved groggily.

Rett left his finger in Cory's ear for a few more seconds for the hell of it, then removed it and resumed running his finger up and down the tightly muscled cords in Cory's arm. Cory shifted over even closer to Rett and gripped at him even tighter for a moment before drifting back into sleep. Rett silently promised himself to never let go of Cory ever again.

He slid down into the warm bed, and in his sleep, Cory pulled him up against his chest and he felt Cory's nose pressed into his hair, and felt his steady, moist breath on the back of his neck.

For the first time in too many days, Rett fell into a peaceful sleep.

Chapter 27

Rett needed to finish getting dressed and to go on over to the Portyards, but he found it too easy to procrastinate. He and Cory had showered together that morning, and things seemed very good again. In the bathroom, he was even able to complain about how frazzled Cory's beard had gotten in the meantime, likening it to a bed of pine straw. But he secretly loved being able to shave him and trim his beard once again, making it presentable for him. Cory was distracted throughout the grooming and his hands were all over Rett's naked body, not caring how he got in the way of what Rett was trying to do. Rett fussed at him and his wandering hands, but patiently took his time just so he could stare at Cory's face, feel Cory's skin under his fingers, have Cory's undivided attention, take the most mundane of daily rituals and turn it into one of the most intimate moments they could share. Just the two of them.

Rett reminded himself that he would really need to call Cory's dad and thank him for the talk about second chances. It had given him a lot of the determination that he didn't have on his own to put things back. But none of that made him eager to go face George and beg for his job back. He knew he stood a good chance of getting it back, but his heart didn't like facing up to the cowardly way he had quit so suddenly to begin with.

Cory left to go to the Portyards first thing in the morning and Rett drove to his apartment to change clothes. But once he got home, he started thinking up stupid reasons to delay. He stripped down to his boxers, and allowed himself to be distracted by the picture Cory had taken on his phone the night before. Their eyes were so ringed in red that they both looked like possums. He couldn't help but smile at it. God, he loved having that picture.

Cory was his first, in a way. Cory was the first man he had ever said the words "I love you" to. He had had feelings for others in the past, with a couple of the guys he had dated over time, but had never said it out loud to their faces. Well, he had admitted out loud to being in love with Mike, which was true, but only in retrospect, after they had broken up. Rett spent a few minutes trying to decide if there was a single reason he had never said it before, or if there was a different reason each time. It didn't really matter in the end. He had the one he really wanted, and had told him so.

And he hoped he never needed a third chance with him.

Rett didn't bother putting any clothes on and stepped out into his den and flipped the TV on. He had been burning to see what was on the news about the game the night before, but Cory had been absolutely determined to not let that interrupt their night together.

On ESPN, he didn't have to wait long. The analysts and anchors were like chickens clucking all on top of each other talking about it, all while showing the trick play that ended the game from multiple camera angles. There was speculation that the whole phone call was part of the strategy to create just enough confusion to be able to pull it off. Then they discussed how clubs weren't supposed to allow any cell phones or other electronic devices on the field, the dugout or in the bullpen, but technically, there wasn't an actual MLB rule disallowing their presence or use in a game.

They showed a brief interview with Cory afterwards, a very serious looking Cory, one whose mind looked like it was in a far different place than the game that had just ended so spectacularly. Cory distractedly mumbled something about owing the Reaper an out and wanting to make sure he got it.

Rett was especially pleased to see that Devin "Reaper" Templeton suddenly had no interest in mouthing off to ESPN or anyone else about the game and refused to be interviewed.

Rett loved that Cory had gotten something of a second chance as well in the game, his chance to put Devin Templeton in his place and show him what it was like to play against a "little leaguer."

Rett flipped over to CNN and as soon as they got to covering anything about sports, it was there, too. Then he tried the Today Show on NBC. Again, it was the big sports story of the day. It boggled his mind to think that there probably wasn't a single person who followed sports that didn't know who Cory Pritchart was by this point. Rett couldn't be more proud of him. And this time, he didn't mind as much how all these hordes of people wanted their little piece of him; Rett felt better about sharing now.

After wasting time flipping through all the sports news he could find, Rett had run out of excuses. He dragged himself back into his bedroom, put his clothes on and faced what he needed to do.

He sent Cory a text once he arrived at the Portyards, and Cory told him to go out to the loading dock and he'd get someone to let him in so he could see George. When the door in the loading dock opened, Rett was happy to see that it was JJ who came to get him.

JJ grinned and said as he let Rett in to follow him, "So now you come crawling back, huh?"

Rett said, "What can I say? I miss Skunk too much. The man's been on my mind..."

JJ laughed and said, "He's been pining away since you left, for sure. You two deserve each other."

"Bullshit! Low blow!" sneered Rett. "And if you tell him I said that I missed him, I swear to God, I'll kick you in the balls!"

"For real, though, you're gonna get your job back? You got whatever was going on straightened out?"

"I'm going to try. It's up to George, really," said Rett. "And yeah, I think I got my shit finally pulled together in a nice, neat pile. I'll show it to you sometime; it's impressive."

"I deal with your shit too much as it is," commented JJ. "I guess you heard about it, but the game you missed last night was something else," he added. "After his last few games, no one in the world expected something like that from Cory. If it hadn't been for him showing that he still had the ball in his glove before firing it off at me to get Templeton out, I probably would have gotten my mask smashed into my face."

Rett said, "I'm glad Cory took that cocksucker to school last night. He deserved it."

"You know, there's all kinds of speculation about who Cory was talking to on the phone. That was some kind of ballsy stunt right there, walking out onto the field on a phone call," laughed JJ.

They arrived at the clubhouse, and as JJ let him in, Rett asked, "So who was he on the phone with. Does anyone know?"

JJ stopped in the hallway and looked closely at Rett for a moment. He said, "Cory said it was his business manager."

Rett wanted to ask him if he believed that or not, but kept his mouth shut.

JJ said, "I gotta get back to practice. Watch out for Cthulhu Rose in there; I think she's behind on her soul-devouring quota. And good luck with George!"

Rett waved JJ off as he walked back down the hall towards practice.

Rett stood outside for a moment, steeling his nerves. When he had pulled himself together all he could, he walked directly into Rosemary's office, who looked shocked for a split second before she glared at him.

"How did you get in here? You no longer work here! Where do you think you're going?" she spat.

Rett completely ignored her, walked right past her, and into George's office, not giving Rosemary a chance to stop him.

George looked up when Rett entered, and then he saw Rosemary standing in the doorway behind him. She was probably about to claw Rett's jugular vein into a spurting fountain that she could bathe in, but George smiled and said, "Rett? Thanks for showing him in, Rose! Come on in and have a seat, Rett!"

Rosemary slunk back to her desk and Rett sat down across from him.

George winked at him and said, "*Now* you finally decide to come ask for some free tickets?"

Rett laughed and said, "Still no, George."

George leaned back and said, "So... what can I do for you then, Rett?"

Rett looked around at the pictures on the wall. George's messy desk. The placard sitting there. Rett decided that maybe he'd like to have one of those sitting on his own desk. *If* he got his desk back.

"I want to come back, George. If you'll let me, I want my job back."

George raised an eyebrow. "Ohhh, so *that's* what you want. Hmmmmm..." George considered the request for a moment or two.

Rett started to get concerned, but George cracked another smile.

"Sure, Rett. I'm glad you came back. Even if it was just me making this decision, I'd welcome you back. I hope you got everything worked out ok, though?"

"Yeah, I think so, George. I'm sorry about that. I'm sorry about bailing on you so suddenly."

George shook his head to dismiss Rett's concern. "Bah, don't even mention it! If you had trouble in real life you had to deal with, you gotta go deal with it, right? Bala and I were trying to figure out how we were going to squeeze some more interviewing in for a replacement. We'd about made up our minds to just go without for the rest of the season. So seeing you here in my office today is good news for both of us!"

"Thanks, George. You're the best, you know that?" said Rett. "Uh... what did you mean, though, about 'even if it was just *you* making the decision?'"

George sat back up in chair again and looked thoughtful. "You know, as much as I want to think I'm the one that makes these kinds of decisions, I get a little dose of reality at times."

Rett stared at George, not understanding.

"This morning, when I got in, I had Cory in my office telling me that there was a chance you might come back and that I'd better *very* seriously consider it. Honestly, to have Cory in here saying that after the play he pulled last night, after what he's done for ticket sales since he started, I'm kind of wondering who really runs this team." George had that good-natured grin on his face again.

Rett was shocked to hear this. "Cory? Really?" he asked.

"Well, Cory, yeah. But JJ, Josh, Arthur, Luis, and Sebastion, too. All of 'em crowded in here."

Rett was even more shocked. Cory had pulled all of them together to demand Rett be allowed back? He felt like he could burst inside.

Then Rett remembered someone else. "How's Gunnar?" he asked.

George shook his head. "Not good. He went to the hospital last night. I think Bala had him seeing a specialist today. We'll know soon. It's pretty serious, though."

Rett felt terrible. If he had pushed back on Gunnar, maybe this wouldn't have happened. If he had refused to help Gunnar hide what he was doing to himself after all those games, maybe this wouldn't have happened. If he had just pushed back and stood up to Gunnar.

George said, "So, are you good to start back today? Can you go to Minneapolis with us this evening?"

"I'm ready," said Rett through a happy smile.

"And George," added Rett, "I won't do this to you again. I promise. I was in a bad spot, but... well... I won't do it again. I really missed being here with the Joes. It was hard seeing them on TV out in Dallas and not being there with them."

George stood up to see him out, and told him to go ahead and go get his badge back. As he was leaving, Rett could swear he almost heard Rosemary's head explode when George told her to reactivate him on the payroll.

On his way to the security office to get his ID badge back, Rett stepped out into the stands for a minute so he could see all of the Portyards around him, see the Joes out on the field warming up under a sky of sun and wheeling seabirds. He touched one of the seats nearest to him and smiled to himself. All of this was his again. He was back where he belonged. He closed his eyes and thanked Val for pushing him over the edge.

Rett wondered at how strange it was — that being pushed over the edge could put you on top of the world.

~~~~

Rett sat down on the floor of the treatment room in front of the cabinet and tried to wrangle the supplies and instruments back into some sort of reasonable order. He was a little dumbfounded that Dr. Bala and the trainers could let it all slip into this much chaos in the little bit of time he was gone. And that was with being on the road part of the time. No matter how it came to be, it was driving him crazy and he wasn't going to be able to set his mind to packing for the trip until he had the mess cleaned up a little more. He wished he had come in there and found all this earlier so he'd have more time before he needed to be ready to bug out to Minneapolis.

Rett had spent the first three innings of the game running back to his apartment to pack for the road trip. But as soon as he got back to the Portyards, he had found that no one had been putting therapy notes and plans into the computer; all of that was still scribbled up on the whiteboard in the office he shared with the trainers, at least the bits that hadn't been obliterated by Rikky's attempt to draw a portrait of Freddie. Rett didn't remember Freddie having a blue tongue that could reach down to his Adam's apple as was depicted on the board. Getting the notes transcribed into his laptop had taken another big chunk of the game.

He finally did get to watch a tiny bit of the end of the game, where he got a warm welcome back, accompanied by the requisite teasing, in the bullpen by several of the trainers and players. The game had been tied with 1 run apiece until the 8th inning, when the Joes scored a couple of runs off a hard line drive by Bert Cardona that looked like it was going to be foul, but hit the pole and stayed fair. The Joes wound up winning the game 3 to 1.

All the fans were hoping to see Cory back to his old self and out of his slump, and they weren't disappointed. He had given up only a small handful of hits and only the one run for the whole game. When Rett had started watching at the start of the 9th inning, Cory had sung "Itsy Bitsy Spider" to himself, and then held the ball up over his head, just like he always did. Rett looked around at the tens of thousands of fans in the stands who also saw Cory hold the ball up over his head, and the hundreds of thousands more, if not millions, watching him do that on TV. But it was for him, him alone, that Cory held the ball up. Knowing this, having Cory tell him the night before that he loved him, finding out that Cory belonged to him heart and soul, made Rett feel like his own heart wanted to leap out of his chest.

As soon as the game was over, Rett had helped Dr. Bala with a few things before he started packing for the game, which was repeatedly interrupted by the welcome-backs from the players as they realized he was there. Dr. Bala was *very* happy to have Rett back, especially since he wouldn't have to worry about packing supplies for the road trip or to try to keep everything organized any longer.

Just as Rett was finishing organizing the treatment room and was ready to pull things together that needed to go on the road, Cory came in, showered and in his street clothes, and laid back on one of the exam tables.

"I want a massage," he said.

Rett glance through the open doors of the treatment room to make sure no one was in earshot and asked, "A 'now' massage now or a 'later' massage later?"

"Both."

"Can the 'now' one wait just a few? I gotta get this stuff pulled together or I'll catch hell for making the bus to the airport late again. And the 'later' one is gonna have to wait until we're back from Minneapolis."

Cory ginned knowingly and said, "Oh, maybe not."

Rett looked at him curiously and was going to ask what he meant by that when JJ walked past the door to the treatment room. He stopped and stuck his head back in and said, "Hey, I need to talk to you two."

They followed him as JJ led them down the hall and into the family lounge, which was empty now that the game was over. Rett and Cory had exchanged glances, wondering if the other knew what JJ wanted to talk about. Rett and Cory sat down a couple of feet apart on one of the couches in the lounge while JJ closed the door and then sat across from them in a club chair.

JJ's face was very serious and he said, "Look, I need to talk to you two, but I can't say what I'm pretty sure I need to say without *you* saying something first."

Rett froze, almost certain of where this was going, but not daring to say anything. When no one said anything else, Rett ventured a glance over at Cory, who looked terrified and locked up. Rett hated seeing Cory scared like that, especially when he knew, and had tried to convince Cory before, that there was no reason for him to worry about opening up to JJ. But still, Cory had to be the one to take this step, not Rett.

JJ looked uncomfortable, but tried again. "Do either of you know what I'm getting into here? We *gotta* talk about this a little, but I can't go first."

Cory sat forward on the couch, locked his hands together between his knees and didn't take his eyes off of them. Rett saw how the color had drained completely out of him. He looked as white as a fresh, clean baseball.

"No?" asked JJ, looking from Cory to Rett and then back again.

JJ ran his hand across his mouth, trying to figure out a different tactic before he started again. He reached down into his shirt and pulled the cross out that he always had around his neck, the one he always touched to his forehead before an at-bat. He carefully put it down on the coffee table between them.

Rett and Cory stared at the cross on the table and tried to understand where JJ was going to go with this. JJ pointed at the golden cross on the thin chain and said, "That cross belonged to my granddaddy. He always had his bible with him, and that cross was on the red and gold bookmark that he kept in his favorite passages. It belonged to my father's father since he was a little kid."

JJ watched to make sure both Rett and Cory were listening to him.

"The thing is, what nobody knows is that Dwayne Troyer, who everybody thinks of as my father, isn't actually my father. He's a good man and I love him, but he's not my father. He's my step-father. My *real* father, Aaron Jones, died when I was about 10. It was *his* father, Isaac Jones, that this cross belonged to."

JJ took a deep breath before continuing, "In 1956, my granddaddy and grandmom, Isaac and Cora Jones, were walking into town, into Okolona, Mississippi. They were moving their family, which included them and my dad, Aaron, when he was a small kid and my auntie, Ada, from Houston to Tupelo. They didn't have a car, so they were walking." JJ had now stopped paying attention to Cory and Rett and instead was focused on the cross sitting on the table in front of him.

"My dad was probably only about five at the time, and auntie Ada was, I guess, two or so. Before they got into Okolona proper, they ran across a lady having car trouble on the side of the road. My granddaddy, being the strong Christian he was, offered to help her. She was nervous at first because he was a black man, but finally let him take a look at her car. At some point, he reached into the car, I don't know what for... to try the ignition again or make sure the car wasn't in gear or whatever. Right as he did so, a truck with four white men came across them."

JJ stared at the cross for a minute before his eyes shifted over to his forearm for another moment.

"Those men accused my grandfather, a God-fearing man whose most prized possession was his bible, of trying to rape that white lady." JJ paused again. "Those men beat him to death, right there, in front of his wife and two young children and the lady with the broken down car. When they finished, when he was dead, they pushed his beaten and shattered body into the ditch. But then they took my father, my aunt, and my grandmother... and they... they took knives and they cut deep X's in their arms, cuts that would heal to scars no matter what. Those men told them that if they ever told anyone about what they had done, they'd hunt them down and kill them, too. They pointed at the cuts in their arms and told them, 'All you niggers look alike, but we can find you now, so you best watch yourself. We'll come for you and you'll wind up just like him if you breathe so much as a word.'"

"Those men killed my granddaddy in cold blood, when all he was trying to do was help that lady. Nothing about it ever appeared in the paper and that lady never said anything. I remember growing up and seeing the scar on my daddy's arm and my auntie's arm, hearing them tell the story of what happened, the truth about his murder. I remember when my mama buried him, in his coffin, she left his left sleeve rolled up so we'd all see and remember what happened. My daddy, before he passed, always told me it was better to be put to death and left by the side of the road for being a man like my granddad than being admired for being one like those murderers."

JJ stopped talking. He took the simple gold cross in his hands and rubbed his thumb reverently across it.

He breathed deeply again and only now looked across the table at Rett and Cory. "I don't tell people about this. This story, this part of me, is for me and not anybody else. But I'm trusting the two of you with it."

"So, you see, I've given you a secret of mine. But more than that, I want you to know that I know how other people can be. I know how people can still be kicked into a ditch for something they don't control or decide on their own, no matter how good they are on the inside."

Rett was absolutely speechless. He couldn't look at JJ or even over at Cory. The most he could manage was to watch JJ slowly run his fingertip across the cross.

Rett heard a throat clear next to him, almost like it was in the distance, not even realizing it was Cory.

"Uh... I..." started Cory. "I'm, you know... I'm gay, JJ." Cory's voice sounded like he had wadded up newspapers stuffed in his throat.

JJ continued to hold the cross in his hands while he smiled weakly.

He finally said with a faint laugh, "Oh, get on out of here!"

Rett laughed, too, then looked at Cory to see how he took it. Cory remained pale and wary, but tried to laugh with them.

"Am I that obvious, JJ?" asked Cory.

"No, but I hang around the two of you a fair amount. And knowing about Rett put me halfway there already. That, plus what happened after Rett left didn't make it too hard for me to suspect."

Cory reached out and put his hand tentatively on Rett's back. "Rett and I are... kind of... seeing each other."

JJ put the cross back around his neck and inside his shirt. He leaned back into the leather chair and nodded his approval. "You two are good for each other."

He teased Rett and said, "Skunk'll probably be a little disappointed..."

"So," said JJ, "now that we've all shared something with each other that we don't want to go beyond this room, I did want to tell you guys to be careful. I'm completely comfortable with you guys. But Ahab? No. And Skunk would freak out. Probably some others, too."

"Are people starting to make comments? Ask questions?" asked Cory.

"No, everybody knows you guys have become pretty much best friends and see you as nothing more than that. But you're on tricky ground for a little while given the timing of Rett leaving and Cory's slump and all that. Just be careful."

JJ smirked a little and said, "Rett can obviously come and go on this team and it's no big deal, but Cory, we'll be in bad shape if something happens to you."

Rett sat up with a start and shot a sharp look at JJ. "Oh, yeah? No big deal? JJ, you can kiss my alabaster ass! We can go on out to home plate right now and you can just kiss it!"

JJ started laughing, followed by Cory a moment later.

"Yeah? You assholes think I'm joking around?" insisted Rett.

Cory rubbed Rett's back a little more to calm him down. "Don't worry, JJ. I'll be more careful now. I, uh... I'm sorry about your father and your grandfather. God, what a terrible thing to have happen!"

"The tattoo on your arm?" asked Rett, remembering JJ's reluctance to talk about it the one time he had asked.

JJ ran his finger across the faint "X" on his left forearm. "Yeah, the tattoo reminds me of my father. The gold cross is my reminder of my granddaddy. I never knew my granddaddy, but I sure do wish I had."

"With all that's happened to your grandfather and your dad, why do you put up with Skunk, JJ?" asked Rett.

JJ studied the tattoo on his arm again for a moment. He said, "Having this... in my family gives me perspective. Yeah, Skunk's a racist. Yeah, he's a homophobic dick. Yeah, he's a multidimensional fuck-all. But he's got no one here on his side. His bullshit doesn't amount to anything. I can get upset and make a stink and give Skunk *exactly* what he wants by doing so. Or, I can rise above it, ignore it, let him know that he doesn't have any power over me. I can be the kind of man that would make my granddaddy proud... and I choose that."

Rett said, "I think you're pretty awesome, JJ."

"Don't go gettin' all teenage girl on me," said JJ sarcastically.

Rett sighed dreamily and said "Can I have your autograph?" which made JJ flip him off.

JJ focused back on Cory. "Everything's fine, man. I was hoping we'd get this all out in the open sooner, and I was hoping you'd take the first step. But I couldn't really wait any longer with Rett back. I've got your back any way I can, we just needed to get it out in the open."

Cory nodded, "Sorry. I'm just terrified of what will happen if it gets out."

"You're right to be that way and you gotta be careful. But now you've got one less person to worry about around," said JJ. "It would be awesome, though, to have you come out at some point. I mean *really* come out. Everybody would totally shit their pants. Maybe someday, big guy, maybe someday. Like maybe after you get a couple of All-Star games under your belt."

JJ stood up and said, "This is good. This turned out good. Come on, guys, the bus is probably waiting on us, and blaming Rett for making us late will only get us so far."

Chapter 28

The waters of the Mississippi River flowed silently past in front of Rett and Cory, winding its way south. Rett's eyes followed it downstream to where he could see a place that looked like actual waterfalls in the middle of the river, in the middle of Minneapolis. He wondered if that could be right since he had no idea that the Mississippi had waterfalls. While he waited for the call to connect, he wondered if maybe the falls were manmade. They looked like maybe they could be manmade. There was no answer on the phone, though, and he ended the call without bothering to leave a message.

Cory was seated a few feet away and leaned back on the steps where they had perched, steps that led right down to the edge of the river's water. After their dinner, they had found themselves here and decided to sit and watch the view for a few minutes. Rett wished he could go be up against Cory, to touch him and seek a little comfort from him while they were watching the river make its way through the city, but the days of doing something like that together in a public place were over. It made their night out on the Brooklyn Bridge that much more precious, back before Cory was on every single sports program on television. Rett could miss those days, but he didn't begrudge them. This was part of the small sacrifice he had to make for Cory. This was part of what he did for Cory's sake. It didn't help that it would be a few more nights before they got back to Mobile and could have real alone time, but at least it was just this one series against the Twins before they were home again.

"She didn't answer?" asked Cory.

"No. Still no answer."

"You didn't want to leave a message?"

"No, the one I left a few days ago is good enough. She's sticking it to me hard this time," said Rett. He looked at his sneakers stretched out in front of him, watching the boats pass the gap between his feet, like they were lined up in a gun sight. "Maybe I really blew it with her." He sighed and pulled his knees up to his chest, wrapping his arms around them. He felt like a door was slowly closing, and once it finally clicked shut, no key in the world would reopen it.

Cory sat up and leaned forward as well. The sun was sinking lower behind them, causing the shadows of the buildings downtown to slowly reach across the river like sneaky fingers. Earlier, for the game, there hadn't been a single cloud in the sky and the temperature was much more pleasant than what they were still putting up with in Mobile. It was starting to cloud up in the east some as Rett looked off in the distance. The only cloud really hanging directly over him was Val. She was flatly refusing to respond to Rett's calls, voicemails, texts, emails, whatever.

"She'll come around, Rett," Cory said, trying his best to reassure him. "Y'all've been friends too long for her to really have ended it. Maybe you just need to back off for another week or so and let her start to miss you."

Rett didn't respond for a few moments.

"It's a shame you don't have a baseball with you right now," said Rett, changing the subject.

Cory looked over at him. "Why?"

"You see that guy on the front of that boat?" said Rett, indicating a commercial boat about forty yards away and headed upstream. "I bet you could bean that guy with it if you had one right now."

Cory laughed and said, "It's a good thing I don't have one. Why do you want to hit that guy with a baseball?"

"You're the one beaning him, not me," shrugged Rett. "I couldn't even hit the water from here."

Cory said, "You being hurt by Val, but taking it out on random dudes on boats isn't good, Rett."

Cory smirked and shook his head. He added, "And your excuses for not being able to throw a ball are getting old. We need to have another pitching practice session. One that doesn't wind up with you getting all rapey and playing my hormones against me."

"Rapey?! Ha! You set up that whole night just to get in my pants! I was just a helpless pawn in your little mind-fuck!"

They grinned at each other, waiting to see how much further they could carry the teasing about this.

It was Cory that blinked first. "I didn't, you know."

"Didn't what?"

"I didn't set out for any of that to happen that night. I was still a little terrified of you telling me to go get bent. I almost didn't try the thing where I stood up against you to step you through the pitching motions. But... I'm glad I did."

Rett leaned back against the steps behind him. "Bigfoot, I wouldn't trade a single thing about that night for all the home runs in the world."

"Me either," said Cory.

They sat in silence for a few moments before Cory stood up and said, "Let's go, chief. I don't want to wander around downtown Minneapolis after dark."

Rett joined him and they began their walk back to the hotel where the team was staying while playing at Target Field. They wandered around the streets and tall buildings of downtown, looking up at a lot of the skyway pedestrian bridges that linked so many of the buildings. While they wandered, a man with his wife and two young sons approached Cory, recognizing who he was, and nervously asked if he could have an autograph for his sons, both of whom were staring wide-eyed at the massive pitcher in front of them.

A shy look crossed his face, and the man told Cory, "I feel bad, you know... I'm actually a Twins fan. But it's really awesome to meet you in person!"

Even in Minneapolis, it seemed Cory had become an easily recognized face. Rett waited patiently while Cory gave a little piece of himself to these people.

When they resumed their walk, Cory insisted they take a street that wasn't the right route back to where they were staying, but Rett walked with him anyway. About halfway down the block, Rett looked back to see Cory standing, waiting, with a grin on his face. He looked up at the hotel they were in front of and told Cory, "That's not our hotel."

Rett walked back to him, and Cory said, "No, it's not. But it could be. For tonight. Away from the rest of the team, if you know what I mean." Cory was still grinning when it hit Rett what he was suggesting, and it was suddenly Christmas in August.

"Are you serious?" asked Rett.

"Sure! Why not? We can have a good night here, together, then go back to our hotel and get ready before the buses leave for Target Field tomorrow."

Rett looked back where they had come from. "You planned this, didn't you? You've had this idea for a while, haven't you?"

Cory looked innocent, but said, "Maybe."

Rett felt like an idiot that they hadn't thought of doing this sooner. He glanced up at the tall hotel again; it was a very sleek, modern one, with a lot of stone and glass. "This looks like a pretty expensive hotel, though. You sure you want us to spend this kind of money?"

Cory eyed Rett in exasperation. "I've got money, Rett. More money than I know what to do with. We've never talked about any of that stuff, but Jimmy wrote into my contract that for every inning I pitch and don't allow any hits, I get a ten thousand dollar bonus. Not bad, huh? My base salary is low compared to most ball players, but I make it up with a lot of bonuses if I do well. I made an extra $90,000 in that first game that I started. I think I can swing a hotel room for a night. Hell, for you, I'll get the fucking Presidential Suite if you want." He emphasized again, "Anything you want, Rett."

Rett had to hold back from wrapping himself around Cory out on the street he was so excited. He beamed at him and said, "This is an awesome idea!"

Cory gave him wary look and said, "But, there's a catch."

"What? Are you going to make me yell 'play ball!' before we fuck?" asked Rett, his eyes narrowing in suspicion.

"No, but you can kiss my ass instead! Just to be safe, and probably paranoid, *you* should get the hotel room, to keep it out of my name. I'll pay you back for it," said Cory. Then he teased, "That is, if you trust me that I'll actually make good on the debt."

Rett said, "Whatever. I'll add it onto the fifty dollars worth of head you still owe me for the sofa."

"Are you nuts? *You* owe *me* fifty dollars worth of head for that! I got you the discount, remember? You haven't even *begun* to pay that off, boy!"

"That's not how I remember it," said Rett, still grinning. "It doesn't matter. The shitty job you do giving head will take you *forever* to pay off a night in a place like this."

"The sooner you get your blinding white ass in there and yell 'play ball!' chief, the sooner we can start clearing off *both* sides of the blow-job ledger," said Cory.

The instant they got into the room, they slammed the door shut and were all over each other. Rett practically was climbing up on Cory so he could kiss him, touch him, feel his body pressed against him. Rett no longer gave a marshmallow-flavored unicorn poop if Cory paid him back for the room or not.

Cory's arms locked around Rett as he leaned back against the door to the room, almost lifting Rett up off of the floor while they kissed hard. This was going to make Rett actually look forward to road trips with the team if they started doing this on an occasional basis.

Cory groaned happily and let Rett back down to the floor and they walked into the room the rest of the way. It was big enough to have a sitting area and a huge king sized bed that Cory would be comfortable in. And best of all, the room was high enough up that it had a view of the Mississippi River through its wall of windows.

Cory put his hands on Rett's shoulders and directed him over to the windows where they could see the river. Rett stood there, looking out at the view, and felt Cory's arms wrap around him from behind, pulling him back against his chest. The soft hair of Cory's beard tickled against the back of Rett's neck where he kissed and nibbled at him delicately. With the view in front of him and Cory behind him, holding and nipping him, Rett felt like he was flying out over downtown Minneapolis.

Cory whispered in his ear, "You're gonna have to get used to me wanting to spend some money on you, Rett. I want to make you happy."

Rett said, "Your money has nothing to do with my happiness, Cory. You better know that."

"I know. But you're gonna have to get used to it anyway. It'll make me happy to do it for you."

Rett leaned back harder into Cory's chest. God, how he loved that feeling, of being surrounded by Cory, of being wrapped up in him. He said, "You being happy is important. But I guess this means turnabout will have to be considered fair-play."

Cory reached down and stuck a hand down the front of Rett's short pants. He growled into Rett's ear, "I love the turnabout!"

They watched as another commercial boat made its way down the river in the fading light and lengthening shadows of the downtown buildings thrown across the waterway.

"It's one of the things that impressed Jimmy the most about you, you know," commented Cory.

"What did?"

"Not one single time that he ever talked to you was my fame or money or any of that stuff something that seemed important to you."

"I didn't think Jimmy was really impressed by anything about me," said Rett.

"He likes you more than I think you realize, Rett. He's just very protective of me. But believe me, you have his blessing, even if you have a hard time seeing it," said Cory, his beard grazing against Rett's neck again.

Rett turned around to face Cory while still wrapped in Cory's arms. He looked up at him and said, "Val said that you were the best thing that ever happened to me, and it didn't matter if you were a ball player or a genetically engineered florist."

Cory laughed out loud and his eyes sparkled at the thought.

"And you know what?" asked Rett.

"What?"

"She's right." Rett sighed, laying his head against Cory's chest, "She's always right."

Cory kissed him on his forehead and said softly, "She'll come around, Rett."

~~~~~

"Holy shit, Cory, all of downtown Minneapolis heard that groan!"

"Harder! Push harder!" demanded Cory.

Rett dug in as hard as he could.

"Fuck... that spot, right there! On my God, that's... how did you find that spot?!" Cory yowled again and Rett wondered how long it would be before the hotel management was banging on their door.

"More!" begged Cory.

Rett rolled his eyes. "How about I switch to the other foot?"

"Yeah, yeah, find that same spot! Where the fuck did you learn this? How come I haven't gotten a foot massage from you before?"

Rett ran his hands along Cory's calf before putting it back down on the bed and switching to his left foot. He started kneading the bottom of it gently at first before increasing the pressure on it.

"Vow of silence. I'm supposed to kill anybody that discovers my superpower," said Rett drily.

"Foot rubs are your...? Ooooooh, shit! God damn, Rett, I'll do anything! Just don't stop!"

Cory was writhing on the disarrayed sheets of the bed, totally naked, while Rett continued to work on his foot. *Wonderful,* thought Rett, *we'll never have sex again. It'll be nothing but foot rubs from here on out. I've become a foot rub slave.*

Cory twisted on the bed from the sensations Rett was sending through him by merely rubbing his feet. He said, "Wait 'til the guys on the team hear..."

"You say one *motherfucking* word about this to *anybody* else on the team and I'll rip your foot off and feed it to the seagulls outside the Portyards' loading dock! One word, cocksucker! This isn't in my job description!" warned Rett.

"Not even..."

Rett snapped, "Do I look like I'm shitting around about this, Bigfoot?"

Cory snickered right as Rett's phone started ringing. Rett answered the call while Cory begged, "Don't stop!"

Rett put the phone between his ear and shoulder and resumed rubbing Cory's foot while he said, "Hello?"

"Rett?"

Rett's hands froze where they were on Cory's foot.

"Rett?" said the voice again. "It's your father."

Rett still said nothing. He couldn't seem to move or speak. He suddenly found it hard to pull breath into his lungs.

After another pause, his father said, "Look, I wanted..."

Without doing it consciously, Rett grabbed the phone from his ear, hung up the call and threw the phone on the bed. He stared at it like it had tried to sting him.

"What happened? Who was that?" asked Cory, getting concerned when he saw Rett's face.

Rett turned away and sat on the edge of the bed, a million things wheeling through his mind and spilling over themselves. He never expected to hear that voice again. That was a past life that he had given a second chance, a second chance that had been wadded up like a used tissue and thrown back at him by his father when he had seen him in that hospital room weeks ago.

Cory sat up, his concern growing even worse. He put his legs on either side of Rett and closed his arms around his bare midsection.

"You ok, Rett? Who was that? Talk to me, chief!"

Rett looked anxiously at the phone, wondering if it was going to ring again. He felt displaced and his heart was pounding. He had his life back together. He had gotten all of his life put back the way he wanted. Why was this happening now and trying to disrupt all of that?

Rett felt Cory's arms tighten around him, trying to get his attention. "It was my dad," he answered.

"Your dad? Really?" asked Cory. Rett stared at the phone like it might sprout stubby little legs and come chasing after him.

"What did he want?" Cory asked carefully.

"Uh... I... I don't know. I hung up on him."

Rett could feel the muscles under his eyes start to twitch. He tried to decide if it was anger, or fear, or maybe even garden-variety pain he was feeling, but he couldn't pick them apart.

"You ok?" asked Cory. He buried his face into Rett's neck and held him from behind, letting Rett know he was safe.

"I wonder if Bo told him anything. Said we were talking again," said Rett, still in a fog. Rett thought, *because if Bo did, maybe Dad thinks...*

Rett shuddered.

Cory pulled Rett back onto the bed and made him lie down. He put Rett under the covers and got under them with him, snuggling up against him, kissing his shoulder and neck and ears.

He tried to soothe Rett, "It's ok, Rett. I'm here with you. Always with you."

Rett realized how fast his heart was beating. Even now, the physical reaction his body had to any kind of contact with that man was extreme. Even after all this time, and even after writing his parents off for good, no matter how much he told himself they had no power over him.

Cory shifted down under the covers and put his head on Rett's chest. He ran his hands along Rett's body, across his stomach, over his bare pelvis and down his legs, then back up, trying anything he could to calm Rett.

Rett's heartbeat finally slowed back down to normal and he put his hand on Cory's head, running his hands through the soft hair that was the color of pecan shells, the soft hair he loved so much.

Cory ventured, "Maybe he was calling to say he was sorry about the hospital."

Rett sighed wearily.

"Well, you don't think he'd call to start being nasty to you again, do you?" Cory asked gently.

Rett thought, *it kind of depends on Bo.*

He continued to thread his fingers through Cory's hair. "I don't know. Maybe."

A moment later, he said, "I need to call Bo."

"You sure you're ok? Your heart started beating like crazy. How you react to your parents scares me to death, Rett."

Rett kissed the top of Cory's head and said, "Thank you for being here. If I'd been alone and gotten that call, I probably would have flushed my phone down the toilet out of panic."

They lay in the bed for probably another ten minutes, Cory continuing to run his hands slowly up and down Rett's body, before Rett picked his phone up again.

He had misgivings about calling Bo in case he was there with his father at the moment, but he hit the call button anyway.

"Hello?"

"Hey, Bo. It's Rett..."

"Hey, Rett! I was thinking about calling you pretty soon. How's Mobile?"

"Uh, actually, I'm in Minneapolis for work right now."

"Minneapolis? For physical therapy? You get shipped around the country just to do physical therapy?"

Rett didn't want to get into all that at the moment. "Mmmmm... it's kind of a long story. Look, are you with mom and dad right now?"

"They're not in the room, but I'm at their house. Mom made dinner tonight, and since I'm still pretty broke until..."

"Bo, did you tell them you and I had talked, that we were back on good terms?" asked Rett.

"Nope. Haven't said anything at all to either of them. I know you're still a little weirded out about them and I don't want to make that any worse."

Rett sighed in relief. "Dad called me just a few minutes ago. You didn't ask him to call me, did you?"

"Dad? Really? Just now? No, definitely not. He's been back in their room resting for the last hour after dinner. He still gives out pretty quickly. Mom's been in the kitchen cleaning up. What did he want?"

Rett said, "I was hoping you knew. I, uh... well, I kind of hung up on him before he could really say anything."

"I don't know, Rett. He hasn't mentioned you at all. Mom was the one that told me you came to the hospital that day. He's been real quiet, though, but... you know... he's had a bad heart attack, so... He wasn't the same after you left, like I told you, but after this heart attack, he's even more different."

Rett thought about it for a moment. He asked, "He hasn't asked you about me at all? Has mom mentioned him talking about me?"

"No, not a peep."

Rett tried to understand what was behind the call he had gotten earlier. Cory had stopped rubbing and instead listened carefully to Rett on the phone.

Bo said, "Rett, give me a chance. Let me see if I can find out what's going on, ok?"

Rett threw the covers off of himself and stood up at the thought of what Bo was suggesting. The idea made him extremely uncomfortable. He went and stood in front of the windows, the city lights and the Midwestern evening glinting on the river, and the last bit of sunset in the west was reflecting beautifully off the heavier clouds that had steadily built in the east. He said, "No way, Bo, I don't want you getting..."

"Just give me a chance, alright?" said Bo. "I'll do it carefully, so he doesn't know we've talked. It may take me a few days to think through how to do it, but just let me give it a try."

Rett considered whether he wanted to drag Bo into any of this. Maybe even calling him at all had been a bad idea.

"Ok, Rett?"

Rett knew he should drop this entire thing and let his relationship with his parents be the mangled pulp of road kill he saw in his rearview mirror, but he couldn't quite leave it alone.

"Ok, Bo."

Bo said, "It's good to hear your voice, Rett..."

"Bo?"

"Yeah?"

"You still have your Hot Wheels cars?"

There was a pause on the other side of the phone. "Yeah."

Rett grinned to himself. "You still play with them, I bet."

Another pause. "Maybe. You still eat those frozen waffles?" said Bo, giving it right back.

"Never mind," said Rett. "You answered my question already, squirt."

"Man, having a big brother sucks nuts," said Bo. "Uh... no offense, I guess."

"My work schedule gets a little crazy," said Rett, "but I want you to come see me sometime. I'd love to have some time with you. I really miss you, man. I'll even make us frozen waffles. Just watch out with dad, please. I really mean that. This is trickier than you realize."

"I miss you, too. But I'll be careful and I'll be in touch in a couple of days. Just hang tight 'til then, alright?"

Rett agreed and hung up the phone. He continued looking out the window, now doubting his decision to let Bo try to get some information. There was lots of room for error, and the repercussions of a mistake could be graver than what Bo understood. He debated calling Bo back and telling him to stay out of it after all, that he'd call his father back himself. But he really wanted a little more information first. He didn't want to have a third round with his dad end the same way that it did the previous two times. If there was to be a third round.

Cory got up from the bed and stood behind him while they both looked out the window, his bare body against Rett's.

"Bo doesn't know anything about the call," Rett explained. "He's going to try and see if he can pull some information out of mom or dad about it in the next few days."

Cory rubbed up and down Rett's shoulders. "It'll be ok, Rett..."

~~~~~

From this height in the hotel, it was hard to tell that it was raining unless Rett looked down at the streets below. He bunched himself up into a ball in the sitting area sofa and watched it anyway, his mind years in the past.

Rett sat at the small dinette set they kept in the kitchen, one foot tucked up under the other leg on the green vinyl chair cushion while he poked around groggily on the family laptop. It was 3am and he had no reason to be on it other than giving himself something to do instead of sitting up in bed while the thunderstorm outside finally died off.

He bit at his lip when he saw his dad shuffle barefoot into the kitchen, his black bathrobe open, exposing his white t-shirt and boxer shorts underneath. His dad was squinting against the kitchen light and said, "Shoulda guessed it'd be you in here. 's raining, after all."

Rett didn't take the bait. It was better if he never took it. He never won any argument even remotely resembling the one about his insomnia during thunderstorms in the 15 years he had been alive.

Instead he lied, "Just realized there were a few emails I forgot to send before I'm in a rush tomorrow morning."

His dad pulled a glass out of the cabinet and began filling it with water from a pitcher in the fridge. He said to his son, "You talking about which boy band you like the most with that girl you hang out with all the time?"

His dad began to drink, but kept his eyes on Rett, who was now looking at a blank spot on the table in front of him. Rett could feel his father's eyes on him, judging him. He barely ever hung out with Charlotte and they weren't even really close. Rett even hated boy bands. But it was better not to take the bait.

His dad put the glass in the sink and mumbled to himself, "Man, I wish I knew what it was going to take to make something worthwhile out of you."

He crossed his arms over his chest and said to his son directly, "Turn it off and go to bed, Rett. You two can compare notes on lip gloss tomorrow."

Rett closed the lid on the laptop and left to go back to his room without looking at his father, fearing there'd be more humiliation from him if he did.

He climbed into his bed, the wind causing the windows in his room to creak from the pressure. There was another brilliant and erratic series of flashes outside his window followed a few seconds later by a bone-rattling crash of thunder. He'd never sleep with all that going on, so he resigned himself to sitting up and staring at the foot of his bed until the storm wore itself out.

He had almost drifted off when he was jerked back awake by more thunder, and he noticed someone in the room with him. Without a word, Bo came over and got under the covers with Rett and snuggled up against his older brother, comforting him.

Having the flannel of Bo's pajamas against his skin made him feel better.

Bo whispered to him, "It's ok, Rett. I heard dad talking. I'll clear out of here before he wakes up in the morning."

A motion on the bed brought Rett back to the hotel room. Cory was sitting up and watching him.

"Is the rain bothering you?" asked Cory.

"No, it's just rain."

"You're thinking about your dad, aren't you?"

"Yeah."

Cory pulled himself from under the covers, walked over and sat next to him on the sofa. He said, "Come on back to bed, Rett. Give Bo a chance to find something out for you."

Rett nodded, but didn't move.

Cory leaned his head over onto Rett's shoulder and whispered to him through a stifled yawn, "It must be awesome to have a brother."

Rett set his jaw and said, "You've got Jimmy, Brick and Zee. You've got a big family."

"Yeah, they're as much family as anyone could hope for, I guess," said Cory. "But they're not blood. You and Bo share blood."

Rett bit at his lip, for the first time realizing he had something that Cory didn't. Something that Cory perhaps even envied a little.

And despite the downsides to what could happen with Bo talking to his dad, it felt good to have someone like Bo. Someone he trusted to be on his side with this, who had always been on his side. Someone he knew from his earliest memories. It felt good to have someone who shared his blood.

Chapter 29

JJ said nothing, but rather stood and looked at Rett with a discontented smirk.

"What?" said Rett, turning off the music on his laptop but leaving his earbuds in his ears. He shifted in the office chair at the big table in the locker room. "I'm just sitting here," he said defensively.

If he had to hear JJ tell him to cool it with respect to Cory again, he was going to go out, buy a feather boa, fuck-me-silly high heels, and a number 72 jersey, and wear them in to the Portyards just to be done with it. Ever since their last talk before they went to Minneapolis, Cory and Rett had made a habit of speaking to each other in the clubhouse only minimally; they couldn't cool it any more short of getting into fistfights with one another.

JJ silently reached in the pocket of his faded jeans and pulled out a wadded up $100 bill and dropped it in front of Rett on the keyboard of his laptop.

Josh Kilfoyle had passed through earlier and so had Rolly Duvauchelle, but right now the locker room was empty. Rett gawked at the money, and then looked around as if the meaning of the $100 bill was taped up on someone's locker station.

"If you're giving me money just because I'm an amazing guy," said Rett, "you owe me a lot more than this."

JJ said, "You know what that's for."

He walked a few feet away, behind where Rett was seated, and leaned up against the divider between a couple of the locker stations. Rett looked at him blankly, then squinted at him, trying to understand why he'd given him a hundred bucks.

JJ pointed at the station next to him. "This locker isn't empty," he said.

It was Skunk's locker station.

Understanding finally dawned on Rett. He started to laugh. "Oh, shit! I forgot all about that!"

"Hey, if you want to forget about it, I'll be happy to take that money back," said JJ.

"Hell, no! You're lucky you paid on time! I charge a lot of interest! Fall behind on those payments, and Cory's gonna come after your knees with a baseball bat." Rett grabbed the money and pocketed it before JJ tried to get it back.

He glanced at the locker station and frowned, "For what it's worth, JJ, I'd rather have lost that bet."

"It's not too late to give me that money back."

"I don't want to lose that bad."

JJ crossed to his locker and started to change into his running shorts and favorite red sleeveless t-shirt for his usual run around the stadium before he needed to be in uniform for practice.

"You wanna bet again he's still here tomorrow?" tried Rett, enthusiastically.

JJ pulled his shorts on and said, "Forget it, cricket. I'm not paying you $100 every day Skunk's still on this team."

Rett laughed and said, "Sounded like a good deal to me."

"Yeah, I'm sure it did," said JJ as he finished tying his sneakers and left to go on his run.

Rett's laptop started to act glitchy after JJ left and he was in the process of shutting it down when Skunk walked into the locker room wearing baggy shorts and a dirty, wife-beater undershirt. He was glad they had finished their conversation when they did because he didn't want to put up with the attitude he'd get if Skunk found out about the bet between him and JJ.

"Where's your little Disney Princess best friend, faggot? Huh?" said Skunk while he opened up a drawer.

Rett turned and glanced briefly at Skunk, and was about to say something. But then he thought about what JJ had said about not giving him what he wants, not giving him the reaction. Since he had the earbuds still in, he pretended to not hear anything and turned back around to his laptop, completely ignoring Skunk. He wished that JJ hadn't left so quickly, though.

Skunk sneered at Rett, "I know you and Cory Pure-And-Clean both gotta be packers."

Rett continued to pretend he couldn't hear anything coming from Skunk.

"Hey, I'm talking to you, faggot!" said Skunk as he stripped his shorts and jockstrap off.

Rett's laptop had shut down, and in the reflection of the dark screen he could see Skunk standing naked and threateningly behind him. But as Rett was about to take his laptop and leave, Rosemary strode into the locker room from Ahab's office, cutting through to the hallway back to her office.

Rett froze, but could see in the screen's reflection where Rosemary stopped and gave an acidic look at the naked Skunk standing there.

Skunk smiled and turned his attention to Rosemary. He opened his arms and said, "Rose, if you want to check out my junk, all you gotta do is ask, sweetheart. I'm not used to chicks being shy, especially ones with a little experience under their belts, like you!" He spread his legs open a little further so she could get a good look.

Rett shuffled a paper or two on the desk, but continued to watch both of them in the laptop screen's reflection. Rosemary's upper lip began to draw up in fury, like a rabid wolf. Even with Skunk standing there naked, she stepped over towards him, grabbed his jockstrap off the chair, and produced a cigarette lighter from a pocket on her skirt. With her eyes still glued to Skunk, she proceeded to light his jockstrap on fire, and then dropped the filthy, flaming fabric to the carpet.

Skunk had backed up a step when he saw what Rosemary was doing, afraid she was going to fling the burning jockstrap at him.

Rosemary said in a soft voice that would give a grizzly bear nightmares, "Next time, you'll be *wearing* it when I light it on fire, child." The ice in her voice when she called Skunk a child sent shivers down Rett's spine.

Rosemary calmly walked out of the locker room and Skunk finally managed to move. He started shouting "Shit! Shit! Motherfucker!" and tried stomping on the burning jockstrap with his bare feet for a moment, and then reached for a sneaker to try to beat the fire out.

As he grabbed for the sneaker, Ahab walked into the locker room and saw what was going on. Rett busied himself with his papers again because he knew there was about to be a serious explosion. And sure enough, as soon as Ahab comprehended what was happening, he blew up.

"What the fuck are you doing, Skunk?! Are you trying to burn the goddamn stadium down? Are you out of that goddamn pea-sized brain of yours?" Ahab was shouting at the top of his lungs and he stepped over and stomped on the burning carpet and jockstrap a few times until the fire was out. All that was left were a few bits of the charred jockstrap and a sooty, burned spot in the carpet about the size of a baseball mitt.

At the shouting, Rett finally took his earbuds out and turned around to watch Skunk get reamed out.

Ahab's head looked like an overinflated red-balloon that was about to pop any second. "What the fuck is wrong with you, shithead?! Do you think this is funny? Is this what you have to do to get attention now?"

Rett would have found it pretty funny if it weren't for the fact that Ahab was terrifying when he got this angry.

Skunk was stuttering and stammering, trying to explain that it was Rosemary that actually did it. Ric Velasques, D'Angelo Cheatham, and Kevin Ostergaard appeared and crowded into the door of the locker room to see what the shouting was about.

Ahab continued yelling at Skunk at the top of his lungs, "Do you think I'm fucking stupid? Are you *really* going to try to blame this on Rosemary? That woman's in her 70's, for fuck's sake! Why would *anybody*, much less Rosemary, touch your goddamn jockstrap, asshole? The thing's a fucking Petri dish for STDs!"

Skunk tried again, "She did! Rett! You were here! Tell him! Tell Ahab what happened!"

Rett turned red at suddenly being dragged into this.

"To be honest, I was busy with my laptop and had my earbuds in. I wasn't paying any attention to whatever was going on in here," said Rett.

"What?" said Skunk, turning very pale. "No, you know Rosemary came through here! You saw what she did! You heard what happened!"

Rett shrugged and held up the earbuds in his hand for Skunk and Ahab to see. "Sorry. I don't even remember Rosemary being here."

Ahab had had enough. He told Skunk to clean his mess up and that the team would probably fine him to repair the carpet. Ahab stormed out of the locker room muttering about worthless prima-donnas as he went.

Rett didn't wait around for Skunk's reaction and he followed Ahab out.

~~~~~

Rett avoided Skunk as much as he could the rest of the day leading up to the game. Throwing him under the bus was only going to make Skunk that much harder to be around, no matter how good it felt to do it to him and even with the plausible deniability. Everyone else was on him like gnats on an open cut trying to get the truth of what happened, and he could barely get work done for all the questions. Rett stuck to his story that he hadn't paid any attention to what was going on in the room, though. He was pretty sure that not a single person he talked to believed that to be the case, though.

Out on the field during practice, Rett managed to get Cory and JJ alone long enough to tell them the truth about what had happened. Cory was sorry that Skunk wasn't wearing the jockstrap at the time after all, and JJ decided he liked Rosemary a lot more than he ever had. Once they went back to finish practice, Rett felt a hand on his shoulder, and he sighed at having to tell yet another person he didn't see anything and knew nothing.

He turned around and found Gunnar there behind him. Gunnar's right arm was in a pretty serious sling meant to immobilize the arm most of the time. Rett immediately noticed that Gunnar had more lines in his face than he remembered, and that he looked paler than he had ever seen him before. He looked ten years older.

"Hey, Rett," said Gunnar.

"Gunnar!"

"It's good to see you back. I heard you had come back."

Rett nodded and said, "You got a minute, Gunnar? I want to talk to you."

Gunnar nodded, and they walked up into the stands a few rows, back behind the team's dugout and sat down in the seats to talk.

Rett said, "How's the arm doing?" Dr. Bala had already put Gunnar on the 60-Day DL, which meant he wouldn't return for the rest of the season. Rett still felt a lot of responsibility for what Gunnar was going through.

"Shitty. First surgery was last week, and I've got another in a few more weeks," said Gunnar, which Rett already knew also. "The pain meds are pretty sweet, though," he added, trying to be a little more upbeat and making Rett laugh.

Rett's smile faded and he said, "I feel pretty responsible for this, you know. I shouldn't have let you keep hiding what was going on..."

"No, Rett," said Gunnar, butting in.

"Bullshit!" said Rett, more forcefully than he intended. But it got Gunnar to let him finish. "Your job is to play baseball. But *my* job is to look out for your health, and I let you down."

Gunnar tried to speak again, but Rett raised his voice and kept going, "*Even if...* even if you want to play through the pain and damage, it's my *job* to not let you do that to yourself. I let you down, Gunnar. And I did a piss poor job of what I was hired to do."

"I know you feel responsible," said Gunnar, "but I manipulated you into what you did, Rett. I did this to myself. Part of me avoiding Dr. Bala was because I could push you to let me do what I wanted. But part of it, too, was that I could talk to you about everything I was going through. I regret forcing you into a bad position. But... I don't regret talking to you about the pressure and the fear."

Rett decided not to wrangle over it any harder with Gunnar. They could both sit there all afternoon, trying to take the blame and not getting anywhere.

"I'm not coming back," said Gunnar, his eyes turning distant.

"I know," said Rett with a nod, knowing full well how the 60-Day DL worked this late in the season.

"No," said Gunnar, "I'm retiring. I'll have the surgeries, but the specialists have said my shoulder will probably not fully heal back the way it was. And I'll be much more likely for another complete tear like this one if I put stress on it. This is... *was...* my last season in baseball. I've... pitched my last game in the majors. I probably won't be able to pitch so much as a wad of paper into the trash again. It's over."

Rett pressed his lips together and stared at the seatback in front of him. Gunnar's career was ending. And Rett played a part in it.

"Only Ahab and George know," said Gunnar. "So please keep it to yourself. I know you will because you kept everything else to yourself so well. But I thought you deserved to know before anyone else."

"I'm so sorry, Gunnar," said Rett, barely able to get the words out of his throat. He swore to himself that he'd never let a player do this to himself ever again if he saw the signs. He'd man up and stand his ground with the players from now on. No matter how much they wanted to be the hero.

He deeply wished it hadn't taken the end of a fine pitcher's career for him to learn that lesson.

Gunnar shook his head and took a deep breath colored by an even deeper resignation. "Nah. I had a good run. Far longer and better than a lot of guys in the majors. That game where we beat the Orioles 1 to nothing, that'll be the last game I pitched. And at least I can point to it and say I won it for the Joes, even if it was Cory that made the Orioles the laughingstock of the MLB that night."

He pointed to the field and added, "At least I know I've left the Joes in good hands."

Rett looked out at Cory on the field, where Gunnar had pointed. He wasn't starting that night, but he was pitching to the batters for their pre-game practice. Somehow, the responsibility for the Joes was shifting from Gunnar to the newest, youngest member on the team.

Rett said, "The Joes were in good hands *before* Cory came along. I'll miss you a hell of a lot, Gunnar."

Gunnar took his uninjured left hand and gave Rett a couple of pats on his back. He stood up to leave and said, "I'll miss you, too, Rett."

Rett thought back about how hard it was on him for the short time he had been away from the team, and he was the least person on the team. Gunnar practically *was* the Joes. It would have to be a hundred-fold that feeling for him knowing he'd never be back.

Rett said, "The *Joes* are gonna miss you a hell of a lot, Gunnar."

Gunnar wandered off and Rett sat in the seat watching the players out on the field. Many of them would do the same thing Gunnar had done, all for the game.

And Rett had to be man enough to no longer let them get away with it.

~~~~~

Cory sang loudly, "Too late, my time has come; sends shivers down my spine..."

Rett refused to sing along. He rolled his eyes and looked at Cory's face in his lap as he drove to Cory's apartment after the game. Cory was in a good mood, even though he hadn't pitched that evening. Ric Velasques had been the starter that night, and the Joes had beaten the Rays 3 runs to 1.

Cory gave Rett a caustic look and stopped singing long enough to say, "Don't roll your eyes at me. This song's a classic!"

Rett sneered and said, "This song's a classic example of trying too hard! It's practically a novelty song, for shit's sake! Put the Psychedelic Furs back on."

Cory jerked up out of Rett's lap and looked at him in horror. "Blasphemer! 'Bohemian Rhapsody' is a high hymn of the classic rock religion!"

Rett sighed and said, "Oh, dear God."

Cory resumed singing in a painful countertenor, "I see a little sillhouetto of a man; Scaramouch, scaramouch, will you do the fandango..."

Rett grimaced and yelled over the singing, "Will you listen to yourself? Psychedelic Furs, now, please!"

Cory reached over and started playing with Rett's crotch and asked, "What will you promise if I put something different on? Huh?"

"I promise to not wreck this piece of shit car just to stop this music!"

"Hey," said Cory, "The deal was... when I'm in your car, *I* pick the music. Otherwise, why would I ever let you drive? This thing smells like somebody dropped a deuce in here."

"Duh," said Rett. "Of course it does. Dog shit air freshener."

"What?" said Cory.

Rett reached down and dug around under his seat, finally pulling something out and throwing it at Cory. It was a tree-shaped cardboard air freshener plainly labeled with the scent "Dog Shit."

Cory gawked at it. "Why the hell would you have a *dog shit* air freshener in your car?"

"Val gave it to me a while ago."

"But whyyyyyyyyy keep it, dipshit?" Cory sniffed at it tentatively and jerked his nose away. The smell had faded, but the air freshener was correctly labeled.

"Why not?"

"Because it makes your car smell like dog shit? Is that what you were trying for?"

"The car already smelled like dog shit. Smelled like that when I got it. Worse, actually. You never complained about it before."

Cory said, "I was trying to be nice, before I knew it was *intentional*. If it already smelled like dog shit, *why* get a dog shit air freshener?"

"Go big or go home," said Rett, matter-of-factly.

Cory said, "I'll never understand you and Val."

Rett sighed again and said wistfully, "Whenever I think of dogs with bowel problems, I think of Val."

"And what reminds you of me?"

"Big piles of greasy crab claws, mostly."

"That's the most romantic thing anyone's ever said to me," said Cory. He reached over and played with Rett's earlobe.

Rett turned down the song. He said, "Look, I need to say something. I want to give you fair warning."

"About what?" said Cory.

"I don't want to have what happened to Gunnar happen to you, Bigfoot."

Cory considered it, then chuckled. "I don't think you have to worry about *that*."

"I'm just giving you a warning. If I think you're overdoing the pitching and putting your arm or yourself at risk, I'll get Dr. Bala involved. Ahab, too, if I have to. I'm *not* going to sit by and see what happened to Gunnar happen to you. You're too important to me to let that happen. I'm *really* not kidding about this."

Cory was silent for a moment and then he put his head back down in Rett's lap. He looked up at him and said once again, but more sincerely, "That's the most romantic thing anyone's ever said to me, chief."

Rett took one hand off the wheel and stroked the beard along Cory's jaw line. Cory closed his eyes and gave a satisfied purr. Rett wetted his finger in his mouth and then stuck it in Cory's ear, holding it there.

Cory sighed in gentle frustration. "Get your slimy finger outta my ear."

"Ah ah ah!!" admonished Rett. "Whatever I wanted, remember?"

Cory left Rett's finger where it was and closed his eyes again. "Yes, dear."

Rett took his finger out of Cory's ear and instead pulled up on the front of his own shirt, pulling it over Cory's head so he could use the hem to dry out his ear for him. Cory squirmed some, then rolled over so he could kiss and tickle Rett's bare stomach under the shirt with his whiskers.

Rett left his shirt over Cory's head, but reached under it and stroked his face gently again. He kept his eyes on the road, but his fingers traced along Cory's nose, around his lips, out to his dimples, then back down through the soft walnut whiskers on his chin. It earned him another satisfied grunt from Cory.

"I love you, Cory," he said quietly.

"I love you, too, Rett."

Chapter 30

Even with the gentle rain falling, Rett could see there were still some serious fans waiting it out up in the stands. Not many, probably only a small handful sprinkled around, holding out hope that the rain would end and the game would go on. He closed the dugout door and walked back down the tunnel towards the indoor pitching and batting cage where Cory was keeping warmed up in the event the game started after all.

He entered the cage and slouched down against the wall as Cory hurled a pitch at JJ at the far end. The readout said the pitch was only going 78mph, which meant Cory was still pitching changeups at JJ.

Yesterday, the day when Skunk got chewed out for attempting to torch the clubhouse, the weather had been great. But today's game against the Rays was almost certainly going to be called due to the mild but steady rain that had come in from the Gulf and settled over Mobile.

Rett turned his phone over and over in his hands while Cory continued to pitch at an easy pace. He wondered if he should try to call Bo, or wait a little longer. Five days earlier, on Tuesday, was when Bo had promised to try to find something out about the phone call from his father, but Rett had heard nothing since. The waiting was making him antsy.

He punched the speed dial on the phone and called Val instead. It rang several times with no answer before rolling over to voicemail. Rett frowned and ended the call without leaving another message.

"Val or Bo?" asked Cory as JJ threw a ball back to him.

"Val. I guess I should give up." Rett sighed heavily and felt very cooped up.

The door to the stairwell banged open and Topher stepped around to the pitching tunnel. He said, "Hey, guys... news from upstairs I thought you'd like to know about."

Cory stopped before pitching again and turned towards him. JJ stood up and propped his catcher's mask up on his head.

"Skunk got traded to the Rangers this morning."

Rett could see Cory glance back towards him without turning all the way. "That was fast. Because of him burning a hole in the clubhouse yesterday?" asked Cory.

Topher scratched behind his head and said, "Look, everyone on this team knows Rosemary is capable of worse than setting fire to a jockstrap, even if that one there didn't see anything." Topher pointed at Rett and then put finger quotes around the phrase "didn't see anything."

"The fire didn't help," he added, "but we all knew this was coming. They've been hashing out this trade for a week now. I think Skunk was the only one that didn't think it would happen. Couldn't see it coming because of his own big, fat ego being in the way. Trading him for something better was far more worthwhile than making him inactive."

JJ asked, "Who'd we get in return?"

"Tomas Arevalo. We had to give them Skunk and a little cash to get him off our roster, though, which hurts. So, Cory, if you can pull off any more fancy footwork to embarrass another team and fill even more seats out there, well, then rock on, my man."

Cory glanced uneasily over at JJ, and Topher added, "No pressure, though," with a sly grin.

"Are we gonna play this game or not? What's taking them so long to decide?" asked Cory.

Topher shrugged. "Just gotta wait for the refs. Who knows why they're sitting on this like it's just a thunderstorm passing by. That stuff looks pretty socked in right now. How fast are you pitching?"

"Just changeups lately, plus a few split changes."

JJ said, "He had one hit 102 earlier."

Topher laughed and shook his head. "You spending your whole paycheck on steroids, Cory, or just most of it?"

Cory tugged down at the back waistband of his uniform. "Hey! You can come examine my ass up close and personal for needle tracks if you think you can find some."

Topher laughed out loud and turned to go back upstairs.

Rett caught JJ scowling at him at the mention of Skunk being traded. He immediately stood up and started to rush to the gate to the cage, saying, "I forgot something I need to do."

JJ started running from the far end of the tunnel, trying to catch him, and yelled, "You're not going anywhere, you little punk! I want my money back! Gimme my money back!"

Rett laughed and tried to dodge JJ's grasp. "No way, Jose! That bet was fair and square!"

"The trade was already in the works!"

"He wasn't off the team until today, loser! Shoulda taken my new bet yesterday!"

Cory looked at the two of them, wondering what was going on.

JJ started to explain to Cory, loudly, "That cracker got my money!"

Rett was about to re-assert that the details of the bet were totally clear-cut, but his phone rang. When he saw that it was Bo calling, he walked out of the pitching cage so he could answer it.

He answered with "Hey, Bo" as he walked down the tunnel back towards the dugout.

"Hey, Rett. You got a minute?"

Rett stepped out and took a seat on the long bench at the back of the empty dugout. "Yeah, I'm at work, but I can talk."

"On Sunday? Do you *ever* get a day off?"

Rett wanted to know what he found out and didn't have a lot of patience for small talk. "It's not as bad as it sounds. Did you find anything out?" He was on edge hoping Bo had managed to be subtle about everything.

"Uh, look, Rett..."

Bo paused, and Rett immediately got worried.

"Dad's here with me," said Bo.

Every pore in Rett's body felt like live electrical wires had been jammed into them without any warning.

"Bo, what the hell happened? You were supposed..."

"Rett, hold on. Dad wants to talk to you. Just listen for a minute, ok?"

Bo's voice wasn't panicked or worried.

Rett frowned. He said, "Bo..." as a long, low growl, communicating exactly how much he thought this was a bad idea.

"You got my word, Rett. Just talk to him for a second."

Rett wavered, trying to decide whether he wanted to get hit with this so suddenly. Despite how he felt like his skin was crawling with electrical currents, Rett scrunched his face up and said, "Put him on."

Rett continued to frown and looked out at the rain that was now tapering off across the baseball field. His breath was shallow. So shallow that he closed his eyes and forced himself to slow his breathing down.

"Hello, Rett," said his father's voice on the other end of the phone.

Rett's lips tightened and his teeth ground together, but he kept control. He said, "Start talking. I'm listening, but I make no promises about what I'm going to do with whatever you say."

His father began, "This way, on the phone, really isn't the right way to have this..."

"On the phone, now, or forget it," said Rett, leaving him no other option. He stood up and began pacing the wet cement that ran the length of the dugout.

There was a silence, followed by a heavy breath on the phone, and then his father began, "I... know that things ended badly between us. But I... I can't leave it like that, even with it being so long ago. Maybe it's hard for you to believe it, but it hurts me to know our family is broken this way."

Rett had to fight harder to keep control. "It hurts you? It hurts *you?* I'm gay. You seemed to think that *that* was the thing that broke *your* family. But it's not changing, so what do you want? Huh? You want me to say I'm sorry and turn straight so you... what... get *your* family back? Clear your conscience? Stop feeling humiliated? Have the world work the way *you* expect it to?"

"Your mom and I have talked about this," said Rett's father, ignoring the acid coming across the phone at him. "I don't get the gay thing, Rett. It was hard for me to see you choosing this life..."

Rett decided this conversation was worthless. He started to interrupt loudly, but his father's voice intensified to force Rett to listen.

"*...and I know, now, and I accept,"* continued his father, "that it's not really a choice. It's hard for me to get my head around, but I'm willing to accept it, ok? I'm dealing with it! I just don't want you to have a bad life, and it's been hard for me to see the gay lifestyle as anything that could bring you happiness. But I get it, ok?" He paused again, and then said, "I get it that, gay or straight, finding happiness for you was never something that I could do for you. You have to find it for yourself, wherever that may be. I get it, that I spent too much time kicking and shoving you down the path I thought was right, the only path I knew. The only path I thought that mattered."

Rett's clenched jaw started to relax slightly. For the first time ever, he thought that maybe his father was starting to understand it some. But there was still a hell of a lot that needed to be explained.

"So, anyway..." his father continued, almost reading Rett's mind, "I know this doesn't fix everything between us. It's a start, though. I had to at least start. I'm willing to put time and effort into this if you are, son."

Rett involuntarily blanched at the use of the word "son."

It was tempting to accept all of this at face value. It would be so easy to accept this as some sort of closure, even if neither of them went any further with it. Part of Rett wanted to ignore what really happened that night, the night he left, just as his dad was doing. But then, he'd be no better than his father. And this attempt, whatever the hell his father thought it was, would be a complete waste of time. It would be no more than meaningless arm-flapping so they could both could face the other way and say they tried.

Rett wasn't going to let himself or his father off the hook that way. Rett had just been through hell learning that the easy way out rarely got you anywhere worth anything.

Rett said, "Are you by yourself? Or is Bo still there with you?"

"Uh... Bo's here with me."

"Go to another room, or outside. We're not done. Not by a long shot."

"Rett, I don't underst..."

"Do it, *Newton*, or this call was a waste of breath and cell phone minutes," spat Rett.

Rett could hear his father walking around. He heard the back door open and then close as his father went outside.

His father said, "Ok, I'm out on the back step, away from Bo."

Rett began, "So that's it? You're gonna leave it at that for now and ignore the fucking elephant in the room, *Newton?*"

"I'm not sure what..."

"Bullshit!" shouted Rett. "You know *exactly* what I'm talking about! God knows it's burned into *my* memory from that night! And I'm sure it's burned into *yours* as well! I could see it in your face that night. So don't you dare act like you don't know what the hell I'm talking about!"

His father, Newton, faltered, "There's... that's... I don't know that I can..."

Rett spat, "This whole talk means zero to me if we can't get past the rest of this. All your newfound good intentions mean absolutely zero if you want to stop there."

Rett heard his father choking on the other end of the phone some. Newton finally came back on and said, "This is hard enough without getting back into that, Rett. I'm really trying hard here."

"That night... you told me," said Rett, grinding the words into the phone, "that if I *ever* touched Bo..."

He finished, "That if I ever, you know, *touched* Bo... you'd kill me."

Rett listened and heard each labored breath, each one a wheezing, forced sound of air, from his father. "Didn't you?" he demanded. "This is the only chance you're going to get, Newton. So, I'll ask you right now, did you really think I'd do something like that to Bo?"

When he spoke, Newton sounded like he had run a mile sprint. He was struggling to catch his breath. "I don't... I, I wasn't sure... I wasn't sure how the gay thing... you know, worked."

"Do you think I ever touched Bo sexually? It's a yes or no question."

There was a significant pause, then, "No."

"Do you think I will now? Bo and I are brothers again. Do you really think that the only reason I went to the effort to get him back in my life was so that I could... fuck him? Is *that* what you believe?"

His father audibly gasped. He said, "That's a horrible thing to say..."

"What's fucking horrible is realizing your father really thinks you're capable of something like that!" shouted Rett into the phone. "Is that what you're worried about?"

"No. No, it's not. I understand that you'd never... I let my worst fears take over that night, Rett. I understood the gay thing so little, and it scared the hell out of me. That's why I said that. I'm ashamed to say, in the heat of the moment, I meant it then."

Rett waited.

His father sighed, "From that day forward, son, I've never regretted saying anything as much as I regret that."

His father coughed again and his voice was noticeably weaker.

"No one should ever have to regret something the way I regret that. It's eaten away at me every day."

Rett felt like pushing even harder, to make sure, but he was becoming genuinely concerned he'd trigger another heart attack given how his father sounded.

Rett said, "Ok." He took a deep breath and repeated, "Ok, then."

The silence continued, his father fighting to breathe and coughing too much in the process.

"So what now?" asked Rett.

Newton took a few more breaths. "This shouldn't have been over the phone. I thought we should have done this face to face. But maybe it was best we started out this way. I know this doesn't magically fix it, Rett, but if you're willing to work on this with me, I want to. Hopefully in person."

Rett rubbed his hand over his face. Out in the stands, there wasn't a single spectator left. He decided they must have finally officially canceled the game. He couldn't decide if he really wanted to go through this even more with his father or not.

Newton asked, "How come... how come you never told Bo about this? About what I said that night... what really drove you away?"

Rett had never told anyone. Not Bo. Not Val. Not Cory. No one. It had even cost him his friendship with Val because she thought he had merely chickened out on his family.

"I don't know," he said. "I... maybe... maybe I thought there was a chance you didn't mean it. That maybe you didn't actually see me as being some kind of monster like that."

"I don't," said Newton.

Rett sat back down on the dugout bench. His eyes unfocused and he tried to decide what he wanted now. This still felt a ways from being settled. But what was the point of all this if he didn't push all the way through with it?

Back and forth.

"Rett?" his father queried.

Rett breathed in deeply to prepare himself. "I tell you what... Why don't you and mom and Bo come to Mobile, say next weekend if you can get away. I have to work, but I'll get you tickets to the Joes–Angels game. We can probably talk a little then, but won't have to if we don't want to."

His father laughed feebly, "Baseball? You hate baseball!"

"Yeah, well, life's pretty fucked up, right? Turns out I'm the physical therapist for the Joes," said Rett.

There was a pregnant pause. His father finally managed, "Wait, are you saying you *work* for the Mobile Joes?"

"Yes, that's what I said. I'm the physical therapist for the team."

"Uh, are you pulling my leg?"

"No. It's a long story. But it turns out I've come to like baseball pretty well."

"Wow! I never thought someone that's gay would want..."

"You're pushing your luck, Newton," interjected Rett, hotly. "You want to come or not?" Rett walked out of the dugout and onto the field, past first base and towards the mound.

"We'll be there," his father said, still sounding rather astonished. He added, "It'll be good to see you. At least, not while I'm doped up and in a hospital bed."

They hung up and Rett stood out in the infield, staring up at the lumpy gray sky overhead. There was no longer a single person visible anywhere. He stood alone in the entire stadium. During school, he had once stayed up for three days straight during finals for a particularly tough set of classes. He felt like that now, after a single phone call that lasted only a few minutes.

He couldn't deny that his father, for once, seemed sincere about respecting Rett for the person he was, rather than demanding he be the person he thought Rett should be. His father even recognized that one phone call didn't make everything right. It didn't erase a lifetime of being ground under the heel of his father's shoe for failing him.

And it was true for both of them. Rett still didn't entirely feel good about his dad. And his dad still was trying to understand him. Succeeding at this was far from guaranteed for either of them.

But now they had taken a step.

Rett stared at the pitcher's mound a few yards away. He needed to hear that he had done the right thing. He needed to know that this was worth what he was going through. He needed to talk to Cory, right then.

Back inside, the pitching tunnel was empty; Rett went upstairs to the main clubhouse to find him. In the locker room, there was no sign of Cory, but several of the players were hanging around, relaxing and watching the overhead TV's. They had all changed out of their uniforms and were waiting around since they would be leaving for the airport not long after when the game was supposed to have ended had it not been rained out.

Rett asked Arthur if he had seen Cory or JJ. Arthur hadn't seen them, but Wally, one of the trainers, walked in as Rett was asking.

Wally said, "I think some of the PR people grabbed them once the game was canceled. They wanted to take advantage of a little extra time and do a little team goodwill at the cancer wing at the hospital. They took today's lineup over there for a little while."

Rett was really disappointed to hear this. He desperately wanted to talk to Cory about what had happened. He desperately needed the reassurance.

But this was part of how he had to share Cory. This was part of the price of the best thing in his life.

Instead, he sent Cory a text asking him to call him when he got a free moment. That done, and with nothing else going on, he walked down to the dining room to get something to eat before the team went on the road.

Right before he got to the clubhouse dining room, he saw the entrance to George's office. He detoured from the dining room and went in.

Rosemary looked up at him with her usual icy stare. Rett closed his eyes and said, "I need to see George."

Rosemary's response was to say, "Why do you always smell like that?"

"Never mind," heaved Rett. "I'll do it myself."

He started to go around her desk, but Rosemary jumped up and blocked the door to George's office. She stuck her head in for a moment, then left the door open as she sat back down without acknowledging Rett at all. As he walked behind her desk, Rosemary took out a can of spray air freshener and started spraying it across her desk where he had been standing.

Inside, George looked up. He frowned and said, "Awww, nuts. You're not going to quit, are you?"

Rett laughed and said, "No. *Definitely* not. I'm coming in to ask for a favor."

"Whatcha need, Rett?" said George, relieved he wasn't going to be short a physical therapist.

"I finally want some tickets, if you've got any you can spare. My, uh, family is coming in town next weekend, while we're playing the Angels. You got any tickets you can front me for Saturday night?"

George leaned back in his chair, looking very smug. "Well, well, well. You couldn't hold out forever, after all, could you?"

Rett grinned politely and let George tease him. "No, I guess not."

"You've held out way longer than anybody else has, though. Hang on, let me check something."

George put on the glasses he used when he worked on his computer and looked at his laptop screen for a few moments.

He said, "I tell you what, Rett, you held out so long, and it's your family... Why don't you take the Owner's Suite that night? Will that work ok?"

Rett was a little shocked. "The Owner's Suite? Are you sure? Won't Mr. LeBayonne be using it?"

George shrugged. "Charles LeBayonne? He's a strange fellow, Rett. He's never been to a single game, and he's never loaned the suite out to anyone else. I know because he goes through me and Rosemary for the arrangements. If he comes up and wants it, I'll get you tickets instead, but I've given it out to plenty of other people in the past with no problem. Take it!"

Rett realized how awesome it would be to use the Owner's Suite that night. "He's never been to a game?"

George put the Owner's Suite in Rett's name for the night and took his glasses off. He shook his head at Rett, "I've only met him a couple of times. Older guy." George chuckled and said, "Even older than me! Most owners take some kind of interest in running the team, which can be a good and a bad thing. Charles, though? Gives it to me and Ahab one hundred percent. Baseball doesn't seem to be his thing at all. And yet he owns a franchise and a stadium, so go figure! If he wants the suite, it'll be the first time in two seasons he's wanted it."

"George, you're the best, you know? I really appreciate everything you've done for me. My family will flip out over this!" said Rett.

"Better to use it than let it sit empty all the time," said George. "And I'm happy to let you have it. Dr. Bala's so glad to have you back on staff that I think he would have paid for it himself for you if he had to!"

Rett stood to go, and George called to him before he walked out, "Just let Rosemary know how many tickets for the suite and whose names to put them in. Tickets will be at will-call when your family shows up. I hope we win for them that night!"

With that out of the way, Rett grabbed a salad and some barbeque chicken for a late lunch. Halfway through, Cory called him back.

"What's going on?" asked Cory.

It wasn't his preference to talk about it over the phone, but Rett said, "That call I got? It was Bo."

"I thought it might have been, the way you ducked out. What did he say?"

"Well, that's the thing. It's not so much what he had to say. He put my dad on the phone, Cory. I wound up talking to him."

There was silence from Cory's end, and then he said, "Hey, I need to call you back, ok?"

Before Rett could respond, Cory ended the call. Rett felt very disappointed that Cory wasn't willing to talk to him about what happened, or even to just listen to what happened.

A second later, he got a text from him:

In the car with others, so no good for talking about this. I want to know everything, tho. Hold on. Back at the Portyards before long.

Rett understood now. He still wanted to talk about it, but Cory couldn't. It was frustrating, but he knew it wasn't that Cory didn't care or didn't want to hear about it. He texted back:

No problem.

A moment later, Cory replied again:

All ok, tho? Youre not mad at me for not talking, r you?

Rett replied: *It's ok. Not mad. Do your thing at the hospital.*

Then he added in another message: *Try singing Rapture to them*

Cory texted: *Ha! You must be ok. Will be back before long*

Rett went back to his food and started thinking about everything his father had said. With Bo, there was never any doubt that he had missed him, even if his brother was afraid to let him back in his life. It all came down to manning-up enough to demand that Bo let him back in. With his mother, he was ok with it. Growing up, he never felt like she actually had a problem with the fact that he was gay, but she never stood up for him. Even the night when it all blew up, she seemed like she was simply supporting her husband. She was just a kite tail; wherever his dad went, she went, too. But his father... he was still on the fence regarding him. If all this was nothing but an attempt by his dad to sooth his own conscience after a near death experience rather than any true desire to have Rett back in his life, to accept Rett as a whole person on his own, then this wasn't going to work out. Rett hadn't gotten a clear feeling about which it was. But he was willing to go a little further with it to see. Suspicious and wary, but willing.

Besides, if things went bad during the game, Rett could walk out of the Owner's Suite and go down to the clubhouse and be done with it.

His phone rang, and it was Bo calling again.

He answered, not wanting to go another round with his dad already, "Hey... you're not going to..."

Bo wasn't listening and started talking all over him, "Are you fucking kidding me?!"

"What?" said Rett.

"You work for the Joes? Is that all just some line of bullshit to rub in dad's face?"

"Are you with dad?"

"No, I'm in my car going back to my place. After he hung up with you, he said we're coming to Mobile next weekend to see you. And then he told me you worked for the fucking Joes!"

Rett felt some relief. He picked at the remnants of the salad in front of him, pushing the tomato chunks around in the bowl. He grumbled, "Why is it so incredibly hard for everyone to believe that I work for a baseball team?"

"It's freaking awesome!" said Bo. "It's just that it sounds like something you'd probably make up just to get under dad's skin."

Rett had to laugh a little bit, despite how unnerved he was still feeling. "I really do work for the Joes. We're heading to Pittsburgh tonight for the series against the Pirates, then back in town on Thursday for the home series against the Angels on Friday. I've already got tickets lined up for you guys for the Saturday night game, by the way."

"Shit, that is so sweet!" said Bo, the excitement in his voice busting out of Rett's phone. "I knew having a gay big brother had to be worth something, somehow or another, but I never thought it would be this!"

"Kiss my freckled ass, Bo."

"Seriously, Everetty, next weekend is going to rock! I mean, I guess if you and dad are ok now. He was quiet after the call. Wouldn't talk about it. I felt a little bad about springing him on you, but he really seems like he wants to fix things. Did it go ok?"

Rett had forgotten how Bo used to call him "Everetty" years ago. He said, "Yeah. It's not all fixed all of a sudden, but it was a start, I guess."

"Why did he leave the room? I wanted to hear what you guys were saying."

"It's between us, Bo. Just some heavy stuff we needed to start clearing the air over."

"Mom and dad started talking about it privately after you hung up. Dad looked pretty exhausted after the call."

"I'll bet he did. I'm worn out, too," said Rett, pushing the rest of his food away from him once and for all.

"But you like working for the Joes, right? You're not, like, going to quit between now and next week so you can go get a job as a professional drag queen or anything, right?"

Rett was a little amazed at Bo. It was still the same Bo, but an older, more advanced version than the one from years ago.

"Well, I *was* happy... until you gave me what sounds like a pretty good idea."

Bo paused and then said, "I'm glad you can let me joke around with you about it, Rett. I've missed being able to laugh with you about stuff. I almost forgot what it was like."

"You were the only one that never made me feel like I was doing something wrong, Bo. Not one single time," said Rett. "You earned the right to joke about it and tease me a long time ago."

He hung up his call with his brother and Rett laid his head down on the table, thinking about all of it.

He hoped Cory showed up soon. And as soon as they got to Pittsburgh, they were going to go find another hotel they could spend the night together in as damn fast as possible.

Chapter 31

Rett dug around violently in his overnight bag, pulling things and tossing them aside, before he finally dumped the entire contents out onto Cory's bed. He grunted a little as he dug around the splayed out clothes, picking through the shirts, shorts, underwear and socks.

"Dammit," he said and pulled at his hair. "Where the hell did that purple Joes shirt go?"

He picked up a cream colored knit shirt and held it up.

"Should I wear this one instead? Maybe I should wear this one instead."

Cory started to say something, but snapped his mouth shut when Rett barked, "What the fuck did I do with the purple one? That's the one I want!"

Cory sat in the easy chair next to the tall mirror, his arm propped up and his chin resting in the palm of his hand while he watched Rett.

There was enough of a pause that he finally felt safe saying, "You mean the purple one you wore this past week while we were in Pittsburgh?"

Rett stopped and stared at Cory, like he was intentionally trying to make trouble.

"Yeah, that one. Shit, I knew I should have been doing laundry yesterday instead of doing you all morning."

Cory stayed quiet, weighing whether Rett was making a joke or was deadly serious.

"The white one will have to do," said Rett.

"You mean the cream colored one?" asked Cory, with a twinkle in his eye.

Rett glared at him. "Oh, *now* you decide to turn queer on me?"

Cory tried to hold back the grin, but failed miserably.

"What's the weather like? Maybe I should wear jeans today," said Rett, refusing to let Cory bait him any further. He ran his hands through his hair again, and looked at the pairs of shorts scattered across the bed. "Jeans that I don't have here. I'll need to run back by my place before going in. Maybe I should wear shorts, but take the jeans to change into."

Cory said, "Ok, that's it." He stood up and walked over to Rett, putting his arms around him from behind.

"As much fun as it is to watch your little freak-out, I'm getting worried about you."

Rett squirmed a little in Cory's arms, not wanting to put up with the condescension, but Cory held tight.

"I'm fine," said Rett sharply.

"Yeah? Then why are you obsessing over what you're going to wear today? You never give a flip about that kind of stuff."

"You know why."

Cory grabbed Rett by the shoulders and pushed him down onto the peaks and troughs of the rumpled white comforter on the big bed. Rett continued to squirm, but Cory climbed on top of him, pinning him down with his arms on either side.

Cory carefully dragged the whiskers of his beard across Rett's nose, touched their lips lightly together, and rubbed their bare chests together. His face only inches from Rett's, he whispered, "It'll be fine, Rett. They're coming to see *you*, not a fashion show."

Rett finally slowed down. He reached around and put his hands on Cory's ass, only a thin layer of underwear separating them from Cory's bare skin.

"You're right," he said. "I'm just anxious."

Cory lifted up a few more inches off of Rett, but didn't let him go. He said decisively, "I'm gonna talk to Ahab and see if Ernie or Sebastion can start tonight so I can be with you for this. This has you all tensed up in a way I haven't seen before and I don't like it."

Rett fought off the instinct to tense up even further at the suggestion. "We talked about this once already," he said. "And, as much as I love that you're willing to be there for me, until I know more about how my dad's gonna react, I don't want to get you involved. It may be a mistake we can't take back. So no, you pitch tonight just like the lineup says, buster."

Cory sighed and rolled off to the side. He draped one arm across his eyes and said, "I'm still unsure about letting you handle this by yourself. You're making me feel like I'm leaving you to the wolves here. Look at how worked up you already are this morning."

Rett rubbed the planes of muscle in Cory's chest, his hand gliding across the soft brown hair coating them. "I'll be fine once we get to the Portyards. Besides, remember, if things go to hell with this tonight, I can walk away. I wish them goodnight, walk out the door and go down to the clubhouse."

Cory gave in. "Ok, fine. But if you change your mind, you just say so, and I'll be there with you."

The two of them lay on the bed next to each other in silence for a few moments before Cory rolled onto his side to face Rett. He traced a finger around Rett's bellybutton and kissed Rett's shoulder, nuzzling him. He said, "I'm proud of you, chief. What you're doing isn't easy for you at all. You know I'll be there with you through the whole thing, even if I'm not in the room with you."

Rett nodded slightly to acknowledge Cory's comment. He didn't feel particularly worthy of anyone's pride at the moment.

Cory pulled up closer to Rett and whispered, "But that's true all the time, not just tonight."

Rett lay there quietly, melting. He wondered what in the world he would have done if he hadn't gotten Cory back. He felt like he had been the biggest chump in the world to let him go in the first place. He'd do anything to deserve Cory.

Rett said, "I didn't mean it, Cory."

"Mean what?"

"When I said I should have been doing laundry instead of you."

Cory laughed. "Oh, ok. That's sweet. I know you didn't mean it."

"I should have been out buying new sneakers," said Rett. "I'm looking at those over there, and they're ratty. I can't wear those tonight... I need new ones."

Cory jerked up and rolled over on top of Rett again, this time pinning him down with his full weight and grinning at him wickedly. He started to tickle Rett, making Rett jerk uselessly beneath him. Rett wheezed trying to laugh and catch his breath at the same time, but unable to do so with Cory's full bulk on top of him. His face turned bright red while he pushed on Cory, trying to get away from him.

Cory finally stopped and lifted up off of him so that he could breathe again. Rett looked up at those deep, brown eyes that he loved so much, the eyes he had almost lost because he had been such a coward. He lifted his head up and kissed Cory deeply, pushing his tongue into Cory's mouth, savoring the feel and flavor of the man that set off sparklers in his stomach every time he did so. Cory returned the kiss by sucking lightly on Rett's tongue, pulling him further into his mouth.

Rett figured they had time, and pulled Cory's full weight back down on top of him.

~~~~~

"Rett," said Dr. Bala, "why don't you go ahead and take off to go get ready for your folks."

"Hmm?" said Rett, distracted.

Dr. Bala pointed at the laptop Rett had been putting notes into while Dr. Bala was checking out Fred Lipscomb's neck and shoulder for a neck stinger.

Rett ignored his laptop and said, "I'm fine, really."

Dr. Bala looked at Rett over his glasses and said, "Read back that last bit."

Rett looked at the notes and read, "Neurapraxia of the left-side lateral cord, brachial plexus."

"And?" prompted Dr. Bala.

Rett looked back down at the laptop. He said, "Oh... recommend amputation at neck, between C5 and C6."

Rett turned red and looked at Dr. Bala. "Did you really tell me to write that down?"

Dr. Bala cocked his head to the side and looked at Rett.

Rett said, now playing along innocently, "So... do you want me to get a scalpel or a reciprocating saw or something?"

Fred started laughing, and Dr. Bala insisted, "I've got this, Rett! Go get ready for the game!"

Rett handed him the laptop and was about to walk out when Dr. Bala said, "But go warm up that band saw before you go."

Fred said, more seriously, "Shit, that was only funny the first time."

443

Rett wandered out of the treatment room. He didn't really want to go sit in the empty Owner's Suite yet. It was still a little over an hour before the game was to begin, and Bo had called him about ten minutes earlier to let him know they were about forty-five minutes away.

But as Dr. Bala had managed to point out so eloquently, he was distracted.

He walked into the locker room and saw Cory in his usual place, in the darkened player lounge, sitting quietly with his eyes closed and preparing himself for a night of pitching. Rett was about to turn and leave, but Cory opened his eyes and spied him standing there. He motioned Rett over, so Rett went and sat down next to him.

"You sure you're good?" asked Cory.

"Yeah. I'll be fine. It's not like I've got to go out and pitch nine innings against the Angels or anything."

Cory smirked. He glanced up at the clock in the locker room and said to Rett, "You ought to head on up to the suite. I've got a surprise for you there."

Rett said, "A surprise? What?"

Cory said, "It wouldn't be a surprise if I told you, Einstein."

Rett stood up to go, but Cory stopped him. "I'll still go with you if you want."

"Thanks, Bigfoot, but I don't want to risk you in there," said Rett.

Cory continued to eye him solemnly. Rett added, "Plus, this is my mess. This is part of me becoming something better than what I was before. This is how I, uh, you know... really earn the best thing that's ever happened to me."

Cory's hand started to reach out for Rett, but he pulled it back. He said softly, seriously, "You don't make this any easier on me when you talk like that."

"I gotta do this myself," said Rett.

~~~~~

Rett had never been in the Owner's Suite before. He'd been in a few of the other suites at times, but not this specific one. It was the same size as the other luxury suites, and generally laid out the same, but the furnishings sure were a lot nicer. The main part of the suite was a sitting area with two large gray leather couches facing each other and with an exotic wood coffee table in between. On the walls were three huge flat TV's that would show the closed-circuit version of the game. There was a wall of plate glass facing out over the field with a black stone bar stretching across and five or six barstools arranged in front of it. A door led to the outside with two private rows of stadium seating, enough to seat probably 16 people or so.

Rett looked around and wondered what the surprise was that Cory had in store for him. There didn't seem to be anything there that looked like it was intended for him specifically.

He relaxed into one of the couches and thought through what he wanted to say to his father when they showed up. He spent several minutes mulling it over his head, much like he had done on and off for the last week, but still wasn't sure what he wanted his father to hear and understand. He rubbed his eyes and gave up.

He stood back up and walked over to the window and looked out across the field. The Angels were on the field finishing their batting practice. The stadium was looking probably fuller than he had ever seen it. Back when he had first joined the Joes, back in June, he remembered how the stadium would probably be only half full, at best. These days, it was typically three-quarters full. And when Cory was pitching, it was often closer to ninety percent full. He smiled to himself at the thought.

A noise behind him shook his thoughts away. One of the catering people backed into the suite with a cart loaded down with food, drinks and serviceware. For a moment, Rett wondered what was going on since he hadn't ordered any food for the night. Then he understood and smiled again.

The waiter nodded to Rett and started setting up the spread on the buffet counter along the back of the suite. He said to Rett, "You guys must be more VIP than the usual VIPs."

"Why's that?" asked Rett.

"It's not every day that the Joes' star pitcher personally orders and pays for the catering in one of the suites."

Rett was tempted to correct him and tell him that the Joes' star pitcher had *never* done that for anyone, but he checked himself and merely smiled and nodded to the server.

The caterer finished setting up and directed Rett's attention to the phone on a side table. He said, "If there's anything else you need, sir, just pick up the phone and press the Catering button. Enjoy the game!"

When the server left, Rett pulled his phone out and gave Cory a quick call to thank him.

When Cory answered, Rett said, "Thanks for the great surprise! The food was really nice of you. It's a pretty awesome spread, too."

"I'm glad you like it. Pretty good timing, too. But you should know..." said Cory.

Rett heard the door to the suite open and looked over.

Cory stepped into the suite, his cell phone still at his ear. He had a huge grin on his face and said, "The food's not really the surprise."

Rett frowned knowing what Cory was trying to do and started to say, "Cory, we..."

Cory held up his hands in defense and said, "Relax, I'm not staying. I just wanted to bring you something."

He stepped aside and when Rett saw behind him, his knees almost gave way. He blinked, sure he was seeing something that wasn't really there.

Val stepped into the suite, smiling shyly at Rett.

Rett was unable to move at the sight of her. His eyes glassed over and he choked suddenly and had trouble holding back. He gave up and let the tears drop from his eyes as he grabbed Val and held her tightly, letting loose the joy and relief of having his best friend, the person that had kept him going all those years, back. Neither said anything for a while; they cried together and rocked each other back and forth for a long time.

Rett finally sobbed into Val's ear, "God, Val, I've missed you so bad. I'm so sorry for what I put you through."

Val stood back, dabbed at the tears under her eyes so she didn't mess up her makeup, and said, "You should be!"

Rett started sobbing and laughing at the same time.

He said, "Do you really forgive me? Do I have my Val back?"

Val's breath caught in her throat again and she said, "Yes, Rett. I can't say no to Cory. How can anyone say no those goddamn dimples of his?"

Rett turned to Cory and put his hand on his chest. "Thank you. Thank you for this!"

Cory's smile grew even larger. "If I can't be here with you tonight, I thought maybe having Val would be the next best thing."

Rett nodded. It would be good to have Val there for support, especially since he had forbidden Cory from participating.

Val said, "Cory called me and told me everything that's happened. He told me how much you've changed. How much you missed me. He asked me to be here."

Rett looked at Cory again, sublime love radiating in his face for his boyfriend in the teal pinstripes.

Cory adjusted the cap on his head and said proudly, "I'm just hoping this will get me to, say, maybe third base with Rett later tonight."

Val's smile faltered. Rett wrinkled his nose and said, "Ugh" at the same time Val said, "Ewww!"

Cory looked between them, confused. "What?" he said.

"Third base is felching!" said Rett.

Cory looked even more confused. "It is? Uh... I don't even know what that is."

Val pulled him down and she whispered in his ear.

Cory's confused look turned to a frown and he stood back up. "Oh, dear God! That's disgusting!" He looked horrified and said, "*That's* third base?!"

He looked confused again and said, "Well, if that's third base, then what's second base?"

Rett said, "Anal sex," like it was the most obvious thing in the world.

Cory's eyes narrowed. "Anal sex. So what the hell is first base, then?"

Rett repeated, "Anal sex!"

"First *and* second base are anal sex," said Cory, trying hard to make sure he had it straight. He stared at them for a moment longer, and then asked, "Sooooo... if both of those are anal sex, then what the hell is like a, uh, blow job?"

Rett said, as if it was common knowledge, "Oh, that's just being polite."

Cory eyed Rett and nodded slowly. "Mmmm hmmm..." he said skeptically.

Val's eyes were sparkling. "I've missed this so much!" she sighed.

Cory said, "Ok, I've got to get back downstairs. Remember what I said, Rett... I'm here with you."

Rett wanted to kiss Cory, to grab him and squeeze him in two, but held back. He touched his shoulder instead and walked Cory to the door to see him off and wish him luck in the game.

When he turned back, Val was already at the buffet that had been set out, cramming her mouth with a piece of beef tenderloin.

Rett said, "Did you miss me, or did you just hear there was going to be free food at this?"

Val said, her mouth stuffed full, "You want the honest answer?"

They sat down on the couch next to each other, Rett's arm around Val's shoulder, "I'm glad you're here."

"I know I put you through hell, Rett. I'm sorry, sort of, I think. I was really frustrated with you because, well... seriously, only somebody with brain damage would walk away from Cory, and I mean like cerebral hypoxia type damage. And worse..." Val sighed before continuing, "I wasn't surprised that you had done it. And I was genuinely wondering when you were going to do it to me."

She snuggled a little closer to Rett and said, "All I ever wanted, was for you to not run away. To stand your ground. I never thought you'd wind up at this point with your father, though, of all people. Are you ready?"

Rett thought about it a moment. "We'll see. I mean, I'm not afraid of him anymore and I'm not going to let him make me feel like less of a person. But whether we can really be a full family again? That's touch-and-go."

"Cory and I talked about you on the phone for quite a while. That boy is fucking crazy for you, Rett. I mean like he would rip his own pitching arm off with his bare hands and hand it to you if you asked," said Val.

"I know."

"And if I ever again hear you talk about leaving him, I'm going to get a tire iron and beat you with it until the cops have to clean up your remains with a wet-vac!"

Rett sighed. "Have you been watching *Goodfellas* again?"

"It's Tony's favorite movie! We've watched it, like, ten times lately!"

"Perfect. You've been on a *Goodfellas* binge and eating red meat right before my family shows up," he said. "How can tonight possibly go wrong?"

Rett reached over and wiped his thumb at the corner of Val's mouth where a little grease from the beef tenderloin had smeared. "I need you to let me handle this, Val. I have to do this myself."

Val nodded and said, "Mmm hmm!"

"I need you to promise me, Val."

"I promise! Cross my heart and hope to die!"

"Show me your hands and promise again," insisted Rett.

Val huffed, pulled her hands out from under her legs and uncrossed her fingers. "Dammit! I promise."

She added, "You've known me too long! That trick still works great on Tony."

"And another thing..." started Rett.

Val rolled her eyes. "Couldn't you have typed up a list for me?"

"Cory's off-limits around them," he growled. "Yes, I know him. Yes, I work with him. But that's it. Got it? I'll *not* risk him around them. I'll do anything to protect him." He was practically snarling by the time he finished.

Val quipped, "Ok, tiger, got it! Do you tinkle on his leg, too, to mark your territory?" Her eyes glazed over for a second and then she said, "Actually, that sounds kinda hot."

Rett's phone buzzed in his pocket. He answered the call and said, "Hey, Bo... how far away are y'all?"

Bo said, "We're here. We just got our tickets. Hey, am I imagining things, or do these tickets say 'Club Level' on them?"

Rett laughed nervously, "Yeah, they do. I'm here waiting on you guys."

Bo said, "Oh, you gotta be yanking my crank! Awesome!" And then more softly, "Hey, look, before we get there... Dad and mom are both pretty nervous, and I know you probably are, too. Just remember dad's had a bad heart attack. Don't be too hard on him, ok?"

"Yeah, ok," said Rett, like he wasn't already navigating a tricky minefield here.

Rett hung up. His lips pulled together grimly.

"They're here," he told Val.

Chapter 32

As always, there was the waiting.

In the last few minutes before Bo and his parents showed up at the Owner's Suite, Rett started to lose his nerve. He had just enough time to think back over how his father always cowed over him, made him feel like an embarrassment, like a failure. He thought about how he was 25 years old now, he didn't need them anymore, and nothing would change what happened in the past. So what was really the point? He still had no real idea exactly what he hoped to get out of this. He had no real idea what his father hoped to get out of this. But probably more than any of that, Rett started to wonder if he'd really be able to forgive his father. And tolerating him wasn't the same as forgiving him.

He looked down at the floor and started planning a route out of the Club Level and back down to the clubhouse where he wouldn't have to come face to face with his father. He could leave right now and not have to see him at all. Ever.

Val saw the look on his face and said, "Hold your head up, Rett. Don't let him make you look down."

He looked over at his friend and she smiled at him, giving him her full support. That was why he was here... to show his father that no matter what he thought about him back then, or perhaps even still thought about him now, he wasn't worthless and he had made a place for himself.

Rett grabbed Val's hand and whispered, "Thank you."

The door to the suite opened up and Bo entered first, all smiles, followed by their mother and father. His mother wore an expression that mixed something of awe and nervousness and hesitation, all visible under the neat reddish-blond curls and thin eyebrows. His father looked a little more determined, but what struck Rett was how much older he looked. It had hit him in the hospital for the brief moment he saw him there, but here, up and moving around, it was even more pronounced.

Bo came up to Rett and grabbed him, hugging him tightly. He said quietly to Rett, "Man, you've totally made up for all seven years by getting this suite right here!"

Rett had to smile as he leaned his forehead against Bo's and put his hand around the back of his brother's neck. He also couldn't resist stealing a side glance at his father to see how he would react to the affection between him and Bo. He had to stem the memory of his father, the night Rett had left, threatening him by saying, "If I ever see you touch him that way, I'll kill you." His father was looking at both of them fixedly, but didn't react otherwise.

Rett hugged his brother again and then turned his attention to his mother, who was still unsure how she should behave around her son, what was ok and what was off-limits. Rett felt a little unsure, too, but the look in his mother's face made him decide to give her the benefit of the doubt.

"Hi, mom," he said. He stepped forward and hugged her as well, even if it was a stiff and reserved one.

His mother seemed like she was on the verge of breaking down in tears and she said, "Oh, Rett, it's so good to see you! To be here with you! I've missed you so much, darling!"

Rett didn't allow the embrace to linger long, though, and he pushed back from her.

He stepped tentatively towards his father, who definitely looked thinner, gaunt even, compared to when he had been at home. But there was something more. Rett looked him in the eye. It was his eyes. His father's eyes, which he always remembered to be an intense blue, were faded and pale now, like a bright blue birthday card that had been left out in the yard, now weathered and wan from being in the rain and sun for weeks and weeks. But despite all that, he could see his father looking back at him, and setting his jaw firmly.

Rett kept a little distance from his father and leaned forward just enough to shake his hand. He said, "Hi, Newton," as civilly as he could.

His father ignored the more formal use of his first name said replied softly, "Hey, son. It's good to see you. To... you know, have this opportunity."

Rett stood back and said, "Oh, and this is Valerie Papadakis." He pointed to his family in turn so she could greet them. "That's my brother Bowen, or Bo, who you saw before but didn't really get to meet. This is my mother, Jaye. And of course, this is Newton."

Val politely shook each of their hands and demurely greeted them. She was so polite, that Rett started to get worried for a moment. He knew Val well enough to wonder if maybe she would put his dad in a headlock until he cried uncle. But the quiet politeness was almost more disturbing to him.

Rett put his arm around Val's shoulder and said, "Val and I were friends through all seven years of PT school. She and I lived together for five years, at least until I moved down here to Mobile earlier this summer."

Newton looked confused and said, "You had a *girlfriend* this whole time?"

Rett sighed. He made a decision right then that he needed to be the one to set the tone of this.

He gestured at one of the sofas and said, "Look, everybody get comfortable for a minute. I've got something I want to say up front before the game starts."

Bo and his parents sat on one of the couches. Val took a seat on the other couch and Rett pulled out one of the barstools. He turned it backwards and sat where he could rest his arms on the back of the stool and address everyone.

Rett began, "I referred to Valerie as my friend. Don't read anything more into it than that. I love her to death, and I wouldn't be here without her support for the last seven years, but she's not, and never was, my girlfriend. She's a friend, and we shared an apartment, that's all."

Rett took a breath and watched as the tiny glimmer of hope in his father's eyes snuffed out. He had bristled at that glimmer and was glad he could wipe it off his face. He said, "Valerie's here because she pretty much knows everything anyway, and I want her here. But that's not really what I wanted to say right now." He paused again, fixed his gaze on his father, and said, "Everything that's happened, all... happened because I'm gay. Not bisexual. Not confused. Not rebellious. I'm gay. If any of this is about 'fixing' me, or convincing me to play straight, or condemning me, or... or sinking into some family-wide denial about who I am... the answer is no. I know where I stand with Val and Bo, so this really falls to you two to decide how you want to proceed given these ground rules." Rett looked specifically at his parents, who were quiet, and his palms began to get a little sweaty. There was a tremendous amount of tension between Rett and his parents as he finished speaking.

His father quietly said, "Understood," though, which caused everyone in the room to relax slightly.

"I'm not going to bring any of this up again," said Rett, "and I'm not going to force this to be a big group therapy session or anything like that. We can catch up with each other, or watch the game, or whatever. But those are my rules," he said. "We've got the use of the suite, and there's a ton of food and stuff back there you can help yourself to... provided you don't let Val get to it first."

Val murmured, "Traitor," at the same time that Bo enthusiastically raised his hand with a question.

Rett scowled at him and said, "Bo, knock it off."

"Can you get this suite anytime you want it?" Bo was practically bouncing up and down in his seat in excitement as he asked the question.

"No... I don't know. I haven't tried. I could probably swing it every once in a while, maybe. George is a pretty cool guy," said Rett.

"Who's George?" asked Bo.

"George Hastings. The Joes' GM. He let me have it tonight. That's the guy I work for," said Rett. "Actually, he's a great boss. I love working for him!"

Val said, "And I notice that the last time I came, I had to buy my own ticket!"

Rett snapped, "And you ate your ticket price's worth of Moon Pies for free, too, so it sorta worked out."

Things gradually relaxed even more after that and they wound up talking through a variety of things, even if they avoided the trickier subject of a broken family.

Bo wanted to know all about how he got the job with the Joes. He wanted to know about the players and which ones Rett knew the best. He wanted to talk baseball stats and strategy, which Rett was secretly surprised to find out he knew much better than he thought he did. He noticed that his father paid close attention to this, but never said anything and didn't join that part of the conversation, instead choosing to sit back and study his sons interacting.

Rett asked his father about what kind of therapy he was going through after his heart attack. He and Val compared notes on their opinions about the therapy and what they might suggest to help with it.

His mother steered the conversation as close to the night of the family crisis as possible, wanting to know what happened after he left and how he got into school. His father wanted to know how he managed to pay for seven years of college, and Rett told him point blank that it was through the modern magic of a hundred thousand dollars' worth of debt. His father got very quiet after hearing that.

They spent time talking to Val about her experience with school and with Rett, about where she worked and lived. She took the opportunity to once again express her opinion that Rett didn't deserve the job he had, which led Rett to point out how he had to work long hours pretty much seven days a week during the season. His mother seemed very pleased that he would have nothing but free time around the holidays, no doubt hoping to have all of them together for the first time in far too long. Rett remained mute on the subject, and wasn't sure if that was going to happen or not.

The more he watched and listened to his mother, the surer he was that she was very different than when he had lived at home. She seemed more there, more involved and interested. He pulled her aside at one point and asked her if she was taking anti-depressants, which she admitted to. He told her that was a good thing and that he was glad she was there. She hugged her son again, a long time this time, and told him that she regretted not going on the medication a long time ago, that maybe things would have been different. His mother didn't bring up anything specifically about him being gay or the night he left, but she seemed so genuinely happy to have both of her sons together again that Rett didn't force the issue.

All through the conversation, they watched the game unfold outside the glass windows of the suite. As always, Rett kept a close eye on how Cory was pitching, and what he saw down on the mound started to concern him some by the 3rd inning.

By the 6th inning, the Joes were leading 4 to nothing, but Rett was still worried, and not very happy with what was happening down on the field. At a moment where Rett and Val were alone at the buffet counter, Val asked discreetly, "Are you seeing what I'm seeing out on the mound?"

"I know, I know! He keeps looking up here towards the suite. JJ even had to wave him down one time to get him to pay attention to his signals. I'm surprised Ahab hasn't pulled him out of the game. I know he's curious about what's going on, but, Jesus... I'm gonna kick his ass for not focusing like he should. And I don't care what the score is," whispered Rett.

By the 7th inning, Rett started to feel a little regretful about his promise to not bring anything up about what had happened. He started to feel like maybe it had been a bad promise to make. The evening was feeling a little bit like a waste of time if they didn't clear the air as a family.

He pulled Val aside and asked her, "I feel like I'm wussing out and not talking about what's still wrong in this family. Was it bad to promise to not bring it up?"

He knew what Val was going to say, but she totally surprised him and instead said, "You and your dad had a heavy talk on the phone last week, right? So don't force it. Besides, I think it's good you can catch up with them about everything and leave the problems to the side this time. They'll still be there to talk about. Plus, I'm here for you, but I'm not sure they'd be comfortable getting into the hard stuff with me here."

Rett really didn't expect her to let him off so easily. But he'd take any slack he could get from her. It made him feel better about letting go for this time.

Val added, "And can I say that Bo is adorable? He's like the perfect version of you."

"You mean straight," said Rett stoically.

"Straight, and with longer eyelashes."

The last two innings of the game made Rett almost panic. The Angels managed to rapidly gain some ground and score some runs, one in the 8th and two in the 9th. And it seemed pretty clear that it was because Cory was preoccupied out on the field. Rett would have sent Cory a text message to tell him everything was ok and to stop looking up at the suite, except Ahab now made Cory give him his cell phone at the start of every game. Ahab was serious, but it had become a huge joke across the team.

When Cory got the final strike of the 9th inning, the score was 4 to 3, with the Joes still leading. At least Cory and the rest of the fielding team held it together enough to win the game.

The win gave Rett the opportunity to show his family the miniature Mardi Gras parade that made its way along the outer warning track when the Joes won at home, something that was rarely shown on the televised games, and something that Rett's mother seemed to enjoy very much.

Rett was relieved it was all over, and they had all managed to be civil to one another, and he felt maybe they could get together again sometime. Rett prepared to see his family off so he could get back to his regular life. He could go back down to the clubhouse and smack Cory around for his performance in the game. Better yet, he'd turn Val loose on him.

Outside the suite, over the normal noise of the crowd leaving the Club Level, Rett heard an unusual burst of applause and a lot of additional voices. He was about to open the door to see what was going on outside, when it opened anyway. And in stepped Cory, still in his uniform, dusty and sweaty from the game, and even a little out of breath from running from the clubhouse to the suite.

"Holy shit! That's Cory Pritchart!" shouted Bo.

Val's eyes got big and both of Rett's parents turned to see what was going on. They both seemed as shocked as Bo to see one of the players suddenly in the suite with them.

Rett said, almost angrily, "What are you doing here, Cory?"

Bo was beside himself, crying out, "That's awesome that you got Cory Pritchart to stop by!"

Cory shut the door behind him and started shaking his head violently from side to side. "I can't sit this out, Rett! Not gonna happen!"

Rett took a step back from Cory and warned him through gritted teeth, "You know what we talked about!"

Cory's face, though, was fiercely determined. "No! You've put so much to the side for my benefit, Rett, and I've let you. I can do this little bit for you. I can be by your side for this! And I'm going to!"

The initial surprise that Bo, Newton and Jaye had at Cory's arrival gave way to confusion about what was going on between

Rett and Cory, but they clearly could tell that there was something more happening than just a visit from one of the players, or rather, *the* player.

Cory reached over and grabbed Rett by the wrist roughly, before Rett could back away from him further, which caused Newton to stand up from the barstool instinctively. Cory pulled Rett in front of him and wrapped his arms tightly around him, pulling him back against his chest. Rett said nothing, allowing the look of frustrated resignation to say everything for him instead.

Cory said over Rett's shoulder, "Mr. and Mrs. Dougherty... I don't know exactly how you feel about your son. I know you have your differences and have had trouble accepting him as he is. But you should know that your son means more to me than anything in this world, including baseball. Your son... is the sun and sky and green grass on a summer afternoon to me. And if you call him faggot or think him less of a person, or worthless, then you need to know, you're missing out on someone truly amazing, and it's your loss. You can call him queer or look down on him, but you'd better do that to *both* of us."

There was absolute silence in the suite and not one single person seemed to be even breathing.

Cory leaned around and kissed the side of Rett's head, and Rett closed his eyes and his expression softened. But even still, there weren't enough words in the world for Rett to express how he felt towards Cory at that moment, for Cory putting himself in this position, all for him, even when he hadn't wanted him to.

Rett's mother gasped and put her hand up to her mouth. Bo's mouth was hanging open in shock. Bo said faintly, dreamily, "Oh, sweet Jesus! My brother is doing Cory Pritchart, and I think I just super crapped my pants! This is the best fucking day of my *life!*"

Rett's father looked even paler. He finally spat, accusingly, "You... you're having *sex* with my son!"

Cory said without hesitating, "I'm very much *in love* with your son!" His arms pulled tighter around Rett protectively.

"You're in love..." began Newton, trying to comprehend.

"And he loves me," said Cory, defiantly.

Rett knew there was no point in fighting it any longer. "I do. I love Cory," he said in resignation as he put his hands on top of Cory's and held them. He pulled to the side so he could look up at Cory's face. He said to him, "I love him more every single day... that I don't kill him."

Newton seemed to be in complete shock as he stared at Cory holding his son. He started to say, "What would your father..."

Cory's voice suddenly had a razor sharp edge to it. "*My father,* and my mother, have known I'm gay since I was 14. *My father,* and mother, love Rett like they love me. Be careful of going down this path, Mr. Dougherty!" he warned.

Newton began grasping around at everything about this situation he couldn't fit together. He began, "Gay guys don't play..."

"Yeah? Are you *really* about to tell me I can't play baseball?" shot Cory.

Bo turned red and said out of the side of his mouth, pleading with his father, "Daaaaad, that's Cory Motherfucking Pritchart! You're embarrassing yourself!"

"You watch your mouth, Bo!" snapped his mother.

"Stop!" shouted Rett. Everyone stopped and stared. "That's enough! From everyone!"

It felt to Rett like the ground he and his father had covered was slipping away rapidly, and he couldn't leave it like that. All the visiting and catching up during the game was fine, but he refused to let his father backslide this way. Not if they were going to continue this in any way.

Rett pulled away from Cory and said to his father, "I think I need to speak to you alone, *Newton.*"

"Not without me," insisted Cory. "I don't like where..."

Rett turned to him and said softly, "Cory, stop. I have to do this. Myself. I can't do it with you there, or Val, or Bo, or anyone else."

Rett rubbed his eyes for a moment and had to come to a quick decision. Did he want to end this now between him and his father, or keep trying? He could cut his losses now before things got worse. Or he could be the bigger man.

He looked at his father for a moment. Bigger, even, than his own father.

He pointed at his dad and said, decisively, "You, I need for you to come with me, please. Mom, Val, Bo... you guys hang out here for a little bit longer. Cory, I want you to come with me, too."

Cory seemed much more pleased now that Rett wasn't excluding him. They left the Owner's Suite and Rett led the three of them out of the Club Level concourse and down to the field itself. His father seemed in wonder at what kind of conversation they were going to have out on the field. He said, "What's this about, Rett?"

Rett turned to Cory and asked, "Do you have a ball with you?"

Cory pulled one out of his pocket and handed it to him, and Rett faced his dad again.

"You and I are gonna toss this ball a little bit, and talk, one on one. Just you and me. Cory, I need for you to wait over in the dugout, please."

Cory frowned, and with a sharp glance at Rett's father, said, "I'll be in the dugout."

Rett walked his father out and placed him on the pitcher's mound. Newton turned around once, rather in awe of where he found himself.

Rett tried to figure out where he wanted to start, but when his father faced back to him, his father was the one that spoke first.

Newton said, the mocking tone evident in his voice, "Since when do you toss *any* ball around?"

Rett tossed the ball to him and he said flatly, "Since Cory."

"His father really knows what you two, uh... do?"

"Yes. And if it means anything to you, his dad is the chief of police in his hometown, and an ex-Army Ranger."

Newton tossed the ball back to him and Rett said, "Cory isn't out, obviously, but cares enough about me to not let me go through today by myself. I want this next point to be very clear... If you start talking about Cory to other people, to anyone, I guarantee you that you will regret it. And that's on top of losing any chance you might have of repairing *anything* with me in the future. Is that absolutely clear?" He glanced over at the dugout where Cory had stationed himself and was watching like a bird of prey for the first sign of trouble.

"Who'd believe me if I told them?" said his father.

"That's *not* what I asked you!" snapped Rett.

"Yes, it's clear," said Newton.

Rett threw the ball back to his father, who added, "I'm pretty amazed anyone managed to teach you to throw a ball." Newton held the ball against his chest and winced slightly at his comment. He backtracked, frowned at himself, and said, "Wait... I didn't actually mean that the way it came out." He threw the ball back to Rett. He tried again and said, "I think it's good to see you've learned to enjoy something like this."

Rett was glad his father corrected himself, because he was teetering on the edge of walking away. But his father's comment, and thinking about Cory standing out on that very pitcher's mound led him to what he decided he really wanted to say, even if it was going to be hard for his father to hear it.

"I know this kind of stuff was always important to you," said Rett. "Sports, cars, 'man' stuff... a bunch of shallow nonsense in the end. You want to know what I've really learned, though?"

Rett threw the ball back to his father, who caught it and nodded.

"What I've learned is that you've really grown up, really become a man, when you realize it's ok to fail, and you're still willing to bear the cost of that failure. Because no matter what... no matter how hard you try to succeed, or worse, just try to avoid failure by avoiding trying, you're *still* going to fail. Part of manhood is what you do after you blow it, after you screw everything up. It's taking responsibility for it, not running away and not blaming others."

"Seven years ago, I turned my back on you and mom and Bo, and I probably shouldn't have. Even after the things you said to me, I shouldn't have. But I'm here right now, throwing this ball back and forth with you, trying to make that right, if I can. So, I'll tell you I'm sorry for being a coward seven years ago, and I mean it. I was wrong to do it. I think everybody in this family paid a price for me doing that, and I will try to make it right. I want to be the kind of man that recognizes that mistake, accepts my responsibility for it, and tries to fix it."

Newton continued to hold the ball at his side, listening to his son and letting him speak.

"Here's the hard part, though," continued Rett. "You had a part in this, too. *You* failed, too. You need to become a man, too. You should get the chance and I'll give it to you, but you *have* to do your part to make things right."

Rett's father's arms remained at his side, limp, and he was no longer looking at his son. Instead, he stared emptily at the edge of the pitcher's mound in front of him.

Rett wasn't sure if he was getting through to him or not. He said, "You can think of me as a faggot, as a waste of your time, and you can think I'm full of bullshit if you want. You can cling to whatever opinion of me you want to and insist you did everything right while all I did was disappoint you. You can blame me for everything in the past, and I'll let you. But what you will *not* do, to me or Cory, is come back into my life to salve your own conscience while still refusing to accept me as anything less than a whole person anymore! Those days are over."

Newton was silent for a long time, not looking up and not moving. And then he suddenly threw the ball at Rett, genuinely more at him than to him, but Rett caught it anyway. When Rett looked back at him, his father's face was contorted trying to hold the pain in. He put his hands on his hips and turned away from Rett while he tried to regain control.

When he turned back to face Rett, he was using his thumb to wipe the tears away roughly. It was the first time Rett had ever seen his father cry in his entire life. Rett couldn't remember all the times he had been yelled at for crying by this man. His father said, "You make it *so hard*, Rett. *Not* because of the gay thing..." he hastened to add. "I come here today and see everything that you've done for yourself and the life you've built. School, people who care, a career, even the things you've said just now. I mean, Christ, look at where we're standing right now! I see so clearly now how I did *nothing* for you the whole time you were in my house. But once you were out on your own, you did *everything* for yourself, everything you needed. You became a man without me. You stand there and all I see is how I've failed completely at this, how I did nothing but hold you back. But..."

The drops kept falling from his father's eyes, trailing down his cheeks. "But then you tell me how I deserve a second chance to fix it. It rubs my face in how badly I screwed it all up, but you... you let me know it's ok and that it can still be made all right. Made right if I'm finally enough of a father to do it. You've become something I never could have made you. All those years ago, that night, I said that you were nothing but a waste of my time. But that wasn't true. *I* wasted *your* time. You were far better off without me."

His father was crying openly now and had wrapped his arms around his chest as it hitched with his broken breaths.

"When I had... my heart attack," he said, his voice cracked and dry, "I flatlined twice. I died twice. And all I could think about was that I'd die for good, I wouldn't come back, and... and I'd never know what happened to you. I'd never know how things turned out. I woke... woke up in the hospital room, and your mom and Bo were standing there. And there was an empty chair next to the two of them. All I saw was the place where you should have been. The place that I drove you away from out of some stupid fear on my part. Out of my fear of not having the control over my family the way I thought I should. I threatened your life because of it, and today I watched you with Bo, as comfortable with each other as any two brothers could possibly be. And it reminds me that I was the one that created that empty chair. All this was about, me trying to reach you after all these years, was just to know what happened, to try to fill that empty place that I created while I still had a chance."

Newton shook his head, his eyes squinted closed trying to stop the flow out of them. "But you've managed to make me see how bad I failed, how selfish I've been, and yet you're still willing to look past it, to work to fix it. And I don't know if I can. I don't know how, son. Things seem backwards between us now... the wrong way..."

Rett's hand felt his face, felt the dampness there that matched that on his father's. He said, "Someone I very much love and respect once told me there's got to be a two-way street between parents and their kids. You and me, we just didn't figure that out in time. But better late than never."

"Show me, Rett. Help me make this right. Bear with me, and I'll understand the gay thing. I'll understand about you and Cory, somehow. I swear to you now, I'll get there with you."

The two faced each other on the field under the intense lights of the Portyards, Rett still unsure of how to proceed. But as unsure as he was, he could see that his father was far more unsure, that his father was the lost child. Rett sniffed again, his eyes still burned and stung, and he caught a glimpse of Cory out of the corner of his eye, still watching them.

His father was right; things were now reversed between them — Rett had to be stronger than his father. He had to be bigger than him. He had to... he had to surrender the decision to his father. He rubbed his shoulder across his cheek to wipe the tears away and stepped forward to him. He held out his arms from his sides, giving up the decision to the man that had only ever seen an act like this as a weakness. He let the ball fall out of his hand and roll away while he waited to accept whatever decision came from the man he faced.

His father took a small step forward, hesitated, and then held out his arms, too, finally wrapping them around his son, gone too long now. His chest racked again and again with choking sobs as he held his son.

Rett returned the embrace, holding his father up, being strong for the both of them, and said, "We'll fix it, dad. We'll fix it."

They stood on the mound, under the lights of an empty stadium, and took the first real step, clumsy and uncomfortable as it was, but real nonetheless, towards fixing everything that was broken between the two of them.

Chapter 33

Everyone tends to think of October as being an autumn month. Not so much in south Alabama, usually. There, it's another warm, if not hot, summer month. But the Alabama summer heat will sometimes get broken by cooler days. The haze of the depth of summer lifts, the humidity backs off, and the sky takes on a clearer, sharper blueness that the more languid summer days rarely could manage. And sometimes, there will be a day where the temperature gives a clear peek of what's coming.

Rett pulled at the long sleeves of his thin Joes sweatshirt as he slouched up against the backstop fence out in the junior high baseball practice field. The day after the end of the regular MLB season was one of those days that had been brilliantly clear and the warmth of the day had given way to what felt like a downright cool evening. He put his arms around Cory, who was in shorts and the tight white knit Polo shirt, the one that was Rett's favorite. Cory was slouched down between Rett's legs, lying back against Rett's chest.

It had been a strange day for both of them, with nothing to do since the regular season was over. It felt like playing hooky after the manic schedule of the past several months. Still, with school back in, they had waited until almost midnight to come out to their field to enjoy each other and the cooler evening. There'd still be plenty of hot days ahead, but this one felt special.

Rett buried his nose in Cory's hair, smelling him and kissing his head slowly. Cory reached into his pocket and pulled out his phone, which had begun buzzing. He looked at who it was, laughed once, and answered it.

"Hey, Bo, what's up?" he said. "No... no, no, it's not too late... Nothing, just hanging out."

There was a pause, then Cory said, "Sure. Oh wait, no, we're gonna be in Lawder for a few days seeing my folks, so that's probably no good. What about the weekend after that?"

Rett sighed. He stuck his finger in his mouth, then plugged it into Cory's free ear and wiggled it around a little. Cory made no attempt to stop him or pull away from it, having given up on fighting the wet-willies months ago.

Cory said to Bo, "Ok, we'll probably see you then, buddy."

Cory hung up his phone and said, "Bo wants to come hang out again. He wants to come watch some of the playoffs with us."

"Hang out with you, you mean," said Rett. "My brother has the worst man-crush in the history of the world. It's pathetic."

Cory wrapped his hands around Rett's legs on either side of him and began to lightly stroke his calves. Cory said, "Your little brother is hot. Those eyelashes of his haunt me."

Rett laughed and Cory tilted his head back so he could grin up at him.

"I feel a little weird about sleeping with you in your parents' house when we go to Lawder to visit," said Rett.

"Why?" said Cory. "You know they don't care at all. Besides, they sleep there together, and that's way grosser than you and me sleeping together there."

Rett mulled it over and then grunted, "Hmm! Good point."

He added, "I should probably go ahead and plan on spending a few days with my folks, too. I can tell mom wants me to, but she's still too afraid to come out and ask."

"You should," said Cory. "You need that time with them, especially your dad."

"It'd be a done deal if you'd go, too."

"You and I both know that's still not a good idea. Your dad still gets a little freaked out by me, even despite the progress he's made. I really think that when I show my face, all he sees in his head is me bending you over the table in the Joes' locker room and felching you."

Rett sighed. "Christ, I so totally regret ever teaching you that word."

The laugh started small and spread from Cory's gut to the rest of him, shaking Rett in the process.

"Maybe it would help if you tell him *you've* been the one bending *me* over and ruthlessly felching me half the time," offered Cory through his subsiding chuckles.

"Oh yeah, that'd make him feel *much* better!" said Rett, his words laced with sarcasm.

They sat in silence for a moment, Cory still rubbing Rett's calves and Rett running his lips through Cory's hair.

"Maybe," suggested Cory softly, "you could point out that I was named Mobile's most eligible bachelor."

"Mother*fucker!*" shouted Rett. "I *knew* you were gonna bring that goddamn article up! I *cannot* wait until you're yesterday's news so I can have you all to myself again!"

Cory leaned his head back again and gave Rett a conciliatory kiss. He said, "I defy you to name one single day where I was anything other than 'all yours,' Rett."

Rett only grunted in reply, but pulled his arms a little more possessively around Cory.

There was another silence between them before Rett felt Cory tense up. Cory leaned forward and to the side so that he could pull a folded-up piece of paper out of the back pocket of his shorts.

As he unfolded it, he said, "In fact, I've got something for you."

Rett sensed the sudden unease in Cory as he took the paper from him. It looked like some kind of certificate. He read it and found that it was a gift certificate "good for one (1) pitching lesson from MLB star pitcher, Cory Pritchart."

Rett thumped Cory's ear hard and said, "Are you back on this horse? And 'star pitcher?' Really? You wanna go get a wheelbarrow tomorrow to carry that ego of yours around in?"

Cory didn't reply, and began biting at one of his fingernails nervously instead.

Rett noticed that there was another sheet of paper underneath the free pitching lesson certificate. He started looking at it and wasn't sure what it was.

"What's this?" he asked.

He continued to read down the page because it took more effort to figure out exactly what it was. By the time he studied it and got to the bottom of the page, Rett's face flushed red.

He pushed up violently on Cory and jumped up from behind him, like Cory was a huge sack of flour that had spiders crawling out of it all of a sudden. He stood up and glared at Cory, his temperature rising rapidly.

"What the hell is this?!" he demanded furiously, waving the paper at Cory.

Cory watched him, but didn't answer.

"What gives you the right to do this? Huh?"

Cory still didn't answer, but his silence spoke volumes.

"You really did this, didn't you?!"

Cory said, "I told you a while ago that you'd have to get used to me doing things like this, chief."

Rett shook the paper at him. He shouted, "A hotel room is one thing! But paying off a hundred thousand dollar debt?! Are you out of your *fucking* mind?!"

Cory said quietly, but firmly, "I love you, Rett. I'm limited in the ways I can show you that. Getting rid of your student loans is one thing that I *can* do."

Rett seethed at him and then sank down to his knees next to Cory. "You show me you love me in all the ways that matter! But this... this is over the line!"

"It was actually Jimmy's idea, which'll probably piss you off even more. He warned me you'd probably not be happy with it, but I don't care. You've yelled at me before." Cory started to grin. "You're short, so I can barely hear your belly-aching way down there, anyway."

Rett sat fuming. Cory had no right to do this.

Cory reached out and pulled at Rett, who resisted. Cory said gently as he continued to tug at him, "You wanna be mad? Be mad. You'll get over it. *I love you, Rett.* I *wanted* to do this for you. And I could, so I did."

Cory won the tug-of-war with Rett so that he fell forward onto his chest, and Rett stopped fighting it. Cory was right; Rett could rant and rave all he wanted, but it was done, and it was just how beautiful a person Cory was. And that was that. Cory put his arms around Rett and held him.

"You're a stinking bastard!" snarled Rett into Cory's chest.

"I know."

"You're gonna have to bust your ass making this up to me!"

"I know."

"You're the most amazing fucking bastard in the whole world."

"I know," whispered Cory.

Rett relaxed and wrapped his arms around him. He sighed, "I love you so much, Bigfoot."

"I know." Cory slipped his hand up under the back of Rett's sweatshirt and slowly rubbed his thumb around on the smooth skin in the small of his back, which Rett had found was one of Cory's preferred places to touch him.

"You really are the best, you know?"

"I'm Mobile's..."

Rett yelled, "I swear to God! If you refer to yourself as Mobile's most eligible bachelor again, I'm gonna bite somebody's ear off!!"

Rett looked up at Cory, who was smiling broadly at him. He scooched forward across Cory's chest and they kissed. They kissed and Rett couldn't help but think about Jimmy's advice — love him and you'll get one of the biggest hearts you'll ever run across in return. Sometimes, like now, it felt like too much. Like he could never measure up to what Cory deserved, like he could never give back as much as Cory gave him. But he loved him with every ounce of his being, and hopefully that was enough. Hopefully the man that Rett was, what he had become, was enough to be worthy of him. If not, then he'd have to become even more for him. Anything, for him.

The kiss slowly trailed off until they were only looking at each other from a few inches apart, Cory's eyes holding tight to Rett's in the yellow streetlight. Rett reached up and stroked the side of Cory's face slowly, silently thanking him and telling him with his own eyes that he'd do anything for him. Anything.

A contented, satisfied grin swept over Cory's face while Rett watched him closely, both of them looking forward to as much time together as they could get in the off-season months. Cory brushed the side of Rett's face delicately with his hand, sending a brief hint of glove leather to Rett's nose. Cory's eyes glinted in the faint light of the field. He grabbed the baseball in the dirt next to him and began to push himself up. "C'mon, chief, let's toss the ball back and forth a few times."

"Just you and me."

~~~ The End ~~~

Other Works by JF Smith

Falling Off The Face Of The Earth

After his big-shot life in New York tragically falls apart, James Montgomery returns to his small hometown in south Georgia a defeated and broken man. All he has left is his mother to help him heal and regain his confidence before he's ready to get back out and re-conquer the world.

But being big-city gay in a small southern town has its own challenges. In addition to coming to grips with what happened in New York, his hometown of Lawder throws its own curveballs at him. James is confronted with a bitter enemy from his school days, and frustratingly can't seem to avoid the guy. His mother suddenly wants to expand the family. The one guy James takes a liking to and starts dating has a lot of hang-ups about being gay. And he watches almost helplessly as a new young bully starts to repeat the kind of abuse he suffered during his own school days.

Here where he grew up, the one place he should feel safe, James feels maddeningly off-balance. He starts to think that maybe going home was a bad idea after all. Maybe he'd be better off moving on and really starting over, completely from scratch. Maybe he should walk away from Lawder, just like he walked away from his life in New York.

But maybe, if he'd give it a chance, he'd re-think everything he ever thought he wanted out of life. And maybe what he thought was important, isn't so important after all. Maybe he could have everything he never realized he wanted, if he just looked around himself for a moment.

Latakia

Matthew likes his life in Richmond. He has his friends and his softball and his volunteer work. And he has a very good-looking boyfriend, Brian, who he's been happily dating for over a year now. So what if his friends tend to question just how good his boyfriend is, and so what if Brian tends to have inexplicable mood swings. And so what if Brian seems to invite Matt's suspicions on occasion. If he just shows a little faith and trust, he'll appreciate what he has with Brian the way he should. Right?

But suddenly, Matt finds himself in a desperate life-or-death situation on a trip overseas, and he realizes just how much he misses home, and Brian. He's luckily rescued by a team of US Special Operations Forces, only to immediately find out they're a bunch of bigoted jerks. Worse, a quirk of his situation forces him to spend time with them that he'd rather not. And that's when he finds out that first impressions can be misleading. When called upon, he steps up when every fiber of his being tells him not to, and discovers something deep inside himself that he didn't realize was even there. And his life will never be the same. He finds that he can, after all, make some very overdue changes in his own life.

What Matt doesn't realize is that the bond of brotherhood runs both ways. And he winds up changing the lives of several of the men on that SpecOps team as much as they changed his.

All it takes is faith and trust.

The Sticks (A Short Story)

Percy's given up. He's given up and wants to be as far away as possible from the place that has been the source of his troubles all his life. But to his disappointment, he finds himself in the last place he expected. And a chance encounter with a redneck and a stubborn hound dog aren't helping, either. That is... until they do.

Invincibility can be found in the strangest places.

About The Author

JF Smith spends large portions of his spare time lighting bottle rockets and firecrackers in his bare hands, exactly like he's been told not to do, and then flinging them at people around him, exactly like he's been told not to do. It's not a great way to earn respect or friends, but it surely keeps people a guarded distance away from him. The rest of his time is taken up with writing and trying to figure out ways to pay for his liability insurance, which has a gallingly high premium. If the spirit so moves you, feel free to contact the author at:

jfsmithstories@gmail.com

www.facebook.com/jfsmithstories

Made in United States
North Haven, CT
06 April 2022

17966856R00295